THE GREEN EYE

THE GREEN EYE

BY
PETER BYRNE

PILGRIMS

PILGRIMS PUBLISHING
◆ Varanasi ◆

THE GREEN EYE
Peter Byrne

Published by:
PILGRIMS PUBLISHING

An imprint of:
PILGRIMS BOOK HOUSE
(Distributors in India)
B 27/98 A-8, Nawabganj Road
Durga Kund, Varanasi-221010, India
Tel: 91-542-2314059, 2314060, 2312456
E-mail: pilgrims@satyam.net.in
Website: www.pilgrimsbooks.com

PILGRIMS BOOK HOUSE (New Delhi)
9 Netaji Subhash Marg, 2nd Floor
Near Neeru Hotel, Daryaganj
New Delhi 110002
Tel: 91-11-23285722, Fax: 91-11-23285081
E-mail: pilgrim@del2.vsnl.net.in

Distributed in Nepal by:
PILGRIMS BOOK HOUSE
P O Box 3872, Thamel,
Kathmandu, Nepal
Tel: 977-1-4700942
Off: 977-1-4700919
Fax: 977-1-4700943
E-mail: pilgrims@wlink.com.np

Edited by Christopher N Burchett
Layout by Asha Mishra
Cover design by Stephen Lau

ISBN: 81-7769-208-9

Printed in India at Pilgrim Press Pvt. Ltd. Lalpur Varanasi

DEDICATION:

This book is for everyone who enjoys
a rollicking good tale of
adventure and challenge,
danger and daring do,
intrigue and mystery,
love and passion
and
the triumph of good over evil.

This book, though based on the experiences of the author, is written as a work of fiction. The background to the work is factual, as are place names in both India and Nepal and as was the dreaded cult of thuggee, in India. But with the exception of those persons who have given permission allowing the author to use them as models for the characters in the book, it has no relation to any person, living or dead.

CONTENTS

THE GREEN EYE OF THE LITTLE YELLOW GOD.
(The poem). ix

BOOK I. Wildman. 1
BOOK II. The Mission. 57
BOOK III. Bombay. 75
BOOK IV. The Road North. 91
BOOK V. Capture. 117
BOOK VI . Sunita. 169
BOOK VII. Nagpur. 193
BOOK VIII. Ghose. 207
BOOK IX. The Clutterbuck Hotel. 219
BOOK X. Gael. 239
BOOK XI. Hide And Seek. 257
BOOK XII. Katmandu. 307
BOOK XIII. The Temple Of The Yellow God. .. 355
BOOK IV. Epilogue. 381
ACKNOWLEDGEMENTS 383

The Green Eye of the Yellow God

There's a one-eyed yellow idol to the north of Kathmandu,
There's a little marble cross below the town;
There's a broken-hearted woman tends the grave of Mad Carew,
And the Yellow God forever gazes down.

He was known as "Mad Carew" by the subs of Kathmandu,
He was better than they felt inclined to tell;
But for all his foolish pranks, he was worshipped in the ranks,
And the Colonel's daughter smiled on him as well.

He had loved her all along, with the passion of the strong,
The fact that she loved him was plain to all.
She was nearly twenty-one and arrangements had begun
To celebrate her birthday with a ball.

He wrote to ask what present she would like from Mad Carew,
They met next day, as he dismissed a squad;
And jestingly she told him then that nothing else would do
But the green eye of the little Yellow God.

On the night before the dance, Mad Carew seemed in a trance,
And they chaffed him as they puffed at their cigars;
But for once he failed to smile, and he sat alone awhile,
Then went out into the night beneath the stars.

He returned before the dawn, with his shirt and tunic torn,
And a gash across his temples dripping red;
He was patched up right away, and he slept all through the day,
And the Colonel's daughter watched beside his bed.

He woke at last and asked if they could send his tunic through;
She brought it and he thanked her with a nod;
He bade her search the pocket, saying, "That's from Mad Carew,"
And she found the little green eye of the god.

She upbraided poor Carew in the way that women do,
Thought both her eyes were strangely hot and wet;
But she wouldn't take the stone, and Carew was left alone,
With the jewel that he'd chanced his life to get.

When the ball was at its height, on that still and tropic night,
She thought of him and hastened to his room;

As she crossed the barrack square, she could hear the dreamy air
Of a waltz tune softly stealing through the gloom.

His door was open wide, with silver moonlight shining through,
The place was wet and slipp'ry where she trod;
An ugly knife lay buried in the heart of Mad Carew,
'Twas the "Vengeance of the little Yellow God."

There's a one-eyed yellow idol to the north of Kathmandu,
There's a little marble cross below the town;
There's a broken-hearted woman tends the grave of Mad Carew,
And the Yellow God forever gazes down.

J. Milton Hayes

BOOK ONE

WILDMAN

When Wildman saw the big Indian truck straddling the highway, he instinctively sensed trouble. He had just powered the 4X4 International Scout through a long, sweeping corner and was touching seventy-five when the vehicle suddenly came into view. The road was narrow here and the truck, a big Tata diesel ten-tonner, parked sideways on the centreline, almost completely blocked it. Jamming his left foot hard on the brake pedal, he began to bring the Scout to a tyre smoking, screaming stop. But even as he did so, something nagged at his mind and he eased his foot on the pedal. Something was odd about the truck. Something was wrong. It was not the fact of its being parked on the centreline and blocking the road. It was something else.

It was not unusual, on the highways of India, he knew, to find cars, buses and trucks like this one parked right in the centre of the road. It was the common and accepted practice of Indian truckers. Sometimes the reason was a breakdown. When this happened, drivers simply allowed their vehicles to roll to a halt in the middle of the road. They parked them there and then, with the assistance of the oilers and loaders who always accompanied them, got out and tackled the problem.

Sometimes drivers simply stopped for a rest, or to chat with other drivers. When they did, it was invariably in the middle of the highway. The hazards this presented to other truck drivers, all of them travelling at high speeds and most of them grossly overloaded, never seemed to occur to them. Even Wildman, with years of driving experience in the subcontinent behind him and a knowledge of the country and its people equalled by few, still could not fathom the blank, unthinking mentality behind this custom, one that annually caused hundreds of accidents.

One eye on the truck ahead, Wildman subconsciously noticed the Scout's speedometer needle drop out of the seventies and into the sixties.

Pasang, his stony-faced Nepalese companion, sitting on his right, spread his feet on the floor of the Scout and with a stiff arm braced himself against the forward thrust of the braking. His eyes darting from side to side, the tough little mountain man leaned forward to study the abandoned truck, his mind reading and quickly analysing all that he saw. The narrow openings on either side of it. The road beyond. The dense cactus hedge that enclosed it on either side. Like Wildman, he too sensed that something was wrong. But he also was unable to put a finger on what it was. Behind the Scout, dust swirled in the hot afternoon air and an early winter sun, pouring its harsh light down from the dark blue bowl of the Indian sky, created a simmering haze. A haze that hung in the flats on either side of the road and swept up into the black rock hills behind them; the *ghats,* through which they had just come, the three thousand foot ranges that separated the plains from the coast and the huge, sprawling city of Bombay.

Wildman wrestled with the wheel of the lurching, sliding vehicle. They were still in the high fifties and sizing up the narrow openings on either side of the truck, and estimating the distance left against his speed, he was wondering if he could get the Scout through one of them when it suddenly hit him. In the same instant, perhaps a split second before him, Pasang also saw what was strange about the abandoned truck and in a voice sharp with urgency snapped at Wildman. "Off the road, *sahib*. Leave the road. *Chitu!* Quick!"

Wildman did not hesitate. With barely a glance at the dense hedge that bordered the highway, he wrenched the steering wheel of the Scout to the right and swung the vehicle off the road. At the same time he floored the throttle and, reaching down, flipped the four-wheel-drive lever into its locked position.

With its engine screaming, the big gold and white Scout burst through the cactus hedge and in an explosion of shattering green cactus leaves and splintering thorn, plunged down a five foot embankment and dropped into the soft black surface mud of an abandoned rice field. The six-thousand-pound vehicle landed with a heavy, squelching impact and Wildman thought for a moment that they might founder. Then the massive Off Road tyres, locked into four-wheel-drive, took hold and in high, pluming arcs of black mud the big vehicle roared across the field and away from the highway. As it did Wildman heard shouts and glancing quickly in his side mirror saw men pouring out from behind the truck, rifles and clubs in their hands. Pasang heard the shouts too and whipping around, hissing urgently at

Wildman, "Thugs, *sahib*. Keep going. That was an ambush. Keep going. Don't stop."

<<>>

As he spoke, they both heard shots from behind them. Wildman, fighting the wheel of the Scout on the slippery mud surface of the field, mentally registered the crack of Lee Enfield .303 rifles. Even as he did, a bullet punctured the rear door of the vehicle and, with a sharp ping, lodged in the steel of the upturned back seat behind them. A second round bounced off the rear bumper bar with a sound like a blow from a small hammer. Then, with a lurch that lifted the Scout's front wheels in the air, they bounced over a small dirt bank and out of the field and into a little grove of trees. With the tyres fighting for a hold, Wildman twisted the vehicle through the trees, sideswiping one, smashing down another that was unavoidable. Then the grove came to an end and the ground dropped sharply into a shallow, muddy river, running at right angles to their line of approach. Wildman, with an experienced eye for the water, guessed that it was about a foot deep and unhesitatingly plunged the Scout into it, at the same time whipping the wheel hard to the left. The big vehicle instantly responded, Pasang being flung against the right-hand door by the sudden ninety-degree turn. Then they were off, roaring up the stony streambed in bursting clouds of spray, water pouring over the hood and streaming down the windshield.

Within two hundred yards the river swung right. On the left was a small sand bar. Seeing it and estimating his distance from the now unseen road, Wildman swung the Scout towards it. They ploughed through the sand and emerged into another rice field. In this the mud was slightly deeper than in the first field and the big tyres picked it up and hurled it up into the air, ahead and behind, coating the vehicle with the black, glutinous clay. Then they were at the edge of the highway. To the left, about five hundred feet back, Wildman saw the truck and, as it came into view, he saw men running down the road in his direction. He instantly floored the throttle, aimed the Scout at the roadside cactus hedge, smashed through it and was back on the highway. Swinging the Scout to the right and accelerating hard, he saw more men running, kneeling, aiming at the Scout. But there were no more shots and, noting the fact, he wondered if the ones that had hit them when they first left the highway had been mistakes, or had just been meant as a deterrent. Roaring away, he saw the kneeling men rising quickly and running back towards the truck. One or two looked

The abandoned truck that Vask's men used to try and ambush Wildman and Pasang. Credit: Bombay Province Road Traffic Police.

On the Indian roads trucks that are damaged in an accident often take days or even weeks to repair, during which time they are left on the roadside. They are seldom abandoned, however; this one has four men sleeping in the cab.

back over their shoulders while they ran. But none of them attempted to shoot again, and this convinced him that the roadblock had not been set up with the intention of robbing him, or killing him, but probably as part of a plan to stop and hold him.

Coming around that corner on to it, unexpectedly, he could have been met with a fusillade of shots. Eight, ten men, with .303 rifles at close range? He might have got through. But he undoubtedly would have taken shots through the windshield. And maybe through the radiator, which would have put the Scout out of action very quickly. How far could he have gone on a dry radiator? Not far, and then the truck would have been after them and would quickly have caught up. No. The roadblock was set up to stop them. And, he guessed, to capture them. And hold them and then deliver them to...who? Vask? The thug that old Lord Carew had warned him about?

<<>>

Wildman cursed quietly. Damned fool, he said to himself. Must be getting old. Would never have allowed yourself to get that close to an obvious trap five years ago. Pushing forty now. Yes, maybe that's what it was. Over the hill and starting down the other side. Damn it, with your experience you should have realised what was odd about that truck the instant you saw it. An abandoned truck on an Indian highway! A truck with no people around it, sitting in it, sleeping underneath it? No sir. Not in India. To leave a vehicle on an Indian highway without attendant guards was to invite instant and total theft. Theft that would start with the outside mirrors, then the windshield wipers, then the fuel caps and anything else that was quickly and easily removable. After that, if the driver or owner did not turn up, the wheels, the fuel tank, the engine, the lot, down to the bare chassis. And if the thieves had something to tow it with, the chassis too would disappear.

Damn! He should have seen it instantly. No people. Not one. Not even the usual bunch of curious villagers gawking and standing around, one-legged, like bloody storks. Pasang saw it before he did. Good thing he did. Good man. Quick. Alert. Probably tough, too, if it came down to it. But they had only been together a few days and that part of the little hillman still remained an unknown. How would he be in a tight spot? Probably damned good. Wildman glanced at the impassive-faced Sherpa sitting next to him. The harsh winter light, bouncing off the hood in front of them, emphasised the hardness of his flat cheeks and lit the russet brown of his skin. His eyes, black, quick, under their hooded Mongolian lids, watched the road ahead. Yes, he'd probably be damned useful. Certainly he'd stayed very cool when they did their little dance in the field back there, .303 bullets buzzing like bees around their heads. Lord Carew's bodyguard. His best man, he had said, when he'd asked Wildman to take him along on the mission.

And the mission. Was it really only ten days ago that he had been sitting in the East India Club in London, when the call came through? The telephone call that he had almost refused to answer. The one that had taken him from the comfortable confines of his favourite club away to hell and gone up into the wilds of the Scottish moors, to old Lord Carew's home, Himalaya House, to hear an old man's extraordinary story? A story that had set him out on a very dangerous mission, one fraught with unique and unusual hazards. One that, were it successful, would enable him to accomplish a long awaited ambition, after which he might well retire. Or one that, were he to make any more stupid damn mistakes like this last one, would end with his bones mouldering in some forgotten rice paddy, deep in the Indian jungles.

<<>>

The dining room of the East India Club was crowded. Ex-tea planters from north Terai country Bengal, and Assam, tall, thin men in their sixties and seventies, impeccable in their Austin Reed, Harris tweed jackets and club ties, rubbed shoulders with one-time rubber planters from Malaya. Jute farmers from Bihar and the Santal Parganas country, their faces bearing the marks of the tropic years, chatted with teak men of the Irrawaddy forests of northern Burma, the old malaria-yellowed elephant men of the hill jungles. Ex Indian Forestry men, from the great sub continent and Ceylon, their faces carrying the stain of uncountable monsoon days, shared tables with retired government men of the British Indian Civil Service. Scattered throughout the big dining room, their ramrod straight backs catching the eye, sat the old military men of the army of colonial India, an army that had fought and died to help carve an empire out of a savage wilderness.

At two tables set slightly apart from the others, sat the box *wallahs.* Although members of the club, they were not quite part of the camaraderie of the men of the Raj. These were the office and businessmen, the ten per cent commission *wallahs* of the company agency houses of Calcutta, Bombay and Madras. And over in a corner, at a special table that was always reserved for them, a table that seemed to bear an invisible sign that said, **DO NOT DISTURB**, huddled four old indigo men from Bihar, all in their nineties, the last of a breed, survivors from another age.

Outside, in St James Square, pigeons flared between the neatly manicured trees and, from behind the stately buildings that lined the walkways, London's crawling traffic rumbled faintly. A weak autumn sun filtered through the glistening panes of the tall dining room windows, laying soft fingers on the portraits of Wellington, Napier, Clive and Nelson, men who conquered and then ruled the far-flung empire of the Raj, of which, now, the East India Club was a last outpost.

Wildman, one of the very few American members of the club, was lunching with his guest, Tom Dadras, a tall, handsome, elegantly dressed American with whom he had shared a few adventures. Dadras, at one time a Senior Vice President of Universal Studios, had since gone into what he smilingly called wheeling and dealing, mainly in the Middle East. He was a man of many secrets, many facets. Wildman called on him from time to time, for an introduction, or for information that might in some countries be regarded as classified. He was a useful friend.

16, St. James's Square,
London, SW1Y 4LH

4th March, 1977.

I have the honour to introduce

Mr. M. Wildman.

a member of The East India, Sports & Public Schools Club, Ltd.

If you will extend to him the privilege of Reciprocal Membership, it will be greatly appreciated.

The Secretary,
Stephen's Green,
Dublin.

P. H. WALLACE
Secretary.

Reciprocal (exchange membership clubs) membership request for Wildman from the Secretary of the East India Club, Wildman's club in London, to the Stevens Green Club in Dublin, Ireland.

He and Wildman had dined well on Scottish salmon, flown in fresh from the north early that morning, with new potatoes from Ireland, washed down with a bottle of Fumé Blanc. They were rounding off the lunch with a glass of port when a white-jacketed club servant approached and asked Wildman if he would like to take a long distance call. When Wildman asked who it was, he was told that the caller, a man, had refused to give his name. Wildman felt like having the servant tell the man to call back later. But, on reflection, he changed his mind. He had only that morning arrived in England. From the airport he had made one call, to Dadras, inviting him to lunch. And from the airport he had come straight to the club and, since booking in had made no other calls. Whoever was calling him must have learned of his arrival in England from Dadras, or else had inside knowledge of his movements. He turned to his companion. "Tom, did you tell anyone that I was coming into the country, or that I as in London? I mean, after I called you for lunch. A friend of mine, perhaps?"

"No, old chap. Nobody. For that matter I didn't know that you had any friends."

Ignoring the sarcasm, Wildman nodded to the hovering servant that he would take the call. He rose, told Dadras not to drink all the port and followed the man out of the dining room and into the club's front hall, where half a dozen old-fashioned, oak-doored phone booths were reserved for club members.

"Cubicle number four, sir," said the man, and left.

Wildman stepped into the phone booth, closed the door, picked up the big black telephone and said, "Wildman here."

In reply he heard an operator say, "Very good sir. Just a minute," and after about thirty seconds of the usual whirring and clanking and groaning noises of the British telephone system, heard a man's voice say, "Wildman?"

"Wildman speaking. What can I do for you?"

The voice that answered him was that of an elderly man. The tone was cultured and the words that Wildman heard were spoken with a slow and careful deliberation.

"Now listen to me, young man. Listen carefully and do not interrupt. I have something that I want to say to you and I have to be brief about it. Walls, as we used to say in the war, have ears." Which war, Wildman wondered, as the voice continued.

"I want to see you. I want to talk to you. I have something very important to tell you and after you have heard what it is that I have to say, and if we can come to terms about it, then I will tell you more and we will discuss something that is in your line of business. All right? No. Don't speak just yet. Let me continue and let me do so by saying that while you do not know me, as a result of which you may hesitate to meet with me, I know all about you. More in fact than many people do.

"I'm talking about what you might call your credentials and to give you an idea of the extent of my knowledge of these, let me quote you a few examples. Baroda, India, 1953. Yes? A job well done! and also very well rewarded by the ruling family there. The Ceylon crossing, 1958. Made by the skin of your teeth with half the Indian customs service on your tail. Tanganyika 1958. They almost got you that time, yes? Good thing they didn't. Very nasty what they do to people they don't like in that little country. But you got out and came through for your sponsors, yes?"

Christ, thought Wildman, how did he know all that! There were only three men involved in the Tanganyika caper and two of them were dead now. Why, in '61… But the old man went on.

"Will that convince you? Show you that I have enough interest in you to have done a considerable amount of research on you? Yes? Good. Then here is the first part of my proposition. Tomorrow morning there will be a car and a driver outside the club, back entrance, Duke Street, at six thirty. The driver will have instructions to bring you here. He will be under orders not to speak to you, other than in an emergency situation. Pack a bag and be prepared to spend the night with me here. If you are interested in meeting me, use the car."

There was a click as the man hung up and Wildman, his mind racing, only then realised that his caller had not given his name or said where he lived. He waited a moment and kept the receiver to his ear. After about five seconds he heard another click. A second receiver being put down? Someone listening on the line? It could be. Though, he thought, with the mechanical eccentricities of the British telephone system, one could never be sure. Pondering on the call, and still slightly shocked at the depth of his caller's knowledge about him—how much else did he know?—He walked back into the dining room and rejoined his friend.

"All the port gone, Dadras, you old soak?"

"Yes. And I just talked with the head waiter and he said there was no more in the cellar, but for a consideration he might smuggle you in a Coca Cola."

"That will be the day, when they allow Coke in here. I should imagine, when they carry the first cans in through the door, that Napier, Wellington and Nelson will leap right out of their frames in horror."

As though he had overheard, a waiter appeared with a decanter of port and filled Wildman's glass. Dadras waited for a while to see if his host was going to tell him about the phone call. He knew better than to ask questions and when Wildman called for the check, he knew he was not going to be told about it. Later, perhaps. But not now.

They parted company in the high ceiling foyer, Dadras to be privately driven to his country house in Berkshire, one of several he maintained in different countries and Wildman to retire to his room upstairs, to sleep off his jet lag. There is a ten hour time difference between London and Anchorage, Alaska, from where he had just flown in and if he was going to be up early next morning—that is, if he decided to follow up on his telephone caller's rather mysterious offer, he wanted to be alert and aware, something that in his business was a useful contribution to the business of staying alive.

<<>>

Wildman. Six foot three in his stockinged feet. One hundred and ninety pounds, dripping wet. No fat. Strong, physically, but not overly so. Lithe, sinewy, limber. Long-legged. Deep chested. A shock of dark brown hair framing a wide forehead set above hard, flat cheeks and a square chin. Even, white teeth that only showed when he laughed. Dark blue eyes that at thirty-eight were already rimmed with fine lines. Desert lines. High altitude lines. Tropical sun lines. A habit of lowering his head when talking with people and looking straight at them over the top of a short, slightly crooked nose.

Several idiosyncrasies. Would not drink alcohol with a man who did not drink it. In cards, played only poker and only for money, never for fun. A strong reluctance to sit with his back to a door in public places. A poor opinion of women generally. In the home, in his opinion, they just about got by. In the outdoors, his world, they had little or no place. When he spoke on the subject of women in the outdoors, he did so reluctantly and, he said, from experience. He had done his best to accommodate them, he said. He had tried. But when they got thirsty in the middle of deserts where there was no water, they complained. And when they got tired on a twenty-mile hike that failed to find a campsite and had to be extended another ten, they nagged. They got cold feet when the temperature dropped below minus ten degrees, and this made them sulky. They were unhappy when they were bitten by solider ants or mosquitoes or tsetse fly, and miserable when they got wet in cold rain. And if they were not fed hugely and at regular intervals, they starting howling for their mummies and demanded to be shipped home. Wildman was flexible on many aspects of his life.

But not on his views about women. They had their place in life, he supposed. But not in his camp. And that was that. And he spoke, he would have you note, from experience.

Even-tempered, outwardly mild-mannered and with a keen sense of humour, Wildman was a difficult man to provoke. But on the rare occasions when someone got under his skin, something savage rose to the surface, from deep inside him, something wild and dangerous. The few men who made the mistake of physically provoking him had done so to their lasting regret. His one hobby was reading and this centred around military history. For relaxation he listened to classical music, his favourite composers being Mozart and Vivaldi. He enjoyed gourmet food and fine wine. But his real passion was the outdoors, his sacred and, as far as he was concerned, womanless preserve—and it lay in the contentment and joy he found in hiking and camping in the deserts, mountains and great forests of the wilder places of the earth. By nationality he was an American; the six other nationalities for which he held passports were simply for the convenience and practice of his profession, that of international courier, a trade that sometimes went under another name...international smuggler.

Born in the mountains of northern Oregon. Mother, American. Father, immigrant British, from old stock. Early schooling, several country towns south of the Columbia while his father, a lumberjack, followed the timber trade. Summers from the age of fourteen working with his father as a "Step and fetchit" in the logging camps, which contributed to his big frame and hard muscles. Tragedy, when his father was crushed and killed by an old widow-maker fir that began to fall one way, changed its mind and went in the other direction. When this happened he moved to Portland with his mother and finished High School. He was a bright student but his teachers called him a dreamer; he had to struggle to graduate. Then, using her deceased husband's accident compensation money, his mother sent him to college. Four years at Reed saw him with a degree in archaeology, an inbred fear of middle class entrenchment, a bank account that registered zero and a yen to travel.

It was about this time that he met a man named Robert Rines. Rines was a retired patent law attorney, from Boston, a genial gentleman with a twinkle in his eye, a healthy bank account and a sandalwood chest full of old family records in Shanghai.

"A what?" said Wildman. "And where?"

It was a long story. But Rines made it short. He and his family were old China hands. His father and grandfather had spent all their lives there, trading with the Chinese and the British. His grandfather had died there and soon afterwards, young Rines and his father had left, a hop, skip and a jump ahead of the Chinese Communists. But in the race to get out and at the same time stay ahead of the advancing red hordes, the family had to leave almost everything behind. Among the abandoned possessions, stored in the attic of an old house on the Bund, in Shanghai, was a sandalwood chest. In it were family records going back nearly one hundred and fifty years.

Rines had recently received a letter from an old family retainer, smuggled out of China by an airlines pilot. The old man had written to say that the chest was still there. Rines wanted the chest, badly, and was willing to pay well, if he could get it. Fifty thousand dollars, in fact. Cash. Twenty-five down, twenty-five on delivery. Plus expenses. Trouble was that the Chinese would not be inclined to let it leave China. Legally, that is. Would young Wildman be interested in having a shot at getting it for him?

Robert Rines of Boston, the man who gave Wildman his first assignment and in doing so set him on his extraordinary career.

Four months later Wildman drove a small van up to an apartment tower on East India Wharf, in Boston, where Rines lived. A couple of men helped him manhandle a big, sandalwood chest in through the front door and into the elevator. An hour later Wildman picked up his second check from the delighted Rines and in the process found himself launched on a new career. Archaeology? Plenty of time for that later, he told himself. Right now, let's see who wants what, picked up from where, and delivered to wherever. And is willing to pay for it.

That was almost twenty years ago. Since then there had been the Baroda caper...five million dollars worth of emeralds across four international borders; the Ceylon affair...a Maharaja's priceless period miniatures smuggled out of the back door from India; the Tanzanian project...ten million in stolen diamonds returned to the de Beers family; the Macao escapade...a Chinese warlord's daughter whisked off the mainland and safely delivered to her family in Paris; and a half a dozen other missions, as he liked to call them, with fees that went as high as two million dollars a time. Archaeology, as a result, had languished by the wayside while his reputation as a courier, like his bank account, grew. And while he personally had little interest in material possessions, he did indulge himself to the extent of a small but luxurious apartment on New York's Fifth Avenue, overlooking Central Park, and a solid, two-story, stone house in the environs of Kathmandu, in the Kingdom of Nepal.

When he was not working, he divided his time between these two places, off time that that grew longer as the years went by. Not from want of offers of work. In a fireproof steel safe, set in reinforced concrete and located behind a magnificent Guy Coheleach watercolour of a tiger, in his New York apartment, was the paperwork of half a dozen pending offers, any one of which would net him a million plus. But whereas in the beginning he had accepted the Rines contract, and one or two others, without hesitation, nowadays he was inclined to take a slower and more circumspect look at the missions he was offered.

He had long since established an ethical code in the matter of his missions and this he always made known to his principals on first contact. One, no drugs. Ever. In his travels Wildman had learned about drugs, had seen what they did to men and women, and children. Two, no gun running and no association with arms deals of any kind. One of his beliefs was that half the wars that were perennially underway throughout the world would come to grinding halt if their arms supplies were cut off. A childish hope, he admitted. But an honest one. Three, no espionage and no association with the same. He considered spying a dirty game at the best of times, a game where people had a nasty habit of disappearing. And his missions were often difficult and dangerous enough without getting involved with the vodka-swilling killers of Russia's OGPU, or the lethal little men of the CIA, or the blundering English funny bunnies of MI5 and MI6.

In addition to these requirements, he had one other, and that was that his principals, regardless of who they were, never asked him to reveal his methods, his *modus operandi*, either before or after a mission. In the matter of payments, his contract required fifty per cent upfront, the balance on delivery of the commodity, whatever it was. Should he fail to deliver the item or items as described in the contract, he would keep the down payment, but forfeit the balance. To date he had never failed to collect the second half of any of his fees.

And this new mission, if that is what it was? Who knows? Might be interesting. The old man sounded lucid enough on the phone. Face to face of course, he might turn out to be something else. An old codger with more money than sense and the family jewels locked in the safe of the Titanic and he'd like to have them back by Friday, if you please. Or a doting old fool needing his daughter rescued from the Moonies in Alabama. Or his ex-wife from a brothel in Baghdad. Or his son from a cell in a penal camp, in northern Siberia. Ah well. He had made no promises on the phone. Didn't have time to, for that matter; the old man had been so brief. So whatever it was, he was clear to accept it or refuse it, as he wished. Meantime, give it a try? Why not. A day in the country would do him no harm and, with a bit of luck, the old boy might really have something interesting to offer. At the same time he would be careful and would take a few precautions. Just in case there was a plot within the plot. Something that he had encountered before. Something that often took a little while to surface.

<<>>

At precisely six fifteen the following morning a large black Daimler car, driven by a uniformed chauffeur, drew up at the Duke Street entrance of the East India Club. The driver parked tight to the curb and, leaving the engine running, sat in the car watching the back door of the club. If he was surprised when Wildman, exercising a know-your-enemy preliminary precaution, emerged from the doorway of a small art gallery directly opposite, rather than the club itself, he did not show it. Wildman crossed the street with long, swift strides and approached the Daimler on the side opposite the driver. He watched carefully as the man opened the door and got out.

"Good morning, sir. Mr. Wildman, I presume. And you have some baggage, sir?" the man said, touching his cap respectfully.

Wildman pointed wordlessly towards the door of the club and when the man went to fetch his bag, which he had left just inside it, had a quick look inside the Daimler. It was empty, apart from a roadmap on the front passenger seat. When the driver returned with Wildman's canvas grip, and opened the trunk to put it in, Wildman watched carefully, noting that the trunk contained only a leather-covered spare wheel and a jack, bolted to the floor with steel wing nuts. Satisfied, he nodded to the driver, climbed into the back of the Daimler and settled himself comfortably in the soft leather seat. The driver climbed into the front, gently closed the door, eased the big car away from the curb and drove carefully up Duke Street. At the junction with Oxford Street he turned left and, twenty- five minutes after leaving the club, swung on to the M1, the great north road that traverses England, south to north, and leads to the Scottish border. Once on the motorway the driver increased speed and when the speedometer indicated 85 miles per hour he set the cruise control and left it there.

Shortly after eleven the car drew into a small country inn, not far from the big industrial centre of Sheffield. The driver parked the car, got out, opened the back door for Wildman and said, "Lunch has been arranged for you here, sir. I will be ready for you when you have eaten. I will be with the car, sir."

Wildman walked into the little inn. A window table had been reserved for him. Seating himself at the table, he was able to watch the driver through the window. The man had climbed back into the front of the Daimler and with what looked like a packet of sandwiches. As Wildman watched, he opened them and began to eat. After a while he reached down and drew up a thermos flask. Hot tea, Wildman guessed. Reassured, Wildman ordered and ate lunch and, as soon as he had finished, left the inn, got back into the car and told the driver to go on.

The driver did not speak again. The big car rolled smoothly north, stopping only once for gasoline. When this happened Wildman got out and watched the car being filled and when this was done, climbed back in again. Ten hours after leaving London they crossed the Scottish border. Within another fifteen minutes, with evening closing in, they turned off the motorway and drove for some thirty miles down a series of winding back roads enclosed with dense Blackthorn hedges. Suddenly the driver slowed and the car made a sharp right turn, into a short, tree-lined driveway. The driveway ended in a massive wrought iron gate, set in a high stonewall. Through the trellis work of the gate, probably half a mile back and set in a stand of huge Scottish pines, Wildman saw the outlines of an enormous estate house made of cut grey stone, its upper stories lined with turrets and crenulated walls. Behind it, light gleamed on the surface of a broad lake. On the wall beside the gate was a sign:

CLOSED AREA. NO ENTRY WITHOUT PERMISSION.
TWENTY-FOUR HOUR SECURITY. GUARD DOGS.

Wildman's driver got out and, as he did so, a big, heavily built man appeared from a small building on the right, behind the gate. The man was wearing a bulging, unbuttoned corduroy jacket, over thick wool trousers. Wildman guessed that the jacket concealed a gun. The driver handed the man a small card and returned to the car. As he did so the gates swung open and they passed through. Immediately inside the gates, though not visible from the road, was a second sign, small, discreet, inscribed on polished brass and set in an oak plaque. It read **HIMALAYA HOUSE**.

As they approached the house, Wildman kept his eyes open. He noticed two men, one with a leashed Doberman, walking briskly through the trees off to his right. As they got nearer to the building, he saw another man standing on a balcony above the front door and said to himself that whatever the old man turned out to be, his security looked tight and efficient. He glanced quickly back at the long stonewall that probably enclosed the whole estate and did a quick estimate of its height. One never knew. In his line of work it was sometimes necessary to leave in a hurry and a good precaution was to know your escape routes.

Tires crunching on gravel, the Daimler drew up to the front door of the house and stopped. The driver got out, opened the door for Wildman and said, "You may go in sir, if you wish. I'll see to your bag."

Wildman thanked him and got out of the car. As he did so the front door silently opened and a man stepped out. He was an Indian, of medium height, slightly built, with very dark eyes set in a thin, sallow face. He was dressed in the traditional garb of an English butler, black trousers with thin, narrow, vertical grey stripes, a black, buttoned up, single-breasted jacket and a spotless white shirt, with a thin grey tie. He stepped forward, exuding, with apparent ease, the traditional false superiority of an English servant, a combination of attempted snobbishness and subdued arrogance. Being an Indian, Wildman thought, and probably a Bengali from the look of him, the pose was not a difficult one for him to acquire and practise.

Wildman watched the man's eyes quickly sweep over him from head to foot, sizing up his clothes and class in one quick glance. Then the man spoke, his voice toneless and flat. "I am Ghose, sir. Welcome to Himalaya House. Lord Carew is expecting you. I will show you to your room."

"Thank you," said Wildman, deciding there and then that he did not like Mr. Ghose.

Lord Carew's castle. Picture taken from the lake.
Photo credit: The Times, London, England.

"I will also see that your bag is brought up," he added with an audible sniff, one that indicated that someone else, not he, would carry it.

Bet you will, thought Wildman. After you've had a quick look in it, probably. He wondered about the 9 mm Glock fixed between the leather walls of his grip. No. It was well concealed. Not likely the man would find it. Unless he had a visual scanning device.

"This way, sir," the man said, stepping back and indicating that Wildman should follow him. "I take it you will be spending the night?"

Sensing the jab, Wildman quickly fired one back. "Not much else I can do, I suppose. Right?"

The butler, leading the way up a flight of wide, heavily carpeted stairs, sniffed again, a sniff that said, American, what else to expect. At the top of the staircase the man turned right and led the way down a long corridor ornately decorated with suits of medieval armour and gilt, framed paintings of men and women in the dress of the eighteenth and nineteenth centuries. At the end of the corridor he stopped at a beautifully carved oak door, opened it and said, "Here is your room, sir. I think you will find everything you need."

"Thanks. Just hope you have my size in pyjamas."

Taken momentarily aback, to Wildman's inner delight, the man quickly recovered and replied. "Certainly, sir. I am sure we will be able to find something. I'll talk to the housekeeper."

"Never mind. I probably have something with me. Just tell me when I get to meet Lord Carew. You did say Lord Carew?"

"Yes sir. Lord Carew. Downstairs sir, whenever you are ready. I presume," and this time the sniff was less than audible, "That you will want to clean up before meeting his lordship."

Christ yes, thought Wildman. After eleven hours on the road one would want to clean up, starting with a quick visit to the loo. The butler closed the door and left. Almost immediately there was a gentle knock and the door opened again. A young boy, no more than thirteen, wearing a grey kitchen apron over black trousers and a blue work shirt, bustled in with Wildman's grip. "'Ere you are, governor. Your bag."

He was gone before Wildman could talk to him, or tip him. When the door closed Wildman walked over to his grip, opened it and ran his hand down the lining in the side. The Glock was there. So much for that. He glanced at his watch. Nearly seven. Might as well get changed and get down to meet the old man. He stripped off his jacket and shirt, went into the small bathroom that adjoined the bedroom, and washed his upper body quickly. Splashing some aftershave under his arms, he looked out of the bathroom window and noticed a stout-looking drainpipe running down the back wall of the house—a nice exit device if needed—and then went back into the bedroom and dressed. He put on a fresh, white, Sea Island cotton shirt and a dark blue string tie, and then slipped into a navy blue, brass-buttoned blazer with the insignia of the Explorers Club of New York on the breast pocket. Running a comb through his hair, he zipped up the

Lord Carew at his castle with one his many dogs.

Lord Carew at his favorite pastime,
fly fishing in the lake behind his castle.

grip, locked it and shoved it under the bed. Then he took a wooden match out of his pocket, splintered it and put one of the splinters between the edge of the case and the leg of the bed. He would not be able to stop someone coming into the room and moving the grip while he was downstairs. A good man would be able to open it, too. But at least he would know if someone had been at it.

<<>>

When Wildman walked into the book-lined study on the ground floor, the shades of night were stretching long black fingers across the parkland in front of the house. As he entered the study, the butler appeared from the shadows and closed the door gently behind him. When he did so, an elderly man turned from one of the tall, draped windows, where he had been watching the last of the sunlight dying behind the trees, and came towards him with a slow but steady gait. He thrust out his hand and said, "I'm Carew. I'm very glad you could come, young man. We have much to talk about and I truly think that you are going to find what I have to say very interesting."

Carew stood, slightly stooped, a shadow under six feet. Flickering light from a log fire in the room's big stone fireplace showed thinning white hair, a craggy, lined face centred around a strong Roman nose and, in spite of his obvious age, the balanced movements of a man who had kept himself fit all his life. His handshake was firm, his gaze steady and penetrating; Wildman took an immediate liking to him.

"I am delighted you are here. Let's make ourselves comfortable, shall we and start with a drink. It'll be Glenlivet, right? With no ice and very little water."

"Right, sir," Wildman replied, wondering how much else the old man knew about him and his habits. Glenlivet, eh? Probably knows, in addition to the little darts that he threw at me over the phone, that I have three scars on my back from Mozambique, 1968. A bullet hole never completed closed in my thigh, 1974. A tooth capped with what might be called some quick, permanent exit insurance. And the number of my Swiss bank account.

The old man went to a small bar built into a sixteenth century Spanish mahogany sideboard, poured two generous measures of Glenlivet into heavy, Waterford, cut glass tumblers, returned, handed one to Wildman and said, "Now let's sit here by the fire and we can talk and I'll tell you what this is all about."

He lowered himself into a big leather chair facing the fire and motioned Wildman to another.

"Cheers."

"Cheers. And thank you, sir."

Outside, night had fallen. But while the old man was pouring the drinks Wildman, with a quick glance through one of the big bay windows, had seen, in the last of the light, what looked like pairs of men walking along the edge of the tree line near the house. Guards? Patrols? He wondered what it was all about. Nice old men living in grand old country houses in England and Scotland did not employ the obvious heavy security that the patrols suggested. Not unless they were afraid of something. Or somebody. And his host did not look like the kind of person who would scare easily.

But then, he had sensed something when he first entered the house. Ghose, the Indian butler, might have been the cause of it. Wildman's experience with people had given him unusual insights into human psychology and he felt that behind the butler's affected superiority lay something else, something sinister, and maybe even dangerous. Whatever it was, it was faint, barely apparent. But it was there, and it touched a chord in Wildman that stirred a few warning vibrations. If anything developed in what the old man might be going to propose, anything that involved Ghose, then the butler would bear watching. Physically he looked as though a strong wind would blow him over and in that area Wildman knew that he could deal with him with one hand tied behind his back. But men like Ghose avoided the physical approach and depended on more subtle methods. Ghose was a knife-in-the-back type, Wildman decided. Yes, he would have to keep an eye on Mr. G. But in the meantime the old man's bearing and air of graciousness reassured him and he settled back in the comfortable leather armchair and sipped his twelve-year-old malt, and waited for him to speak.

The craggy lines of his face under lit by the flickering firelight; Wildman's host now looked at him and said, "I trust you had a pleasant drive up here, then? Not too tiring?"

"On the contrary, sir. Very pleasant."

"And a decent lunch?"

"Most enjoyable, thank you sir."

"Good. I must apologize for my driver not speaking to you. He was under strict orders from me, you see. Not that you would have found him a great conversationalist. But I felt that you might have wanted to ask him questions about why I wanted you to come here, about which he knows nothing. And, being an uneducated man, he might have tried to invent something, and caused you some confusion. Hearing it from me seemed to be the best way. In other words, what you hear will be, as you Americans say," and he smiled gently, "The real McCoy. Without distortion of any kind. Do you understand?"

"I think I do, sir. Certainly I am interested in hearing what you have to say, and what this is all about."

<<>>

The old man settled back in his chair and turned his face to the fire and began to speak.

"The story I am about to tell you, young man, is a strange one. Very strange, in fact, almost to the point of being incredible. But, I assure you,

Lord Carew as a young, British, regimental officer in Katmandu, just before he took the Eye from the temple of the Yellow God, and, as a result, was cashiered from his regiment. Photo credit, Sandhurst Military Academy, Lancashire, England.

every word of it is true and I think you will see this, as we proceed. Firstly, however, before I go, I have a question to ask you. If you give me an affirmative answer to the question, then you will find a credibility basis, as it were, to my story. The question is this. Do you know a poem called the Green Eye Of The Little Yellow God?"

Wildman did not hesitate. He had read it as a boy and had been so fascinated by it that he had memorised whole verses. In his house in

Kathmandu he even had an engraved and framed version of it, illustrated by a Tibetan artist.

"Yes sir, I know it well. It's the story of Mad..."

He stopped and looked across at the old man and slowly an extraordinary thought raced through his mind.

"Yes," said the old man. "It's the story of Mad Carew. The man who stole the Eye, the green eye of the little yellow god. And what happened to him. The colonel's daughter? The temple in the hills? In the dark of a winter's night when the ball was at it's height? Remember? And an ugly knife lay buried in the heart of Mad Carew, the vengeance of the little yellow god?"

"Yes sir," said Wildman, keeping to himself the wild thought that had flashed through his head. "A great piece of poetry, in the best traditions of Kipling and the Raj, even though it was written by...?"

"J. Milton Hayes. Long since dead but a good friend of mine while he lived. He wrote the poem more than seventy years ago and he did it on my behalf, and at my request, to counter the news stories of the time. Stories that seeped out of Nepal and into India and then to this country in various distorted forms. So distorted in fact, that the public did not know what to believe. And in particular, did not know what to think of the rumours that the hero of the piece—the villain, if you like—young Mad Carew, lived or died. Now, are you with me so far?"

"Yes sir. Of course. Please do continue."

"The poem, now, is one that few people read any more and the story itself has long since been forgotten, erased from people's minds by the passage of time. But its little story is true in every respect except one. Have you guessed? I sense that you may have done so. Yes, I was Mad Carew. I was the man who took the Eye, the great emerald, from the temple of the little yellow god. The untrue part? I did not die in Kathmandu. I was not murdered. I was stabbed, and hurt, and lost a lot of blood. But I was young and resilient and I recovered quickly. I escaped. I got out. By the skin of my teeth, I have to admit with, firstly, the custodians of the temple after me, and then the Nepalese police. Then..."

"But you were a British officer, sir. Local police would not have been able to lay a finger on you?"

"Were. Was. I was cashiered by my colonel, the minute I got out of hospital. And that of course lost me the protection of the army. Publicly, what I did was the reason for my dismissal. But there were personal reasons behind it on the part of the colonel. Fellow had decided that he did not want his daughter to marry some young scallywag who stole jewels

Colonel Wilberforce Witherspoon, DSO, Commandant of the British regiment in Katmandu, father of the original Gael, the beautiful young woman with whom Lord Carew, as a young man, fell in love and for whom he stole the Eye. Seen here in London with his sister and her children.

Photo credit, Buckingham Studios, Park Lane, London W1.

from temples in addition to which he had a brigadier at headquarters in mind for her.

"Anyway, I managed to elude the police and get across the Nepal border and down into India. But word had gone out about the great emerald, and within a week every cutthroat and thug in India was after it. And after me. Fortunately I had already served in India and was fluent in Hindustani and I used this, plus a disguise as a *fakir,* a holy man, to get all the way to Cape Cormorin and from there over the straits in a native fishing boat, to Ceylon.

"After that, the Indian Ocean in an Arab dhow to Bahrain and from there on foot, and by whatever means I could find, to Ankara, Budapest, Paris. In Europe I managed to shake off the last of my pursuers and was back in England in three months. They picked up my trail again later and, until I came into my family fortune, and was able to afford proper protection, they gave me a bad time. The prize was, of course, the Eye, the greatest emerald ever to come out of Asia. They are still after me, as a matter of fact. But we'll come to that in a moment.

"In the meantime what is important is this. I was Mad Carew. I am the man who stole the great Eye of the temple deity. Stole it for the love of a woman who, when I tried to give it to her, laughed in my face and would not believe what I had done, would not believe that it was real. Yes. I took it. And...?"

"Yes sir?"

"I still have it. And I want to return it. And I want you to do this for me."

<<>>

Wildman was stunned. The story was ages old. Prehistory. From the colonial days of the Raj. Carew, if he was the man he said he was, the young British subaltern of the epic poem, and if he was in his early twenties at the time, must be...

"Yes," said the old man, reading his thoughts, "I was twenty at the time. The Great War was still seven years away and England was in the heyday of its empire. I am ninety-five now and all this happened seventy-four, seventy-five years ago."

Wildman, deep in thought, looked at his glass. When he did, the old man rose slowly from his chair and took it from him and walked to the sideboard and refilled it.

"We will have plenty of time to talk tomorrow. I hope that you will be able to stay with me for a day or so. Yes? Good. Knowing what I know about you, I think, this affair aside that I am going to enjoy your company while you are here. I hope that you will tolerate mine. I shall try not to be an old bore. But I feel you should know the whole story. Obviously, if you accept as credible all that I tell you, and decide to take on the mission—the task of returning the Eye to its rightful owners—you will have to be thoroughly briefed. Very thoroughly indeed. Yes, I know what you are thinking. Why did I choose you? Right? Well, I can answer that. I chose you after taking a long, careful look at the credentials of several people who operate in fields similar to yours, and then comparing their experience and their record of success with yours. And my findings suggest, without argument, that you are the best person for the mission, the task of getting the Eye back to its rightful place in the temple of the little yellow God.

<<>>

A little later, Wildman and the old man sat at either end of a long, beautifully polished oak table. Candlelight glistened on silver that carried the coat of arms of the Carews. Soft-footed servants came and went, all carefully supervised by the watchful Ghose. Carew, knowing of Wildman's dislike of sitting with his back to a door, had positioned him facing the main door of the dining room and from time to time, when it opened, Wildman was able to see down a short corridor to a second door. Once, briefly, he thought he caught sight of a brown face that was neither Indian nor Caucasian. A swarthy face, broad, possibly Mongolian. But he might have been imagining things and he dismissed the thought.

The presence of Ghose bothered him and he wondered why Lord Carew would employ such a man. Perhaps there was a story behind Ghose. If there was he felt he would hear it from the old man before his visit ended. During dinner the old man continued to talk about the Eye. But Wildman noticed that whenever Ghose came into the room he stopped and changed the subject, waiting until the man left, before continuing.

"I have often thought of returning the stone. My original plan after Gael, the colonel's daughter, jilted me was simply to get it to England and sell it. But soon after I got back, the Great War started up. I was swept into it and was away for four years, four years during which I had a lot of time to think. And the more I thought about it, the more convinced I became that the act I had committed was something more than simple theft. More than just the stealing of a valuable jewel from a temple. You see, the temple of the yellow God in Nepal is a very special place for pilgrims from all over the little kingdom. Losing the eye of their god meant that their deity was defaced, disfigured, as it were. And the more I thought about it, the more I became convinced that the Eye had to go back. But then came the first attempt to kidnap me and, as a result, the first serious delay in my planning."

"Kidnap you, sir? You mean to murder you?"

"No. Not to murder me. They—and I'll tell you who they were in a while—were not after me. They were—indeed, still are—after the Eye. Only I know where it is. No other living soul does, as a result of which, were they to kill me, they would never find it. No. Their plan was simple. They just wanted—and they tried damned hard—to get me into their clutches and make me tell them where the Eye was."

"This happened here, in England, sir? I mean, Scotland?"

"Yes, here, at Himalaya House. Once they had me, their plan was to torture me into giving them the location of the emerald. And that would have been the end of it. And the end of me too. 'Dead men tell no tales' is the motto of these people."

"And these people were, who, sir?"

"Well," the old man continued, "That was, at first, the unbelievable part of it. They were, of all things, Indians. Naturally, when I first realised that someone was after me, I suspected that it must be the priests of the temple, out for revenge, or, at the least, the recovery of the emerald. But then I began to think. Nepalese holy men are not vengeful by nature and the attempt to get me was a vicious one. No. They were Indians. And after my security men picked up a couple of them and using, shall we say, a little persuasion, managed, before handing them over to the police, to get them to talk, we discovered who they were and where they were from. Which is why," he said, as Ghose entered with a bottle of port on a silver tray, "salmon fishing in Scotland is among the finest in the world."

Wildman smiled to himself. The old man, in spite of his age, was quick. At the same time he wondered about the acoustics of the house. What was it Carew had said to him on the phone? Walls have ears?

The old man waited until Ghose had left the room and then continued. "Now, where was I? Ah yes. The ones we handed over to the police. Well, not wanting to attract too much attention to what happened, I restricted the charges against them to trespass with criminal intent. There was no mention in the proceedings of kidnapping, or attempted kidnapping. Had I included these, the next thing would have been the press wanting to know why. And it would not have taken a lot of research for some bright young reporter to dig up the original story. Newspaper files go back a long way in this country. Naturally, the two men we caught also said

The Colonel's lovely daughter, Gael. A photo taken in London on the eve of her departure for Kathmandu to join her father with his regiment there. Photo credit Hyde Park Buckingham Portrait Studios, Mayfair, London W1.

nothing at their trial. Any mention of kidnapping would have added considerably to their sentences. As it was, they got five years each and as soon as they came out of prison were deported, back to their own country. That was five years ago."

"And since then, sir?"

"A year after they were deported, there was another attempt. This indicated to me, quite clearly, that the people who were after the Eye were not going to give up. This time, there were three men. They had been well trained and their training must have included a thorough study of the house here, as well as the estate, and its boundaries. But, fortunately for me, they made a couple of mistakes. The first was choosing a night in October when there was a full moon. Now in Scotland here, one hardly expects to see the sky after the end of August and there was actually heavy cloud the night they made their attempt. But soon after they cut the wires, and got over the wall, the clouds dispersed and the moon broke through. My men—good men, all ex-policemen—were on the alert and most fortunately saw them. They got two of them. Put the Dobermans on them and they surrendered without a fight. Indians are not very good with dogs, as you probably know. But the third man got into the house here and actually got to the second floor before he was, er, stopped."

"Stopped, sir?"

"Well, yes. You see I have in the house here what you might call a backup arrangement to the outside security. We'll talk about what this is, later. All right? In any case, there now arose the question of what to do with these latest visitors. Something different this time, because obviously the enemy had plenty of manpower available and two more men in jail was not going to put much of a dent in their efforts."

"Two men, sir? I thought you said three?"

"Two. The one who was, er, stopped, in the house, succumbed to his injuries. So, thinking about what we should do this time, I talked to my top security man here and took his advice. The result was what you might call deterrent action. They were kept here for a week or so, while I made arrangements with a friend of mine who has an ocean-going powerboat. After their stay here, they were put on board his boat and taken out to sea. A week later they were found by the Turkish authorities, on a beach in Salamanca. They were both alive and in good health when the Turkish police picked them up. But they were each carrying a kilo of heroin sewn into their clothing and I do not have to describe to you the very dim view that the Turks take of drug dealers in that tough little country?

"Quite frankly I do not like being a part of something like that. But when one is dealing with thugs like this, a big stick, shall we say, carries a

Ghose, Lord Carew's butler, probably dishonestly reading one of Lord Carew's private cables before making a copy to send to his real master, Vask.

lot of weight. The main thing was that I not fall into their hands. Had this happened, they almost certainly would have been able to get the emerald because they would have gone to any limit, including the most severe torture. And I regret to say that I do not think that I could take a lot of physical pain at my age. Mad Carew, the man I was seventy-five years ago, might have been able to do it. But not this Carew. I have done a study of medieval torture and believe me, these people would not have hesitated to indulge in it. I feel quite sure that the ones sent to get me would have been experts in their field, fiendishly brutal and utterly ruthless. Hence the guards here, young Mr. Wildman, the security, and the dogs, and the precautions that I take and must continue to take for as long as I live. Or at least for as long as I still have the Eye in my possession. As to who is behind these efforts, and who trained and sent these people…"

The old man hesitated a moment and then touched a little bell on the table beside him. Quickly, too quickly for Wildman's liking, Ghose oozed into the room.

"Yes sir?"

"Ghose, we'll have coffee in the study. Brandy and cigars, please. And after the table has been cleared, you may go."

"Thank you, sir. Good night sir."

The butler's eyes slid towards Wildman. "And goodnight to you, sir."

Wildman felt a shiver of unease as the man passed by him and left the room. When the old man rose, he got up quickly and followed him into the study.

The walls of the study were pale green down to a height of about four feet and below that were covered with dark, panelled oak. A large case, filled with books, top to bottom, was set against one wall. The remaining three walls were adorned with medieval maps and charts. A huge grandfather clock ticked quietly in the corner and on a sturdy brass table, a dark green bottle of cognac and two snifters were waiting for them.

"I have some fifty year old Napoleon, here, young Wildman," said the old man. "And it is time it was drunk. I also have some Burmese cheroots, to which I understand you are quite partial?"

"Right, sir," said Wildman, accepting a thin black cigar.

The curtains of the study windows had been drawn against the night and the only light was from a small wood fire, burning in a little stone grate, plus two small lamps, set on corner tables. When they had lit their cheroots and settled themselves comfortably, with large measures of brandy, Lord Carew spoke again.

"Vask," he said, looking up towards the ceiling through a cloud of pale blue cigar smoke.

"I beg your pardon, sir?"

"Vask. Vask the second, to be accurate. An Indian from Benares. Or Varanasi, as it is known nowadays. An evil man. As evil as his father, the man who led the thugs who pursued me across Indian and down into Ceylon, when I made my run from Kathmandu. Pursued me and damned nearly got me a couple of times. A *bunnia*. A moneylender. And a burning *ghat* operator. As wicked a man as ever put cold steel to a victim's throat. Totally unprincipled, a foul-mouthed lout, a braggart and no doubt a coward of the first order. But, whereas his father was basically a simple thug ‑ kill and rob, rob and kill ‑ Vask the second is different. Vask number two has money, big money, and with it the power to perpetrate crime in its most violent form in a country where, as you know, money will criminals to do almost anything they wish.

"May I know, sir, if you will forgive the interruption, how he made his money? How… thank you, sir. I will have a little more of your excellent cognac."

Replacing the heavy green bottle, Carew continued.

"Vask's father died when Vask number two was quite young. There were two boys, Vask, and another, a younger one, called Gunga. All I know about the second boy is that he was mentally retarded. He is still alive, I am told, and his brother looks after him. And I heard that he grew to be enormous, an oddity in a land where people are traditionally small. But, whereas he might be physically dangerous, because of his size, he is of no consequence to our story.

"After the father died, the mother took both boys from their home village ‑ somewhere near Nagpur, in the Central Provinces ‑ to Benares. There she apprenticed them to a *ghat* operator on the river, a man who supplied firewood to the Brahmin priests, for cremations. The two boys worked there for a number of years. Vask the elder soon established himself as a cunning little scoundrel and soon learned to sit back while his brother, bigger, stronger, but without the brains to see how he was being used, did all the work.

"One day the body of a minor Raja was brought to the *ghat* for cremation. There was a considerable police escort arranged by the family, because the Raja's will stated that his court jewels were to be burned with him and then thrown into the river with his ashes. The Raja had a number of wives, now widows, and these, with their wailing and carrying on, together with their children, and their servants, created considerable and unusual confusion at the *ghat*. No one knows how Vask did it, but somehow or other he managed to get his hands on the jewels. Six months later he sold a diamond pendant in Calcutta for fifty thousand pounds sterling, about sixty thousand of your American dollars, a lot of money in India. The police heard about it and investigated. But he paid them off and the matter was hushed up and quickly forgotten. Using the money, Vask promptly bought out his employer, an old man close to retirement. Then came the dirty part of it and with it the rise of Vask to his present financial prominence.

"Within another three months he asked the owner of the adjoining *ghat*, a young man with three small sons, to sell out to him. The man refused. A week later his youngest son disappeared. Vask repeated his offer. The man saw the light and sold out. In spite of this, his child was never seen again.

"Vask's next move was the property on the other side of his. The owner, a powerful *bunnia* who had spent all his life fighting off people like Vask, told him what he could do with his money. Vask made him a second offer and told him that it was his last. The man refused to be intimidated. A week later, his house was rocked by a huge explosion and completely destroyed. He was out at the time, fortunately. But his wife and children were not and they died in the wreckage of the house. The *bunnia* did not hesitate. He went immediately to see one of Vask's managers, handed over title of his property, took a tenth of what it was worth and departed quickly for safer climes. This was all thirty or forty years ago. Today Vask owns a hundred *ghat*s, has the firewood rights to a hundred more and, I am told, takes a ten per cent commission on all offerings made to the priests of the temples ¯ some two thousand of them ¯ along the river. Money? The man is a multimillionaire, ten times over. A rupee millionaire, true, which means rich within his own country. And so Vask has become an Indian tycoon.

"With his wealth, naturally, has come great power and, in Vask's case, being the person that he is, he uses it to control a veritable army of thieves, embezzlers, arsonists, strong-arm men and murderers, throughout the length of the subcontinent. You have already guessed, I should imagine, what this is coming to? Yes, it was Vask who organised the attempts to kidnap me. It was Vask who trained the thugs who, twice, have come close to getting their hands on me. And it is Vask and his evil empire that you will be up against if—might I say when—you agree to take on the mission of getting the great emerald, the Eye, back to its rightful owners in the hills of Nepal."

A small glowing log fell from the fire into the stone grate in front of it. Wildman moved swiftly from of his chair, picked the burning ember up with his bare fingers, flipped it back into the fire and, with a lithe movement, sat down again and reached for his cognac glass. Lord Carew, seeing the way he moved, seeing the indifference with which he handled the burning piece of wood with his bare hands, smiled to himself. Yes, Wildman could do it. He was the one to get the Eye back to Nepal. The question was, would he take on the mission…

"Well, young man, what do you think? Would you like to talk a little more tonight or would you like to sleep on what we've discussed so far?

Wildman looked into his brandy snifter for a moment and then spoke. "I think, sir, if you don't mind, I'd like to sleep on it, tonight. It's been a longish day and, quite frankly, I am finding your story quite stunning, to the point where I am having difficulty putting it together in my mind, and shaping it into a cohesive whole. There is, I feel, more to discuss. A few little holes in the fabric, so to speak, which I would like to see repaired, and also some questions that I would like to ask."

"About my butler, Ghose, and about what I meant by my back-up system in the house here?"

"As a matter of fact, yes, sir. But those can wait until tomorrow. If you will excuse me now, sir, I will head for bed. But before I do I would appreciate some fresh air. Would it be permissible to have a walk around your meadow? Blow some of the cobwebs out, so to speak?"

The old man hesitated for a second and then said yes. "Come. I will walk you to the front door. The security will need to be alerted. Then I'll get off to bed myself. Don't need much sleep these days, I find. But nevertheless, need to get a few hours. Keep the old batteries charged, so to speak."

They left the study and walked through the sitting room into the entrance hall. The old man led the way, his footsteps silent on the thick pile of the hallway carpeting. Before opening the front door, Carew flicked a switch that operated a powerful outside light. Then he opened it and stepped through. Wildman, following, his pupils contracting against the glare of the strobe, was just in time to see a shape moving away, out at the edge of the light. It looked like a small man and it moved quickly and soundlessly, out of the light and into the darkness. Someone caught unexpectedly in the strobe? Then his attention was diverted as two heavily built security men, one leading a huge Doberman, appeared around the corner of the house. They walked quickly up to Lord Carew, nodded their heads and said, "Good evening, sir."

"Stains. Wilson. Good evening. This gentleman," said the old man, turning to indicate Wildman, "is my guest, as you know. He will be walking around a little, getting some fresh air. Please pass the word to the others."

The men nodded and walked away, one of them pulling a two-way radio out of his pocket and beginning to talk into it. Carew turned to Wildman. "Good night, young man. I am going to close the front door. But when you come back, one of the men will let you in. Just come up to the light here and make yourself visible. Have a pleasant walk, sleep well and we'll talk again in the morning."

Wildman took a few paces away from the glare of the strobe light and then stood for a moment, savouring the clean cold night air. A thin moon was rising through the trees to the east and a high, strong wind sent billowing cloud scudding across the dark blue bowl of the sky. He looked carefully around and, when he was satisfied that he was alone, walked quickly across the parking lot that fronted the house and out into the meadow. The grass was beginning to dampen with dew and this, together with its thickness, made his swift progress almost silent. He headed for a small thicket of trees that he had noticed when he arrived. There would be dark shadows in there and although he did not really feel that he needed the security that their cover would give him, his natural instincts as an outdoorsman made him prefer to walk in cover, rather than in the open. He did not actually feel that he had anything to fear. Nevertheless, what Lord Carew had told him about the kidnap attempts, and Vask—an incredible man with criminal tentacles that could reach all the way from India to Scotland—made him wary. Vask's men had twice actually managed to get into the estate. The Eye, the great emerald, was the magnet that drew them, like moths to a candle. Wildman did not doubt that they would try again.

Reaching the shadow of the trees, Wildman paused and stopped. Behind him, from the direction that he had come, the meadow was silent and empty. There was no sign of the security men; hopefully all of them had been alerted to his presence. If he were to bump into one who did now know him, well, he could probably handle it. Ex-British policemen were dependable chaps on the whole. But if the ones that he had seen were examples, they were probably all heavily built and, as a result, not too quiet on their feet. Wildman, who could move fast, and as silently as a ghost, felt that he had the ability to avoid a confrontation, if one threatened.

For three or four minutes he stood in the shadows of the trees and slowly, as his eyes grew accustomed to the light, he was able to see all the way across the meadow to the other side, and even a few feet into the trees there. He was standing like this, still, watching, when his eye caught a movement. When he first saw it, his immediate thought was that it was one of the guards. But when he analysed what he had seen, he felt it was too quick to have been one of the big security men. More like an animal, a fox, perhaps, or a badger. Then he saw it again, tight to the edge of the tree line, away over on the far side of the meadow. This time, vaguely, blurred in the thin light of the early winter moon, he caught the outline of a man. A man, moving quickly and silently towards Wildman's left. A small man, broad of shoulder and...But suddenly the figure faded into the tree line and was gone.

Wildman stayed where he was and studied the layout of the meadow and its boundary vegetation. The trees that fringed it curved all the way around it in an unbroken line, eventually coming to the little grove where he was standing. He surmised that if the man he had seen continued to move in the direction he had taken, he would ultimately arrive at the little grove. He hesitated a second or two and then turned, moved quickly to the left, and, being care to keep in the shadow of the trees, walked fast for two hundred and fifty yards and then stopped. He chose a massive oak with a thick trunk and, hunching down into its shadows, froze into immobility. He was now directly in the path the man would take if he kept coming from where Wildman has last seen him. If the man had already detected him and was now homing in on him, he would expect Wildman to be in the little grove of trees, and not where he was now. In which case, hopefully, Wildman thought, he would make contact with him. What would happen then? Wildman decided to wait and see.

For ten minutes Wildman sat, silently scanning the trees in front of him. The night remained silent and nothing moved. He was at the point of moving to change his position when suddenly, from behind him, directly behind him, and no more than twenty feet away, he heard a stick crack. Long training prevented him from moving quickly. He waited for a full sixty seconds and then slowly, very slowly, began to turn his head in the direction of the sound. When his head was fully turned he was able to see all of the ground directly behind him. The trees, a little thinner here, allowed more moonlight to seep through and the leafy corridors between them were softly illuminated. Nothing. He strained his eyes to see further back into the trees. Nothing. Nothing in the shapes and shadows of the forest that even suggested a human form. No movement. *Nada*. He remained motionless, looking back over his shoulder, for another five minutes, moving only his eyes to search the dark lanes between the trees. Then, just as he was starting to turn his head back and resume his original position, came the crack of another stick, sharp and brittle in the damp night air. This time the sound came from in front of him, the direction his body was facing. Without hesitation he snapped his head around to the front and was just in time to see a dim figure moving swiftly away from a big oak, no more than thirty feet away. Small, broad of shoulder, clothing that seemed to be dark brown in colour and with something that gleamed briefly from the front of his body, about where a belt buckle would be. Something that glimmered like gold in the moonlight; a blurred glow that was quickly gone, like the figure itself, into the blackness of the forest.

All right, my friend, Wildman said to himself, you want to play games, do you? Well, two can play your little game and if you want to play with me you'll find yourself with an able opponent. He bent down and quickly untied his shoes and took them off. Ten feet away was a little stump. He walked quickly over to the stump and put his shoes on it—easier to find later than in a single tree like a hundred others—and then, turning, took off at a fast, near silent run, away from where he had seen the figure disappear. He ran for a hundred feet, cut to the right, ran for another hundred, cut right again and then, slowly, to make his approach as quiet as possible, moved quickly forward for another seventy-five feet through the trees.

The ground cover was light and he made no sound in his final approach to a place that he estimated would put him within twenty or thirty feet of where he had seen the figure disappear. Now, he thought, we'll see how good you are, whoever you are. We'll see if you know that to gain the advantage of surprise, in a situation like this, there is nothing like running away from the man who is tracking you and then, when he is least expecting it, come at him from a totally different direction. He covered the last few feet of his approach bent over, very carefully placing one foot in front of the other and then, in absolute silence, lay down flat in the moist grass. Raising his head slowly, he began to scan the ground ahead of him.

The moon cruised slowly down the sky and off to Wildman's right an owl hooted twice. As the night grew, the temperature dropped, and Wildman felt it now, seeping into his clothes, the damp cold of a Scottish October night. He shivered in his light wool blazer. He was not dressed for the great outdoors, nor for games of hide-and-seek in the Scottish woods, he told himself. At the same time, he had not expected anything like this. Was he dealing with one man? Or two? Or three? Whoever was out there was exhibiting what were obviously some excellent skills in woodcraft. Twice he had tried to get close to the man, or men, and he had been outfoxed. Was it by accident that he had failed to close with him? Or just luck? As if to show him that he would have to start rearranging his thinking, if he imagined it was luck that had prevented him from coming to grips with the unseen stick cracker, or stick crackers, another snap suddenly broke the stillness, directly behind him.

This time Wildman did not hesitate. He came up off the ground in a single fast movement, whirled around and hurled himself in the direction of the sound. Although he had been facing the other way when he heard it, he was able to pinpoint its position at twenty yards away and directly behind him. He ran the twenty yards in two seconds, stopped, went down on knee, froze into immobility and listened. Nothing. Nobody. Not a sound. But there had to be somebody. Or something. There just had to be. Though big, Wildman was quick and he prided himself on being able to move as fast and faster than most men. Dammit. There had to be someone there. There had to be…unless his twig snapper had simply moved off with extraordinary speed. Wildman decided instantly that this is what he must have done. Gathering himself, he leapt up and raced another fifty feet through the forest in the direction that the man or men must have taken; the direct line of exit from the place of the sound, the only line of exit that he, or they, could have used and remained unseen.

With another fifty feet of forest behind him, Wildman skidded to a halt and again froze to watch, searching intently in front, to either side and behind. As he did so, he caught a quick movement from fifty feet away, back in the direction he had just come from. Swinging around to bring his eyes to bear on the spot, he was just in time to see the blur of a small figure dropping from the limb of an oak, hitting the ground and literally bouncing off it to disappear into the trees. Again, as before, Wildman saw the touch of gold at the man's waist. Again, as before, the figure was gone in seconds, into the darkness of the forest.

For a second Wildman considered pursuit. Then he cursed, gave up the idea and slowly began to make his way back to where he had left his shoes. Now, in anticlimax, and in spite of his exertions, he felt the cold seeping through his body. His feet were soaked from the wet grass and he could not but help feel a slow anger at being outwitted, as it were, in his own bailiwick. At the same time he felt a sneaking admiration for someone who would do what his adversary had done. Allow himself to be seen and stalked at close quarters, and then to climb into and conceal himself in a low tree, a tree under which he must have known Wildman would run.

Five minutes later Wildman was at the stump where he had left his shoes. They were gone and, for a moment, his anger surged again. Then he smiled. All right, you little bugger, whoever you are, he said to himself, you and I will have a day of reckoning. Then we'll find out who the better man is and just how smart you think you are.

<<>>

Dawn. Wildman had slept well. But his experience in the woods bothered him. He attached no menace to the little game of hide-and-seek that his stalker had played with him. Nevertheless, before he went to sleep, he propped a heavy chair against the door and balanced his grip on top of it. And he slept with the Glock under his pillow. Loaded, close to hand.

With the first light of day etching the eastern sky he was up and, dressed in a dark blue tracksuit—and carefully watched by a new group of security men—was pounding the gravel driveway from the house to the front gate. Eight times up and down the half-mile driveway and he was ready for a hot shower and breakfast. Now, with a weak October sun shedding a pale light though the tall windows of the dining room, he sat drinking coffee and tucking into scrambled eggs and toast. He always ate like a starving Irish schoolboy after his run. Lord Carew, seated in front of him, gently sipped from a steaming cup of Darjeeling tea.

"I still import it myself. That's the only way to get the real thing—Flowery Orange Pekoe—and make sure it's not blended."

The old man had some notes in front of him and, when he put his teacup down and looked up, Wildman guessed that he was ready to resume last night's conversation. So he leaned back and listened.

"Should you decide to accept this mission, your main problem will be Vask. And you must not underestimate the man. True, he is a braggart and a coward. But he is also clever. He will not hesitate to play the fool, or even act like an idiot, when he feels the occasion demands it. He will do this to psychologically lower his opponent's defences. Then, when the moment is right, he will pounce. And when he does, it is with the speed of a striking cobra. The man is uneducated and, when it comes down to it, I would not give him high marks for intelligence. But he has something that balances this, a low native cunning, and it is this that has brought him to where he is today.

"He controls, as I have told you already, a huge organization and its tentacles are far reaching. And he wants the Eye and will stop at nothing to get it. He will kill, maim and torture if need be and, using his money, and the power that goes with it will, in pursuit of his goal, order his minions to do the same thing. His reason for wanting the Eye? Simple greed, of course. But also something else. Something that I will come to in a moment.

"With his people, and in case any of them ever dared to wonder why so rich a man would want more, he has created a rationale that has turned the securing of the Eye into a kind of crusade. He has done this by telling them that the Eye, which they must all help him secure, belongs to a Hindu temple in south India to where, when he gets it, he will be returning it. Thus, their assistance, in addition to the monetary rewards that he promises them, will in time gain them the greatest reward of all, the blessings of their gods in the hereafter. And for a superstitious people, this is a powerful incentive to help him achieve his aim. He has of course promised them that the minute he gets it back, he will return it to the temple in question. Most of them believe him; anyone who does not, and makes his doubts known, quickly goes the way of all of Vask's enemies. They simply disappear.

"As I said, the man has great power. This includes a veritable army of men, either working for him or working with services that are available to him, via payment, coercion or bribe. Using this power he will always be doing his utmost to stay abreast of anything connected with the Eye. For instance, he may even know, after all these years, my intention, now, to return it to its rightful owners. If this is true, then he will be ready to act the minute we move.

"As to his weaknesses, and what you might be able to exploit to your advantage, there is not much I can put my finger on, so to speak. Only one comes to mind. This is his caste and its great importance to him. Vask is a Brahmin, the highest caste, as you know, of Hinduism. It is something that he reveres to the point of obsession. More so than the average Brahmin. Why? Because becoming a Brahmin was for Vask, next to gaining his great fortune, the greatest achievement of his life. Yes, I know what you are thinking. One is either born a Brahmin or one is not, with nothing in between. But not in the case of Vask. Vask's Brahmanism was purchased. That's right. He bought it.

"Mostly, it is taken for granted by students of the Hindu religion that caste is established by one thing, by being born to it. One is born a *harijan*—a sweeper—the lowest of the low, or a Brahmin, highest of the high. Or into any one of the hundreds of other castes in between. And that is it. There are no alternatives. But this is not the case. Caste can be purchased from the Hindu priests of any of the bigger temples. The price is high. There is one temple in Benares, the priests of which demand a fee of a cow made of solid gold. The cow must be larger than life-size and big enough, at least, for the gift giver to able to crawl right through it, in one end and out the other.

"Anyway, soon after he made his fortune, this is what Vask did. He did it quietly and without publicity. One day he was a low caste *harijan*. The next, a holy Brahmin, the highest of the high. Now, I am told, next to his money this is the most important thing in his life. Certainly the way he uses it would suggest this. He never ceases to flaunt it in the faces of others of lower caste than himself, which, as you can imagine, is what all—one hundred per cent—of his employees are. It is therefore an integral part of his power. But, as you know, in power there is always weakness, and sometimes within a man's greatest strength may lie his greatest weakness."

The old man paused for a moment and when Wildman did not speak, continued.

"As to his real reason for wanting the Eye, remember what I said about his being rich, but only rupee rich? This is exactly what he is. Rupee rich in a country where rupees, if you have enough of them, can purchase a great deal, but outside of which, out of India, that is, they is useless. His dream, which is the dream of many a wealthy Indian in a country with tight, impossible to circumvent currency regulations, is to be hard currency rich, something that gives instant access to the riches of the west, whether the currency be dollars, pounds, yen, marks or francs. The Eye is his key to this and there is no doubt in my mind that within days of getting it, should he do so, it will be for sale to the highest bidder on the American or Japanese markets. With its sale, Vask's dream in this direction would be realised. I had the stone confidentially appraised five years ago. Its value was set at thirty million dollars and there are collectors, American, Japanese, French, who would probably pay three times that, to add it to their collections."

Wildman whistled softly, poured himself another measure of the strong black Tanzanian coffee that he loved—yes, the old man seemed to know all of his secrets—and sat silently for a moment. The he leaned forward and said, "Lord Carew, I'll take the mission. But before I do there is some additional information that I would like to have, which I believe you can supply. And a point I would like to make clear to you about my method of operation."

"Your method of operation? What you want to tell me is that it is to remain absolutely confidential, before, during and after the mission. Is that right?"

"Yes sir. But then, I should have known that you would be aware of my needs in that respect, and that you would realize the importance of their confidentiality. When you know a man's methods, the paths that he follows, the information can put you and keep you one step ahead of him. In my line of work that is something that I cannot afford to have happen."

"I understand. In fact I came across those needs, as you call them, quite early in my study of you. And the information that you would like to have from me?"

"I really seem to have only one and that concerns your staff here, in particular your man Ghose."

"My servants. All right. Now let me see. There are three gardeners, both village men, in their sixties. There is Mrs. Widgeon, the cook. She's also from the village and, like the gardeners, has been with me for decades. There are two under-maids in the kitchen and the houseboy, the boy who brought up your case when you arrived. Then there are the gate men; there are four, all from the village, and they work in shifts. Then the security and heaven knows how many of them there are. They are all from the Regional Security Agency in Glasgow, all British ex-policemen, all bonded and all of excellent character. They own and run the dogs, of course, and I think," he said with a smile, "That even the dogs are bonded. Then there's Ghose, my butler."

"Yes sir. Ghose. I'd like to know all about him. How he came into your employ, how long he has been with you, what his background is."

<<>>

"Ghose. Well, now we must go back a long time. To the First World War. I went into it as a junior officer. I was, as you recall my telling you, cashiered after the Kathmandu affair. So when the call to arms came for WW1 I had to re-enlist. I only managed to get a commission because there was a demand for trained men. I went in as a subaltern and came out four years later as a Brigadier. But in the meantime I was wounded. In fact it was at one of the worst periods of the dreadful trench warfare, at Ypres. I was with a Gurkha unit attached to an Indian engineer regiment when I got it, half a dozen chunks of shrapnel from a German mortar that almost took my leg off. I passed out and, when I came to, they told me that an Indian *sepoy* named Ghose had seen me go down. Without waiting for orders, he had gone over the top, straight into the vectored machine gun fire of the enemy, picked me up and, though hit twice, managed to carry me back. They took me back to a field hospital and as soon as I could, I made inquiries about the man. I wanted to thank him for saving my life. Eventually I found him. He was also in a field hospital behind the lines and when I got to him, he was almost gone. Gangrene. Riddled with it. Right up one leg and into his buttocks. And in those days, before antibiotics, gangrene was a killer.

"The man was close to death and he knew it. But he was conscious and I was able to talk with him. And he knew who I was. Just before he died he took my hand and said, '*Sahib*, look after my son. His mother is dead. He is alone. He has nobody.' And then he died.

"To cut a long story short, as soon as the war was over I charged my lawyers with the task of finding his son. It took them nearly a year, working through Indian army records and lawyers in India. But eventually they found the boy. In a village near Nagpur."

"Nagpur, did you say, sir?"

"Yes. Nagpur. Anyway, eventually, we got him to England. The boy was eighteen when he got here, too old to go to school and for that matter showing no inclination to do so. All he wanted to do was live in the house here and work for me. His English was fair and so I put him to work, staring at the bottom, in the kitchen and eventually, well, you know the rest. Today he holds a position as butler and I must say that in that position he performs his duties efficiently and satisfactorily."

"That's it then, sir. That's the complete staff?"

"Well, not quite all. There is one more, one who, if you decide to take the mission, I would like you to take with you."

Wildman was startled. "Take with me, sir? You mean, to Nepal? To actually accompany me? But sir, you know that I always work alone."

"I know that, Wildman. I know well that you are a loner in your work. And I know also how skilled and competent you are. But I wonder if you realize what you are up against, if Vask and his thugs get wind of your mission? If they do, once you are on the subcontinent, every man's hand will be against you. You will be able to trust no one. Not a single person. Anywhere. A man's eyes are set in the front of his head, yes? If Vask gets on your trail you will need eyes in the back of your head. And what I am offering you is just that, a pair of eyes for the back of our head. But that is all that I am doing. Just offering them to you. Not forcing them on you. I will simply introduce you to them and then you can make a decision about taking them with you. Or not. All right?"

"Very good, sir," said Wildman, "I think that is fair," thinking that he had absolutely no intention of taking one of the old man's servants along with him, but that for the moment, to please him, he would meet the fellow, whoever he was.

The old man got up from the breakfast table. "Let's go into my study now and you can meet the man in question, my 'back-up' system…remember what I told you…that I keep in the house here in case security fails to stop someone getting through? Come. Follow me."

<<>>

They rose from the breakfast table together and walked across the main hallway to Carew's study. The old man motioned for Wildman to precede him into the study and, just before he followed him through the door,

Wildman heard him whisper to someone behind them. Wildman entered the study and then politely stepped aside to allow Lord Carew to pass him, so that he could close the door behind them. But when he turned around the door was already being closed by another man, a small man who had come into the room behind Lord Carew, moving as smoothly and silently as a panther, a little, brown-faced man with board shoulders, muscular arms and a shock of thick black hair.

Wildman froze. The man was dressed in a dark, double-breasted jacket and tight, grey trousers that tapered into the tops of black, felt Tibetan boots. Around his waist was a dark red cotton sash. In the front of it was tucked a huge knife encased in a black leather sheath, a *kukri,* the fighting knife of the mountain men of Nepal. The man stood about five feet four inches in height and probably weighed no more than a hundred and thirty pounds. In comparison to Wildman he was small. But there the comparison stopped, for there was something about him that made Wildman think of a coiled steel spring, wound down tight and ready for instant release. Now he stood, his gaze on Wildman, his hands down at his sides, his eyes steady and still. Wildman took his gaze and held it. The man was a Nepali and, as his clothes suggested, a Himalayan mountain man, possibly a Bhutia, or Sherpa.

Lord Carew spoke. "This is Pasang. My personal bodyguard. My most trusted man and indeed, after all these years, my friend. Pasang, this is Mr. Wildman."

The man stepped forward quickly, extending his right hand towards Wildman and said in Nepalese, "*Namaste, sahib*. Greetings. I hope that I find you in good health."

As he did so the hilt of the big *kukri* gleamed gold in the morning light coming through the study window, and suddenly Wildman knew who it was that he had been playing hide-and-seek with in the meadow the night before. He smiled, stepped forward and took the man's hand in his, returning the greeting in fluent Nepalese. Instantly the man's second hand came up forward to join the first and seizing Wildman's right hand in both of his he gripped it firmly in the traditional Sherpa greeting that signified respect and friendship.

Lord Carew spoke again, smiling a thin, tired smile. "I think you two have already met, yes? Pasang told me about last night and he is willing to apologize for what happened, if you wish. But he knows I want him to go with you, knows that you might be reluctant to take him and he wanted to show you, as it were, that he is not without certain expertise, especially in woodcraft.

Wildman looked at the little hillman and smiled. "There is no need for him to apologize, sir. And I acknowledge his expertise in the woods. As to his coming with me, well, it's breaking a golden rule. But I have never been a stickler for rules and, yes, I'll be happy to have him come along."

"Excellent," said the old man. "I know that when the times comes, as it very likely will, that you will find that you have a valuable asset for the success of your mission."

Turning to the hillman he said, "Pasang, it has been decided, then. You will go along with Mr. Wildman. He will start the journey soon. Tomorrow, I would think. And you will stay with him until the task at hand is completed. When it is finished, over and done with, completely, you will act on the instructions contained in a letter I shall give you. It will be a sealed letter that you will carry with you at all times and that you will only open when, as I said, the mission is fully completed. You may go now."

The little hillman nodded, bowed to Lord Carew and turned to leave. At the door he hesitated and then stopped, turned to face Wildman and said, even white teeth showing in an impish smile, "Your shoes, *sahib*. The maids have cleaned them and they have been replaced in your room."

Wildman turned to smile at Lord Carew and when he looked back the man was gone. Now he knew without a doubt that the little hillman was the fleeting figure who had outwitted him in the woods, and also the shadowy person he had seen—sensed rather than seen—in the house and grounds. Lord Carew's personal bodyguard. His back-up system that had effectively stopped the thug who had managed successfully to evade the outside security system and get into the house. The old man's shadow, faithfully watching over a beloved master.

<<>>

"Well, young man. You'll take the job, yes?"

"Yes sir. I will."

"Good. Then there is only one other small thing to attend to, and that is the matter of your fee. We can come to an agreement on this in one of two ways. Either you can tell me how much you require, and I will give it to you, or you can let me make what I think you will find to be a generous offer."

Wildman looked out of the study window at the big meadow in front of the house, soft now under a curtain of falling rain. Then he turned to the old man. "There will be no fee for this mission, Lord Carew. For me, sir, there will be something of a special motive involved in this particular task. And," raising his hand gently towards the old man, "I would deem it a favour if you did not ask me what it is."

Lord Carew looked directly at the younger man for a moment. Then he advanced, took Wildman's hand, shook it warmly and, still holding on to it with a firm grip, said, "Young man, they used to say you were a dreamer when you were at school. Yes, my research on you went back a long way. Now, without my asking what your motives are for refusing a fee for the mission, let me just guess that you are looking towards the possibility of having a dream come true. Yes?"

Wildman, looking into the old man's age paled eyes, nodded slowly. Yes. Carew had certainly done a thorough job of research on him. But had his inquiries really gone that far back, to his father, and his father's father? Time would tell.

"Then let us adjourn for the moment," his host said. "I have reading to do, and some writing. The letter for Pasang, and also something for you, the little poem that I told you about, that you will find very useful when you get to the end of your journey. No more discussion now. We will meet at lunch. One o'clock. Let's plan on that. As to departure, would you like to plan to leave about three? That will put you into London pretty late, but I should imagine that you can stretch out in the back of the Daimler, if you wish, and I'll arrange dinner for you on the way down at the place where you had lunch coming up."

"Three will be fine, sir. In the meantime, I think you have a map room? May I use it? I can start my planning there and then round it off when I get to London. May I also use your phone to call my club and let them know that I need a room, and will be coming in late?"

"Certainly, my boy. One o'clock it is, then. I'll alert Mrs. Widgeon to come up with something nice and we'll dig in the cellar for a vintage bottle of wine to celebrate our contract, and your departure. And we can round off our discussions then and also talk about Gael and plan for our liaison, while you are on your journey."

"Gael, sir, did you say?"

"Yes, yes," said the old man, easing him out of the study. But we'll talk about that at lunch. The map room is upstairs, second door on the right. Until lunch then."

Wildman's mind raced. Gael? Who the hell was Gael? Not the original Gael? Not the Gael of Carew's time in Kathmandu? No. That was not possible. Or was it? Carew was still alive from then, at ninety-eight. She would be the same. Or close to it. Wildman's mind conjured up a vision of a wild, toothless, white-haired hag, locked up in some attic room in the huge old house, tearing at the walls of her cell, a prisoner of Lord Carew. Then he dismissed the fantasy, crossed the hallway and ascended the stairs to the map room. He was almost at the top of the stairs when he heard a door closing softly behind him. He had noticed it when he crossed the hallway, open half an inch or so. Peering over the banister from the landing, at the head of the staircase, he was just in time to see Ghose walking quickly, furtively, towards the kitchen. He waited until the man disappeared and then turned and walked down the corridor to the map room.

<<>>

Three hours later, Wildman, his work in the map room completed and his head crammed with facts and figures, distances, elevations and driving times on the route he was considering taking through India, to Nepal, completed his packing and joined Lord Carew downstairs. The old man met him in the hallway and, as they walked into the dining room said, "We'll have a light lunch. Does that suit you? A little smoked salmon with some good black bread to be preceded by one of Mrs. Widgeon's favourite soups, fresh mushrooms from Inverness, with black Zanzibar pepper. And we'll wash it down with a bottle of Dom Perignon '67, with which we will also toast the success of your mission. After lunch we'll meet in the meadow and round off our business."

Meet in the meadow? What the heck does he mean by that, thought Wildman. First the mention of someone called Gael. Now, 'we'll meet in the meadow.' But he held his tongue. In the brief time that he had known him, he had learned that the old man was highly intelligent and at the same time endowed with plenty of good common sense.

As they sat down at the massive oak dining table, Wildman thought this might be an appropriate time to ask Lord Carew about Pasang, and how he came into the old man's service. He was just about to do this when Ghose entered the dining room, followed by two kitchen maids. Both the maids carried silver trays. One held dark green earthenware bowls and spoons, the other a big silver bowl with the soup. Ghose came to the table and proceeded to ladle the soup into the bowls. Close up, Wildman noticed a curious yellowness around the man's eyes and faintly, barely detectable, but nevertheless present, a strange, acid body odour. He found it disturbing.

The soup dispensed with, Ghose returned, with the kitchen maids carrying the smoked salmon and the black bread. He himself carried the

Dom Perignon, which he proceeded to open with considerable care. Neither Wildman nor his host spoke when Ghose was in the room and Wildman decided that Ghose, unless he was a complete idiot, must notice the lapses in their conversation. Wildman just did not feel like making substitute conversation—yes, great salmon fishing in Scotland at this time of year sir—and Carew was by now probably tired of doing it.

Wildman wondered about Ghose and his background. What Lord Carew had said about his not wanting to go to school—a splendid opportunity for a young, uneducated man straight from India; and his statement that he was content with the menial work of a servant. There was something odd about it, and he made a mental note to start a little dart flying in Mr. Ghose's direction. One that would commence its trajectory with a call to a friend of his in the Office Of Public Records in New Delhi, fly from there down to the Central Provinces of India, Ghose's supposed place of origin, and then ricochet through some of the villages around Nagpur, where he claimed he was born. A little dart ball that with sufficient velocity might well puncture the little balloon that was the supercilious Mr. Ghose.

"Gael," said Lord Carew.

"I beg your pardon, sir?"

"Gael, my granddaughter. My last and only relative. And," waving a delicate, blue-veined hand to indicate the house and all that went with it, "The sole heir to all of this. All to be hers one day, if, that is, my attorneys can persuade her to accept it. Will not take anything from anybody, this young woman. A free spirit, Wildman. A unique young woman, just as you are a unique young man. And—and this is where she comes into your part of the picture, as it were—the only other person living, apart from you and I and Pasang, who knows about the Eye and about my intention of trying to return it to its rightful owners. A unique and unusual young woman, Wildman," he concluded, with a look towards Wildman that was penetrating and meaningful.

"Yes sir?" said Wildman slowly, thinking, oh no, not a woman, not some chattering female. Some—what was it he called her—free spirit? That was just what he did not need on a mission like this one, some giggling girl stumbling along behind him and tripping over his heels.

As though he could read Wildman's mind, Carew said, "No. I am not going to force her on you, for the mission. Not at all. All that I want, all that I am asking, is that you meet her and have a chat with her. You see, until I met you, Wildman, I have not known anyone who could, shall we say, match up to her in intelligence, wit and humour. Certainly not any of the young men who have come by here, inquiring about her from time to time. Young men who have met her just once, become instantly ensnared by her beauty and vivacity, and then found themselves sent on their way with a few barbed and witty words. And that is where they are usually left while the young woman herself moves on."

"Yes sir," said Wildman, struggling to keep his disinterest in Lords Carew's 'free spirit' from showing.

"She is the only daughter of my only daughter. I never had a son, as I think you know. Her mother, my daughter, met and married a Group Captain Moseley, an Australian Air Force pilot, early in the last war as a result of which Gael, my granddaughter, was brought up in Australia. The name Gael? I would hardly expect you to recognize it," he said, his eyes flickering up to Wildman's face and down again. "But that was the name of the colonel's daughter, the young woman who, shall we say, was the root cause of all of this. My granddaughter was given the name at my request. Her mother had no objection and her father did not disagree. The odd thing is that she looks extraordinarily like the original Gael, a great beauty in her day, let me tell you. And even though memory fades with the years and my mind's eye is obviously not as sharp as it used to be, I can still see that beauty, touch it, feel it...I would ask you to meet her, Wildman, that is all. Will you do that?"

"Very good, sir. I'll do that," said Wildman, wondering if the old man was playing at match-making and if he was being set up as a marriage candidate for someone who, he seemed to be saying, made men run for cover within minutes of initial contact.

"By the way sir, how old is she?"

"She is thirty-one, Wildman. A delightful, healthy and happy thirty-one, as you will find when you two meet."

"As for Pasang," the old man continued, "you must be curious about how he came into my service here. Pasang is a high mountain Sherpa from northern Nepal. When he was young, he walked down from the mountains to the British Gurkha recruiting centre, in eastern Nepal. Passing some initial tests, he was accepted into the Fifth Gurkha Regiment of the old British Army of India. After training as a rifleman parachutist, he was posted to Singapore. When Singapore fell to the Japanese, he managed to get out in the company of some Australians, and together they made their way down into the East Indies and from there across to the Australian mainland. In Australia they were regrouped. In those hectic days, with the Japanese rolling back the frontiers of the Empire, and when manpower was the great need, all sorts of odd postings were made. Pasang wound up with the Australian Air Force and after a series of minor postings, and a little promotion, found himself appointed batman to the aforementioned Group Captain Moseley, Gael's father. At the end of the war, Moseley very much wanted to reward Pasang for his service by getting him into Australia. But immigration laws proved too strict. So they contacted me, I took him in here and he has been with me ever since. A little more salmon for you, young man?"

"Thank you, sir, no. I have had what I believe was an elegant sufficiency."

"Good. Then we'll quaff the rest of the champers here and toast the success of the mission and you can be on your way. Pasang is all packed and al that remains now is for us to walk down to the meadow together."

"A toast then. A Sherpa one. *Tashi delay*! Long life and happiness and, in your case, success."

They raised their glasses and drank.

<<>>

A little later Wildman and Carew met at the front door of the house. Wildman watched as Pasang brought out his grip and handed it to the chauffeur of the Daimler. The hillman went back into the house and came out with a small bedroll. He was dressed in his traditional dress with his *kukri*, the gold tip of its handle gleaming in the pale winter sunlight, solidly lodged in his red waist sash. Wildman wondered if he ever allowed himself to be separated from it and he experienced brief shiver of apprehension as he guessed what must have happened to the thug who managed to get into the house, on the last kidnap attempt.

Now six security men appeared. One of them stationed himself by the Daimler. Two, with leashed Dobermans, took up positions on either side of the parking lot in front of the house, while the remaining four, obviously acting on Lords Carew's instructions, separated and walked quickly down to the four corners of the meadow. There they halted and took up positions facing outwards. Lord Carew waited until the men were all in position, then took Wildman by the arm, and, motioning for Pasang to follow, walked down into the centre of the meadow.

"What I have to say to you now, Wildman, is for your ears only. That is why I have chosen this place, where there are no listening walls, nor, shall we say, softly closing doors? Yes. I know what you think about Ghose. You do not trust him. You worry that he might be connected with Vask in some way? All right. Just keep this in mind. This is my bailiwick here. My territory. I can handle things here and, although I am in my nineties, I am quite capable of doing this. More capable than some people might think, including Ghose, on whom I have been keeping my eye for some time now. If Ghose were to leave here, as he may, one of these days, then I would lose what control I have over him. So, quite simply, it behoves me to have him stay here, where I can keep an eye on him. All right?"

"Yes sir. I think your approach—of keeping him here and watching him—is a good one."

"Good, now, two last things to discuss. One, where you are going to meet Gael. That will depend on which route you take out of England or, if you are going to meet somewhere in Asia, which route you will be using there, to get to Nepal?"

"That's right sir. And as I have not yet completed my planning on this, what I will need to do is get a message to you, when I have. How do you suggest I do this?"

"Gael is in Sydney right now. I will call her and alert her…"

"From here, sir?"

"No, from a friend's house, a safe house. About twenty miles from here. A house with a private phone that we will both use, from now on, for any further communication. Here," he said, handing Wildman a small card, "is the number. Use it to call me when you have your plans in hand. You will be at your club in London? Good. Then call me at the house here, just to say something like thanks for the nice visit and as soon as I hear from you I will go immediately to my friend's house, and call you at the club from there."

"Very good, sir. Then that seems to be all, with the exception of the stone and the piece of poetry that you mentioned. Where do I pick up the stone, and how?"

The old man reached in his pocket and took out a heavy leather wallet. From it he extracted a small card and handed it to Wildman. The card was blank except for a seven-digit number, handwritten on one side.

"Give this card to the manager of my bank, Grindlay's Bank in St. James Square, just next to the East India Club. He will give you a small, sealed leather bag. He does not know what the bag contains and there is no need for him to know. You may check the seal if you wish. I hardly think there is any need. I have been banking with Grindlay's for seventy years and my father before me. Thoroughly dependable people. Not the kind of people to go poking through one's private deposit box. The bag contains the Eye and I do not need to tell you that once it is handed over to you it becomes your responsibility, in total?"

"Very good, sir. And the poem?"

From an inside jacket pocket the old man took out a small, folded piece of paper.

"This is the word key to the temple of the Yellow God. You will need it. When I went there, when I broke in, as I am ashamed to say now, the temple had only one door. I had no trouble with it. I simply broke the lock with a stone and forced it open. Soon after that, the priests there, worried about their security, changed things. They employed a group of engineering technicians from Japan to build them a foolproof security system. Now the whole complex is enclosed within a high stonewall, twenty feet high or more, and very smooth, so that it is impossible to climb. And the old single door has been replaced with three new ones, all in the front of the temple, side by side. One of the doors, only one, allows access to the temple. The other two are dead ends, traps for the unwary and the unwanted with each, I am told, holding potentially fatal consequences to anyone foolish enough to try and gain entry through them.

"It has taken me years to get what is written on this piece of paper, the key to the riddle of the doors, a riddle in itself, from the priests of the temple. When they refused to answer a dozen letters, I sent Pasang to see them. After he had gained their confidence, he told them, binding them with oaths of great secrecy, that I had the Eye and that, if I could, I would one day return it to them. They gave him this piece of writing, these verses and what I want you to do is to learn them by heart, carefully, every word of them, and then destroy the paper. I would not want it to get into the wrong hands, even though, being a riddle that is a key to another riddle, I am not sure that it could be used by anyone else."

Wildman looked at the little piece of paper. There were five verses in all, written with an old fashioned, steel-nibbed pen in jet-black Indian ink. He folded it and put it carefully into an inside pocket of his jacket, resolving to read it, and learn the verses, as soon as he could.

The old man stepped forward and seized one of Wildman's hands in his, at the same time resting his other hand on Wildman's arm.

"Goodbye then, young man. We may meet again. We may not, for my days are numbered now. But that is not important. What is important is the success of your mission. And I know that you are going to be successful. Godspeed to you.

"And Pasang," he said, motioning to the Sherpa to come forward, "here is the letter that I want you to take and carry with you. It is addressed to Mr. Wildman. I want you to carry it and I want you to give it to him when the mission is completed. What is in the letter will, you will see, affect and shape your future. Carry it carefully. Now go. Go in safety."

The old man shook hands with both of them and then, turning, walked briskly up the meadow, towards the house. He did not look back. Wildman, followed by Pasang, walked to the Daimler and there stood back to allow the Sherpa to enter. But the little mountain man, instantly establishing his new status with Wildman, shook his head and said, "After you, sir."

Wildman got into the back of the car and settled himself in the big leather seat. Pasang carefully closed the door behind him and then got into the front, with the chauffeur. The big car purred into life and rolled swiftly down the driveway. The estate gates opened and closed behind them and when they did, the security men in the meadow relaxed and started back towards the house. At the house itself the front door closed softly behind the frail figure of Lord Carew as, smiling gently to himself, he made his way towards his study and what he considered a congratulatory and well-deserved glass of cognac.

BOOK TWO

THE MISSION

On the drive down to London they made one stop, for dinner, at the inn where Wildman had lunched on the way up. Pasang indicated that he would prefer to eat with the chauffeur and did so. After Wildman had eaten, he ordered a cognac and, taking out the little piece of paper that Lord Carew had given him, laid it on the table in front of him. There were five verses in all and they were titled.

THE RIDDLE OF THE GOLDEN DOORS

Forward stride, count not the cost,
He who hesitates is lost.
For those who come to the golden doors,
The question arises, which one is yours?

Is it the left one, or middle, or right,
And can entry be made both by day and by night?
But the left must be wrong if the right is right,
As in the opposite, regardless of might.

Herein lies a deadly riddle,
Is death awaiting in the middle?
Or are all three doors but a lethal warning,
From each of which there is no returning?

A man of wisdom might quickly see,
That entry lies in number three,
But the doors their numbers do not say,
How then know the one safe way?

The faint of heart will never know,
But those who dare will onward go,
Provided that their cause is just,
And in their hearts no evil lurks.

Wildman read the verses through twice. At first, the wording meant nothing to him at all. Then, reading it through for the third and fourth time, he suddenly realised that the verses were exactly what Lord Carew had said they were. A key to the door, the one safe door of the temple, the key that Wildman would need when he eventually reached the temple, to get inside it and return the Eye. The key that would protect him from whatever dreadful fate lay in wait for someone opening, or trying to open, the wrong doors. But "*the left must be wrong if the right is right,*" meant nothing to him at this point, any more than *"as in the opposite, regardless of might."* But there was plenty of time to work on the riddle. He would memorize it first and work on it later.

Arriving in London, Wildman booked in at the club and, with a little difficulty, managed to get a room for Pasang in the servants' quarters. Not done, you understand, Mr. Wildman. Not normally, that is to say. But as long as your man uses the back door, the ladies entrance, that is, and in consideration of the very healthy contribution you annually make to the upkeep of the premises, we'll make an exception in your case. Bet you will, thought Wildman.

Next day Wildman was up early. There was much to be done. Having agreed to take the mission, his one aim now was to get started as quickly as possible, to get underway. If word were to be leaked to the enemy—and already he was beginning to think of Vask and his thugs as the enemy—they too would be making preparations and plans, with the intention of separating him from the Eye. A quick exit from England, he thought, might give him an initial edge.

Long before the traffic had started to build up in the streets of London, he was working on plans for the mission. The first of these took him to the Royal Geographical Society in Kensington Gore. An early morning call to one of the society's directors, a friend of his, had set certain wheels in motion. When he and Pasang arrived at the ancient brick pile facing Green Park, a young man in an old Etonian blazer, ruffled corduroys and a pipe, was there to meet them. Pasang elected to wait outside and for the full three hours that Wildman spent in the building, he sat on the front steps, his dark brown eyes watching and carefully appraising the people who came and went through the ancient courtyard, nodding in reply to an occasional good morning and scowling to himself, inwardly, when a trio of simpering Indian students walked past. Nepalese, traditionally, do not like Indians.

Inside the building Wildman was quickly led to a small back room. It contained a large table and a single chair. On the table were seven bulky files tied with red ribbons and, beside them, four large tomes bound in leather. The young man closed the door softly as he left.

Wildman picked up the first file. It was entitled, ***AN ACCOUNT AND HISTORY OF THE CULT OF THE THUGS OF THE CENTRAL PROVINCES OF INDIA. BY HENRY SLEEMAN. FILE ONE. 1734 TO 1791***. He opened the file and began to speed-read through the ancient and dusty pages.

The file began with a history and description of the practice of *thuggee* by the criminal tribes of Central India. It told how male members of the tribes were enrolled as boys and trained through early childhood in the sinister and murderous practices of the *thuggee* gangs. All members of the cult were worshippers of the goddess Kali, the Hindu deity of death and destruction. After taking solemn oaths of secrecy and dedication, both to the goddess and the leaders of the gangs, it was instilled into them that their sole duty in life, their only reason for living, was to supply the goddess with human victims. To this end they were required to kill, wherever they could, and as often as they could, anyone outside of their own villages who was not a member of the cult. If there was a choice, they were to pick Christians and Muslims. The reward for their services would be a share of whatever loot the killings generated and, of course, the blessings of Kali.

Their method of killing was to be, always, by strangulation and they were taught how to use a silk scarf—a *rumal*—for this purpose. The *rumal*, a piece of cloth about a yard square, was folded into a single strip, and a heavy coin, in this case a single silver rupee, was knotted into the end of the strip. Victims were approached from behind. The thug—the strangler—would hold his right arm across his chest, with the unweighted end of the strip locked in the fingers of his right hand; the other end, the weighted end, dangling down his left side. To make the kill, the band of silk was whipped around the victim's neck, from left to right, in a lightning-fast, backhand movement. When the coin-weighted end came around the victim's neck, the strangler would reach across and seize it with his left hand. Thus, when pressure was applied from behind—pressure assisted by a knee in the victim's back—it was a form of cross-pressure centred on the victim's throat, and the sides of the neck. When applied with force, blood circulation through the carotid arteries was instantly cut off and the result was immediate loss of consciousness, followed by death.

Most of the victims of the cult of *thuggee* were travellers, and when a party was encountered on the road, the rule was for every man, woman and child to be strangled. After strangulation the bodies were stripped and everything of value was taken. Graves were then dug for the victims and they were placed in these, side by side. But before the graves were closed, a bamboo stake was driven through the heart of each and every one. The motto of the stranglers may well have been, dead men tell no tales.

Rupert and Rara, the little children who escaped the thug attack when travelling through India by running into the jungle and hiding. Their mother-Gael, the colonel's daughter-and her husband, Brigadier Wildman, were murdered in this tragic incident. Picture taken on the children's return to their family home in Ireland. Photo Credit, J.E. Stanley. Artists & Photographers, 22 Westmorland Street, Dublin, Ireland.

It took Wildman an hour to read through the first file. When he was done he closed it and opened the second. This one was dated 1702 to 1853 and he went through it in thirty minutes. The third file was dated 1854, three years before the Indian Mutiny and it went all the way through to 1914, the first year of the World War 1. He was two-thirds of the way through it when he suddenly stopped, leaned forward, read a yellowed page for a second time and found the information he was looking for.

It was all there. The tragic story of a British family travelling by train through India. Of a breakdown, at night, in the jungles of the Central Provinces. Of a band of thugs who descended on the wretched and defenceless passengers. Of a vicious gang leader who had every man, woman and child murdered. Of two little English children who fled into the jungle, and lived to tell the tale. The name of the leader of the thugs... Vask. A man, who, the file said, was probably responsible for three thousand murders in the Central Provinces. A man who, when he was arrested and hanged for his crimes in Bombay, six months later, left behind a wife and two sons...

Wildman closed the file and sat back. Sunlight filtered through the dusty panes of the tall windows of the little room and from outside came the faint rumble of London's traffic. Slowly a plan took shape in his mind. It would be a plan for the mission. But it would also encompass a private plan of his one, one based on what he had just read in the ancient files.

He would go to Nepal via India. Lord Carew would not like it. Pasang might not like it. There could be difficulties in making contact with the old man's so called 'free spirit', Gael. In addition there would be added risks. But what he had seen in the files convinced him that this is what he should do. For the ancient archives had confirmed a story that his father had whispered to him as a child. Now the time had come to act on it, to seek a reckoning with the criminals who had wantonly murdered an innocent English woman, all those years ago and who, according to Lord Carew, were still practising their vile trade. The original Vask was long gone. But again—and the files confirmed that Lord Carew was right—a similar organisation, one that dealt in torture and death, was now being led by one of his direct descendants, a man who, because of the power of his wealth, was above the law. He hesitated for a moment more and then made up his mind. He would go through India and he would go by road. He could be running into a hornet's nest. But at the same time it might give him a chance to draw Vask out of his lair and into the open, where he might be vulnerable, and where a reckoning could be affected.

Emerging from the Society building, he collected Pasang, and together they found a small tavern and had lunch. It was a buffet meal and after each had collected his food, Pasang took his to a corner of the pub and ate alone. Wildman said nothing. When they got to India he hoped that things would be different. But for now, if this was what the man wanted, a master and servant status between them, then this was what he could have and until they got to India, he would respect the little Sherpa's wishes.

Lunch over, Wildman told Pasang to take the afternoon off. Did he have some money? Yes. They would meet later that night.

Wildman returned to the club and, making his way to his small, upstairs room, sat down and made a number of phone calls. The first was to a travel agent in London, where he made reservations for two persons, First Class, British Airways, London to Bombay, for the following day, and reservations, on arrival in Bombay, at the Oberoi Tower Hotel. Did he want the tickets delivered? No, he would pick them up the next day. Then he called Lord Carew and told him that he was calling to thank him for a delightful visit, and that he hoped he would be able to come again soon. When he had finished talking he listened on the line for a moment before putting the receiver down. Yes. As before, a double click. An extension phone in the house? Or a tap on the line?

He then wrote out two cables. The first was to his housekeeper in Kathmandu. It read: ***ARRIVING SOON. SAFEGUARD HOUSE. NO VISITORS UNDER ANY CIRCUMSTANCES. EXPECT GIFT PARCEL BY REGISTERED MAIL, AIR. GOOD WISHES YOU AND FAMILY. WILDMAN.*** The cable was addressed to Mr. Tashi Kirong, Julia Cottage, Jawalakhel, Kathmandu.

The second cable was addressed to **MODI, 56, MAHATMA ROAD, COLABA CAUSEWAY, BOMBAY, and it read, THIS CABLE PRIORITY RATING ONE. ARRIVING IN TWO DAYS. NEED FAST, RELIABLE, FOUR WHEEL DRIVE VEHICLE FOR ONE MONTH. COST IMMATERIAL. RELIABILITY ESSENTIAL. WILL CONTACT YOU ON ARRIVAL. WILDMAN.**

The cables completed, he left the room and walked downstairs to the club lobby where he gave the cables and two ten pound notes to the Hall Porter. "Immediately, sir, at once."

Then he walked out of the club, turned left and, with long strides, quickly covered the fifty yards to Grindlay's Bank on the corner. Inside he asked to speak to one of the assistant managers and was guided to a quiet back room. There he presented his credentials for his foreign currency account and asked for fifty thousand dollars in one hundred dollar bills. He also requested and was given, as a special client of the bank, two nylon money belts and a locking canvas sack. When the money arrived, he placed two hundred and fifty bills in each, placed the belts in the canvas sack, thanked the bank official and left the building. He returned to the club, went up to his room and put the canvas sack in his grip, and shoved it under the bed. Then he stripped off, showered, put on a dark blue cotton bathrobe and lay back on the bed to await Lord Carew's call.

The call came an hour later. Wildman had been dozing, but he was instantly alert when he heard the old man's voice. The line, for once, was

NATIONAL AND GRINDLAYS BANK LIMITED

(AMALGAMATING NATIONAL BANK OF INDIA LIMITED AND GRINDLAYS BANK LIMITED)

INLAND & OVERSEAS TELEGRAMS
MINERVA · LONDON

TELEX NOS. 22368-9

TELEPHONE: LONDON WALL 4040

26 BISHOPSGATE LONDON·E·C·2

IN REPLY PLEASE QUOTE

1st January, 1959.

Dear Mr. Wildman.

CHANGE OF NAME.

Please note that in accordance with a resolution passed by the Bank's shareholders at an Extraordinary General Meeting held on 25th November, 1958 and duly approved by the Registrar of Companies, Board of Trade, London, our name has been shortened with effect from 1st January, 1959 from "National Overseas and Grindlays Bank Limited" to:-

"NATIONAL AND GRINDLAYS BANK LIMITED"

Yours faithfully,

Assistant Secretary.

Letter to Wildman from his bank in London. He also banked with Grindlays in Bombay and Calcutta.

good and he heard the old man gasp when he told him that he had made a decision about his route to Nepal, and that he was going to go via India. He did not tell him that he was going to go by road. That, he felt, might be a little too much for the old man to accept. As it was he detected a note of concern in his voice. But whatever he felt, the man was too well bred to question Wildman's decision and when he spoke, he did not comment on it.

"Very well. You have made your decision. I will cable Gael this afternoon and ask her to fly to India at once. I have already alerted her and she

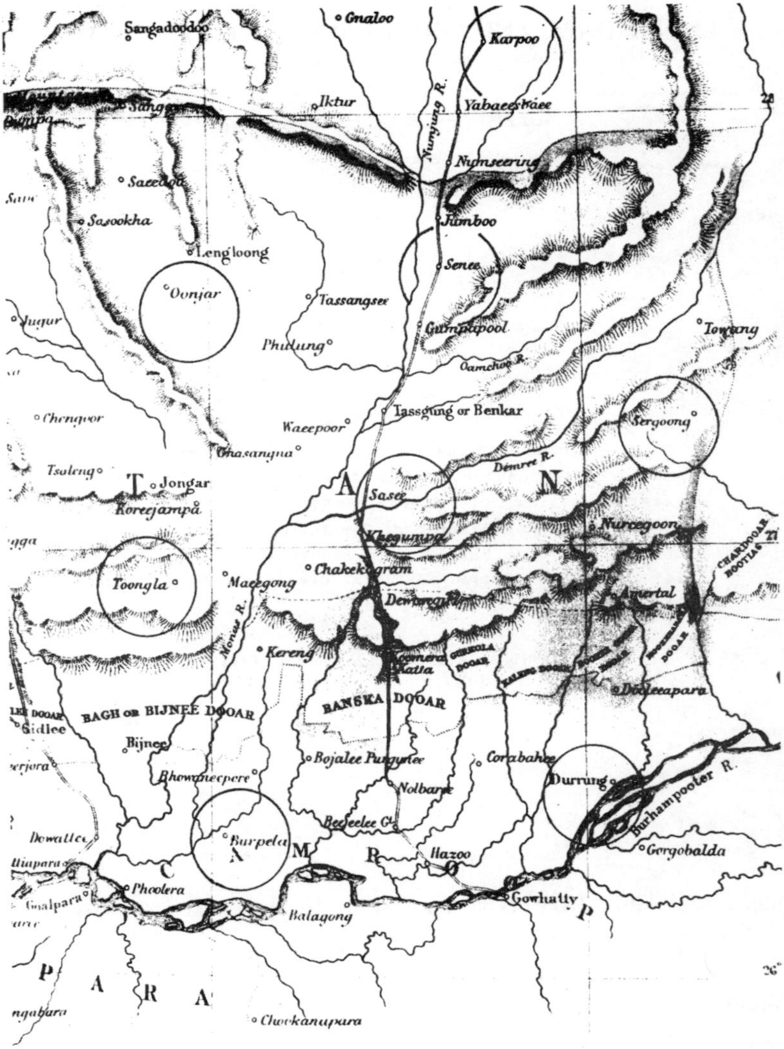

Historical map of part of north India showing, ringed, locations were the original thugs, Vask's ancestors, committed their atrocities.

Photo credit: House of Commons, London, England. Feb 15 1865.

is ready to leave without delay. Now, what about a meeting place? Where and when?"

Wildman thought for a moment and then said, "How about the front of the Taj Mahal in Bombay, three days from now, nine in the morning? Tell here to look for a four-wheel drive vehicle, probably a Jeep or a Land Rover. Tell her to be ready to leave at once and that I will wait fifteen minutes, no more. Does she know Pasang? Will she recognize him when she sees him, sir?"

"Yes, she knows Pasang. All right then. Front of the Taj in three days' time. Nine in the morning. I will tell her that. And Wildman?"

"Yes sir?"

"Be careful."

The line went dead and this time there was no double click. Wildman hung up the receiver, shrugged off his bathrobe and dressed quickly in flannels, a cotton Tattersall shirt and a dark blue cravat. Slipping on a navy blazer, he left the club and walked across the square into Haymarket Street. Crossing the road, he entered a little street that ran behind the Haymarket theatre. He walked down the street, stopped under a little sign that said, JOE ROBINSON. JUDOKWAI, entered, descended a flight of stairs and was greeted at the bottom by a huge man dressed in a black-belted judo robe. They shook hands and the big man directed Wildman to a dressing room, where he changed. Emerging, he spent the next three hours with the big judo teacher, and several of his companions, working the judo mat until, exhausted, bones aching, he stopped. The club closed as he showered and, at his invitation, the big man and a couple of his equally brawny friends joined him for dinner at a nearby pub.

Nine that evening saw him back at the club. Pasang was tucked in his cubbyhole in the servants' quarters at the back. Wildman looked in on him quickly, said goodnight and told him to meet him early next morning. The he went to his room and retired for the night.

Next morning he was up soon after dawn. He dressed in his tracksuit and left the club by the back door. As he expected, Pasang was waiting for him outside the club and gave him a cheery good morning as he swung into Duke Street and then, at a fast pace, with the little Sherpa effortlessly padding along behind him, ran uphill to the end of the street. At Regent Street he swung left towards Hyde Park, ran down to Hyde Park corner and then into the park itself. Two hours later they returned to the club.

Wildman, noticing that the little Sherpa was not even sweating after two hours of running, told him to pack and to be ready to leave at nine. When Pasang headed for the servants' quarters, Wildman entered the club through the back door and walked to the front hall. There he checked with the Hall Porter about an answer to his Bombay cable. There was none, the man told him, straightening his tie and raising his eyebrows fractionally at the sight of a tracksuit in the front hall of the club.

Wildman returned to his room, showered, changed and descended to the main dining room for breakfast. After breakfast he returned to his room again and took the Glock 9mm out of his grip. From a small plastic bag he took an oiled cloth and wrapped the Glock in this. Then he took the canvas bag that the bank had given him, emptied it of the money belts, and put the Glock inside and locked it. This done, he picked up the phone and called Harrods, London's famous department store and, using his credit card, placed an order. Did he want it sent somewhere? Yes. But he would come by later in the morning to check it and would they kindly hold the packing until he did?

At his request the Hall Porter had sent up an old steamer trunk of his from storage; now he opened this and commenced pulling out clothing, boots and camping equipment. He thought quickly about what climates he might encounter on the trip and chose his clothing accordingly. Central India in late October and early November would have day temperatures in the sixties to eighties, nights down into the forties. A road journey would take him though the Central Provinces. North of there would be cooler, and when he got to Nepal he could expect, at altitudes of up to five thousand feet, days in the forty to fifty range and nights that would drop the mercury to freezing. Five thousand was as high as he expected to go.

To start with, he would travel dressed as he was. Medium-weight cotton shirt, grey flannels, his standby navy blazer, regimental tie, medium weight Orlon socks, and black loafers. For Bombay, he chose a lightweight tropical suit, khaki colour, polyester-cotton mix, with two sets of trousers. Opening his travelling grip he put in the suit, folding it carefully, adding two shirts, underwear, extra socks and leather shaving kit with a standard Schick razor and extra blades. He added soap, toothpaste and extra toothbrush, then zipped up the kit and packed it in the grip. Then he turned to the question of outdoor gear.

From the trunk he pulled out a medium weight, fibre-filled sleeping bag and a thin, self-inflating ground pad. He stuffed these down into the grip and with them jammed a heavy, oiled-wool L.L. Bean sweater, dark blue, with long sleeves. Reaching into the trunk again he found a heavy, black, five-cell flashlight. He opened it up and loaded it with five new Duracell batteries, made sure that it had an extra bulb stored in its base cap and then added it to the gear in the grip. He considered but decided against several other items in the trunk, among them running shoes and down-insulated clothing. There would be little time for early morning running once he started up through India and where he was going, he would not need the down clothing. An old pair of corduroy trousers and a worn corduroy jacket with leather elbow patches were next. Two unopened bottles of Glenlivet scotch followed. He wrapped one in the corduroy trousers and the other in the old jacket, and packed them carefully in the centre of the grip.

He looked at his watch, a slim gold Omega, to check the time. Then he took it off and replaced it with his field watch, a steel Rolex, ten years old and rather battered, but looking just as good as the day he won it from a hard-faced Australian journalist named Steve Dunleavy in a poker game in Macao.

Next came waterproof matches in a small, screw top waterproof container. A medium-weight, two-bladed, locking Coleman knife, one blade with a serrated edge, accompanied by a small sharpening stone in a leather case. And a pair of Leitz 10X40 Trinovid binoculars. This left just two other items. His bush hat, a heavy, double brim, felt Terai hat from Nepal, with a khaki band. And a pair of leather boots. The boots were knee high, made of Brazilian buffalo hide by the Gokey Company of St. Paul, Minnesota and, like the hat, he never went on a mission without them. Checking to see that the leather was well oiled, he wrapped them in a thin cotton towel and put them in with the other things. This done, he zipped up the grip, closed and locked the trunk and then called the front desk.

Within a few minutes one of the hall porters came and took the trunk. Wildman waited until he left and then took out the money belts from where he had concealed them behind a couch cushion. He tied one around his waist and then, the second money belt in one hand and the canvas sack containing the Glock in the other, descended the stairs to the front hall. At the reception desk he checked again for a cable from India. There was none. He gave the hall porter the canvas sack for safe deposit, and tipped him generously. Then, with the grip in one hand and the money belt in the other, he left the club by the front door and joined Pasang outside. Pasang hailed a taxi. One quickly drew up to the curb. Wildman threw his suitcase into the front and waved Pasang into the back. But the little Sherpa stepped back and said, "After you, *sahib*", and Wildman with a smile climbed into the back of the cab.

When Pasang joined him, Wildman handed him the money and showed him how to tie it around his waist under his clothing. At the same time he directed the taxi driver to take them to a little street in Soho.

"We are off, Pasang," Wildman said, as the taxi swung into Piccadilly and swung around the famous fountain of Eros, the goddess of love, and into the maze of streets that is London's sleazier night club area.

Lowering his voice, Wildman continued. "First, Pasang, we have to pick up our tickets. Then we go back to the bank, where I have to collect a small packet. Then to Harrods, for some gifts for my Sherpas in Kathmandu, the people who look after my house there."

"*Tik cha, sahib*. Very good."

"Good. By the way, I notice you are not wearing your *kukri*?"

"In my bedroll, *sahib*. Otherwise trouble at airport, you know."

"All right. And you have your passport ready?"

"Yes *sahib*. All ready."

The taxi rolled to a stop under a sign that said, BOND, TRAVEL SPECIALISTS. Wildman told the driver to wait and jumped out of the taxi and entered the travel agency. He was out again in five minutes, six thousand dollars poorer but with two first class air tickets on Pan American, London to Bombay, one way, and a voucher for a week's stay for two at the Bombay Oberoi Tower.

Re-entering the taxi, he told the driver to return to St. James Square and stop at Grindlay's Bank, in the corner of the square. They were there within twenty minutes. Again Wildman told Pasang to wait and, leaving the taxi, went into the bank alone.

Entering the bank, Wildman went straight to one of the seated officers and asked to speak to the manager. Within a few minutes he was ushered into the manager's office and, as soon as he was seated, after the briefest of introductions, he showed him the numbered card that Lord Carew had given him. The manager, an older man with many years' service behind him, hesitated a moment and then rose and asked Wildman to follow him. Unlike his previous visit, when his transaction was carried out in a small backroom, this time he was led all the way back to the main bank vault. Following the manager, and accompanied by a uniformed guard, he passed through a massive steel door with computerised locks. After this came a second steel door, equally massive, and here the manager asked him to wait.

Wildman watched as the elderly man entered a small room lined with numbered steel boxes. He quickly selected one of the boxes, opened it with two keys and, reaching in, took out a small leather bag. The bag had a yellowed, tattered label attached to it on which was written, in faded black Indian ink, a number. The man compared the number with the one on the card, muttered something about it being in there for a long time, then closed the box and came out, beckoning Wildman to join him at a small table set against the wall. On the table was a single item, a fat ledger bound in gold-embossed black leather. Opening the ledger, with the security guard standing behind him, the manager began turning and scanning the pages. Eventually he found the entry he was looking for. The notation said, simply, ***CAREW. ONE LEATHER BAG. SEALED. OCTOBER 25TH 1907.***

"Here you are sir, all intact, as per the register. Would you care to sign here, please? The bag is still sealed, as you can see and as we have no idea what is in it, that is all that you are signing for, one sealed leather bag."

Wildman read the entry, signed his name, added the date, took the bag from the man, thanked him, dropped the bag in his pocket, nodded to the security guard, walked back upstairs, left the bank and rejoined Pasang in the taxi. He told the driver to take him to Harrods, in Knightsbridge. While the taxi crawled down through Hyde Park Corner and fought its way through London's incredible traffic, he resisted the impulse to take the little leather bag out of his pocket and open it and look at its contents. He did, however, run his hand across its surface several times and what he felt inside—something that was something round and smooth and about the size of a golf ball—set him to wondering about its extraordinary value and, in turn, old Lord Carew's great trust in him.

Harrods. One of the great stores of the world. With a doorman in a uniform that looked like a cross between an Argentinean admiral and a Vatican guard. A giant of a man whose moustache bristled when he saw Wildman's taxi parking in a **NO PARKING** zone and continued to bristle until the ten pound note thrust into his hand eased the problem and produced a hearty "Good morning sir," as he ushered Wildman into the huge store.

Wildman walked quickly to the nearest elevator and was whisked to the top floor within seconds. The order that he had phoned in, the gifts for his housekeepers in Kathmandu were ready. For his Sherpa, Tashi, shirts and Levi trousers, a sweater and canvas-sided working boots. For Tashi's wife, half a bolt of pure silk and another of brocade. For their little girl, a huge doll dressed in a bright, Irish green full-length dress, a diamond tiara with plastic diamonds, large blue eyes that opened and closed when it was picked up and laid down and, courtesy of the latest in electronic wizardry for dolls, a built-in voice system with a vocabulary of a hundred words. Wildman winced when he saw it and heard it speak. But his housekeeper's little daughter would love it.

The salesperson was a pleasant young Englishwoman and, Wildman guessed, rather new to her job. Good, he thought. Just what I need. He approached her and picked up the doll.

"Nice, isn't it," he said, smiling at the young woman.

"Yes sir," she replied. "One of our nicer models. And all the other things you ordered are ready for you. All we have to do pack them and then get the address of where you want them sent."

Wildman smiled again and lifting the doll held it up to the light, and then, making sure that she was watching him, suddenly changed his expression to one of painful surprise. He froze, grabbed his stomach and bent over.

"Oh God," he said. "Sorry. It's cramps. Damned malaria. Takes you unawares, you know."

Still bending over, his face began to turn red and the young woman saw to her alarm that his eyes were beginning to water.

"Sir, are you all right?" she said, her eyes wide with concern. "Can I help you? Shall I call a doctor?"

Through gritted teeth, his face twisted in pretended pain, Wildman muttered. "No, just a loo. That's all I need. A toilet, you know? Can you…what, over there? Thanks. Hope I can make it."

Clutching the doll and visibly staggering, he made his way down between the laden counters, knocking over a stack of show boxes and a clutch of schoolgirl's hockey sticks. The minute he disappeared, the young woman reached for her phone and called for her supervisor. It took an under manager a little while to find the supervisor. "He looked terrible. I thought he was having a heart attack. Said it was cramps though, something about malaria."

The supervisor, an older woman, with many years of store experience in everything from coronary arrest to epilepsy, listened until the girl had finished and then commenced to tell her what to do. But before she could finish, the young woman interrupted her. "Oh dear. He's coming back. Yes, he looks better. I think he's all right."

She put down the phone and addressed Wildman.

"Sir. Are you all right? I can get a doctor if you wish. You're feeling better? Oh, thank goodness. You really had me worried for a minute there."

"Sorry luv," said Wildman. "Malaria, you know. Brought it back from Africa. Brings on the cramps and takes you unaware at times. Not contagious, however. So nothing to worry about. Now let's see. Everything here? The silk. The sweater? Good. Then here's the doll and what I want you to do is pack it all very securely—I suggest a strong wooden box—

and then send it by registered mail, by air...got your little pencil ready there?...to Mr. and Mrs. Tashi Kirong, Julia Cottage, Jawalakhel, Kathmandu. Don't forget now, registered mail. OK? Now what do you think it will cost?"

The young woman looked at the assortment of goods on the counter and picking up a calculator began to try and estimate weights and airmail costs. Wildman waited a moment and then, looking at his watch, pulled out his wallet and laid five ten-pound bills on the counter.

"I think this should cover registered airmail, OK? The rest of the costs are on my credit card. If there is a balance you can keep it, all right?"

"I think fifty pounds is really too much, sir. Twenty pounds at the most. And we are not allowed to accept tips here. I think..."

"In that case, if there's anything left over, just make a donation in my name to the Flat Earth Society."

Saying which he smiled and walked away, leaving the young woman, charmed by his smile and totally perplexed by his suggestion about the Flat Earth Society, in a state of utter confusion. Down five flights of stairs, a cracking salute—five more pounds worth ‾ from the doorman, into the taxi and they were off to the airport.

At the airport, just before boarding, Wildman made one last call to the hall porter of the East India Club. Had there been any reply to his cable to Bombay? No, he was told. Nothing had come in. When he heard this he left the phone booth and together with Pasang walked to the first class check-in counter. Their bags whisked away, they then made for immigration. There was no outgoing customs check and forty-five minutes later the big Pan Am Boeing 747, in vast plumes of spray from the rain-soaked tarmac and belching black kerosene fumes from its four huge engines, lifted off and climbed smoothly into the grey October sky. As it did, three hundred and fifty miles away to the north, the sallow-faced Ghose carefully closed and locked the door of his room and sat down to read the packet of cables that Lord Carew had given him to send from the local post office.

There were three cables in all. The first was to the Dusit Thani Hotel in Bangkok, requesting a reservation for a suite for two persons, arriving within twenty-four hours, in the name of a Mr. Wildman. The second was to the manager of the same hotel, requesting special services for Mr. Wildman as a V.I.P guest. The third was to the manager of the Shangri La Hotel in Kathmandu, advising him that a Mr. Wildman would be arriving within thirty-six hours from Bangkok, and advising him to cable the Dusit Thani for details of Mr. Wildman's flight number and arrival schedule. He too was to reserve a suite for Mr. Wildman and arrange for V.I.P services. As in the cable to the Dusit Thani, all invoices were to be sent to Lord Carew via Grindlay's Bank, London.

An hour later Ghose sent the cables at the little village post office a mile from Lord Carew's estate. This done he walked down the street of the tiny village to its single pay phone. Sliding into the little red phone booth, Ghose carefully closed the door behind him. Then, pushing a handful of coins into the steel phone box, he dialled a number in London. When his connection came through he spoke in Hindustani.

"It is moving. Bangkok. Tomorrow. The Dusit Thani hotel. Then through to Kathmandu. Most probably Thai International into Nepal but maybe also Burma Air or Royal Nepal Air. Wildman. American. About six foot two. A hundred and eighty pounds. A professional smuggler. And a Nepali. A Sherpa. Small. About five foot six. Wears traditional Sherpa dress. Age about fifty. Carries a knife."

Ghose smiled. At last. His job was finished, the assignment completed. He returned to the house, quietly packed and that night, when everyone slept, slipped through the security men, climbed the wall of the estate, walked to the village and caught a night train to London. Twelve hours later he was seated on a plane for Bombay. From there he would go by train to Nagpur. Home. Home again after long years of servitude. Home to the long-awaited reward from his lord and master, Raja Vask.

BOOK THREE

BOMBAY

Bombay, with the first cool winds of winter sweeping in from the Indian Ocean. Bombay, a giant among cities. A seething mass of people, of colour and noise and dirt and squalor. Wide avenues graced by the massive stone structures of the British and the Raj, and behind them narrow streets where the houses leaned together and almost touched. And layered in the humid air, the powerful, all pervading odours of cooking food, of curried meats and dried fish—Bombay Duck it was called—of vegetables and fruit and ginger and garlic and cardamom and saffron.

Wildman and Pasang took a taxi from Bombay's Santa Cruz Airport into the city. At the Oberoi Tower Hotel, on the waterfront, Wildman asked for and was given adjoining rooms on the fifth floor. He saw Pasang checked into his room and after the porter had left, made a call to his Bombay contact, Modi, a man vital to his plans for the journey north by road. After some waiting he was put through to the man's office in the city. A secretary spoke. Yes, they had received Mr. Wildman's cable. But Mr. Modi was in Japan on business. And at the moment he was actually out on a fishing trip in the northern islands and unreachable by phone.

Wildman hung up and swore. What now. He needed Modi to get a car, for the drive north. He could fly to Delhi, of course and from there to Kathmandu. But that would distort the aim of the plan he had made when he visited the Royal Geographical Society in London. He could go by train. But that too would not fit his planning, and what he hoped it would produce. No. He had to have a car and he had to have one now, without delay. He opened his grip and took out a small combination journal and address book. The journal was almost empty—Wildman did not believe in leaving written trails behind him—and the address book was written in code. He flipped the pages. Under B, which stood for Bombay, he found just two notations. One was for Modi, his address and phone numbers.

The phone numbers carried a Calcutta prefix and not a Bombay one. Not something to baffle the CIA for very long. But enough to stop an Indian policeman from getting anything at a quick glance.

Under Modi, in the second notation, was another name but no address. Wildman remembered writing this in the book three years previously. The name was Chatterjee and beside was written, Hippie Haven, Third Best.

Wildman thought for a moment. Hippie Haven? For second or two he could not recall what it meant. Then it came to him. Hippie Haven in those days was the nickname for Goa, the old Portuguese colony, down the coast from Bombay, where hippies by the thousand came for the cheap food and lodging. In this case, however, Wildman's code told him it was the name of a street, and not the city. Goa Street was what it meant. And Third Best? Number three.

He put the address book back in the canvas bag and locked it. Then he took a box of matches from the hotel's writing desk and, breaking one into two pieces, put one of the pieces between the grip and the wall. Any movement of the grip would cause the match to fall down behind it. He left the room, pocketing the room keys, knocked on Pasang's door, told him that they were going to take a little trip and then together they took an elevator down to the huge lobby of the hotel.

Walking out through the hotel's huge, plate glass, front door, and getting one of the turbaned doormen to call him a taxi, Wildman thought about his room and wondered if he should have set some more matchstick traps. But there was not much point. The Oberoi Tower was the kind of hotel where the soap and towels were changed twice a day, where innumerable staff would have master keys and would be in and out of the room every hour or so. In any case, if someone did get in and do a search, it was doubtful that they would find anything to connect him with his mission. The only piece of contraband that he might have been concerned about was the Glock. And that was safely locked away in a security box at the East India Club.

Wildman told the taxi driver to take them to St. Michael's Cathedral. From there they would walk across to Goa Street. On the way to the cathedral, in a voice too low for the taxi driver to hear, he outlined his immediate plan to Pasang. He told him that his main Bombay contact was out of town and that they now had to deal with another, an unknown one, for a car. Pasang listened carefully and, when Wildman came to the part about the car, he glanced quickly at the big American. Wildman caught the glance and realised that, until then, he had told Pasang nothing about his plan and, in particular, nothing abut how they were going to travel to Nepal. He gave his companion's impassive face a quick look. If the hillman was surprised, his face did not show it. He simply nodded in agreement to what Wildman was telling him, and if there was any question in his mind as to the wisdom of what Wildman intended to do—to travel across India by road carrying something as valuable as the Eye—again his face showed nothing.

"Very good, *sahib*," was all he said, and Wildman wondered if his little companion's self-imposed discipline was a carryover from his years of military service, or something that had a basis in his absolute dedication to the old man, Lord Carew. Or a combination of both.

The taxi pulled up in front of the cathedral. Wildman paid the driver, waited until he had left and then set off a brisk pace into a maze of narrow streets. At an intersection, Goa Street was marked with a rusting metal sign hanging from a leaning wooden post. It was a street of small shops selling everything from bicycle parts to shoes and sewing machines. There were a couple of sleazy restaurants. With Wildman leading, they stopped at the first one, went in, sat down at a battered, metal-topped table, and ordered tea. A thin-faced boy in a torn, grease-spattered shirt brought them two glasses of milky tea. Wildman's had a large black fly floating in it. But the tea was not Wildman's real interest at the moment. He wanted to see if they were being followed and together they waited for five minutes, watching the street carefully, as a precaution.

When he was satisfied that there was no one taking an interest in them, he threw some coins on the table and left the tea to the flies. Followed by Pasang, he walked quickly out of the restaurant, across the street and into the gloomy hallway of an old house, the sagging, open front door of which bore the number, 3. Once inside they climbed a flight of grimy stairs, picking their way through piles of refuse. A large rat scurried ahead of them. At the top of the stairs was a single door. It looked a little stronger than the one down at street level. Wildman knocked and waited. When he heard a movement behind the door he knocked again.

The door opened about two inches and part of a man's face and body appeared. He was small, no more than five feet, dark faced and dressed in a faded blue shirt and a once-white pair of cotton trousers. Wildman leaned forward and smiled. "Mr. Chatterjee, isn't it?"

The man looked up at Wildman warily, his face a mask of suspicion, and, as he did so, Wildman slid his foot sideways into the narrow opening between the edge of the door and the jamb, at the same time moving his body imperceptibly forward.

"We want to talk to you, Mr. Chatterjee. Just for a few minutes. May we come in?"

Applying pressure with his body, Wildman eased the door inward. The man, his face frowning, stepped back and, as he did so, Wildman and Pasang moved swiftly through the doorway and into the room, Wildman closing the door behind them with a quick thrust of his hand.

The room was bleak and bare, the furniture consisting of a bed, two old wire chairs and a tale with a pile of papers on it. There was a cheap transistor radio on a shelf above a sink. In the corner was a large, open tin trunk bulging with tattered clothing and under the bed were stacks of old newspapers. The walls were nearly completely covered with garish Indian calendars and pictures cut from Indian movie magazines. Wildman smiled. "Mind if we sit?" and promptly sat down in one of the wire chairs.

The little man, visibly nervous, remained standing. "What you want?" he said. "Where from you come?"

Wildman leaned forward. "We'll tell you what we want in just a minute, Mr. Chatterjee. In the meantime, you have a brother in Calcutta, yes?"

"Yes, I do. But what has that got to do with you?"

"Why don't you sit on the bed there, Mr. Chatterjee," said Wildman, motioning the little man towards the bed. "And then we can talk."

When their reluctant host was seated, Wildman began. "About three years ago your brother did a little job for me. A simple thing. I needed some, shall we say, official papers. He got them for me, no questions asked. In return he was well rewarded. When I met him he was working as a grease monkey in a dead-beat garage in the back of Ballygunge. When I left him, or soon afterwards, he had his own place on Chowringhee road, a block and a half from the Grand Hotel. I understand that since then he has done very well for himself?"

Wildman had been watching the little man's face as he spoke, and now he saw the beginnings of recognition creeping slowly across it. Suddenly, with a movement that caused Pasang to tense, the man sprang forward, pointed a grimy finger at Wildman and in a voice hushed with awe, said, "You are the wild man yes? The same one? And my brother must have..."

"That's right. Your brother gave me your name and address here and said that if ever I needed something in Bombay, something a little out of the ordinary?"

Wildman was cut short by another quick movement by the little man, who now spun around, took three quick steps to the door and locked it with a big metal key. Turning, he hurried to the single window that looked out on to Goa Street and pulled two thick wooden shutters across it. He secured them with a latch and then scurried back to the bed and sat down. Then, raising both hands in front of him in a gesture that was almost supplication, he said, in a voice hissing with excitement and expectation, "Oh mister wild man sir, for you, for your friend, anything. Oh sir, after what you did for my brother, anything. Just tell me what I can do for you."

Wildman talked and, when he had finished, to make sure everything was clearly understood, he had the man repeat what he said. "A four wheel drive vehicle in thee first class condition, yes? A good vehicle that will not let the *sahib* down? Yes. But certainly sir. Absolutely. Within twenty-four hours at the latest and no later."

And did Mr. Chatterjee, Wildman asked, actually have something like this readily available? To which the little man replied. "Available, sir? But of course not. A poor man like me. How in the name of the gods would I have something like this?"

"Then?"

"Ah, sir. Friends. Cousins. And cousins of cousins. Family members, you understand, sir. With favours owing here and there and with the anticipation of the reward. Much reward of course sir, for in this case there will be many people involved. Isn't it pleeze?"

Wildman, who had dealt with cousins of cousins and 'Isn't it pleeze' in India before, nodded.

"But of course," he said, rubbing his thumb and forefinger together in a universal gesture that brought a smile of understanding to the little man's face.

An hour later they were back at the Oberoi. Chatterjee had the hotel number and their room number. He would call.

Pasang ate dinner in the hotel's café and, noting the four-hour time difference between London and Bombay, went to bed early. Wildman promised to wake him if anything developed and, after telling him to make sure his door was locked and bolted, went and dined in the hotel's French restaurant. An hour later, after a nightcap at the hotel's Bengal Lancers bar, he collected his key from the reception desk and went up to his room. There he checked his booby-trapped grip, found it untouched, stripped off, showered and was easing himself into bed when the phone rang. He picked it up and said, "Yes?"

It was Chatterjee. "Ee's ready, sir. All fixed. Can you come my house six morning?"

"Yes."

The line went dead. Wildman checked his Rolex. It was still on Greenwich Mean Time. He moved it forward four hours, set its alarm to five a.m., slipped into bed and within minutes was asleep.

<<>>

At three minutes before five Wildman woke up, turned off his watch alarm, picked up the phone and dialled Pasang's room. The Sherpa answered instantly and when he did Wildman told him to join him in his room for coffee, and to be ready to leave the hotel immediately afterwards.

"With bag, *sahib*?"

"No. We'll be coming back here. It's just a visit. To where we were yesterday."

Then Wildman called for room service, ordered toast and coffee and croissants for two, showered and was dressed when, a few minutes later, Pasang knocked on the door. Twenty-five minutes later they left the hotel and at five forty-five a taxi dropped them behind the old cathedral. As its ancient bell tolled six, they again climbed the stairs to Chatterjee's room and knocked on his door.

The little man was waiting for them. He shook Wildman's hand warmly, hesitated, shook Pasang's hand and then scurried out through the door, beckoning them to follow him. Locking it carefully behind him, he hesitated for a moment and then turned and looked earnestly at Wildman. "Sir, these men you will meet. They are, as we say in India, cousins of mine, yes?"

"Yes?" said Wildman, knowing that in India anyone who has the least association with anyone else, even though there is no family relationship at all, is a cousin.

"Well sir, I, how can I say this? I just want to say, sir, remembering how good you were to my brother, for you to be careful with these men, especially their headman. He is, what you say, *chelac,* which in the English I think means the cunning. Yes sir?"

Wildman nodding thoughtfully and when he did, the little man scuttled off down the stairs and out into the street. He waved at a crawling taxi—another cousin, Wildman wondered?—ushered them into the back, leaped into the front and then with a wave of his hand told the driver to take them across the city to Colaba, the peninsular end of the city that forms one of the long arms of its bay.

A mile down into the huge causeway, Chatterjee stopped the taxi and then, with what looked like practiced precaution, waited until it had disappeared before darting off down a long, gloomy alleyway. Wildman and Pasang stayed close behind. The three walked fast and when the waterfront came into view, their guide led them into a narrow lane between towering tenement buildings.

At the end of the lane was what looked like a big storage shed, fronted with double doors made of corrugated metal. A smaller door led into the shed from the side and Chatterjee walked up to this and knocked and waited. After half a minute the door opened. Chatterjee immediately went inside, beckoning for Pasang and Wildman to follow him. When they were in, he carefully closed the door behind them and flicked on a light switch. Above them three neon light bars flickered for a moment and then came on, filling a big concrete-floored shed with light and revealing to Wildman and Pasang two vehicles. One was a black, metal cab Jeep and the other a big, four-wheel drive International Scout Traveller. Standing in front of the vehicles were five Indian men. One of them, wearing a black leather jacket, was big, unusually big for an Indian, and he cradled in his arms a double-barrelled, twelve-gauge shotgun.

Wildman tensed when he saw the Indians in front of them and he felt Pasang stiffen beside him. But then Chatterjee stepped forward, waved towards the standing men and with a toothy and nervous smile said, "These are my cousins, sir. All cousins. All friends."

The Indians nodded, Wildman relaxed and Chatterjee, waving his arms and skipping from one foot to the other, said, "Two vehicles, sir. Both very good. For you to choose whichever, sir. Isn't it."

Wildman walked forward and looked at the Jeep. It appeared to be in reasonable condition. But a small sign riveted to the body under the door caught his eye. It said, **MAHINDRA & MAHINDRA, CALCUTTA**, and he knew immediately that the vehicle was manufactured in India and therefore would not be of the quality of one made in the US. He had had experience with things made in India and he quickly decided that he would only take the Jeep if there was nothing else available.

The Scout looked better. It was one of the Traveller series, an extended version of the original Scout made by the International Harvester Company in the seventies. Wildman walked slowly around it, looking it over carefully. The paint job was two-tone, a gold body with a white canopy and roof. Apart from a few scratches and a couple of small dents in the front bumper, it showed no damage. The tires looked good. They were heavy duty, six-ply, off-road radials. Bolted to the steel front bumper was an 8000-pound Warn winch and in the roof, at the back, was a glass hatch.

Wildman went down on one knee and looked under the vehicle. There was a thick steel protective plate welded to the frame under the steering rods and the engine sump; another one protected the fuel tank in the rear. He decided to look inside and tried the door handle. The door was locked. He looked questioningly at Chatterjee, who immediately gestured to the waiting men. When he did the one with the shotgun stepped forward and with an oily smile said, "You are interested in thee car, yes?"

Wildman nodded and when he did the man handed him two keys. Wildman took the keys and walked around to the driver's side door and opened it. A faint musty smell filled the interior and he guessed that the car had been standing for some time. He opened one of the windows and then climbed in and ran his eye over the inside fittings. In the front were two single seats, cloth-covered, with a console between them. The back seat was folded forward, and Wildman gauged the space behind to be about six feet long, ample to stretch out in, he thought. In the back, carefully wrapped in canvas and small bags, he noted a jack, a wheel wrench, a coil of nylon tow rope, a tree strap, a set of battery jumper cables, two cans of automatic tire inflator and a long narrow box marked **SPARES.**

He turned to the front and looked around. Mounted on top of the carpet-covered transmission case was a big compass with black and white figures. Behind it, snug against the bulkhead, was a red fire extinguisher and between the two was a seven-cell flashlight. He opened the console. In it were was a twelve volt, plug-in coffee pot and packed around it were some road maps of India, a pair of heavy leather work gloves, two enamel mugs, an assortment of wire, nylon cord, water proof matches, a US Army water bottle and other odds and ends.

Next he looked at the instrument panel, which contained the ammeter, fuel, oil and temperature gauges. The speedometer was marked in miles per hour and the odometer indicated a mileage reading of 15,500. The transmission, as he could see from the numbered dial set in the instrument panel, was automatic. Beside the transmission lever was a second lever, for four-wheel drive.

Wildman, wary of the five Indians watching him, turned carefully to Chatterjee and speaking to him through the window said, "I'm going to start it up, OK?"

Chatterjee looked questioningly at the big man with the shot gun, who shook his head, which in India means yes, and when he did, Wildman pushed one of the keys into the ignition and gave it a quick twist. The engine turned over slowly, coughed once, hesitated and then burst into life. A small cloud of blue grey smoke belched out of the twin exhausts at the rear and then they ran clean. The engine coughed again a couple of times and then settled down into a deep, rumbling purr.

Wildman let the engine run for a few minutes, his eyes on the gauges. The temperature gauge stayed motionless for a while and then, very slowly, began to move up. The oil gauge needle swept immediately to a vertical position and then settled back to within a fraction of the red line that indicated normal pressure. The ammeter indicator whipped over to its charging position the instant the engine started, showing that the battery had not been used for some time and needed charging. It also showed that the alternator was working for, as Wildman watched, the needle slowly began to move towards the thin green line that indicated a full charge. The fuel gauge showed the tank to be about a quarter full.

Wildman touched the throttle and revved the engine. The steady purr quickly rose to a deep, throaty roar that filled the shed. He watched in the rear-view mirror for exhaust emission as the twin exhausts blasted out the hot engine gases. But there was no sign of smoke. He touched the brake pedal and heard the hydraulics sigh. Power brakes. There was also power steering and, when he slid the transmission lever into Drive, the big vehicle immediately inched forward. He eased the vehicle forwards and backwards, testing the gears. All worked smoothly. He touched the horn and it blared across the shed, bringing a start of surprise and a scowl from the man with the shotgun. He checked the headlights and indicators and, when he was satisfied that they all worked, revved the engine again, let it drop down, slammed the transmission lever into Park, turned the engine off, opened the door and stepped out.

There was silence in the shed when the engine died and Wildman could hear the group muttering among themselves. Chatterjee inched up to him with a nervous smile.

"'Ees all right then, yes, everything 'ees OK?"

Wildman looked at him and nodded. "OK, here's what we're going to do. You and I are going to take a short ride around the streets so that I can check the vehicle on the road. Just the two of us, OK? And then if it's all right we'll come back here and we'll talk business. OK?"

Chatterjee gave him a nervous look and then said, "Yes sir, I think so. But first I must talk with my cousins, isn't it."

An hour later Wildman and Chatterjee were back in the shed again. The cousins, after some muttering, had agreed to let Wildman take the car out for a run with Chatterjee. Pasang had stayed behind, a hostage of sorts, although the group seemed to be happy enough with Chatterjee's word as a guarantee, accompanied no doubt by a rendition of Wildman's former dealings with his brother in Calcutta. Wildman had driven the car about five miles and run it through its paces. Everything seemed to work well, including the winch, which he tested by pulling out the cable and tightening it to full tension on a solid post. Now they were all back in the shed again, the doors were locked and the time for 'the beezinees talks' had arrived. Chatterjee opened the proceedings by asking if Wildman was satisfied with the car and if he was going to take it.

"Yes. It's OK. And if we can come to agreement I will take it. I'm willing to pay anything reasonable for it. Anything reasonable, I say and you can tell your smiling cousins here that I am not a tourist, that I am not new to India and that I know the ropes when it comes to wheeling and dealing in this country."

"The ropes, sir?" said Chatterjee, with a puzzled look.

"Never mind. Just get with the gang there and find out how much they want and where and when and so on."

Chatterjee turned and walked over to the huddle of men and then together they all walked away, down into a corner of the shed. Wildman heard subdued muttering. He smiled at Pasang who flashed him a brief grin and then scowled at the group in the corner. Wildman noticed that not once, since they met them, had Pasang taken his eyes off them, particularly the big man with the shotgun. He obviously trusted them about as much as Wildman did and watching them, he wished that he had the Glock tucked under his arm, just as, he guessed, Pasang wished that he had his *kukri* to hand.

Then the group had come to an agreement. They turned in a body and walked back to where Wildman and Pasang were waiting. Although he seemed to have little standing in the group, Chatterjee seemed to have been appointed their spokesman. But then, Wildman was not sure that any of the others spoke English.

"Sir, they want very much money for thee vehicle."

"OK. How much?"

"Sir, they want fifty thousand dollars. Dollars cash that is. Green dollars, sir."

"Fifty, did you say?"

"Yes sir. 'Ees much money and…"

"OK, here's what I'll do. I'll give them twenty-five thousand. In cash. Green dollars. They'll get it in one hundred dollar bills, which will give them the best return on the black market, which, I imagine, is the only market they know. I will have to have the car today. Now. And the way we'll do it is this. You and one of them, one other, that is a total of two only, will come with me to the hotel, in the car. We'll put the car in the hotel garage and we'll go to my room and I'll get the money immediately, and pay you immediately."

Chatterjee turned to the waiting group and explained Wildman's terms. There was more muttering and when it had subsided Chatterjee turned back to Wildman and said, "All right *sahib*. They will take twenty-five. But they want it immediately, and they want three of them to come to the hotel with you. That is me and two of them, one of which will be the big man there."

Wildman hesitated. He gave the big man a quick look. He was big. But he moved slowly and Wildman felt that he could handle him, if push came to shove. He nodded assent and reaching into the Scout, lifted the back seat to its upright position. Then the five of them piled in, Wildman at the steering wheel with the big man beside him, the shotgun wrapped in a blanket, the other three jammed in the back with Pasang. One of the other men opened the doors of the garage and Wildman fired the motor and drove through them and out into the street.

Within thirty minutes they were driving into the hotel's big underground garage. Once inside, Wildman parked the Scout and, when everyone was out of the vehicle, he locked its doors and waved to a couple of the garage's security men. When they came over—big, turbaned Sikhs in tight-fitting hotel uniforms—he told them that he would like them to stay close for a few minutes while he concluded a small transaction. Then, with the gang leader scowling at what he suspected was some kind of ruse, he pulled up the front of his shirt and took out a fat money belt. With the Sikhs watching carefully, he withdrew two thick packets of hundred dollar bills, each of them containing a total of one hundred bills, and put them on the front of the Scout. Then he broke another packet and counted out fifty singles and added these to the pile, at the same time beckoning to the gang leader to take the money and count it.

The big man did not hesitate. Shouldering Chatterjee aside he grabbed the money and with his two partners watching carefully, counted it twice. Satisfied, he stuffed the money into his pockets and with a shout at Chatterjee, made for the garage exit, the blanket-wrapped shotgun tucked under his arm. Wildman let him go, happy to see the last of him, but as Chatterjee, somewhat bewildered by the speed of the proceedings, started to follow him. Wildman reached out and grabbed him by the arm.

"Wait. Let them go. I want to talk to you."

They waited until the men, warily watched by the two Sikh security men, had left the garage. Then Wildman spoke again. "They're not really your cousins, are they?"

"Well sir, not really. But this is India, you know and here..."

"By that you mean, they are not family members, right?"

"Yes sir. That is right."

"And so how much of that money will you be getting?"

Chatterjee shook his head sadly. "Well, sir, there is no agreement. I am sure that I will get something. They promised me that I would get something."

"That's what I thought," said Wildman, remembering the way the other men had treated Chatterjee in the shed and the way he had been shouldered aside when the money appeared. All of this told him that down the road, when the money was spilt, the little man, the person who had put the deal together, was going to be left out in the cold.

He still had the money belt in his hand. He opened it and quickly counted out fifty one hundred dollar bills.

"This is between us. OK? Nothing to do with the others. This should help you get set up in something that will bring you an income. Maybe you can join your brother in Calcutta? Yes? Then take care."

Leaving the little man standing with his mouth open, Wildman turned to the two Sikh security men and gave each of them a handful of rupee bills. "Keep an eye on that nice new car of mine," he said and, with a parting wave to Chatterjee, and accompanied by Pasang, headed for the hotel elevator.

<<>>

In his room Wildman looked at a big road map of India that he had taken from Lord Carew's map room, at Himalaya House. Using a pair of callipers set to a scale of five miles to the inch, he walked their steel points in a line up the highways from Bombay, through Nagpur and Varanasi, and on through the northern province of Uttar Pradesh to the border of Nepal, just south of Kathmandu. About a thousand miles.

From the Nepal border to Kathmandu, depending on which route he took, another two hundred. Twelve hundred miles. One long day's driving in the US, if you were in a hurry. Two, at a push, in most of the countries of Europe. In India, on the narrow, crowded highways, fighting the truck traffic and the people with their buffalo and bullock carts, their rickshaws and bicycles and the sheep and goats and cattle and dogs...six days at least, probably more. Two hundred miles was a more than good daily average on an Indian highway. On the back roads, with their broken and shattered surfaces and with potholes big enough to swallow a cow, half, or even a quarter of that, if one was lucky.

He looked at his watch. Four hours since he had picked up the Scout and paid the owners. Owners? He wondered. There had been no paperwork involved and Wildman had a sneaking feeling that the car might have been stolen. From whom, he had no idea, but from the appearance of the vehicle he guessed it might have been someone's safari car. The glass-viewing hatch in the back and quality of the spares suggested an American or a European owner. There were no license plates. Well, later he could have a friend at the FBI check the engine and chassis numbers for him. Not that it mattered. He had what he wanted, and in the meantime it was secure in the garage of the hotel. Its security was made all the more intact by a tough little Sherpa who, half an hour after the transaction in the garage had been completed, had moved out of his room and into the vehicle. Pasang did not trust Indians that was obvious. But then his people, the hill people of Nepal, had no love for them, from time immemorial.

<<>>

At five forty-five Wildman picked up the phone. When his call was answered he asked to speak to one of the chefs in the kitchen and, on being connected, he made a simple request, which was a traditional Nepalese dinner, for one. Could they do that? Yes, of course. This was the Oberoi and whatever it was, if you were prepared to pay for it, you got it. The dinner was to be accompanied by a bottle of the best quality beer. And it was to be delivered to his car in the garage.

"The garage, sir?"

"Yes. The garage. And make sure the beer is cold."

Later that night Wildman went down to see Pasang and give him orders for the following morning. The big, underground garage was cool, dimly lighted by fluorescent ceiling bars. Two uniformed security men nodded to him from a small cubicle at the entrance, as he went in. Pasang was sitting in the front of the Scout, reading a small English Nepali dictionary by the light of a hand-held flashlight. He saw Wildman in the rear-view mirror when he was coming down the entrance ramp and jumped out to meet him.

"Everything OK, Pasang?"

"Yes *sahib*. Everything *tik cha*. Also very good dinner. I thank you *sahib*."

"Good. I'm glad you enjoyed it. And you're OK to sleep here?"

Wildman looked into the Scout. Pasang had raised the back seat and folded it forward and in the spacious rear, had spread out his bedroll. This consisted of a thin mattress and a light woollen blanket. There was no pillow. A slight bulge in the mattress showed at the head of the bed. His *kukri*, Wildman surmised.

"OK then, Pasang. Here's the plan for the morning. I would like to get out of the city early. But we can't. We have to meet Lord Carew's granddaughter at nine. By the way, Pasang, you do know her? I mean, will you be able to recognise her when you see her?"

"Oh yes, *sahib*. I know the *memsahib*. She is tall and fair. And very beautiful, *sahib*. I meet her many times when she comes to Himalaya House, to visit with the good Lord Carew."

"OK. Tall and fair. And er, attractive, you say? Good. There may be a few tourists around the Taj Hotel at this time of year. But we should be able to spot her. Problem is, however, that we cannot wait. By making contact with the boyos we got the Scout from, we have exposed ourselves to the bazaar grapevine, if you know what I mean. And the Indian grapevine is as fast as anywhere in the world and it would not surprise me if certain people were already alerted to our arrival. In other words, once we leave here, we are going to have to hoof it. Tomorrow morning it's going to be a quick refuel—there's an Exxon station just near here—and then over to meet this young lady. When we meet her we have to decide whether we are going to take her with us, or not. I hope it's not, because she may be a smart kid but a woman on a trip like this is nothing more than an encumbrance. Personally I think the best thing for her will be to get on a plane and head for Kathmandu on her own and meet us there. In any case, the main thing for us is, after meeting her, to get out of the city as fast as possible. So I'll send some breakfast for you early and we'll take a couple of packed lunches from the hotel. I want to try and get a hundred miles at least under the wheels by tomorrow evening."

"Very good *sahib*. The morning, then. Eight half."

"Yes, Pasang. I'll be checked out of the hotel by about eight-fifteen and then we'll fill up and go straight over to the Taj. By the way, you know how to lock those doors from the inside, yes? Good. Sleep well then. Until the morning."

BOOK FOUR

THE ROAD NORTH

The morning air was cool and damp as Wildman pounded down the two-mile length of Bombay's Marine Drive in his running shoes. The sun was still not up, the traffic was thin and the shapeless bundles that lay tucked in against the sea wall had not yet turned into the whining beggars of later in the day. Returning to the hotel he spent forty-five minutes in its big swimming pool, steadily lapping back and forth in the green, heavily chlorinated water. A shower, breakfast in his room, tea and toast and eggs sent down to Pasang, a ten minute study of a road map of the city of Bombay, a quick packing of the grip and he was ready to leave.

A quarter to nine and a murky sun trying to pierce the morning haze saw the big gold Scout moving quietly through the streets of lower Colaba, twenty gallons of gasoline gurgling in its steel plate protected tank, the engine purring smoothly. Wildman had topped up the oil and purchased an extra three cans of Thirty Weight Detergent and he had also had the tires inflated to thirty-five p.s.i. With the big vehicle carrying a minimum load, this would make for harder riding. But it would also minimize the possibility of a tire being punctured by something sharp on the road.

Wildman was dressed in a worn pair of corduroy trousers tucked into his Gokey boots. He had not worn the boots for a month, and they felt a little stiff when he put them on. But they soon warmed up and as the leather softened, it shaped itself to the contours of his legs and feet. Over a long-sleeved khaki shirt he wore on old corduroy jacket with leather elbow patches and, sitting firmly on his head, its brim snapped down to shade his eyes from the glare of the morning sun, his double-brim Terai hat.

Pasang wore his traditional clothing. But now, back on the road, and off the streets of the city, the big *kukri* was back in place, firmly angled into the front of his waist sash, its dark, hardwood handle gleaming with oil, the gold tip at its end softly pulsing in the morning sun.

Thirty minutes after leaving the hotel, Wildman looked at his watch. It showed three minutes to nine as he turned towards the waterfront of the inner bay and drove down an esplanade dominated by a massive stone monument of the Gateway of India. Here he swung left, into the mean and narrow street on to which the huge Taj Mahal hotel faced. At nine precisely, he pulled into the curb, switched off the engine and rolled down the window.

There was the usual scattering of tourists moving in and out of the hotel. Two beggars approached the car immediately it stopped; a fierce scowl from Pasang sent them scurrying. The streets were filling now, with taxis, cyclists and pedestrians. Traffic was beginning to build, as the day grew.

Wildman watched the hotel entrance for anyone who looked at all like what he expected. Australian. Tall, fair, probably tanned and well-dressed and no doubt loaded down with fifty huge suitcases and all ready to jump in the jolly old Scout and join him for a jolly old joyride up the jolly old road to Kathmandu. Women! Wildman ground his teeth.

Nine five and no sign of her. Nine ten. Nine fifteen. Wildman began to swear. Goddamit. Probably up in her room putting her hair curlers in, or powdering her face. Or trying to get her suitcases closed. Or having a nice cup of morning tea before going out to join the funny man her dear old grandfather had told her about, for a fun trip up to Nepal. Probably got the time wrong. Probably got the day wrong, goddamit. And this, right now, was just what he did not want. A delay. The big car sitting in the public street, obvious, conspicuous, attracting attention. Unwanted attention. He whipped the keys out of the ignition, said, "Pasang, two minutes," leaped out, locked the door behind him and raced into the hotel. At the reception desk he flashed out two twenty-dollar bills and got immediate attention.

"A cable form. Quick. Overseas, that's right."

He scribbled hurriedly: *Lord Carew. Grindlays, London. No sign Gael. Suggest you advise her contact me Sheraton Hotel, Varanasi, three days from date. Wildman*. He marked the cable Urgent to route it for twelve-hour service and threw it across the desk at the clerk.

"Very good, sir. We can send that at once. But what about your receipt?"

"Keep it for me. I'll pick it up later. And you can keep the change, OK?"

He raced back to the Scout. Pasang leaned over and unlocked the door.

"Any sign of her, Pasang?"

"No *sahib*. No one. No sign."

Wildman swore, started the engine, dropped the gear into Drive and surged out into the traffic. Goddam women. They were all the same. Late. Perennially, incurably late. And irresponsible and undependable. And this one? Probably had a hair appointment and missed the plane in Sydney. Or went to the wrong airport. Or got on the wrong flight and ended up in Terra del Fuego. Ah well, he'd kept his promise to the old man. He'd do the same thing again in Varanasi. Call the Sheraton and see if she'd made it. But that was all that he would do. That would fulfill his promise. With a bit of luck, he thought, she won't be there and after that he'd be clear of her and not have to worry about her.

Three hours later they were still fighting the traffic. But it was thinning, as were the houses and factories and the milling crowds of people on the streets of the enormous city. Ahead of them, dim in the dust and ever-present smoke of cooking fires, and just becoming visible, were the Western Ghats. A low, straggling range of hills that rose east of the city and divided the flat lands of the coast from the central plains, the heart of India, known as the Central Provinces.

Soon they began to climb. Traffic was heavy; mainly trucks, but they made good time up the twisting, zigzagging hill roads. Where the highway broadened, two thousand feet above the coastal plain, Wildman pulled in and stopped. They rested, relieved themselves over the road's retaining wall and ate their packed lunches—fried chicken, bread rolls, a banana, an orange, salt and pepper and a piece of lime. They drank cautiously from a little rivulet dripping out of a rock, climbed back into the Scout and, with the sun slipping down behind them, moved on. It took them five hours of hard driving to cross the rolling hills and start descending the east side. They were moving fast down the last of the long winding hill roads when, rounding a corner, Wildman saw the big truck straddling the road ahead.

<<>>

Vask, Raja Vask to the men standing around him, was angry and in the big, white walled house on the hill, an air of high tension prevailed.

"Fools. Imbeciles. Monkey brains. You eat my bread, you suck on my money and this is what I get in return."

He was a big man. Not tall. But heavily built, and fat. But the fat was well spread, layered across his body and down across his stomach, so that the stomach did not bulge. Five feet ten in height, tall for an Indian, and with his bulk making him seem bigger; he towered over the nervous men around him. His neck was short and very thick, set tight to broad, muscular shoulders. His head was bullet-shaped, almost conical, and covered with a thick growth of carefully-oiled black hair, cropped short and combed flat across the breath of his cranium. His forehead was narrow and its frontal lobes, jutting out over a pair of small, hard, black eyes, would have had an anthropologist reaching for a camera and a measuring tape. A large mouth was set between lips that were drawn back in a look of perpetual disgust—his men thought of it as a perpetual snarl—showing large, even teeth stained dark red with years of betel nut chewing. His voice was low, hoarse, and guttural.

He stood at the end of a long wooden table in a room in the front of the house. It was a large room and easily accommodated the twenty or so men who stood around him. On the table in front of him was a map, some ballpoint pens and a collection of miscellaneous papers. The map, a road map of India, was open, and Vask was pounding on it with a large, hairy fist. He glared at the men around him and shouted at them in a hoarse, loud voice, the voice of a man who has spent a lot of time in noisy conditions, the voice of a man who demands to be heard.

"Does anyone among you miserable collection of toothless old women know where Ghose is now? Anyone?"

The men around him were silent. Then one, with a narrow fox-like face, hard, piercing black eyes, and a hooked nose that suggested a northern origin and with his head bound in a big cloth turban, stepped forward. He was Vask's chief driver, Metha. "Raja *sahib*, he must be on his way here. He phoned after those two devils got through our roadblock and said he was coming. On your behalf, Raja, I told him to come here at once and seek further orders from your good self, Raja."

Vask gave the turbaned one a sour look. The man's gaze dropped and he drew back among his companions.

"All right. You did the right thing, Metha. I want to see Mr. Ghose and I want to see him here and damn soon. He has cost me a lot of money, wasted a lot of my time and he has some big explaining to do. I don't allow mistakes, you know that, Metha. You hear that, you others, you crawling collection of bedbugs?

The men shook their heads from side to side vigorously, looking to each other for support.

"And Mr. Ghose has now made not one but two big mistakes. And he is supposed to be the clever one, the *eesmart* Bengali with the *eesmart*

The loaded Scout fording a river on the way north from Bombay.

The Scout encountering a temporary obstacle on the way north to Nepal.

Wildman's room at the East India Club, St James Square, London, where he did most of the planning for the mission.

English education. Yes. Mr. Ghose has some explaining to do, when he gets here."

Four days previously Ghose's message from England had been received at Vask's house, outside Nagpur. Cabled to Bombay through an agent in London, transmitted by telegram from Bombay to Nagpur and then phoned to Vask's house from there, it had taken eight hours to reach Vask. *The Eye,* the message had said. *Moving at last. Two men. An American and a Nepali. London to Bangkok, Thailand. In Bangkok, The Dusit Thani Hotel. With ongoing reservations from there to Kathmandu.*

Vask had wasted no time. He had instantly put a team together, his best men. Phoning ahead, they had raced into Nagpur where Vask, flashing the great Indian convincer—the hundred rupee bill—in large quantities, had had five wretched peasants and two irate American tourists bumped off an Indian Airlines, Nagpur to Delhi flight by a greedy little airlines clerk…so sorry, sir, madam, a confusion in the computer, you understand, isn't it. Arriving in Delhi, Vask and his men switched flights—another fifty or so of the little blue convincers changing hands—to an Air India flight to Thailand, one that took them direct to Bangkok. There, Vask, working non-stop, had set up intricate and expensive arrangements to waylay the two couriers when they arrived at the Dusit Thani, relieve them of the Eye and have them disposed of, quickly and quietly. He had been in Bangkok twenty-four, time-consuming, money-consuming hours, when another call had came through to him, this time from an agent in Bombay, to say that two men answering the description given by Ghose had just arrived there from London. They had picked up a car from a group who had done business with Vask in the past, and who, knowing where their bread was buttered, made haste to inform his Bombay agent. The two men, he was informed, were already on the road, and heading north.

Vask was furious. He blamed Ghose for the mix-up. He had immediately cancelled the Bangkok arrangements and flown back to Nagpur, via Delhi. The false lead had cost him thousands of dollars. Not rupees, of which he had plenty, but hard earned, hard to come by black market dollars, the only currency with which he could work in Thailand, the only currency, in the form of new, one hundred dollar bills, his Thai associates would accept. The costly transactions he had made brought home to him all the more his need for hard currency, to expand his criminal empire. One could be a multi-millionaire in rupees in India, as he was. But set one foot across the nearest international border and if one did not have ample foreign currency, preferably green dollars, as they were called, one could just about starve to death. The Eye was the answer. With its sale he would be hard currency rich, dollar rich. His mind dwelt briefly on what he could get for it on the international market. A hundred million? A hundred and fifty? And then ten percent as a steady income from that, from one or two greedy but sound Swiss institutions who did not care if the money came from the devil himself. Yes, the Eye was the answer. He had to get it.

Speaking on the phone from Bangkok he had ordered an immediate roadblock of the Bombay to Nagpur road. He told his agent to get hold of Ghose and put him in charge. Ghose had fouled up once. But, Vask had to admit, this was the first time, the first time in many years of loyalty and conscientious work, work that had included an unbroken stream of regular monthly reports.

Ghose had also handled the attempts they had made to get the old man, Carew. True, they had failed. But that was the fault of the bungling idiots who made the attempts. Ghose was smart, he had to give him that. The smartest among the bunch of monkey brains he had working for him. He was finished in England, of course. But perhaps he could be useful here; now Vask would have a chance to find out. Brains were a scarce commodity among Vask's henchmen. But Ghose had them. So he would give him another chance. Of course if he fouled up a second time, then that would be it. Then there would be a reckoning.

Vask had been back a bare three hours from the abortive trip to Bangkok, when another call came in. This time it was Ghose in person. The devil American and his Nepali hillman had broken through the roadblock. They were in a big car with some kind of special drive...they had got into the paddy fields and gone around the roadblock and....

Vask, his eyes half closed to slits, listened to what Ghose had to say. Then, in a voice of ice, he told him to stay where he was, near a phone, and wait. He called a meeting of his underlings and outlined another plan. It was based on the speculation that the American and his companion were now about one full day out on the Bombay to Nagpur road, probably about a hundred miles northeast of the city. That they would probably stop for the night somewhere and then, the following day, head north again. It was also based on their obvious need for fuel along the way, and dovetailed to the number of gasoline and diesel stations that lined the main highway, many of which Vask owned. And it was to be rounded off with five jeep-loads of armed men cruising the highway within the one to two hundred miles radius of where it was estimated the American might be.

The armed highway cruisers were given precise instructions. The American was to be captured alive. This was vital. As to the hillman,

Mr. And Mrs. Gilliam Ween, of Touchen End, Berkshire, England. Ween, a senior investigative reporter for the London Times, was sent to Varanasi to write a series of articles on the ancient cult of thugee, as revived by Vask. He may have delved too deep into Vask's operations; he and his wife Isabelle disappeared there, April 1st, 1985 and have not been seen or heard of since then. Photo credit: Interpol, Paris/London.

bring him along too, but kill him if he resisted. Vask would stay at his house by the phone and the road cruisers were to keep in touch with him by phone, whenever possible. He would make special arrangements with the main telephone exchange in Nagpur for all calls to be put through to him instantly. This time, he warned there would be no failure. If there was, then heads would roll. Or, as he more ominously put it, his eyes sinking back under his protruding eyebrows, the silk handkerchiefs would swing and the stakes would be driven. He concluded his planning by having his driver, Metha, make a call to his Bombay agent to find out what fuel the American's car used, gasoline or diesel. A reply came back in twenty minutes. Gasoline. When Vask heard this he nodded and dispersed his men to their work.

<<>>

Dawn of the second day. In the mango grove, silence. With the first twittering of the birds in the grey, damp light of dawn, Wildman opened his eyes. Without moving from his cramped position in the front of the Scout, he lay and listened for a full minute. Then he slowly levered himself upright and looked through the dew-soaked windshield of the vehicle. Twenty feet away, his thin blanket wrapped around him, his back to a big mango tree, Pasang sat, wide awake, his arms folded across his stomach, his hands resting on the brass-tipped handle of the *kukri* in his lap. His face was like granite in the dawn light; his eyes slits. He caught Wildman's movement and immediately looked across and nodded. Christ, thought Wildman, did he get any sleep?

Wildman unlocked one of the side doors, struggled out of his sleeping bag and eased himself out of the Scout.

"Did you get some sleep, Pasang?

"Of course, *sahib*," the man replied, smiling. "But we had better be driving on now, *sahib*, yes?"

"Yes Pasang, on it is. And if you want to climb in the back now and get some rest we can..."

"No *sahib*, I am unrested. I mean, well rested. Sorry, *sahib*. Still learning the English, you know. Well rested I mean."

"All right then, we'll move on and if you wish we can make some coffee on that little machine there, as we drive."

Pasang rolled up his blanket and tied it into a bundle. Going around to the front of the Scout, he took the keys out of the ignition. He rolled up Wildman's sleeping bag and then, taking both bundles, walked to the back of the vehicle, unlocked the big, steel, upward-opening door, pushed both bundles well forward against the upright back seat, closed the back door, locked it and then returned the keys to the ignition.

Wildman climbed in, opened Pasang's door to let him in and then fired the engine. The Sherpa got in the Scout, closed the door and locked it. As Wildman eased the Scout out through the trees of the mango grove where they had spent the night and up a hard grassy bank on to the main road, Pasang opened the console between the seats, took out the little coffee percolator, filled it with water from a plastic bottle, spooned two heaped teaspoons of coffee into the top and plugged its extension cord into the cigar lighter. He then set the pot carefully between his feet on the floor of the Scout.

At the top of the bank, on the edge of the highway, Wildman paused and let the Scout engine idle and warm up. He glanced to left and right. The tree-lined road stretched away to right and left and was visible for half a mile in either direction. Nothing moved in the grey, damp, dawn light. No trucks. No buffalo carts. No one stirring. It would not be that way for long. He flipped the shift lever into Drive, depressed the throttle and swung hard left and out on to the road.

As the Scout gathered speed, he eyed the dials. Oil pressure, a little off the vertical, but steady. Temperature needle all the way down, the engine cold, but slowly beginning to warm. Voltage ammeter steady after an initial swing into the charge zone to compensate for the downward power surge caused by starting the big motor. Speedometer steady at 40 mph and climbing, with the odometer showing two hundred and six miles of road under the wheels since leaving Bombay. Fuel gauge, low, over the vertical, into the quarter tank area, and sinking. They would need fuel within the next forty or fifty miles. When they filled up he would be able to estimate the mileage they were getting. Back in Bombay, checking the fuel tank under its thick, protective, steel plate in the rear, he had estimated its capacity as close to twenty-five US gallons and he guessed the big engine's fuel consumption to be close to twelve miles to the gallon. Which meant that they had probably about seventy miles left in the tank.

The road remained clear as Wildman pushed the big car up to sixty and then seventy. The engine purred and the wind roared against the shut windows. Pasang leaned forward and unplugged the coffeepot. He opened the console, took out two enamel mugs and filled one three-quarters full with the steaming brew. Placing the pot carefully on the floor he reopened the console, took out a bottle of Glenlivet, added a generous measure to the mug of coffee and handed it to Wildman. "No Pasang, you have it. You must be chilled, dammit, sleeping outside."

"Thank you *sahib*. After you *sahib*," he said, and Wildman, keeping his eyes on the road, sighed and took the mug from him. Pasang then poured himself a mug of the hot coffee and put two heaped teaspoons of sugar in it. He then placed the pot on the floor and, leaning over his mug to avoid spilling it in his lap, sipped carefully. He did not help himself to any of the scotch and Wildman did not offer him any.

Wildman was learning about Pasang. The previous day, when they had loaded the car at the hotel, he had found a bottle of beer in the console. It was the cold beer that he had had sent down the previous evening with Pasang's dinner. Pasang, seeing him look at it, had felt the need of an explanation.

"S*ahib*, I like to drink. Enjoy very much from time to time. But here," and he stumbled for words, "Here is job to be done. Important job, arranged by, what you say, commissioned by, our good Lord Carew. Job is work, *sahib*. We having saying among Sherpas. Work first, play after. So first I do the work, *sahib*. Get job done. Then play. Drink is play for me. Play later. Meantime keep edge of *kukri* sharp, if you understand what I mean."

The previous night there had come the question of where they were going to sleep. There was plenty of room for two in the back of the Scout. But Pasang was adamant. Wildman was to sleep inside and Wildman guessed that this meant he was to sleep inside and keep the Eye safe while he, Pasang, would stand sleep outside. Sleeping outside, as Wildman found out next morning, apparently meant staying awake all night. Wildman glanced at the bronzed faced little man sipping his coffee. Apart from the roadblock, they had not been in any kind of skirmish yet. But if and when the time came, he had a feeling that he had in Pasang a companion whom he could count on. In the meantime, working as a set of eyes for the back of Wildman's head, as Lord Carew put it, Pasang was proving his worth. Wildman felt a growing respect for the tough, silent little "After you *sahib*" Sherpa and made a mental promise that if they came through this together, he would make sure he was well rewarded.

<<>>

An hour later they were fifty miles down the road. Traffic was thickening and, as it did, their speed began to drop. Wildman pushed the big Scout to its limit, accelerating hard, braking hard, diving off the road as the big trucks came at him and thundered past. On the Indian highway, one "Argued" with other cars, with motorcyclists, rickshaws, cyclists, bullock carts, buffalo carts, cattle, goats, sheep and pedestrians. But not with trucks. The highway, like all of India main highways, was single lane. Down this the big trucks thundered, throttles flat to the floor, always vastly overloaded and driven by, as far as Wildman was concerned, lunatics whose single manic belief was that the road belonged to whosoever was biggest and heaviest. When one of these leviathans came at one, at seventy miles an hour, carrying twenty or thirty tons of load on a chassis built for a maximum load of ten, one did not argue. One simply left the road, drove down into the deep dust or mud of the verge, plunged through and then returned to the road when the truck had passed.

When truck met truck on the single lane road, drivers delighted in playing the old, American, hot-rod, teenager game of chicken. Seeing another truck approaching, they would accelerate, switch on their headlights, blast their horns and, leaning out of their cabs, screaming mutual abuse at the tops of their lungs, drive straight at one another. The rules of the game said that at the last moment one or the other was supposed to give way. But reflexes dulled by marijuana, hashish, or alcohol not being in the same league as those of quick-witted young Americans, the end result of the chicken challenge was more often than not spectacular head-on collisions. In the short distance that they so far covered from Bombay, Wildman and Pasang had seen the results of half a dozen of these, with shattered piles of burned and splintered wreckage, and they were to encounter half a dozen more before they reached the Nepalese border. Unlike Vask's roadblock, however, the wrecked metal monsters always had men sitting or sleeping around them to guard whatever was left, worthless though it appeared, from thieves.

In the fifty miles since leaving the little mango grove, they had passed one fuel station. It was unattended, its office door closed and the pumps locked with heavy brass padlocks. Through a grimy window, grey with dust and filth, a large red and white sign, **CLOSED,** voiced its message. Wildman, watching the fuel gauge, was beginning to get a little anxious. Maybe in Varanasi they could pick up some plastic fuel drums and carry them for extra fuel. He hated to carry gasoline in a vehicle; but he might have to do that.

"Pasang?"

"Yes *sahib*?"

"We will need gasoline, soon. Keep an eye out for a fuel station."

"A gasoline station, OK? We're going to have to stop and fill up."

"Very good *sahib*. That last one was more than thirty miles back. There should be another one soon. I am sure you noticed at that last one, *sahib*, that the sign, the one stuck in the window, was clean and new. That

Part of the enormous bus fleet owned by Vask.
Using these, he was able to transport his gang members and keep in touch with a network of spies all over north India.

caught my eye, *sahib*. New and clean in the middle of all that dirt and dust, *sahib*," he said looking at Wildman quizzically.

Wildman said nothing, but bit his lip. Dammit. No. He had not noticed that. He felt like pretending that he had and glanced across at Pasang. But the man was staring straight ahead, not waiting for an answer, not waiting to criticize him with a meaningful look.

"Thanks, Pasang," was all that he said in reply.

The road straightened and ran for half a mile through a long avenue of huge, gnarled pipal trees, their sweeping overhead canopy shading the road from the sun, a relic of the days of the Raj, when British soldiers used them to march to battle.

Pasang suddenly pointed. Far down the avenue ahead of them, a rusting Burma Shell sign hanging from a steel pole marked the site of a fuel station. Wildman slowed and when they reached the sign, swung off the road into the gravelled clearing of the station. There were two pumps, one for diesel and one for gasoline, and he pulled up to the gasoline pump and stopped. Pasang immediately jumped out, flipped the lock switch down on the door, slammed it behind him and, walking away from the Scout, turned and took up a watching position twenty yards away.

Through the grimy glass windows of the station office, Wildman saw three men watching him. He sized them up carefully and then switched off the engine, rolled down the window and waved his hand, palm down, for service. One of the men stayed in the office. The other two came out and walked towards the Scout, side by side, moving slowly. As they approached one of them spat a stream of crimson betel nut juice out of his mouth and raising his hand, fingers open and hand slightly curled, twisted it round and round in an ill-mannered and negative gesture, at the same time shouting, "No gasoline."

The Scout's gasoline tank filler was on the left side rear and Wildman had parked so that it was close to the second of the two pumps, the gasoline pump. This put him, in the driving seat, within three feet of the pump itself, close enough to see that the nozzle and its release handle, clean and shiny, had recently been used. A small drip of gasoline fell from the end of the nozzle as he watched.

"What do you mean, no gasoline? You have gasoline, I know you have."

The arm waver waved his arm *again*. "*No beezly.* You understand *beezly?*" he said, rudely. "*Beezly*. Ee-lec-tric-seety. Pump's ees electric pumps. No *beezly.* Therefore no gasoline."

The man turned and started to walk away. "Wait. Don't you have any in cans?" Wildman said. "What about back there," pointing towards the rear of the station, where a couple of dozen forty gallon drums stood. But the man just waved a hand again, this time over his shoulder in a rude gesture of dismissal, walked back into the glass-windowed office, entered it and slammed its door shut.

Pasang, who had been watching and listening to the whole conversation, walked quickly to the Scout. Wildman leaned over and flipped up the door lock. Pasang climbed in and when he did, Wildman immediately fired the engine and swung the Scout back out on to the road.

"Something bad happening *sahib*."

Wildman considered for a moment before answering Pasang. It was bad that they were now very short of fuel. If it came down to it, of course, they might be able to flag down a passing car, or truck. But most of the trucks had diesel engines, not gasoline.

"Yes Pasang. Something bad? You mean no gasoline and our tank growing more empty by the minute?"

"No *sahib*. Something else. As we are leaving that place did you see those gasoline drums out at the back of the station? From my side I could see them clearly. They had an outside light set above them for the nighttime. For thieves. I mean to stop thieves."

"Yes?"

"The light was burning, *sahib*."

Mentally kicking himself for not noticing the light, which meant that the station had electricity, he mentally registered the way that the little Sherpa had framed what he had said. 'From my side, *sahib*,' suggesting that it had been easier to see the light from his side and phrasing it this way to save Wildman any embarrassment that he might feel by his lack of observation.

"If I may make suggestion, *sahib*. Next gasoline station will require much caution. Maybe we look before we go in? Maybe keep engine running in case of anything bad."

"Right, Pasang. That's if we can get to the next gasoline station. As of now we are beginning to run on the fumes left in the tank, I should say."

In another ten miles the fuel tank gauge swung across the red Empty line and moved into the little blank space below it. Wildman dropped the speed of the Scout down to forty, and then thirty, and then twenty-five, trying to make whatever was left in the tank last as long as possible. Soon the tank had nothing more than a tiny residue of fuel left. But it could not last, and when Wildman suddenly saw a green metal Castrol sign, perched on a leaning wooden pole, a hundred yards ahead, he breathed a sigh of relief. He slowed, listening to the sounds of the Scout's gearbox running down through the intricacies of its automatic gearing. Thirty yards from the station, he brought the vehicle down to a crawl and turned his total attention to a scrutiny of the ugly, square cement bunker that was the fuel station office.

A door, open. A single large window made of small panes, water-streaked, flyspecked. Inside, two men sitting at a table leaning over some papers. At the pumps, a young man of about twenty and a half-naked boy with an idiotic grin. One of the men looked up casually as the Scout swung into the station yard and then looked down at his papers again. Through the filth of the office window it was hard to be sure, but Wildman thought that he leaned a little closer to the other man for a moment, as though to whisper something.

His foot gently touching the throttle, ready for fast exit, Wildman carefully drove the Scout past the pumps and up to the gasoline station office. Easing himself forward, he looked carefully at the area behind the office building. The space back there, between the building and a low concrete wall that ran all the way around the compound of the station, was empty except for a clutter of rusting gasoline drums, oilcans, old rusting car parts and torn plastic bags. A single water tap dripped and beside it a brown pariah dog lay stretched out in the sun. Apart from the dog there was no sign of life. No people. No lurking goons.

Flipping the transmission into Park, Wildman turned off the engine. As before, Pasang immediately jumped out, locking the door behind him and, repeating his action of the last station, walked quickly away from the Scout and took up a watching position. As he did so, one of the men came out of the office. He was small and fat and dressed in a torn and greasy shirt, with a flapping loincloth. Walking towards the Scout, he shouted and waved his arm. "No there. No gasoline there. Over here," waving towards half a dozen red, plastic cans laid out in a row at the side of the office building. "No *beezly*. Pump no working. Gasoline in cans if you are wanting it."

Wildman watched him carefully, at the same time keeping his eye on the other man in the office. The man in the office seemed absorbed in his papers. He hesitated a second and then, starting the engine, slipped the Scout into Drive and eased it forward and away from the pump. As he did so the young man and his idiot helper swung into action. They ran to the red gasoline cans and started carrying them towards the Scout. Wildman nodded at the small fat man and stepped out of the vehicle. He closed the door behind him, but did not lock it and, walking back to the rear of the Scout, unlocked the fuel cap, took it off and kept it in his hand. The young man stepped forward with a funnel. But when he opened the first can Wildman put up his hand, said, "Wait," and, bending over carefully, sniffed the contents. It was gasoline all right. Low grade, low octane Indian gasoline, by its peculiar sour smell. He waved the boy forward and together he and his half-naked helper started pouring the gasoline through the funnel into the tank.

It took twenty minutes to fill the tank and when it was done, with much slopping of fuel over the rim of the funnel and down the legs of the two attendants, almost twenty-five gallons had been poured in. Wildman stayed close to the tank all the time it was being filled, taking his eyes off the two attendants only to swing his head back from time to time to check the slowing rising fuel gauge in the instrument panel of the Scout. Pasang in turn watched the two men in the office.

When the tank was full, the fat man came out of the office again, shouting at the two attendants to clean up and put the cans away. This done, he walked quickly back into the office, with what Wildman thought was an almost exaggerated haste, as though he wanted to be done with the transaction as quickly as possible. When he reappeared it was with the bill—a scribble in pencil on a dirty piece of paper. In a voice that seemed to Wildman to be distinctly nervous, he said, "Nine hundred and seventy-five rupees 'ees total price."

Wildman pushed the self-locking filler cap on and banged it with his fist to make sure it was locked. He then pulled ten one-hundred-rupee bills out of an inside pocket and handed them to the fat man, who immediately turned and scurried back into the office with the money. Opening the driver's side door he got in, at the same time reaching across to flip the lock on the passenger side door for Pasang.

Pasang walked quickly to the car, jumped in and closed and locked the door. Wildman paused to look around the compound. The young man and the slow-witted boy were standing watching him from the shade of the office building. The fat man had gone back into the office and had taken his original place at the table with his companion and was studiously, a little too studiously Wildman thought, reading the papers on the table.

Wildman gave Pasang a quick look and told him to stay in the car. Turning the ignition key, he stopped the engine. He then reached under the dashboard, pulled the hood release, got out and walked around to the front of the Scout and lifted it. He pulled out the oil stick, wiped it on a little oily rag that was tucked under the spring clip of the hydraulic brake fluid tank, replaced it in its shaft, pulled it out again and looked at it. The oil, clear and shiny, lined the FULL mark on the stick. He replaced it, put the little rag back, slammed the hood down and returned to the car. Then he fired the engine, dropped the gearshift into Drive and accelerated hard out of the compound. His last sight of the station was of the idiot boy, giggling and shaking his head from side to side and licking his gasoline-soaked fingers. Christ, thought Wildman, that stuff smells bad enough. What the hell must it taste like?

Once out on the road again, Wildman drove as fast as road conditions allowed. Fast. He had a nasty feeling about the fuel station they had just left. Had there been a trap there? Had it been called off at the last minute? Were more men supposed to arrive? Certainly the ones who were there, a fat man and his office companion and a gangling youth and an idiot boy posed no menace. Indeed, if they had tried anything...He dismissed the thought and kept his foot hard on the Scout's throttle. The big vehicle thundered down the road, its heavy-duty tires whining lustily on the hard bitumen surface. The engine emitted a steady if constrained roar as the speedometer needle drifted back and forth between 60 and 70 mph and, in spite of his foreboding, Wildman felt a familiar sensual pleasure as the pulse and throb of the big vehicle transmitted their vibrations to his body.

The road began to climb and ahead, through the mid-morning haze, they could see a low range of hills against the skyline. A sign said **NAGPUR, 30 MILES**.

"Madhya Pradesh jungles coming up soon, Pasang. And we are going to have to eat something, seeing that we have not eaten since yesterday. What say we find a nice roadside inn, one with air-conditioning and nice clean tablecloths, fine food and good service, where we will avail ourselves of a delicious meal."

Pasang smiled a thin smile. The best they would find, he knew, just as Wildman knew, would be some flyblown *char dukan*, or teahouse, with the usual fare of rice and curried vegetables. But food was food and they both knew that *dal bhat*, as it was called, was what they would be eating, all the way to Kathmandu, unless, as was unlikely, they stopped over in Varanasi at a tourist hotel.

"Maybe some more coffee, *sahib*, in meantime?"

"Good idea, Pasang. And we'll keep a lookout for somewhere to eat at the same time."

Pasang slipped out of his seat belt and turned sideways to get the coffee makings out of the central console between the front seats. As he

The burning ghats at Benares (now Varanasi).
At one time Vask, through ruthless trading, acquired and owned more than 75% of the waterfront property.
Photo credit: Varansi city police.

Ruins of the house blown up by Vask when its owner refused to sell it to him.

did so he suddenly froze. He turned back slowly to face the front and keeping his head facing forward, without looking at Wildman, said, "*Sahib*, can I have the mirror to look in?"

Wildman sensed the tension in Pasang's voice and, without saying anything, reached up and twisted the mirror to his line of view. As he did so he looked into his side mirror and saw what Pasang had seen in his peripheral vision. About a thousand feet back was a grey, canvas-topped Jeep, coming fast, white-clothed figures hanging out of the open, doorless sides and more crouched behind the windshield.

"OK Pasang, I've got it. What do you think?"

Pasang, watching the mirror, body rigid, his fingers curled around the handle of his *kukri*, did not reply. Wildman watched the vehicle behind them for a further three to four minutes as it appeared and reappeared in the clouds of dust sucked up from the highway verges by the passage of the Scout.

"Right, Pasang. Here's what we'll do. You keep an eye back there and I'll keep an eye ahead. OK? It looks as though they are keeping pace with us. If they try to catch up, we'll give them some dust to eat off. Personally I think this chappie of ours will outrun any Indian vehicle on the roads. But their game may be a roadblock ahead. I'll watch for that. You watch them. We'll give them another five minutes or so and then we'll do a tail check on them."

For another five miles Wildman held the Scout at a steady 60 mph. Then he nodded to Pasang, slowed and said; "Now we'll see what they are up to."

Applying the standard method of detecting a follower, he slowed to fifty, and then forty. Sure enough, the Jeep slowed with them, maintaining its thousand-foot gap behind them.

"Keeping back *sahib*. Not catching up," said Pasang, watching the mirror.

"Right," said Wildman, waiting until the road opened up and the traffic thinned a little and then putting his foot down. Forty, fifty, and then, for two long stretches, sixty. Then back to a steady fifty. They looked back. The Jeep was gone.

"Gone, *sahib*. Too fast for them I think."

"Good, Pasang. Now we'll give them another mile or so to see if they are still after us and then we'll find a side road and pull in and let them pass."

A scattering of buffalo carts appeared on the road ahead. Wildman cursed, swung off into the verge and, in boiling clouds of dust, roared down a long, shallow ditch and then back up on to the road. A truck forced him off the road again, then another truck. This was annoying. But they would do the same to anyone following them and it was also possible that the boiling clouds of thick brown dust created by the Scout, which reduced visibility to two or three feet, would also slow the vehicle behind them.

Regaining the road for the third time, Wildman thrust the throttle hard to the floor to rebuild his speed. The needle moved up again into the sixties. Wildman, a natural driver, seldom looked at it, preferring to drive to the allowable speed of road conditions. He was more interested in watching the engine's performance indicators and now, with the road briefly empty in front of him and the speed steady, he gave the panel a sweeping glance.

The fuel gauge was on FULL with twenty-five gallons, give or take a pint or two, in the tank, good for probably three hundred miles. Must try to find a better fuel station next time, he thought; jerry cans and idiot children and half an hour to fill the tank. The alternator needle was straight up and flickering only with the vibration of the engine. The oil indicator...the oil indicator? Wildman looked up at the road and then down again at the oil pressure needle. It was off-centre, off to the left, at an angle of forty-five degrees. Low. Low for the high revolutions of the engine and at the speed he was travelling. But he had checked the oil no more than twenty miles back and it had been well up on the high mark on the dipstick. His eyes flicked over to the water temperature gauge. It too was up, out of its usual position, and within a fraction of being vertical. Well, the speed could do that. That big winch on the front did reduce quite a bit of the airflow in to the radiator. He looked up at the road again, flipped the wheel to miss two rickshaws and a wandering horse, looked down again and swore. The oil pressure needle had dropped another fraction of an inch and, as though keeping company with the water temperature gauge, had crossed the vertical red centre line and was moving—goddamit, the thing was visibly moving—into the red danger area beyond.

Christ. What was happening. Wildman looked up. A huge truck was coming straight at them. He wrenched the wheel and the Scout lurched wildly, thundered off the road into the verge, bounced into a hole, missed a tree by inches and slammed back up on to the road again. Wildman accelerated hard, checked the road ahead and then looked again at his instruments. The oil pressure gauge was continuing to drop and suddenly, to his horror, the needle swung all the way to the left, hit the zero mark and stayed there. The temperature gauge, its little red stick a warning finger, immediately began its own personal dive to the right, through the red danger zone all the way to the high temperature H. At the same time a high-pitched whine, rapidly increasing in volume, came from the engine.

Wildman immediately took his foot off the throttle, flipped the gear lever into neutral and reached for the ignition key. His plan was to get the engine stopped before whatever was happening under the hood could do any serious damage and his actions were quick and smooth and well co-ordinated. But he was too late and, before he could turn the key, the engine noise surged to a hitch-pitched scream accompanied by a horrible grinding of metal against metal and the staccato pounding of overworked valves. The scream culminated in an explosion of steam and oil from under the hood. There was a tremendous bang, dark green radiator fluid spurted out on either side and the engine died. As it did power was cut to the steering and the brakes and for a hundred yards Wildman fought the leaden wheel and the sluggish, powerless brakes, before being able to bring the vehicle to a dust boiling, jarring halt at the side of the road.

Silence, and the only sound the hissing of steam as water and brake fluid boiled on the red-hot manifold pipes of the Scout's shattered engine. A silence quickly broken by the whine of an approaching Jeep coming up behind them, fast. Wildman, his pulse racing, watched the vehicle roar to a stop behind them, watched as half a dozen men in dirty white clothing piled out and ran towards them, two of them with pistols in their hands, another with an ancient Lee Enfield 303 rifle. The two with the pistols ran up to the Scout, pounded on the windows with their fists, shouted and pointed their weapons at Wildman and Pasang. The one with the rifle ran to the front of the Scout and rather stupidly pointed his weapon at the radiator. Wildman looked at Pasang and then, slowly, his eyes on the man nearest him, unlocked the door and climbed out. The man with the pistol immediately used it to prod him in the stomach—another stupid move, thought Wildman, one that gave him the opportunity to floor his opponent with a quick backhand—and shouted at him to move. "Back to the Jeep. Get in the Jeep."

Wildman turned and had started to walk back towards the Jeep when he saw Pasang getting out of the other side of the Scout. The man covering Pasang stepped back when he saw the big knife sticking out of Pasang's waistband. He pointed at it and shouted for Pasang to take it out and throw it on the ground. Wildman saw Pasang hesitate.

"Do it, Pasang. Do as he says," he shouted.

He watched out of the corner of his eye as Pasang slowly took the big *kukri* out of his sash and placed it carefully on the ground in front of him.

The man covering him waved him back with the pistol and as Pasang turned to follow Wildman he picked up the knife and stuck it in the front of his ragged trousers.

Wildman and Pasang were pushed unceremoniously into the waiting Jeep—no body search, smiled Wildman to himself, very unprofessional—and as they were driven away Wildman saw a second Jeep pull up and two men with a towrope run towards the Scout.

BOOK FIVE

CAPTURE

They drove for an hour. As soon as they started, their captors had closed the canvas sides of the Jeep and Wildman and Pasang, crammed in the back, were forced to endure the fetid odour of unwashed bodies. They stopped twice to top up the boiling radiator of the Jeep and each time they did this, weapons were poked into their rib cages by the pistol-packing ones and they were watched with scowling looks. Wildman, watching their comic opera methods, had to restrain himself from laughing. He was very tempted to do so but he knew Indians and he knew that they might construe this, not so much as an insult, but as some kind of loss of face. Then they could be dangerous and while he had a feeling that they would not kill him, not yet anyway, he sensed that they would not hesitate to hurt or even kill Pasang, something to be avoided. Their captors talked incessantly and this plus the noise of the engine and the rattling body of the Jeep allowed he and Pasang to exchange an occasional whisper. In one of these Wildman told Pasang to play along with their captors for the moment and do what they wanted. Later the two of them would form a plan.

After an hour they left the main road and took a gravelled side road that led into an area of small rolling hills. Soon the gravel road petered out and became a dirt track. They slowed and began to climb and suddenly Wildman glimpsed, through the grimy windshield, a white house, one that looked like an old British Indian country house, set on top of a small hill. A little later the Jeep came to a halt in a swirling cloud of dust in front of the house. They were hustled out. Wildman had a quick glimpse of more men in the entrance of the house and a scowling, ugly-faced woman, leaning out of an upstairs window, looking down. Then they were pistol-prodded around the side of the house and marched through a set of high, double doors that led into a small yard that was surrounded by a low wall. The yard contained an assortment of battered looking Indian cars, old, rusting car parts and, in a corner, a small furnace.

They were quickly hustled across the yard, through a stout wooden door and down a long gloomy corridor with what looked like cells, with heavy wooden doors, on either side. Doors to two of the cells were quickly opened and Wildman was pushed into one, Pasang into another. Just before the door of Wildman's cell was slammed on him, he had a quick glimpse of Pasang. Perhaps he expected him to glance back at him, a look of understanding, or recognition. But Pasang, his face a mask, was watching the man wearing his *kukri,* the man who had taken it from him on the road and who was still wearing it stuck in the front of his trousers. Then their cell doors were slammed shut and Wildman heard heavy bolts being slid into metal apertures on the outside. For a while there was a murmur of voices. Wildman thought he heard someone laughing. Then there was silence.

Wildman examined the cell that was his prison. The walls were of hard, sun-baked mud and from what he could see, as he was pushed inside, probably three feet thick. It would be possible to get through one of them with a digging tool, he thought. But unfortunately he just did not have a steel-bladed folding shovel tucked in the brim of his Terai hat. James Bond would have had one, he thought, smiling to himself. But he and James had never met. And if Vask was as evil as his reputation suggested, and unless he and Pasang could find a way to escape, they never would. For he had no doubt that the men who had captured them were Vask's men, and that the house where he and Pasang were now imprisoned, was Vask's stronghold.

Wildman continued to examine his cell. It measured about fifteen feet by fifteen feet. For furnishings, there was a wooden table, one wooden chair and, tucked against a wall, a small rope bed with a wooden frame. Set in the wall above the bed was a small window, about twenty-four inches square with four panes of grimy glass, thick with cobwebs. Wildman walked over to it and, using his fingernails, scraped half an inch of the glass clear. On the outside of the window, set firmly into the hard mud of its frame, he saw what he expected, half a dozen thick iron bars. Each was an inch in diameter, heavily rusted. He looked through the bars and found that he could see, at an angle, into the back yard through which they had come when they arrived. By straining against the glass, he could see three quarters of the yard itself and the double doors that were its only exit to the outside.

Turning from the window, he walked to the door of the cell. It was made of wood. It looked to him like *sal,* the common hardwood of the

Vask's house, where Wildman and Pasang were taken when they were captured. On the left is the entrance to the back yard through which, on arrival, Wildman and Pasang were taken to their cells.

Rear view of Vask's house showing the upstairs room where Vask conducted his interrogation of Wildman and Pasang.

In a restaurant in Varanasi, one of the last pictures taken of Gilliam Ween. On his left is his daughter Tara, who visited him briefly while he and his wife were there. On his right, the well known Paris Match magazine writer and columnist, Fifi La Griffe, on her way back from Assam where her magazine had assigned her to write a series of articles on head hunting.

The Weens in happier days with their children, Mikhail and Tara, dining at the Savoy Hotel, London. Picture credit Scotland Yard Criminal Investigation Division, Pending Files, London, W1, England.

northern Indian forests. He could not see its edges, tucked as they were into the frame, but he guessed it was four inches thick. Two lines of iron bolts were set in the door, horizontally, and Wildman guessed they were what held the bolt structure on the outside. He looked at the heads of the bolts. Originally they had had slotted heads and could be opened with a screwdriver. But someone had filed the slots down and now they were smooth. He stepped back and looked at the door again, measuring it with his eye until he had a mental picture of the position of the outside locks.

The bottom of the door had a gap of about three inches between it and the floor. He put his hand down and felt a faint draft of air coming through. The door itself had one other feature. About five feet from the ground was a small aperture. It measured six inches in height and four inches across. In it were set four vertical bars. He ran his fingers over the bars. Unlike the window bars, they were of hardened steel. He pressed his face against them and found that he could see part of the corridor outside, its ceiling, and part of the floor in front of the door. But he could not see the door locks and, mentally measuring the distance between where he thought they were, and the aperture, he guessed they were too far away for a reaching arm, even if it were possible to get an arm between the aperture bars, which it was not. The door of Pasang's cell, directly opposite, had no aperture.

He examined the ceiling of the cell. In the centre was a small round hole and when he put his hand up to it, he felt a flow of air passing out through it. This accounted for the flow of air coming under the door. One other item caught his eye. Protruding from the wall, beside the door was a large, rusted metal hook. He walked over and touched it with his fingers. It was caked with a dark red, brittle substance. He scraped a little off with his fingernail. It looked like dried blood. He shuddered. Some poor wretch had hung there. Someone foolish enough to defy Vask, or perhaps try to cheat him.

His inspection completed, Wildman walked to the bed and sat down. He was about to swing his feet up and stretch out when he heard voices, followed by footsteps. He sat up. The door bolts rattled, the door swung open and four men quickly entered the cell. Wildman recognised them as the men who had been with him in the Jeep. He looked past them. Another two men, both carrying heavy wooden clubs, stood in the doorway and as Wildman watched, they moved aside to allow a seventh man to step through the doorway into the cell.

Wildman tried hard to hide the surprise on his face when he recognised the man. It was Ghose. The sallow face, the small black eyes set too close together, the surly mouth and the arrogant cast to the head, were still the

At an upstairs window of a house in Nagpur, a rare picture of Vask, believed to be the only one ever taken of the infamous thug and mass murderer. Credit: Nagpur City Police, Nagpur, Maharastra.

same. But now he was wearing Indian clothing, a long-sleeved white shirt that hung over a pair of loose white cotton trousers, with black plastic sanda1s on his feet.

Ghose looked at Wildman and if Wildman expected him to say very much he was disappointed. "Your clothes, Mr. Wildman, please. Everything. Shoes, socks, watch, your hat, belt. Everything. Quickly."

Wildman hesitated, and as he did the two men with the clubs made a movement. But Ghose stayed them with his hand and Wildman, accepting the situation, which was that if he refused he would be forcibly stripped, and probably also beaten, quickly undressed. The men in the cell gathered up his clothing and when they had it all, Ghose nodded and left and they followed him out through the door. Wildman made a quick estimate of the strength of the party as they started to leave. None of them were very big and he estimated that with some fast moves he could knock out the men with the clubs and burst through the others and get down the corridor and....But that would mean leaving Pasang behind. No. If he was going out of here they were going out together. His cell door slammed shut, the bolts were driven home and Wildman was left sitting naked on the hard, string bed.

For a few minutes there was silence. Then he heard locks rattling and, across the corridor, the door of Pasang's cell being opened. There was a murmur of voices. Pasang was being told to strip. The order was followed by a brief silence and Wildman tensed. Pasang would not like being ordered to strip. He would be outraged, in fact. Nepali hill people have a strong sense of modesty and nakedness, in public, among both men and women, is considered shameful. Pasang's reaction was as Wildman surmised. There was a shout, followed by a scream. Then the sounds of a scuffle, several thuds, a groan, and then Pasang's cell door being slammed followed by silence. Good try, Pasang, Wildman thought. But not good enough. Not against six goons, two of them with wooden clubs. He excluded Ghose who, he felt, could, if and when the time came, be knocked out with a good backhand slap in the chops. And he smiled grimly as he heard the group dragging a groaning member down the corridor and out to the back yard.

Half an hour after Wildman had been forced to strip the men returned. The door of Wildman's cell opened and they threw his clothes, socks and shoes in. The money belt was gone from his trousers, as was his Rolex; Wildman guessed that there was little chance of his seeing either of those again. Across the corridor he heard Pasang's cell door being opened and shut. Then all was silent. He dressed and as he did so the dim light filtering through the grimy panes of the cell window began to fade. Then it was gone and the cell was dark. Six o'clock, Wildman estimated. November in central India. Dark at six and a long night ahead.

An hour later Wildman heard the sound of a Jeep grinding up the hill in low gear. It pulled in to the front of the house. Voices drifted down the corridor, clanging of chains, slamming of doors. He recognised the heavy, thudding door sounds. Scout doors. They had towed it here from the highway. The sounds increased and Wildman moved quickly to his cell window. He saw the yard doors being opened and as he watched, the big gold and white vehicle was pushed into the courtyard by a dozen men. He wondered what they were going to do with it. Repair it? Use it? Sell it? At the same time he wondered what had gone wrong with it. He had used a number of Scouts over the years, in the US, in Nepal, in Africa and Australia, and never had one let him down yet. And this one had not just let him down. It had blown up on him. And why? The clock had registered a mere 16,000 miles, nothing for that hefty 3450 cc engine. In addition the thing had been well looked after, something he had seen at first glance, back in Bombay. Well, whatever had happened, there was one thing he was sure of and that was that nobody was going to drive out of here in that vehicle in the next twenty-four hours.

Two hours after dark Ghose and his men came back. The door opened and again six of them. Business thought Wildman and tensed himself. Ghose was precise if nothing else. "Turn around and put your hands behind your back. Any trouble, Mr. Wildman and you will be sorry."

Slowly, and stiffening the big muscles at the back of his neck against a blow, Wildman did as he was told. Ghose made a quick motion with his hand and one of the men stepped forward and with deft, practiced movements bound Wildman's hands behind his back. The instant the rope touched Wildman's wrists he recognised it by its touch. It was woven, coconut-fibre rope. He had used it himself, many times, building blinds and tree platforms for wildlife observation and he knew that given enough bindings, the stuff was practically unbreakable. He also knew that its elasticity greatly contributed to its strength, making it almost impossible for a tightly bound man to free himself.

When his hands were bound to Ghose's satisfaction, Wildman was led from the cell. The men then grouped around Pasang's door. One of them slid the bolts back and the two with wooden clubs stepped into the cell. Pasang was sitting on his bed and when the men came through the door he slid off it and stood, tensed, waiting. The men, sensing trouble, stopped a few feet away from him and looked back at Ghose for instructions.

For a tense moment everyone stood still. Then Wildman shouted, "Pasang, do as they ask. Just do it."

When he did, the two men advanced on the little Sherpa, spun him around and quickly tied his hands behind his back. Then he was brought out into the corridor.

"You come now to meet my master," Ghose said. "He wants to have thee conversation with you."

"And that would be?" said Wildman, pretending that he did not know.

"Vask. Raja Vask to all who know him and to you also."

They were taken down the corridor, through the back yard and around the side of the house, Ghose leading the way, the men carefully grouped around them. Wildman glanced quickly around as they passed through the big double doors of the back yard. It was about eight now and dark. But a glowing moon was climbing up out of the hills to the east, giving him enough light to look around. By it he could see that not far from the small hill on which the house stood, the sloping ground, falling away from the front of it, rose again quickly to a series of jagged rock outcrops. A thinning of trees broken with patches of light brush swept up to the outcrops and Wildman guessed there might be forest behind them. Long dark shadows, running through the outcrops, suggested ravines. An escape route? Possibly. The Central Provinces, of which Nagpur was the capital, still had some wild country in its heart, ravine country and jungle country that was home to bandit gangs whose control of the area, since time immemorial, was legendary. If he and Pasang could get out of the house and into that jungle and ravine country…

They entered the house through the front door. They were pushed down a short corridor and into a big room brightly lit by the glare of a pressurised kerosene lamp. The room contained a long wooden table and a scattering of cheap bazaar chairs with shiny metal seats and legs made of twisted, heavy grade, galvanised wire. Seated at the far end of the table from the door—like a giant and evil toad, thought Wildman—was Vask.

In the doorway the group came to a halt and the guards hesitated. For a few seconds Vask, his eyes lidded against the glare of the lamp, silently watched them. Then, with a flick of a hand he dismissed the men and with the other hand beckoned Wildman and Pasang into the room.

"So, mister wild man, or whatever your name is, thee famous mister wild man, they call you, brought down to thee ground and also brought to visit the Raja Vask by a little sugar in your gasoline tank."

Vask's huge head nodded up and dawn and a heavy grunting noise, that Wildman took to be a laugh, issued from his mouth. "A little too sweet for thee wild man, eh?

View of the back yard of Vask's house that Wildman and Pasang could see from their cell window.

Two of Vask's men working a small furnace in the corner of the back yard of Vask's house. They used it, during Vask's search for the Eye, to cut up the larger metal parts of the Scout.

And suddenly, in a flash, Wildman saw in his mind the idiot boy at the gasoline station licking his fingers as they drove away, and knew how Vask had got him. Got him, the clever bastard, with a little trick as old as the first automobile; sugar mixed with the gasoline that, with the heat of the engine, quickly crystallised and sealed the exhaust valve apertures, causing the engine to literally explode.

"Now, Mr. Wildman, you and I have things to talk about. But firstly, to make you more comfortable, we'll get rid of that rope, yes?"

He clicked his fingers and at once two men appeared in the doorway. He spoke to them quickly. One of them left and returned within minutes with a knife. Stepping behind Wildman he sliced the ropes that held his wrists and set them free. Then he and the other man left the room, closing the door behind them and leaving Pasang still bound.

"Now, come. Sit at thee table here. Down at the end where I can see you. And we will talk."

Vask leaned forward and smiled, showing two rows of large, betel nut stained teeth in a dark red mouth. At the same time he motioned with his hand. Wildman walked to a chair set at the head of the table, at the opposite end from Vask, and sat down. Pasang made to follow him but Vask shouted at him. "Not you. You sit on the floor. Common villagers do not sit at the same table as a high caste Brahmin."

Pasang, keeping in mind Wildman's admonition to do what he was asked and play along with his captors, went to the corner of the room and sat down with his back to the wall.

Vask eased his position in his chair and, leaning forward, put his elbows on the table. He gave the huddled figure of Pasang a quick, contemptuous look, coughed, spat on the dirt floor and continued.

"Thee thing, thee issue, as you Americans like to say 'ees this. You have something that I want. A stone, yes? A little stone. The Eye, it is called. The green eye of the yellow god of Kathmandu. Now, you are not going to play any games with me. Nor do I intend to play any with you, mister. Very simply put, you have it, I want it, and I am going to get it. In fact, no matter what it takes, you are going to give it to me. And why do I want it? Because I am charged by my faith, handed down by my father, and to him by his grandfather, by all that is holy to a Brahmin, to get the Eye and to return it to its place of origin, the temple in Kathmandu. That is where it belongs and that, mister Wildman, is where it is going and nothing, nothing will stop me from fulfilling my appointed task, the return of the Eye to its rightful owners."

Oh yes, indeed, thought Wildman. You'll sell it to the highest bidder faster than I can say bullshit. Vask continued. "As I say, we can be very civilised about this. You hand the Eye over to me and you have my word, the word of a true Brahmin that you will go free. I will order my men to drive you back to Bombay, place you in a hotel of your own choice—all paid for—and from there you can go home, free to, er, continue your interesting career as a carrier, or whatever you call it. To assure you that I mean what I say, here is your money and your beautiful watch."

With a quick movement Vask reached in his lap and produced Wildman's and Pasang's money belts and Wildman's Rolex watch and slid them down the table.

"You see what I mean, then, about being civilised? I am sure that you do, and that you too can be civilised. Then we have an agreement, yes? And we will do thee business together, yes?"

Wildman looked at the hulking figure of Vask at the other end of the table. His first reaction was to tell him to go to hell. But Vask held all the cards at the moment and until he, Wildman, found an ace or two up his sleeve, he thought it might be more prudent to go along with him as far as that was possible and, until he found the right cards, to play for time.

He looked at Vask and spoke. He spoke quickly and it was only after he did that he realised that he might have made a mistake and, with what he had said, given Vask a strategic advantage that he could well put to his own use.

"Before I answer your question, Mr. Vask, I have one to ask you. You talk about setting me free if you, shall we say, get what you want? But what about my man there? Will he be freed with me?"

Vask hesitated for a moment and then, his eyes glittering, spoke. "I think you are fond of that little hillman? How can this be? How can you like someone of no caste? A nothing person from the back hills of Nepal? But then, you Americans are strange and so I'll strike a bargain with you. All right, after you have handed over the Eye, you can go and he can go with you. All right then, we have an agreement, yes? Then just hand over the stone and as I promise, you can both be on your way out of here without delay."

Wildman hesitated. He needed time to think, time to plan. He had watched Vask very carefully as he was speaking, and what he saw in the man's eyes confirmed what old Lord Carew had told him about his deviousness and ruthlessness. It also convinced him that once Vask had the Eye in his possession, his chances of getting out of there were zero. Pasang's chances were even less. If there is something less than zero. As long as Vask did not have the Eye they were safe. And Pasang? Pasang was the problem. Had Vask sensed that Wildman had a bond with the little Sherpa?

Three of Vask's professional stranglers. They were Afghanis and later, when arrested by police, they said that their fee for a strangulation depended on the importance of the person but was usually about Rs250.00. (US $3.50)
Photo credit: Federal Bureau of Investigation, Langley, VA, USA.

Men waiting outside one of Vask's houses in Varanasi hoping to find employment with one of his gangs.

He knew that he was now Vask's only lead to the stone itself and that, because of this, Vask would not, could not, kill him, until he had it in his possession.

But Pasang? Vask would have him strangled out of hand and though Wildman knew that Pasang would die hard and, given half a chance, take a few of Vask's men with him, one can only fight so many men at a time. But Vask might also use Pasang as a pawn in the game and Wildman shuddered to think of what he might do to the little hillman. His mind racing, he decided that the best thing to do now was play for time. Time to think and plan and explore every avenue of escape from the house.

"Mr. Vask," he said, looking steadily at the big man at the other end of the table, "I tell you what I will do. I'll consider your offer tonight. You let us sleep on it, and in the morning I'll give you my answer."

For a moment he thought Vask would refuse. The man gave him a quick, cunning look and for a second or two Wildman thought his little ploy had failed. But then Vask smiled, a slow, ugly smile and said, "Yes, but of course you can have the night to think about it. That is what I would call a very civilised thing to ask and as a civilised man I will certainly grant you your request. Also, as you seem to be so concerned about your little servant there I'll let him stay with you. For a high caste man such as you to be concerned about an untouchable such as him is a mystery to me. But then, you Americans have strange…what is it you call them, sets of values, yes?"

Vask clapped his hands. The door opened and Ghose appeared. Vask beckoned him up to the head of the table and then whispered instructions in Hindi. Wildman's knowledge of the language was fair. But Ghose's replies were as muted as Vask's voice and he could only pick up a few words. One of them, *bhai*, meaning brother, rang a small warning bell, down in the back of his mind.

Ghose left the room and Vask turned his attention again to Wildman. He smiled slowly and said, "Your dinner is being made ready. You will enjoy it, if you like good Indian food. Your room is being made more comfortable. Unfortunately, of course, the door will have to be locked. 'Ees not that I do not trust you, you understand. 'Ees just that at night we would not want anyone bothering you, such as the man whose room is next to yours, down there. My brother. My most trusted companion. The one person I can always depend upon to do whatever I ask him to do. The man who helps me to question people, who assists me, if you know what I mean, in persuading the reluctant to cooperate. Now, stand back from the table, there, over against the wall, beside your little friend there. Because you are about to meet him and my brother gets excited when he meets strangers. In fact I would strongly advise you not to get too close to him."

Wildman rose quickly and moved to the wall next to Pasang. As he did so the door darkened and through it came something out of a nightmare, something that made Wildman's skin literally crawl.

The creature that came through the doorway was, apparently, human. But only just so. Vask's brother stood close to six feet in height, tall for an Indian. But it was his gigantic overall size that captured the eye. The enormous body completely filled the big doorway and Wildman estimated its weight to be well over four hundred pounds. The bulging torso was wrapped in filthy rags that left the arms and legs bare. The legs were short, bowed and covered with thick black hair. The feet were shoeless. Wildman ran his eyes over the body and took in the huge arms, black-haired like the legs and rippling with muscle. But it was the face that snapped him to instant, freezing attention. The face was almost perfectly round. The complexion was dark, almost black, broken only by the bloodshot whites of a pair of small black eyes, set tight together above a huge, spatulate nose. A vast, slobbering mouth was rimmed by thick red lips. Spittle oozed from its corners. The face was crowned with a short, thick forehead and massive frontal lobes that were like something that had just crawled out of the primeval ooze.

In the doorway the giant creature stopped. For a moment it seemed baffled by the glare of the pressure lamp on the table. Then, as its eyes adjusted to the brightness, its massive head slowly swivelled around to look at Wildman and Pasang. It seemed to ignore Pasang, crouched as he was against the base of the wall, and its eyes settled quickly on Wildman. The second it did so the huge head began to nod up and down and a thin, high-pitched whine issued from the drooling mouth. Slowly the huge body began to turn towards Wildman's figure, frozen against the wall and then, nodding its head with increasing speed, the whine growing higher and louder, it began to move towards Wildman. It moved forward half a dozen slow, shuffling, foot-dragging steps and then came to a halt. As it did so five men appeared in the doorway behind it and Wildman, his mouth dry, saw that they were all firmly clutching a thick coconut-fibre rope that was tied around the creature's waist.

You see, mister Wildman? This is my brother, Gunga. Little Gunga, we call him. Who lives, as I told you, in a little room just down the corridor from yours. Locked during the day, open at night. Locked during the day because we can't really have him wandering around. A little slow, mentally, my brother. Retarded is I think what you call it in America? But that's to our advantage, because it keeps him simple, keeps his life simple, so that essentially he is a man with just three needs, three enjoyments. These are eating, drinking—we let him have a little rum from time to time, it helps to keep him quiet—and...."

"And?" Said Wildman, keeping his eyes carefully on the hulking monster straining at the end of the rope.

"And, shall we say, playing with people. Yes, he likes to play with people. Unfortunately he gets a little rough at times and, er, damages them, if you know what I mean. As a result of which we have to make a careful choice of who we allow him to play with. These choices are, as I think you can understand, people we do not like. People who try to double-cross me, for instance. People who try to steal from me. People," and here he looked meaningfully at Ghose, "Who let me down. And also," looking directly at Wildman, "People who do not give me what I want."

Vask eased himself back in his chair to study the effect of the presence of his ghastly brother on Wildman.

"Yes," he continued. "He likes to play with people, my little brother does. But as I say, he can get rough and we have to be careful. Pulled a man's arm off last week. Right out of the socket. Ever seen that done, mister Wildman? A messy business. But in that particular case it did the trick. I needed information. There were two men involved. And, as you can guess, as soon as Little Gunga got to work on the first, the second could not wait to tell me all I wanted to know. Not that it did him much good. I do not forgive people who oppose me and so when we were finished, Little Gunga had two people to play with that day, instead of just the usual one."

Vask smiled his slow, sour smile and looked at Wildman again.

"Well then, my friend. What do you think? Would you like to tussle with my little brother? Think you might stand a chance. Big, isn't he? And therefore slow? Eh? Big men like that are always slow, you think, eh? Well then, watch this."

Vask stood up quickly and, reaching down, picked up one of the heavy, steel, wire chairs and slid it down the table. With a speed that was blinding and, for something so large, quite extraordinary, the giant snatched the chair off the end of the table and then, with three or four powerful squeezes of its massive hands, mangled it to pulp. But while it did so, and what made its awesome speed and strength all the more horrifying, was the fact that it never took its eyes off Wildman's face and the high-pitched whine, issuing from its slobbering mouth, as well as the nodding of the huge head, never ceased.

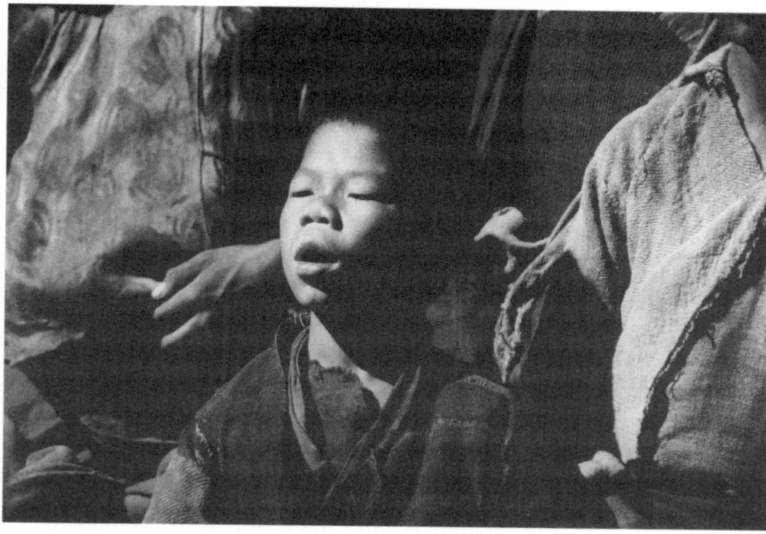

Little Gunga. Photo taken when he was six. At this age he already weighed 185 pounds and possessed phenomenal strength.

Chatterjee, the little man in Bombay who arranged the sale of the Scout for Wildman. With the money Wildman paid him he went to Calcutta and joined his brother in the garage business

Vask clapped his hands and the men in the doorway began to haul in the rope that held the giant. For a moment the giant resisted its pull. But then Vask shouted at it, "Tomorrow. Tomorrow you can play." And slowly, reluctantly, its eyes never leaving Wildman's face until the doorjamb blocked its view, it allowed itself to be led away.

Vask laughed his grunting laugh. "He seems to like you, mister wild man, eh? I wonder how wild you would be if he got his hands on you? Not too wild anymore, I would swear?"

The door opened and Ghose appeared. He told Vask that the room was ready for Wildman.

"And little Gunga is locked up for the moment?"

"Yes, Raja, until the night."

"Then go, mister Wildman and take your servant there with you. My men will show you to your room. You will find food and drink waiting for you and a comfortable bed. Sleep well and remember, if you have any ideas about getting out of there, that Little Gunga walks the corridor at night and as you can see, he is not the kind of thing you would want to bump into in the dark, right?"

With Vask's guttural laugh echoing in their ears, Wildman and Pasang, the latter still bound, were led out of the house, around to the back, through the yard, through the back door into the corridor and then down the corridor to their cell. Eight men, led by Ghose, accompanied them. At the cell door, Ghose waved them inside. One man went in with them and while the others blocked the doorway he cut the rope that bound Pasang's hands. The cell door was slammed shut and they heard the locks being thrust home. Then, through the door aperture came Ghose's voice. "You are a foolish person, Mr. Wildman, thinking that you could outwit my master, thinking that you could outwit me. Where is the Eye? Where are you keeping it? You had better tell me because it is only a matter of time before you are going to have to give it up."

Wildman watched the pallid face in the aperture and said nothing. He wondered what was going on in Ghose's mind? The man was clever, he knew. Was he now looking ahead? Was he thinking of what might be going to happen to all those having knowledge of the stone, when Vask eventually got it? Vask was not a man to leave a trail of incriminating evidence behind him. The sale of the stone in any country in the world would generate enormous interest. Not just among the criminal elements who would be involved in its passage, but also among law enforcement agencies in many countries. These might include India. Fingers would point to a long trail, trodden by many people, a trail that could eventually lead back to Vask. The way for him to prevent this happening would be to simply remove the trail's signposts. In other words, eliminate everyone involved, especial the principals, like Ghose.

Wildman watched the cold black eyes framed in the door aperture. "Well, Mr. Wildman, are you going to talk with me? I could help you, you know. But there is not much time. If you will talk with me—and you know what I mean—it will have to be tonight. My Raja is a man of limited patience. He has given you until tomorrow. But he has only given you that time while he searches your car. That is where the stone is, right? And I think you know, as well as I do, that when he finds the stone that is the end for you and your little friend. You will not leave here. You cannot be allowed to leave here, right? You understand what I am saying? What I am offering you? I am offering you your life. All you have to do is tell me where the stone is. I will get it and come back. I will make sure that Little Gunga is locked in his room and then I will open this door for you. You, and your man, can get out. There are big forests east of here and for a man of your abilities, all you have to do is get into them. Once in there, no one will find you and I know you have enough skill to make your way through them, to freedom. Yes? Come, talk to me. I cannot wait here. Raja Vask will get suspicious if I am not back in the house in a few minutes."

Wildman walked up to the door aperture and looked through at Ghose's face. He felt a cold, hard anger creeping over him as he looked at the thin mouth and the sallow features. He had listened carefully to what the man had said and he knew it to be as empty as was the man himself. Once Ghose had the stone, he would be up and away like the rat he was, leaving Wildman and Pasang to Vask's wrath. He looked at the steel bars in the aperture and for a moment his arm began to rise. But they were set too close together to get more than two or three fingers through, forcing him to abandon the thought of what he would really like to do which was reach through and grab Ghose by the throat and wring his miserable Bengali neck.

Ghose, sensing his anger, backed away from the opening. He turned and spat and then spoke again.

"All right then, you won't speak with me. So you will lose everything. Raja Vask will find the stone, you can be assured of that, and when he does you will suffer the fate of others who have tried to better him, and have failed. Tomorrow you will see what I mean. Tomorrow you will get to play with Little Gunga."

Ghose turned and was gone. Wildman listened to him walking away. Just before the outer door slammed, behind him he heard bolts being withdrawn and iron hinges squealing as Ghose opened the door of Little Gunga's cell. Then the yard door slammed and there was silence.

Wildman turned to Pasang, who was rubbing his wrists. His hands had been bound for two hours and the pain of returning circulation must have been considerable. The Sherpa saw Wildman looking at him and grinned.

"Are you OK Pasang?"

"Yes *sahib*. OK. No troubles, thank you."

"Good, then let's see what these goons have left us."

Wildman turned to the cell. On the bed were his sleeping bag and a single blanket. He turned his attention to the table. Its stained surface had been covered with a newspaper. A single candle guttered in a metal holder, shedding a thin yellow light into the cell. Beside it was a small box of matches. On the table were two metal bowls, with lids. Wildman took off the lids. In one was hot, steaming, boiled rice; in the other a mixture of curried vegetables. A third bowl, smaller, held a mess of yellow lentils. Beside each bowl were two tin plates with separated areas for different foods, a single, small eating spoon and a single fork. Also on the table was a large ladling spoon and fork made of some soft metal. Beside it was a single glass and one of Wildman's bottles of Glenlivet from the Scout. It was the one that he not yet opened. It was full and its seal was intact. Next to it was his cloth-covered, metal water bottle, its weight indicating that it was full.

Wildman told Pasang to go ahead and start eating and, unscrewing the cap of the Glenlivet, poured himself a generous measure in the single glass. He picked up the glass and held it out towards Pasang with a questioning look. But the Sherpa shook his head and, grunting his thanks, began ladling food from the bowls on to one of the tin plates. When he had filled the plate he laid it on the table for Wildman and then prepared another one for himself. This done he picked up his own plate and going over to the wall, under the window, squatted down against it, face to the cell door, and began to eat.

Wildman sat on the bed and ate, sipping the Glenlivet slowly with his food. He had taken due note of the single glass and the single eating spoon and fork. The single bed. The single sleeping bag. Vask was making his point about Pasang's lowliness and the strangeness of Wildman being concerned about him. If anyone were to ask him, Vask would say that it was disgusting to think of sharing a room with a man of no caste, an untouchable. But to those who knew his real background, this would have been nothing but hypocrisy. For Vask was a "bought" Brahmin.

In India it was generally believed that one could only be a Brahmin if one was born a Brahmin. But this was not true. There was another way, and this was to simply to go to the priests at the nearest temple and offer them enough money. This is what Vask, originally a low caste body burner at the *ghat*s, the equivalent of a gravedigger, had done. People said that because of his wealth the priests had made him pay dearly. But that just made his new caste all the more special, and now he revelled in it and proclaimed its holy status for all to see and take note. He also used it, backed by the power of his money, to help maintain his hold on the minions who worked for him.

Lord Carew had put his finger on it when he told Wildman that Vask's caste was, after his money, the most important thing in his life. Hence Pasang's relegation, by Vask, to the very bottom of the caste ladder. Doing this, be believed, enhanced his own eminence and helped to glorify his own lofty status. It also—though Vask did not stop to think about this—showed where his weakness was. Perhaps, Wildman thought, it could be exploited, if the opportunity arose.

Wildman sipped his scotch and watched his little 'low caste' Sherpa eating. 'After you, *sahib*,' he had said, when Wildman told him to eat. And he had refused a drink of scotch, which Wildman guessed, he would have enjoyed. And now, Wildman guessed, regardless of what I say to him, he's going to sit up all night watching that door and staying on guard. Wildman swore a silent oath to himself that nothing, nothing, would make him leave there without his stalwart little companion.

They were hungry, not having eaten for more than twenty hours, and between them they quickly finished the rice and vegetables and the small bowl of lentils. And they were thinking of sleep, at least Wildman was, and Pasang was stacking the bowls on the table and wondering about where to have a pee when they both heard it, a faint whining sound, coming down the corridor, and growing louder.

<<>>

They froze and looked towards the door and as they did so, a huge black face with a slobbering mouth, Little Gunga, filled its single aperture. In the flickering light of the cell's single candle, the face took on a look of dark malevolency and Wildman felt his heartbeat quicken. For about a minute the creature stood still, looking through the aperture, and from the direction of its gaze, Wildman thought that it was looking at the table and the remains of their dinner. Its only movement was the strange bobbing of its head, up and down, that they had seen earlier; the animal whining accompanied the bobbing motion, increasing and decreasing slightly, as the head rose and fell.

Then suddenly the creature moved. It shifted its body sideways and reached up towards the door aperture. At first it appeared as though it were trying to get its hand through the little opening. Then it seemed to realize that the gaps between the bars were too small and it stopped. Then, like a huge child carefully examining the feel of a new toy, it forced one of its huge, spatulate fingers between the bars. When the finger was fully through, it curled it around the base of one of the bars and began to pull. The whining increased and the nodding of the massive head quickened, and while Wildman and Pasang warily watched, the bar slowly began to bend outwards. As it did so, its lower end, encased in the wooden frame of the opening, began to rise out of its socket. Suddenly, with a snap, the end of the bar popped clean out of its wooden socket. The creature immediately wrapped the remainder of its fingers around the bar and with a twist, pulled it right out of the frame.

With one bar gone there was now space for the giant to insert all of one hand into the aperture. Wildman watched the massive hand, with its thick, black covering of hair, seize a second bar and quickly twist it out of the frame. After this it quickly pulled out a third bar and then a fourth. When the last bar had been pulled clear, it stopped for a moment and pressed its face against the aperture. The whining increased and the small black eyes, set in dark, red-rimmed sockets, seemed to be trying to say something. When Wildman and Pasang did not respond to whatever it was trying to convey, the huge face was suddenly withdrawn. For a moment nothing happened. Then, with a sudden movement, a huge arm was thrust right through the opening and into the cell. At the end of the arm a single finger extended itself and pointed towards Wildman and Pasang. At the same time the creature's whining changed, becoming erratic and rising to a higher pitch.

When the huge arm came through the door aperture, both Pasang and Wildman had instinctively stepped back. They were a good six feet from the door and the size of the cell gave them safe clearance if the giant tried to grab them, which is what both of them thought the thing was trying to do. They were both wrong, as they very soon found out. For another minute the arm remained jammed in the aperture, a finger the size of a pinecone sticking out of the vast fist on its end. Then, as Wildman watched, the five fingers of the giant's other hand appeared under the lower edge of the door and both he and Pasang heard a ponderous grunt as the huge creature began to try and lift the door off its hinges.

The door groaned. The grunting increased in volume, interspersed with the whine. Something within the doorframe snapped with a loud crack and Wildman, looking fearfully around for a weapon of some sort in the cell, saw the bottom of the door slowly begin to bend outwards. All this time the other arm, with its pointing finger, remained firmly lodged in the aperture. It was Pasang who suddenly realised what was happening, what the giant wanted. He acted with a speed that was just in time to stop the solid wooden door from being wrenched out of its frame. He leaped to the table, grabbed the Glenlivet and, with a single bound, was at the door. Gently, and being very careful to stay out of the reach of that awful hand, he pushed the bottle of scotch into the grasping fingers. Instantly the hand under the door was withdrawn, the whining ceased the enormous fist closed carefully around the bottle and the arm slowly, almost delicately, drew the bottle sideways through the little opening.

Wildman felt the cold sweat running down his back. Motionless, he and Pasang stood and watched. Through the aperture they saw a hand lifting the bottle to the huge, slobbering mouth, saw the head tip back. They heard a deep, drawn-out gurgling sound as the near full contents of the bottle—something close to a litre of scotch—went down the giant's throat and then heard a smash of breaking glass as the bottle was dashed on the floor. For a second or two there was silence. Then they heard scraping, shuffling footsteps as the creature staggered down the corridor and then a crash of metal springs as it dropped on to a bed in its cell. A little later, a series of thunderous snores stirred the night air. They continued for most of the night.

Before settling down for the night, Wildman carefully examined the door to see if the giant's attempts to open it, before he had been pacified by the scotch, had weakened it in any way. They found that the bottom half was slightly twisted and now leaned out of its frame a few inches, into the corridor, away from the cell. With the bars now gone, Wildman found that he could get his arm all the way through the opening and he immediately pushed his arm through, to see if he could reach the door locks. But try as he might, he could not reach them. They were just too far down.

They looked around the cell for something that they could use to reach the locks. With the metal food ladle that had been left for their meal, they found they could just touch the upper ones. But the bolts were hard set into rusted sockets and again and again, until it snapped off, the ladle bent double under the pressure applied by Wildman. In the end they gave up. They would tackle the problem again with daylight. In the meantime, to help them prepare for whatever the morrow would bring, sleep, rest, was probably the most important thing.

One of Vask's vicious gang members, a professional strangler from Kabul. When captured by police he proudly claimed to have strangled a hundred men, women and children. Credit: Nagpur (Maharastra) City Police files.

The ugly and suspicious looking woman that Wildman and Pasang saw peering from an upper window at Vask's house, when they were taken there by Vask's men.

They settled down to sleep. The night was cold the cell was damp and chilly. Pasang had insisted that Wildman take the bed. Wildman agreed, but only if Pasang would take the sleeping bag. After the candle was put out, the dim light seeping in through the cell's single window saw Wildman covered with the thin, single blanket, stretched out on the bed, and Pasang, the sleeping bag wrapped around his shoulders, propped up against the wall opposite the door. From down the corridor Little Gunga's snores rumbled in the night air and Wildman's last thoughts before he went to sleep were that tomorrow looked as though it was going to be a hard day for both of them.

About five minutes after he had stretched out on the bed, Wildman heard a whispering sound. He stiffened and remained still and listened. It came again and then developed into a scurrying. In the dim light of the cell Wildman suddenly saw several large grey shapes come sliding underneath the door. Rats, attracted by the smell of the cooked food, coming to claim their own, the little bits and pieces of food they would find on the floor. Wildman let them cruise. Rats were par for the course in a place like this. He covered his head with the blanket and when two of them jumped on top of him and gave him a foot pattering inspection, he shrugged them off. He heard Pasang stamp with his foot a couple of times. The rats were bold but otherwise harmless. They leaped up on the table and the rice pot rattled as they turned it over and cleaned it out. The spoon fell to the floor and was promptly carried off. The lentil bowl became the centre of a fight between two big males for a while. Another pair spent some time gnawing at the bottom of the door, where the giant's hand had grabbed it and partially impregnated it with sweat. One of them started nibbling at the end of Wildman's blanket until a kick sent it flying. After that the men were left alone.

Wildman dozed, with the blanket drawn over his face. He was unable to sleep. The pallid moonlight, shafting through the greasy panes of the little window, was getting in his eyes. Getting brighter...He sat up abruptly. The light coming through the window was artificial and it had suddenly increased. As it did, he heard voices from the yard outside. He hissed to Pasang, "Something happening," and stepped to the window and looked out.

In the yard were half a dozen men. The double doors were open and more men were coming through them. Several of the men carried kerosene pressure lamps, the glare of which cast dancing shadows against the mud walls of the yard and the gleaning gold and white of the Scout. Vask, a grey blanket wrapped around him against the night's chill, dominated the scene and they could hear his heavy voice snarling orders. One of the men brought him a chair and Vask positioned it in the centre of the courtyard and sat dawn. Three more men appeared in the yard entrance, dragging an oxyacetylene welding set with two heavy metal cylinders on a small trolley.

Wildman tore some newspaper from the sheets that covered the table and wadding a small piece of it in his hand, spat on it and rubbed one of the panes clear. Now he was able to see the men in the courtyard more clearly. They wore dirty overalls and shirts stained with grease and oil. Some of them wore rags around their heads; some carried blanket rolls or had blankets wrapped around their shoulders. They were garage men, mechanics, and he quickly recognised them as such.

"What is it, *sahib*," said Pasang beside him. "What you think they are going to do?"

Wildman hesitated for a moment and then answered. "I'm not sure, Pasang, but I have a feeling that they are going to do a job on the Scout. And not to repair it, either. Doesn't take ten—how many are there out there, thirteen or fourteen—men to repair one car."

"Then, *sahib*?"

"They are looking for the stone, Pasang. They searched our clothes and I am sure that they searched the cell here, while we were meeting mister Vask and his lovely brother. I am sure that Vask has also searched the Scout. They have not found it, obviously. And so? So it's my guess that they are going to take the Scout apart until they do. Notice Vask there, propped up in his chair keeping an eye on things. That's why he's there, I'm sure of it."

While they watched, Vask gave directions and the motley group set to work on the big vehicle. Firstly, with much grunting and shouting, they pushed it into the centre of the courtyard. More lamps were brought and these were positioned around it; then the men started. Boxes of tools were opened, the furnace in the corner was lit and fired up by two, lean faced individuals who looked like Afghan tribesmen and the Scout was literally attacked from all four corners at once. And from the way the men worked, it was obvious to Wildman that Vask had no intention of ever trying to reassemble the vehicle, or try to get it running again.

Wildman looked at his watch. Eleven o'clock. "Pasang, get some sleep. There's nothing we can do now. Vask is going to be occupied with his search out there at least until morning. Maybe even late morning. I don't think those goons out there know how well one of those things is built. Get some sleep, do you hear me? A little rest will help us face things tomorrow. OK?"

"Very good, *sahib.*"

Pasang turned and went back to the wall and wrapped the sleeping bag around him. But he did not lie dawn. He sat on the floor, put his back against the wall, crossed his legs in front of him and faced the door. Wildman sighed and lay down on the bed and after a while, in less time than he expected, he was able to will himself to sleep. From the courtyard came an occasional shout accompanied by a clank of metal, hammering noises, the hissing of the furnace bellows and the rasping of hacksaws.

The sounds from the yard were still filtering into the cell when a thin grey streak, tight to the line of the eastern horizon, announced the dawn. Soon a sickly light filtered through the cell window and oozed across the hard dirt floor. Wildman opened one eye and listened. He swung his arm up and looked at his Rolex. Just after five. He looked across at Pasang. He was sitting exactly where he had last seen him when he went to sleep. His only change in position was that his knees were up and he had his chin resting on them. His brown eyes, barely seen under the lidded folds of skin that typified the men of the high hill country of Nepal, were set on the door of the cell and Wildman knew without asking that they had been there all night.

When a steady, continuous sound suddenly ceases, the effect on a listener is often the same as a new sound commencing. Wildman sat up quickly when all sounds suddenly stopped in the yard outside. He pushed off the folds of the blanket and stepped to the cell window and looked out. Vask was there, with Ghose, and they were ushering the mechanics and the furnace men out of the gate. Vask was giving instructions to his own men. Then the gates were closed and Vask and Ghose disappeared into the house. A few minutes later Wildman heard the door at the end of the corridor being opened, and voices. He heard a cell door being slammed shut—Little Gunga's cell? —and then footsteps. With a rattle of bolts his cell door was opened. Ghose stood there with half a dozen men, several of them with wooden clubs. Carefully, keeping two men in front of him, he spoke. "You can come now to thee toilet. Both of you. Come."

Ghose stepped back and waved them out. With Wildman leading, and with men in front and behind them, they were led out of the cell, down the corridor, past the giant's cell, the door of which was bolted shut, and out into the courtyard. Except for the gate guards, two of them sitting on stools beside the double doors, the yard was now empty. Had the mechanics been spirited away so that they would not see Raja Vask's guests? Or taken out for a morning meal. Or both. Wildman guessed both. But what took his attention as they emerged into the yard was what had been done to the Scout in the night.

The yard was strewn, wall-to-wall, with a veritable sea of mechanical devastation. In the middle of it stood what amounted to little more than the metal skeleton of the big vehicle. All of its major parts had been removed. They had been unscrewed and unbolted wherever this could be quickly and easily done. But anything that had proved too difficult to remove had simply been cut off with the oxyacetylene torch. The front bumper and the winch were gone. The hood and the front wings were off. The engine, stark without its covering hood, was still in place, but all of its exterior parts—the cooling fan and its belt drive, the power steering unit, the power brake unit, the air filter and carburettor, the heating unit, all of the water pipes and hot air pipes, all of the engine wiring, the plugs, the coil and distributor, the battery, the washer water tank, the radiator and its water pipes, the radiator overflow container—all had been ripped or cut from the engine. The doors were off and lay on the ground beside the frame. All of the fibreglass top had been cut away. The steering shaft had been cut out, the steering wheel was gone, the seats had been removed, front and back, and the flooring had been ripped out.

All this Wildman took in with one glance. And then Ghose was muttering at him and the men were pushing them through a sea of wire and metal plates and pieces of water pipe and glass from smashed headlights, towards a small wooden shed set in the corner of the yard. Inside was a standard squat toilet. Wildman made use of it, with the door half open and two of the men watching him suspiciously. He was made to wait outside while Pasang did the same and this allowed him to look around the yard.

He studied the sea of devastation that was the end of the Scout. He noted what had been done and what remained to be done before Vask would conclude that he was not going to find anything hidden in the Scout, or in its parts. The engine was still in place. It would take them another couple of hours to open it up completely, to get the cylinder head off and the pistons out and check the sump, the oil filter and the oil pump. Then would come the drive system, the transmission case and the transfer case. After that? Well, it depended on how far Vask would go. A thorough search would have to include opening up the front and rear differentials, the drive shaft, the front and rear axles, the wheels and tires—still attached to the frame—and then the chassis, the box-frame construction of which could provide a hundred hiding places for a small leather bag with a single jewel inside it.

Wildman made his estimation of the time needed to search what was left quickly. Another six to seven hours at least and he knew it was important to keep that in mind. Then he turned his attention to the yard itself and how, if the gate were closed and guarded, they could get out of it.

He looked at the gate. The big double doors did not fit well together and through a gap between them he could see the gravelled driveway that swept around to the front of the house. But now they were securely locked with a long, iron bolt and hasp and the hasp itself had a huge padlock on it, closed. Wildman had the feeling that Vask kept it locked all the time and that one of the gate guards kept the key.

He looked up at the walls of the yard. They were of thick, hard, sun-baked mud. The tops were rounded and he guessed that if they were like the walls of the cell, they were probably three to four feet thick. Height? Twelve feet. High enough to keep out, or in, the average Indian. But a Darcy Dugan? Wildman smiled to himself. Years ago he had read of an Irishman named Darcy Dugan who had escaped from Ireland's infamous Mountjoy Prison by going over a fourteen foot wall with nothing more than his wits and his physical ability. Every day, for weeks before, and to the amusement of his jailers, Dugan had run back and forth inside a small exercise yard, always stopping just short of the high wall that enclosed it. One day, to the non-amusement of his surly guards, he had run perhaps a little faster than usual. Arriving at the wall he had hurled himself upwards, placed a foot hard against the wall about five feet from the ground, bounced off the thrusting foot with the momentum of his run, catapulted himself to the top of the wall and then over it. He got away and was not seen again. Wildman, intrigued by the story, had practiced the method himself and had perfected it for walls up to thirteen feet. Twelve feet would not be difficult. But what about Pasang? That was a long way up for a little man like him.

He looked at the corner of the house where it jutted into the yard. Two storeys, straight up to twenty feet, with a grey tiled roof on top. The walls were smooth, with no handholds, no drainpipes. And even if there was something to climb on, what advantage would being up on the roof give them? No, it would have to be the wall. Or the gate. His musings cut short by the emergence of Pasang from the toilet, he turned and allowed himself to be led back through the debris of the Scout towards the cell. Half way across the yard he stopped and pretended to look in despair at the remains of his vehicle. One of the guards immediately snarled at him to get along, and pushed him from behind. He staggered forward, tripped on a metal plate, stumbled and fell. The guard cursed him and shouted at him to get in the house. He stood up at once and continued walking towards the house. But when he did so it was with a small piece of wire concealed in his hand.

When they returned to the cell they saw that the food containers of the previous night had been removed. In their place were two plates stacked with Indian *chapattis*; coarse, unleavened, peasant bread, like a tortilla. There was a bowl of jam, a bowl of strong smelling butter and containers of salt and pepper. A large metal teapot steamed gently through its spout. Wildman opened the lid and sniffed. It was his coffee, from the Scout. There were two tin cups and a single spoon. As they ate they heard the mechanics return. Looking through the window Wildman saw Vask take up his position again in his chair in the centre of the yard, a big *hookah* water pipe perched on the ground in front of him and a tray with a teapot and sugar bowl and mug. He looked angry. But from the way he was making himself comfortable he also looked as though he was settling down there for the day.

<<>>

The sun was gone from the courtyard. The Scout was gone too. In its place lay a jangled heap of cut metal, steel plates, wire, smashed cylinders and broken glass. One man, on Vask's instructions, had taken a sledge-hammer to the radiator and smashed it to pieces. Two more, working with axes, were in the last stages of chopping up the fibreglass cab and roof of the Scout. At the furnace, Vask's two, hard-faced furnace men were heating pieces of metal, that Vask thought might be hollow, to a white hot hew and then smashing them on an iron anvil, with a sledge hammer. Over in a corner, carefully spread out on a large piece of white plastic, were the innards of the transmission case and the transfer case. To Vask's right, three men were cutting the last pieces of the frame into small sections. Two more, using hacksaws, were still working on small pieces of the sealed units that were the ignition coil and oil filter. Of the Scout itself, as a single entity, nothing remained. The space in the centre of the yard, where it had been parked, was now empty, almost as though it had disappeared; the junkyard that had taken its place almost suggested that it been swallowed by a giant shredder and then vomited back up.

Then the work was finished. Vask rose suddenly from his chair, knocking over the tray and its contents. With a savage kick he sent the water pipe flying. The guards at the gate fumbled with the padlocks and opened the gate. The mechanics, standing around, smoking and spitting, watching Vask and, thinking of their money, froze as the big man, closely followed by the cringing Ghose, swept through the double doors and out of the yard.

After a while Ghose returned, told the mechanics to gather up their things and get out. In a sullen troop, they shuffled out of the yard. The two guards closed the doors and then there was silence. In the cell Pasang looked at Wildman. "Trouble now, I think, *sahib*."

But Wildman was busy working on his little piece of wire, doubling it to strength it, twisting it into a straight stem with a hooked end, into something with which he hoped to be able to reach and work the door bolts. He was still working on it when he heard the sounds of men coming down the corridor. The cell door was flung open and Ghose stood there. "Up against thee wall, both of you. Hands behind thee back. Any trouble and heads will be cracked."

Wildman, sliding the little piece of wire under the folded blanket on his bed, nodded to Pasang to do as he was told. Quickly, their hands were bound with fibre rope and they were led from the cell. As they came into the corridor Wildman saw Pasang's head snap to the left quickly. He looked back. The guard who was standing there was one of the men from when they were first captured, the man who had taken Pasang's *kukri*. He was still wearing it, the scabbard stuck in the front of the waistband of his trousers. Wildman saw Pasang's eyes glittering and he hoped the little man would not try anything. He knew how he felt about the big knife. To have it taken from him was bad enough. To see another man wearing it was poison.

They were led around to the front of the house, in through the front door and down the corridor into the front room with the big table. Vask was at the table, waiting for them, a scowl of anger creasing his swarthy face. And once again, acting without thinking, Wildman made his second mistake in the deadly game he was playing with Vask, one that, unfortunately for he and Pasang, gave the thug another ace up his sleeve.

The scene was much the same as their first meeting with Vask. But the atmosphere, Wildman sensed immediately, was very different. Vask's men were jumpy and nervous and they cursed and spat as they pushed their two prisoners into the room. Something, perhaps it was sight his beloved *kukri* in the hands of another man, made Pasang hesitate as he came through the door. Instantly one of the guards turned and cracked him over the head, hard, with a wooden club. He raised the club for a second strike and Wildman, acting with an instantaneous surge of anger, stepped forward, lashed out with his foot and took the man between the legs. The man screamed and collapsed. For a second the guards froze and then three of them of them raised their clubs and leapt towards Wildman. But a word and a raised hand from Vask stopped them in their tracks. They stepped back, pushed Wildman on towards the end of the table and, picking up the dazed Pasang, threw him bodily against the wall. Then, at a nod from Vask, they filed out, closing the door.

Vask looked down the table at Wildman and hissed.

"Sit down."

Wildman warily eased himself into one of the chairs at the end of the table. Vask, his eyes slits in the dark mask of his face, remained watching him for a few minutes. Then he spoke again.

"You are fond of that little man, aren't you, mister? Treat him like a brother, eh? Wouldn't like to see him get hurt? Eh?"

Wildman felt his blood chill at Vask's words and slowly a cold premonition of what was going to happen crept over his body.

"All right then, mister wild man. Here, as they say in your country, is the situation. You have been here two days. You have wasted two days of my time. The time of a Brahmin raja, with important things to do. So what we come to now, is a single question. Where is the Eye? You do not have it on you. It was not in your vehicle. Therefore you have put it…where? Wherever it is, I intend to find it and to have it. I am therefore going to ask you one last time, in thee most civilised manner, to hand it over. But I warn you, now, that this is the last time of my asking."

Vask's voice had changed from its original guttural tone. Now it was harsh, cold, biting. His eyes glittered and he emphasised his words by pounding with his fist on the table in front of him. Wildman guessed, correctly, that there was now more to the situation between them than just Vask's need to have the great emerald. In the eyes of his men, and whoever else was in the house—women too, no doubt that he and Pasang had seen one on arrival—Vask was beginning to lose face. They all knew that he wanted something from the big American *feringhee* and his Nepali servant. Some, a few of the more senior ones, like Ghose, knew what it was. Most did not. But all knew that when Vask wanted something he usually got it very quickly. His method, native cunning backed by brute force, never failed. Now, with this foreigner and his servant, he had not failed but, well, he was taking longer than usual and, to his staff, who watched everything that he did like circling vultures, there was the faint smell of defeat in the air. Very faint, but nevertheless there. Vask may or may not have smelled it himself. But he knew that his men had begun to sense that he was not winning the game with this *feringhee* and this was something he was going to have to put a stop to, right now.

Vask glared at Wildman and then his patience, what there was of it, snapped. He slammed his fist down on the table and roared for Ghose. The door opened and Ghose nervously stepped in. Vask waved to him to come closer and when he did, gave him whispered instructions. Ghose walked back to the door and shouted. At once six of the guards ran into the room. Four of them rushed up to Wildman and stood beside him. The other two ran to where Pasang was and, picking him up, dragged him to the table and sat him down, none too gently, on one of the wire chairs. Vask rose. There was another little door at the end of the room. He walked to it and passed through it. Wildman heard water running and guessed there was a toilet there.

Then Vask came back. But he did not sit. He remained standing, his eyes on Wildman, but flickering occasionally towards Pasang. The main door opened again and two men appeared. Between them, holding it by its metal legs, they carried a metal brazier full of burning, red-hot charcoal. A third man carried a small metal rod, about twelve inches long and with it a thick leather glove. The two men placed the brazier on the floor next to Vask and the other man put the leather glove and the metal rod on the table in front of him.

Vask reached out and picked up the metal rod and drove it deep into the glowing coals. Then he leaned forward and placed both hands flat on the surface of the table.

"Every man has a weakness, mister, and for a while I must admit that I did not know where yours lay. And then you gave it to me. Stupidly, but as I knew you would, given time. Mind you, I will admit that I never suspected where yours might lie and when I saw signs of it, when you first arrived here, I really could not believe them. Men have feelings like what I saw in you for family members, sons, brothers and sometimes wives. But to have them for a servant? Someone who is not even a relative? And not just a servant, but also a low caste one? In fact, one with no caste at all? One who, if he lived in this country, would rank below a toilet cleaner? One whose very touch," he said with shudder, "could defile a Brahmin and cause him to lose his caste?"

Vask glared at Wildman, leaning forward, studying the effect of his words and though Wildman met his gaze and glared back, his heart was cold inside him. And in anticipation of what he suspected was going to happen, he felt the hairs at the nape of his neck beginning to prickle.

Vask continued to stare at Wildman for another half a minute and then suddenly raised himself upright, picked up the leather glove from the table and slid his left hand into it. Reaching down, he pulled the metal rod out of the brazier fire. It glowed a dark red and when he tapped it on the rim of the brazier, hot sparks went dancing into the air. Turning, he walked over towards Pasang. Seeing him coming, the two men on either side of the little Sherpa grabbed him and held him. One took his thick black hair in a hard fist and jerked his head back and the other wrapped an arm around his neck. They have done this before, thought Wildman, noting how they acted without directions from Vask.

Vask walked up to within a foot of Pasang and, reaching out, held the red hot metal rod within two inches of his left cheek. Then he turned his head to look at Wildman. "Well, mister, yes or no?"

When Wildman hesitated, he reached forward and jabbed the rod against Pasang's cheek. As he did so, he looked down into the little Sherpa's eyes and what he saw there gave him a start. As Wildman surmised, this was not the first time he had used a hot iron to make someone talk. But it was the first time that a jab in the face from a piece of red hot metal had produced no reaction, no scream of pain, from his victim. Pasang's eyes were slits in a face masked with sweat. But they glared back at Vask with an intensity that momentarily took the man aback.

At heart, like all bullies, Vask was a coward and when confronted with courage in another man, particularly the contemptuous kind that was now being exhibited by the little hillman, he was momentarily taken aback. To give himself time to recover, he turned and walked back to the brazier and with quick, jerky motions, movements that portrayed his agitation, plunged the rod back into the coals. Turning, he again directed his gaze at Wildman. "Well, mister, see what you are doing to your little friend here. You. Not me. You. And you think this is something, eh? You think a little touch on the cheek is something? This is just the beginning. The beginning, you hear me?"

Vask drew the rod out of the coals. Once again it glowed a dark red. Holding it in front of him he again walked down to Pasang and turned to look at Wildman. "All right mister. Yes or no?"

For an answer, Wildman literally exploded in the grasp of the four men who held him. One went down from a lashing kick that shattered his shinbone. Another sank to the floor when Wildman's knee took him in the groin. But a third man held on and the fourth got behind Wildman and, in the melee, got an arm free and cracked Wildman, hard, on the base of the skull, with a short thick wooden club. The blow took the fight of out him and left him dazed. Vask, shouting for more men, waited until they came pouring through the door and surrounded Wildman. Then he turned again to the seated Sherpa, the men holding him pulled his head back and Vask, with a malevolent snarl, thrust the red hot iron right through the little hillman's left cheek and into his mouth.

One of Vasks's men who Vask said tried to betray him, murdered-strangled-and then hung and left to rot in the forest. Photo Credit: Wildman files.

The men holding Pasang jerked back as a sputtering waft of steam and smoke bore the smell of burning flesh into their faces. Vask, his face a mask of contorted rage, pulled the rod out of the seared and burning flesh, stepped back a pace and shouted, "What now, Nepali hillman. Now you think you can persuade your master to talk?"

As he said this, he looked again towards Wildman to see the effect of his words on the big American. By doing this, he was totally unprepared for what happened next. Pasang, his body twisting in pain but with his eyes still steadfastly locked on to Vask's face, drew his head back a couple of inches against the grip of the man who held him, took a breath, then jerked forward and spat full into Vask's face.

<<>>

In the split second before Pasang acted, Wildman guessed what he was going to do and shouted. But he was too late and despair swept through him with the realisation that Vask would now kill the little hillman without question. But that was not what happened.

For a second Vask froze. It was as though he could not believe what had happened. Then he reacted and his reaction was totally different from what Wildman expected. He staggered back and, pulling up the front of his flapping shirt, began to scrub frantically at the spittle on his face, at the same time screaming at the top of his voice. "Filth! You have defiled me! Defiled me! You have defiled a Brahmin! You have taken my caste…"

Still screaming obscenities, but now in a voice almost incoherent with rage and despair, he charged towards the door, colliding with and knocking down men who were running into the room. The last that Wildman saw of him was as he went through the door, violently scrubbing at his face with the front of his shirt, which he had now completely ripped off. Wildman heard shouts from outside, the roar of a Jeep engine starting up and lastly Vask screaming. "To the temple. The temple, you sons of whores. The temple! THE TEMPLE!"

As the Jeep roared away, Ghose appeared in the doorway of the room, his face pale, his eyes wide, men crowing behind him. He appeared to be severely shaken by what had happened. But nevertheless he quickly took charge of the situation and issued brisk orders to the guards. Wildman and Pasang were grabbed and half dragged from the room and quickly hustled back to their cell. At the door of the cell, Ghose, giving no orders to have their hands untied, waited until it was closed and securely locked. Then he waved the guards away and, leaning forward, spoke to Wildman through the aperture.

"Now you have done it, Mr. Wildman. By defiling his caste you have sealed your death warrant. You have killed yourself, for sure. Your man is dead too, that is also for certain and my guess is that he will die slowly. I would not like to be in your shoes when Raja Vask comes back from the temple. He will get his caste back all right, although it will cost him a great deal of money. But its loss will leave a mark on him, one that cause him to lose face and for that he will have his revenge. You have only one last chance."

Ghose turned and looked down the corridor to make sure that none of the guards were within hearing. Then he put his face closer to the hole in the door and whispered.

"One last chance. Give the stone to me. Do that and you will save your life."

Wildman stood and looked at the cringing Bengali's face.

"Ghose?"

"Yes, Mr. Wildman," the man said, his face taking on a look of greedy expectancy.

"Go fuck yourself."

Ghose looked as though he had been hit in the mouth with a baseball bat. Then his lips drew back and in a hissing snarl he said, "Very well then, mister, if that is what you want. I gave you a last chance. Let us see who has the last laugh when Raja Vask comes back. Although, personally, I do not think you will be laughing. Just in case I am wrong, however, which is doubtful, I plan to be there when you suffer the reward of your stupidity."

Then Ghose was gone. Wildman heard his footsteps retreating down the corridor and there was silence. Hands bound, he moved across to Pasang and sank down beside him. The little Sherpa was squatting, back against the wall, his head hanging down between his knees. Feeling Wildman's presence beside him, he raised his head slowly. A little blood oozed from the hole in his cheek. The hole itself was rimmed with black, seared flesh and a big bruise surrounded it, dark blue against the bronze of his face. When his head was fully up he turned to look directly at Wildman and, to Wildman's amazement, smiled a slow grim smile. "S*ahib*, you did the right thing not to give him anything. Now we have another chance *sahib*. We have bought time, as you say. Yes? That *pugla*, that madman, will be at the temple with his priests all night. Lots of singing and praying and mumbo jumbo and money changing hands to get back his caste. He will hardly, I think *sahib*, be back before morning. But he will be back tomorrow and when he comes, *sahib*, if we are not out of there, then, as they say up in my country, we are down the crevasse without the rope. But for now we have a little extra time."

Saying this, the little man walked to the bed, sat gingerly on the edge of it and slowly, but with grim determination, began to work his wrists back and forth, up and dawn, twisting with all his strength against the fibre rope that bound then.

Wildman, his mind racing, sat down on the bed beside Pasang and, ignoring the pain in his wrists, and the lack of circulation in his hands, joined him in the silent struggle to work their hands free. The cell was dark, with only a faint gleam of light coming through the window and soon the only sound was the laboured breathing of the two men as they fought their bonds, plus the occasional scurrying of a rat or two.

It was nearly an hour later, during which time neither of the two men had made the least impression on the tough, elastic, coconut fibre with which their wrists were bound, that Wildman suddenly had an idea. It came to him when a rat, which had been happily nibbling at the edge of his boot, suddenly moved up several inches and started to take an interest in his ankle.

"Pasang?"

"Yes *sahib*?"

"Is your cheek still bleeding?"

"Yes *sahib*. I think so. A little."

"Here, lean over. I have an idea. Lean back down on the bed here and let me get some of the blood on these ropes."

Gently, and wincing at the pain that he knew Pasang must be experiencing, he rubbed his bound wrists back and forth on the bleeding wound on the Sherpa's face.

"I hope that doesn't hurt too much."

"No hurt *sahib*. Nothing. But what is your plan?"

"My plan is this. I am going to lie on the floor here and see if our little four-footed friends like blood. Know what I mean? There's a chance that if they do…"

Wildman got off the bed and slowly, so as not to startle the big, watchful rodents, stretched out on the floor. He thrust his bound wrists out behind him as far as he could and then lay still and waited. Pasang, silent, lay back on the bed.

<<>>

For a while nothing happened. Then, faintly, Wildman heard a whisper behind him. This was followed by a gentle sniffing and softly, so softly that he could barely feel it, a rat slowly and hesitantly began to gnaw on the bloody ropes around his wrists. Wildman, a surge of excitement running through his body, wanted to tell Pasang that his plan seemed to be succeeding. But he was afraid that if he spoke he might startle the rat that was nibbling at his bindings, and it would get nervous and leave. So he waited, silently and soon another rat joined the first and together the two rodents began nibbling and tugging at the ropes. When a third rat tried to join the first two, there was a brief fight ending in a thin scream. But feeding territory was quickly established and Wildman, originally hoping that a swarm of the creatures would gather and between them rip his bindings to pieces, had to be content with the nibbling of just two and the prospect of a long slow wait for release.

Sometime after midnight, his hands totally numb, and his wrists a torment of pain, Wildman felt the first main strands of his bonds beginning to snap. The rats continued to gnaw on them and Wildman knew that he should let them continue and wait until he was sure that the bindings were weak enough for him to be able to break them. But suddenly his patience snapped and surging to his feet and ignoring the pain that it caused him, he put all his strength into a twisting pull on the ropes. He felt them starting to give and, gritting his teeth with the effort, put the last of his strength into breaking them. The rope on his left wrist suddenly snapped and his hand was free. But it took him another ten minutes, ten minutes of agony, before he could he could use his numbed hands to get the bindings off his other wrist and then free Pasang.

He looked at his watch. Three thirty. It would be light soon. Would the dawn bring to an end to whatever mumbo jumbo Vask was being put through at the temple? Would the first rays of the sun have him back at the house, seething with rage and thirsting for revenge? Revenge that Wildman, for a while at least, would survive. Because he was still the key to Vask's finding the Eye and Vask, enraged though he would be at what happened to him, would still be sensible enough to realise this and would keep him alive. But Pasang? Wildman hated to think what Vask would do to him, shuddering at the thought that, whatever it was, Vask would no doubt force him to watch. Whatever they were going to do to save themselves, it was going to have to be done now, before Vask returned. Once he got back, their fate was sealed.

Wildman slid his hand under the blanket on the bed. The piece of wire that he had picked up in the courtyard was still there, where he had hidden it. He pulled it out and walked quickly to the door. Lowering his face to the aperture, he looked through at the door of the cell opposite. It had a sliding bar lock, similar to the one on the door of their cell. He measured it with his eye. If it lay in the same position as the one on their door, then theirs was set about three feet down from the lower edge of the aperture. He reached through the aperture and, stretching his arm down to its fullest length, with his armpit jammed hard against the rim of the opening, felt back and forth with his fingers. He could feel nothing but the rough wood surface of the door. He pulled the wire out of his pocket. It was about ten inches long. He estimated that this was short of the lock by about six or seven inches. Damn. And the wire was too soft for use as a single strand and too short to be doubled. Nevertheless it was worth a try.

He took the wire and twisted one end into a little loop. The other end he twisted around his finger. Then he ran his arm through the aperture again and, watched intently by Pasang, began fishing for the handle of the bolt.

<<>>

After about thirty minutes, his arm was aching with his effort to reach the lock and he had completely failed to snag it. He had tried looping the wire over it and snagging it with a back and forth movement of his hand. But nothing worked. His arm, its circulation slowed by having his armpit jammed against the rim of the aperture, was beginning to go numb. He pulled his arm out of the hole to rest it and at the same time looked at his watch. Four fifteen. He looked at the cell window. Yes, the light was beginning to grow and even the blackness of the corridor outside the cell was beginning to turn grey. Christ, he thought. Time is running out. There's got to be a way of opening that damn bolt...

Pasang stood silently behind him. He did not offer to help. He had assessed exactly what Wildman was trying to do, what his chances were, and of what little use he would be to him with his very much shorter arms. Like Wildman, his mind too was beginning to ring alarm bells. Like Wildman, and perhaps more so because of his insights into the mentality of the Indian criminal mind, he knew very well what their chances were going to be if they were still there when Vask got back from the temple.

Wildman swung his arm back and forth to restore its circulation. Satisfied that it was limber enough to continue, he stepped to the door again and thrust his arm through. But perhaps it still lacked full circulation and was not as limber as he thought, for as he lowered his arm down the other side of the door to start groping for the handle again, he gave a gasp and then swore. "Dammit Pasang, I've dropped the bloody wire. Now we have a real problem."

Pasang, ever the man of action, rather than words, promptly dropped to the floor and put his face to the gap under the door to try and see if the wire was there. And Wildman still had his arm stuck through the aperture and was standing with his face twisted sideways, to see if Pasang could see the wire, when suddenly the little man leapt to his feet, came up off the floor with a single springing thrust of his powerful hillman's legs, grabbed Wildman around the waist and with a powerful upward lift wrenched him away from the door. They fell back together in a jumbled heap on the floor and, as they did so, Pasang hissed one word into Wildman's ear. "Gunga!"

And as though in answer to his name, the black face of the giant suddenly appeared in the door aperture.

<<>>

For about twenty seconds, Vask's monolithic brother stood in the corridor peering myopically into their cell. Then, in a repeat performance of what it had done the previous night, a performance that for the two men in the cell soon developed into a nightmare, it thrust its massive arm through the aperture, extended a sausage-like forefinger at the end of it and pointed. At the same time the huge, melon-like head began to nod up and down and the creature began its hideous whining.

"It wants whiskey, *sahib*," whispered Pasang.

"Yes, and we don't have any to give it, dammit."

Wildman looked around desperately. The creature's whining was increasing and the huge arm was beginning to wave up and down in time with the nodding head.

"The tea pot, Pasang. Let's give it that. I think it still has a little coffee in it."

Wildman leapt to the table and grabbed the metal teapot. It was empty. Pasang started to say something. But Wildman ignored him and, holding the pot out, allowed the giant to take it in his hand and pull it slowly and carefully through the window. He watched as the creature tipped its head back and thrust the spout of the metal pot into its mouth. It held it there for a moment and when nothing came out of the pot, shook its head from side to side, the spout still stuck in its slobbering mouth. It tipped the utensil even higher and they heard the metal spout grind against the creature's teeth. It held it like that for probably ten seconds, shaking its head from side to side, as though this would give it what it wanted. Then, with a vast hiss of exploding breath it lowered the teapot to eye level and looked at it.

Slowly, in its dim mind, it realised that the pot was empty and as it did, the huge body began to tremble with rage and frustration. The pot was hurled to the floor and the shrill whine increased in volume as it turned and pressed its huge black face, now contorted with anger, against the door aperture.

For a few seconds the giant looked into the cell at the two men. Then its face disappeared from the aperture and at the same time its huge, spatulate fingers appeared under the lower edge of the door. For a moment nothing happened. Then the giant began to pull, upwards and outwards, on the door. Wildman leapt to the bed, swept the blanket off it and, picking it up, drove its end hard against the wall. A leg of the bed cracked. He thrust again and the leg splintered. He dropped the shattered frame and pulled the leg off. "Quick Pasang, make yourself a weapon. That bloody door's not going to last long. Pasang, quick…"

But Pasang was doing something else, sweeping the newspapers off the table and bunching them together and twisting them into a torch.

The door groaned and its bottom slowly began to bend outwards. The movement stopped for a moment while the creature shifted its position, to get better leverage. Then it began again and as it did, Wildman heard wood splintering and cracking. There was a loud metallic snap as one of the hinges snapped off. Wildman, sweat pouring down his body, watched and waited, the wooden bed leg, his only weapon, ready in his hand. But behind him Pasang was moving, and Wildman suddenly heard the rasp of matches, and smelled smoke. Another hinge popped; followed by the metallic screech of screws being ripped out of the hardwood frame and abruptly the door gave way. It went suddenly, and caught the giant off balance. He staggered back into the corridor, holding the door bodily in his arms. Then he hurled it aside, lowered his head and with arms hung low, hands down, huge fingers open, ready to clutch and hold and crush and kill, moved forward through the twisted doorframe and into the cell. As he did, Pasang stepped forward and thrust his blazing newspaper torch right into the creature's face.

To get close enough to the giant, to be able to do this, the little hillman had to step right in front of him, within a couple of feet of the enormous body and its encircling arms. But he ignored the danger and, jamming the blazing newspaper right into the creature's face, held it there, not hard enough to quench the flames that issued from it, but close enough to give them full effect.

Until then, the only sound that Wildman and Pasang had heard the giant make was the heavy whining that seemed to be its only form of speech. That and a grunt or two, while it levered on the door. Thus the scream that it now gave, a deep powerful scream that tore across the cell and rent the air with its power, took them by surprise. It screamed again and hurled itself against the wall of the cell. It bounced off the wall and fell on top of the table, crushing it to splinters, its hands firmly clamped to its burning face and with Wildman and Pasang leaping from side to side to keep out of its way.

The giant continued to scream and now they heard other sounds, shouting, footsteps pounding, doors being opened. "Get beside the door, *sahib*, quick," hissed Pasang, his voice low and urgent.

Wildman, one eye on the staggering giant, leaped to the side of the door as men pounded down the corridor. The first of the guards rushed into the cell, a man with a wooden club. He was closely followed by a man with a ragged shirt, a man with the handle of Pasang's *kukri* sticking out of the front of his waistband. A man who was about to come to a nasty end.

Wildman was not sure, later, of what actually happened then, in the cell. He remembered a blur as Pasang catapulted himself out of the corner of the cell, straight at the man with his *kukri*. He remembered the man giving a single shout of dismay as Pasang ripped the big knife out of his waistband. He recalled a steely flash of light, followed by a scream, and then the sight of the man, his head hanging by a thread of skin from the upper half of his torso, staggering and falling in a bloody heap on the floor. He remembered that the second guard either did not have time to scream, or was locked into instant shock by what happened to his companion, a state from which he was quickly relieved by a single vertical chop that split his head almost in two.

Then they were in the corridor and there was Ghose in front of them, raising his hands in fright, turning to run, slipping, realising that he was too late to get away and then turning back to them, his mouth open and his hands up in supplication. Wildman was first out of the door of the cell. His big, muscular hand grabbed Ghose by the shoulder and spun him around while a second hand, curled into a tight, hard fist and carrying most of the power of Wildman's arm and shoulder muscles behind it, chopped him in the nape of the neck. If he heard Wildman say, 'out of the way, you little Bengali twit' he gave no sign, and Wildman and Pasang, leaping over his falling body, did not wait to find out.

There were two more guards in the corridor. One had seen what had happened to the two who had entered the cell. The other had not. The one who had not, turned to face Wildman and Pasang, swinging a three-foot-long, hardwood club in front of him. Wildman stepped back and allowed

Pasang to pass him. The man with the club, seeing Pasang coming at him, made the mistake of swinging it up and to the left, to take Pasang with a backhanded blow across the face. This gave Pasang the opening that he needed for a cutting, sideways strike that buried the *kukri* deep into the man's neck. The man slumped and started to fall and Pasang, leaping forward, slammed an elbow into his face to hasten him down and get him out of the way in the narrow corridor, and so that he would have space to tackle the second man.

But the second man had just seen his companion make a hasty departure for the happy hunting grounds and was already screaming and running as fast as he could towards the exit to the back yard. He got to the door just three feet ahead of Pasang and, realising that the his pursuers were close, and that he was not going to get through it unscathed, spun around, dropped to his knees and howled for mercy. The *kukri* cut short his screams and sent him to join his companions, as Wildman and Pasang leaped over his falling body and ran on.

<<>>

They were into the courtyard. Ahead of them were the big double doors, closed and locked and, beside them, rising to their feet, the door guards. They were young men and they were close to the end of a four-hour shift, tired and cold and probably hungry. This made them a little slower than they might normally have been, so that when Pasang and Wildman appeared out of the doorway of the cell block, they might have thought for a moment that the figures they saw in the dim dawn light were Ghose and his guards. It took them probably three seconds to realize that the men they saw were not Ghose and company, but the two prisoners, just long enough for Pasang and Wildman to bound across the tangled wreckage of the Scout and close with them.

One of the men shouted something and reached under the stool where he had been sitting. He might have been reaching for a gun, or a billy club. That was a mistake. The *kukri* took him clean across the back of this neck and he was dead before he hit the ground. Wildman did not hesitate with the other man. He had sized him up while closing on him and had seen that the man was weaponless. He simply grabbed him around the waist, picked him up and, continuing with the momentum of his charge, smashed him against the solid wood of the yard doors. He heard something snap, guessed it was the man's neck, and dropped him. The man fell like a sack of bones to the ground and lay still.

Wildman flung himself around to look at Pasang. But once again the little man was ahead of him. He had put his *kukri* carefully on the ground beside him and was rapidly going through the pockets of the door guard he had felled. "The key, *sahib*. The gate key. Look in the other man's pockets. Quickly *sahib*."

Wildman turned and dropped on one knee beside the second guard. Rapidly he searched his pockets. There was no key. "Pasang. No key. What about your man?"

"No key, *sahib*."

Wildman stood, stepped to the double doors and looked at the padlock. It was firmly locked. It was roughly made and could be picked, given a little time. But there was no time. It was also made of steel and, though crude, strongly constructed. Too strong to smash open quickly.

Wildman looked up at the wall. "Pasang, can you make the wall? I think we can get over it, if we can get a run at it."

"Yes *sahib*. But have to clear some stuff out of the way first."

Frantically, one eye on the house, ears open for the sound of approaching men, they set to work to clear an avenue through the debris, for a run at the wall. Metal and wire and glass were picked up and flung aside. Steel plates and chunks of chassis were kicked out of the way. And then it was ready, a narrow lane through the rubble, a foot wide and fifteen feet long.

Wildman positioned himself at the end of the lane and waved Pasang ahead of him. But the hillman, his bloody kukri dangling in his hand, shook his head and with a wolfish grin said, "Thank you *sahib*. But after you *sahib*."

Wildman gathered himself, took a deep breath and then launched himself at the wall. Fifteen feet. Four fast, pounding strides. Then the right foot hard down and an explosion of energy poured into the upward leap. Then the left foot slammed against the wall, the bounce, the powerful surge of the body to the top, a grappling of hands on the smooth surface of the rim and he was up, his body straddling the rim, lungs heaving as they pumped more oxygen into his system. Up, on the top and looking around and waving for Pasang to follow him. But while he was wondering if the little hillman could make it, and still with his arm in motion, waving for him, his companion bounced up out of the yard like a coiled steel spring and landed with a thud beside him.

Wildman grinned at the Sherpa. "Pasang, I think you just bumped Darcy Dugan out of his place in the Guinness Book of Records."

Pasang did not quite understand what Wildman meant. But he grinned and said, "Very good *sahib*. But now we get down from here and run like young yaks, yes?"

He did not wait for a reply, but led the way. Wildman followed him and, hitting the ground together, they took off and with an unspoken decision ran for the bluffs that edged the meadowland, to the east of the house.

<<>>

On the dusty floor of the cell block corridor, Ghose moved. Slowly his senses returned and he sat upright. For a few seconds his dazed mind was unable to grasp what had happened. A heavy thumping coming from further down the corridor confused him even more. Then, with a gasp, he remembered. He heaved himself to his feet and, fighting the nausea and pain from the stunning blow that Wildman had given him, lurched down the corridor towards the door to the yard.

As he passed Gunga's cell he stopped and looked in and quickly discovered from where the thumping noise was coming. Vask's enormous brother was hunched in the corner, his body turned against the wall. His hands covered his burnt face and slowly, and with a dreadful rhythm, he was pounding his huge head against the wall. Ghose shuddered, turned, and staggered down the corridor, stepping over the dead men lying in the dark red pools of their life's blood. Once in the yard his eyes took in the two other guards, one dead, the other still unconscious. Stepping quickly over the nearest, he reached under one of the stools that the guards used to sit on, pulled a key from a crack in the seat, opened the gate padlock, pushed one of the big doors open and staggered through. He was just in time to see Wildman and Pasang, a thousand feet away and running fast for the low cliffs on the edge of the hills.

Ghose was still half dazed. But his lungs were pumping oxygen into his bloodstream and his mind was beginning to function. He shook his head to clear that dizziness that threatened to overcome him and made an effort to think clearly. Apart from the bloody heaps that lay in the cell corridor and the yard, there were more men in the house, probably five or six left from those that Vask took with him to the temple. Enough to organize a pursuit. But Wildman and his man were running hard and were two thirds of the way down across the open land between the house and the cliff edge; within another thirty seconds they would be into the forested hills and once in there they would be difficult to follow. Again, the hills were, for Vask and his thugs, *terra incognito.* The hills were bandit country, the domain of the dacoits of the Central Provinces. The edge of the hills marked their territorial line, a line that Vask and his thugs would cross at peril of their lives.

For a moment Ghose hesitated. He looked again at the direction that the runners were taking and then had an idea, one that he assessed as the only one suitable to the circumstances. He hesitated a moment and then made what he thought was the right decision. Alas for Ghose, it was the wrong decision and it was one that he was to rue for the remainder, the brief remainder, of his wretched life.

Waving his arms and shouting, Ghose leapt forward and ran down the long sloping hill after the two fleeing men. As he did so, Wildman and Pasang reached the wall of the cliffs, hesitated for a moment and then plunged into a narrow ravine that led back into the hills. Just before they raced into the ravine, Wildman looked back and saw Ghose coming down the hill, running and waving his arms, and shouting. He frowned when he saw the man was alone. What the hell was he trying to do? Catch them single-handed? Dismissing Ghose's actions as probably generated by panic, and wishing that he had hit him harder, he swung round and plunged into the ravine with Pasang.

<<>>

Close to the mouth of the ravine into which Wildman and Pasang ran, was a big cattle corral. In it were about a hundred domestic water buffalo, a prized and valuable herd belonging to Vask. Used for milking, ploughing and as beasts of burden, the huge animals were usually docile and manageable. But the Asian water buffalo, in spite of its size, is a nervous creature and it does not take a lot to provoke it to panic. A stranger, a barking, heel-nipping dog, the scent of a leopard wafting out of a ravine, any unusual noise, can quickly stir a group of them into a stampede, particularly when they are locked in a corral and feel trapped.

The massed animals in the corral had seen the two men run past, had picked up their unusual body odours and had recognised them as strangers. This disturbed them and they began to raise their heads and show the whites of their eyes. Now, shouting and waving its arms above its head, came another figure, again a stranger, and among the group the big bulls began to toss their horns and snort and stamp their feet.

Built against the cliff wall, and set close to the corral, was a small shed that Vask's buffalo herders used. Six men looked after the herd; they cooked, ate and slept in the shed at night. Now, hearing the snorting of their animals, they came running out to see what was disturbing them.

"*Jeldi,*" shouted Ghose. "Hurry. Drive the buffalo into the ravine after those men. They must not escape. Quickly, quickly."

The herders did not know Ghose. But they had seen that the man had just come from Vask's house, and this suggested authority. They did not hesitate. Quickly opening the corral gates, they began lashing the huge bovines with long thin sticks, to drive them out of the corral and into the ravine, after the fleeing men. The huge animals, now thoroughly alarmed, immediately stampeded and in a wild, bellowing, horn-tossing mob, surged out of the corral and into the cleft in the rock wall.

Wildman and Pasang were five hundred feet into the ravine and had stopped, briefly, to listen for pursuit, and to catch their breath. They stood and looked back, their chests heaving with the effort of their run, their ears straining back in the direction they had come. On either side of them the grey rock walls of the ravine rose straight up, smooth and unmarked, for thirty feet. They were not climbable and Wildman hoped that as they moved on down the ravine, they would soon find a break, one that would allow them to get out of the ravine and into the forest. Once in the forest their chances of eluding any pursuers, and getting away, would be greatly enhanced; once in there, they both felt they could elude pursuit.

They still did not quite understand what Ghose had been trying to do, running down the hill alone like that and they were puzzling about this and getting ready to run again, when a sound made them freeze. The sound came from the ravine behind them. A deep rumble, like low thunder. Wildman frowned and looked at Pasang. But Pasang, instantly recognising the sound for what it was, leapt forward, grabbed Wildman and giving him a violent push that set him staggering forward, shouted, "Run *sahib*, run! Buffalo coming."

Spinning around, he hurled himself after Wildman and together the two of them raced on into the ravine. The floor of the ravine was sand. But the waters of a thousand monsoons had given its surface a hard, smooth crust, broken only occasionally by the rounded outline of a half embedded river stone. It made for good running. It also picked up and gave volume to the deep rumble of the hooves of the now-maddened herd and a roll of thunder swept down the ravine and enveloped the two men, as they ran for their lives.

They pounded on down the ravine, Pasang with his shorter legs taking two strides to every one of Wildman's. The ravine's high walls continued and nowhere was there a break that offered an exit; and the walls themselves, brushed smooth by the waters of a millennia of monsoons, offered no handholds or footholds that might allow them an escape. Wildman, his heart thumping and his lungs rasping, was beginning to wonder how long the ravine was when, to his dismay, as they rounded a corner, he saw that it came to an abrupt end. Ahead of them, in a perfect *cul de sac,* the walls closed to form a rock amphitheatre that completely sealed them in.

They staggered to a halt and then, instinctively, though each knew it was hopeless, flattened themselves against the curving wall and turned to face the onrushing sea of animals. There was no way out and, although they both thought about it, absolutely no way of slipping past the thundering, wall to wall, herd of maddened animals.

"Sorry about this, Pasang. My fault, I'm afraid. Should have cut south and run down the cliff face, and not into it."

"Not your fault, *sahib.* Mine," said Pasang, and he was turning to shake Wildman's hand in a last goodbye when, without warning, a thick, brown rope made of twisted vines snaked down from the rim of the bowl above them. Looking up, they saw the wizened face of a little old man, beckoning at them wildly.

They did not hesitate. "Up, Pasang, Wildman shouted. "*Chitu!* Quickly."

"No *sahib.* After you, *sahib.*"

Wildman was about to say no, not this time, when around the corner of the ravine a black wave broke and Wildman, leaping for the rope, had a quick glimpse of tossing horns, glaring eye whites and wet black muzzles streaming with saliva. Then he was up and Pasang, a monkey with a leopard on its tail, was up behind him.

The instant they gained the top, the old man hauled up the rope, coiled it carefully over his shoulder and, waving at them to follow him, turned and ran nimbly into the forest that fringed the ravine walls. Without any hesitation, they turned and ran after him.

Behind them, a great pall of dust rose from the rocky bowl that marked the end of the ravine. In it, the thundering herd had run against the solid rock wall that enclosed it. Thrust forward by the mass of the animals behind them, the big bulls, the herd leaders, had smashed headlong into the base of the rock. Some were killed instantly. Those that survived fell back into the oncoming mass of animals behind them and within seconds the bowl was filled with a bellowing melee of crushed and broken and dying animals. Their agonized bawling echoed through the trees behind Wildman and Pasang and rolled back down the ravine to the quivering, nerve-wracked man who had ordered their destruction. And then on, out of the mouth of the gorge and past the frightened group of herders and up across the meadow and up the hill to the house to where Vask, a great rage building inside him, stood with his men around the Jeep that had just brought him back from the temple. A rage that his newly regained caste did nothing to appease. A rage that made his voice cut like a whip and left his men wide eyed and in terror of their lives.

"Ghose. Where is Ghose? Get me Ghose. NOW!"

BOOK SIX

SUNITA

The old man, who might have been well into his seventies, ran like a deer and it was three quarters of a mile before he allowed them to stop and draw a breath. When they did, he turned to them and spoke for the first time. He told them that he was a *dacoit,* a bandit, and that he was with the *dacoit* group of Sunita, the famous bandit queen of the jungles of the Central Provinces. When he heard the name, Pasang looked up quickly and whispered to Wildman, "A Nepali woman, *sahib*. I have heard of her. She will be of help to us."

Sunita, the old man explained, had sent him to spy on Vask and his men. She knew who Wildman was, had heard of his exploits in India in previous years, had heard that Vask had managed to kidnap him and was at this very time in the process of planning a rescue attempt. The rescue would not have been difficult to carry out because it would have meant crossing the territorial line that divided Vask's holdings from those occupied by the *dacoits.* Before doing this she had had to consult with other leaders. This had taken time. Now, he told them, when they came to her camp, she would be very pleased indeed. She would harbour them, they would be safe from Vask and his gangs, and they would be made welcome. Saying this, the little man turned and without another word led them on into the forest.

Soon he slowed the pace and it was a good thing that he did, for it was five hours of a combination of brisk walk and steady half trot before they reached their destination. Five hours that took them through ten miles of deep jungle, across dried riverbeds and in and out of deep ravines. They would have travelled faster had not the old man insisted, each time they crossed a patch of sand or deep dust, on brushing out their tracks with a handful of dried grass. Only once did they stop and that was to drink from a small stream, and for Pasang to wash and dry his *kukri*. Wildman noticed that he had not put it in the sheath since they had broken out of the cells; he also noticed that when he washed the big knife, the little hillman was very careful to keep the sheath separate, away from the water, and dry. Crouched at the water's edge, Pasang felt Wildman watching him. He turned and smiled. "The sheath has to be kept dry, *sahib*. I would like to wash it and then smoke it in a fire, because another man has used it. But I must wait until later to do that."

Wildman felt that there was more to the separation of knife and sheath than Pasang wanted to explain. But no doubt he would learn the meaning of it later. As indeed he did.

Early in the afternoon the hills became steeper and more jagged. There were thin, knifelike edges to the tops of the ridges, with trails just wide enough for the passage of one man at a time. The sides of the ridges dropped away into deep ravines choked with vines and matted foliage. Several times the old man stopped to listen to sounds in the brush. When he did, Wildman and Pasang recognised the scratching of Grey Jungle Fowl among the dry leaves in the ravines, the delicate patter of footsteps as an unseen deer slipped away ahead of them and, once, the crashing rush of a startled wild boar.

They had climbed all the way up the spine of a long, narrow ridge, when suddenly the ground in front of them levelled off. A rock wall appeared and, in it, a narrow opening. They stopped and the old man gave a low whistle. At once they were challenged by two men with rifles—World War 1 .303 calibre, Wildman noticed—and allowed to go forward again only when the old man called out a password. They passed through the narrow opening in the rock wall and found themselves in a small valley, the floor of which was flat and covered with small trees and light brush. The valley was surrounded by high ridges on the tops of which Wildman saw the shapes of watching men. In the trees ahead of them he made out the dim shapes of tents and small, grass-roofed buildings.

Their guide led them forward. There were men among the tents, squatting, eating, and cleaning rifles. They looked at Wildman and Pasang with curiosity. But the sight of the guide satisfied them and the three passed quickly through the encampment to the head of the valley. Here, set hard against a steep rock overhang that marked the upper end of the valley was a large, ornamental tent with netted windows and a wide canvas porch supported by bamboo poles. The tent had a canvas door set in the wall immediately facing them; it was closed with a heavy metal zipper.

Their guide motioned for them to wait and, walking to the door of the tent, called out his name, saying, "It is I. Old Burra. I am back, Sunita Rani."

A woman's voice answered from inside the tent, bidding him enter. On hearing it he reached forward, pulled the door zipper down and disappeared through the entrance into the tent. He was gone for nearly five minutes and when he appeared again he was smiling. "The Rani welcomes you and wishes you to enter," he said.

He waved them towards the tent and with the same movement turned and walked away. Wildman looked at Pasang and then stepped forward and entered the tent. Pasang, his fingers gently resting on the handle of his *kukri*, followed him.

<<>>

Immediately inside the entrance of the tent was a large single room. Its ceiling was of dark blue silk and it soared upwards for more than twenty feet. The walls of the room, also of silk, and patterned with flowers, were ten feet high, and in them were set a number of canvas doors leading to separate apartments. The floor was of a heavy canvas covered with thick, gaily-coloured woollen rugs. In the centre of the room, seated on a pile of cushions, was a young Nepali woman.

Wildman guessed that she was in her mid thirties. She might be tall, standing up. He was not sure; her legs looked long. But from what he could see of her body, she was a woman in superb physical condition. She was dressed in gold, skintight, silk trousers and her legs flowed downwards from a small waist, which was bound with a black sash. Above her waist a she wore a yellow silk blouse, the fabric of which was stretched tight by two ample and perfectly rounded breasts. Her face was small, oval-shaped and its colouring was a creamy brown, a brown that was too pale to be brown, a cream that was too dark to be cream. The face was surmounted by a wide, smooth forehead and it was framed in a cascading torrent of thick, black hair that flowed out over the cushions around her, reaching well below her waist. Her eyes were large and black and set under flowing lashes and Wildman's, noting the full lips that rimmed a wide, sensual mouth, felt a tightening in his groin.

For a few seconds the two men stood alert and wary and took in their surroundings. Then the silence, the sense of safety and the calm face of the woman seated opposite them began to take effect. Wildman felt himself relaxing and Pasang, taking his hand off his *kukri* and bowing, touched his fingers to his forehead and said, in Nepalese, "Greetings, princess."

The woman immediately joined her hands together and raised them in the traditional Nepali greeting. She smiled and beckoned them to come forward. As they did, she leaned forward and looked at Pasang's cheek. It was to him that she first spoke. "You have been hurt, my friend. That wound should have attention. I will have my medicine man look after you."

Saying this, she clapped her hands and a man appeared through one of the side doors. She spoke to him quickly in Nepali and then turned again to Pasang. "Please go with him. He will take you to the medicine man. He will also arrange food for you and a place to rest. You are safe here. Go now and have your wound attended to."

Pasang hesitated and looked at Wildman. Wildman nodded and when he did, Pasang rose and followed the man out of the tent. The woman watched Pasang leave and then, speaking in English, told Wildman to be seated. As he lowered himself to the thick pile of the carpet in front of her she smiled, tossed her hair back and asked him if he knew who she was.

Wildman looked at her and answered her question with one of his own. "And why do you ask me if I know who you are?"

"Because, Wildman *sahib*, I want to see if you know as much about me as I know about you," she replied, smiling an enigmatic smile that made Wildman realise they were going to play a little game together, a game of who knew how much about the other.

"All right then. I'll tell you what I know about you. You are Sunita, the bandit queen. A woman whose fame reaches far across the hills of central India. A woman whose reputation, depending on the source of its description, ranges from the depths of evil to the heights of goodness. The evil side of it is the people who have died at the hands of your men. Died with a bullet inside them, or on the end of a spear, or with a cutlass thrust through them. Or, on occasion, with a noose around their necks as they swung from a jungle tree. Innocent men murdered by your gangs, according to those who cry evil on your name."

The woman smiled and Wildman noted white, even teeth gently touching the insides of sensual lips. She nodded. "So far, very good."

"And the good side of me?

"On the good side, from the people that you protect, the poor among whom you distribute money and gifts, a different story. A story of a central Indian Robin Hood. A story of kindness and concern, of sharing and charity to all who come to you for help. A story that says that those who die at the hands of your gangs are those who prey upon the poor, or try to betray you, to inform on you. A story that has gone far beyond the central hills here and all the way to Cape Cormorin in the south and the borders of Nepal in the north, of a combination of princess and saint. A story that

Sunita the bandit queen, in the Indian jungles, as a young woman in the early days of her bandit career.
Photo Credit, Amrit Bazaar Patrika newspaper files, Bombay.

At Sunita's camp, a sentry watches from the top of a tall tree.

gains more colour and more sensation every time it is told. A story in which the wretched poor of this country find something to believe in, something that is untouched by corruption and vice, something that is for them a dream, a dream of truth and justice."

The woman started to raise her hand, as though Wildman had said enough. But he ignored her and continued. "And a story that sometimes, just sometimes, touches ever so gently on the other side of the bandit *Rani*, of a young lover, a Nepali boy, who was murdered in India. About how you appealed to the authorities, endlessly, to carry out an investigation and find the culprits and bring them to justice. About how, when they did nothing, you turned against them and swore vengeance. About..."

"Enough, enough. You have said enough. Too much, perhaps. You know more than most people, that I must grant you, Wildman."

The woman's eyes had blazed for a moment when Wildman talked about her past, the Nepali boy rumoured to have been her lover. But when he ceased, at her raised hand, a veil came over them and for a moment she was quiet. Then she smiled, drew her legs under her, and, looking directly at Wildman said, "Yes. You know a great deal for a *feringhee,* a foreigner who is not even of this country. But I also know a great deal about you, Mr. Wildman, maybe more than you might suspect. We are not far from Baroda here? Yes? Ah, I see that you know what I am taking about. Yes, your expertise in carrying little presents for people across international borders, and in getting across the same borders at, shall we say, unguarded and unofficial points, is legendary. Yes. You have been in and out of this continent quite a few times and not always by what are laughingly known as the tourist routes. And I have heard about you, indeed, have been hearing about you, for many years. The jungle grapevine, we call it. The problem is that like a vine it grows on itself, twists and turns and climbs and falls and then grows back again, so that the mature vine in the end may be nothing like what it started out to be. So it is, with what I hear of you. Legend and myth. And my problem is to separate the two. A problem that has so perplexed me over the last few years that I half determined to kidnap you on your next assignment and bring you here and find out for myself! And now look what the gods have done for me."

She laughed and with a flick of her head thrust a veritable waterfall of black hair down across the cushions behind her. "And now you are here, at last, and my dream has come true. A dream of being able to find answers to two very important questions about you."

Wildman raised an eyebrow and smiled. The woman was losing her initial shyness and growing confident. With her confidence was building a kind of exuberance and it showed in the quick movements of her long, sinewy body and the gestures of her hands with which she accompanied them.

"Two questions, did you say, Rani Sunita?"

"Yes. And the first of these, Wildman, has to do with your legendary courage. You see I am interested in courage. And with something that is more than a common interest. Here, living the life that I do, it is a vital part of the survival of myself and my people. Thus I take heed when I encounter it here, which I do more often than you might think. In my men, for instance, when they clash with our enemies, when they offer their lives for me, or for the survival of the group. And the vine whispers of your courage and the whisper is of a courage that is icy cold and unmatched.

"I want to see this legendary courage, Wildman. Indeed, I insist on seeing it. I have decided therefore to allow you to give us a sample of it, before you leave here. A chance to see for ourselves, myself and my people, if what the vine whispers is true. You are very much like me, Wildman. Like me you have lived and indeed are living a life that at times takes you out to its thin edge, the edge where lies fear, without which there is no courage. I too have been to the edge and I know what fear is. I too, have been able to conquer it. But whereas my people know this, as they know me and my courage, they do not know you, or yours. They are anxious to see an example of yours, to gauge its strength. By seeing it at close hand, not only do they feel they will learn from it, they believe that they may also be able to absorb some of it. We want this, Wildman. We need it and I think that if you understand our need, you will not refuse this request."

"Well, I am not quite sure how we can go about doing this. But if it is important to you, and to your people, I'll do the best I can."

Wildman wondered where this was leading. A hand-to-hand combat match with half a dozen of her best men? A hunt on foot, with a spear, for a tiger? A raid on an armed police post, which he would have to lead? He also wondered exactly when Sunita's people had talked with her about this. He and Pasang had only just arrived and the woman had not yet spoken with anyone other than their old guide and the man who had taken Pasang away. Were her people really involved? Or was this just a private need of her own? Either way it looked as though he was going to have to go through with it.

"Good. Then it is agreed. I knew that we could depend on you. You can rest. I will gather my people and prepare a feast and when the moon rises you can meet Little Shiva and we will see if she finds you as fascinating as I do, as challenging as my men do. If she does, then your job will be

Sunita's mother, in a village in the Nepal Terai southlands.

Sunita's father. He disapproved of her profession but admired her for her courage, and her generosity to the poor.

to respond to her fascination by kissing her. That is all. But when you do, all will know of the courage of the legendary Wildman and it will be sung in the market places and spoken of in the villages and whispered down through the halls of the jungles for a thousand years."

She clapped her hands and a man appeared through one of the canvas doorways. She turned to him and gave quick, precise orders. Then she spoke again to Wildman. "Go with this man. He will show you where to bathe. He will also give you clean clothes. After you have bathed you can rest. There is a tent for you and there will be tea and bread there for you. The ceremony will begin when the moon comes over the rim of the valley. That will be a good time for Little Shiva. She seems to like the moonlight. It calms her, I think.

<<>>

Wildman followed his guide out of Sunita's tent and down through the encampment. The man stopped at a small tent, asked Wildman to wait, and went in to get clothes for him. Another small tent stood close by and, as Wildman watched, the flap moved gently and a single brown eye appeared and fixed itself on him. A voice whispered, "Everything OK *sahib*?"

It was Pasang. God, did the man never rest?

"Yes Pasang, everything is OK for now. I am going to wash and later on we will meet for a feast where I am supposed to…"

But at that moment his guide reappeared with an armful of clothes and, beckoning Wildman to follow, led him over to the edge of the encampment where there was a small pool fed by a little stream. He laid down the clothes and also a bar of soap and a small towel, told Wildman that the tent where they had just been would be his for resting, and left.

Wildman took off his Gokeys, stripped off his sweat-soaked clothing and washed. As he did so his mind began to dwell again on the question of what the bandit queen's test of courage might be. Or rather, now that he gave it a little more thought, what was probably a test suggested by her and then devised by her people. Little Shiva? God, he suddenly had visions of another "little" Gunga. A female Little Gunga? But no. That was stretching it a bit. Then who? Or what? And he was to kiss this person? Kiss her? It? Them? Tussle with her? Or it? Or them? "Them" he could understand. A fight with two or three others, with fists, or a wrestling match with no holds barred. Or a duel with poles or clubs? But no. He had a feeling that it was something more subtle than that. Then what? A duel in a darkened room then, wrist locked to wrist, with knives? But no. The duel, or whatever it was, had to be in the open, for apparently Sunita's men were going to watch it; in a dark room there could be no audience. Then what?

His mind ranged and, for a moment, it wandered back to Hemingway's fascination with courage and his grim story of the ancient Spanish crones, standing at the doorways of the slaughterhouses after the bull fights, drinking the blood of the dead bulls, the crimson liquid oozing from the corners of their withered mouths as they cackled and screamed at the young men to come and kiss them. To accept that kind of invitation took an iron will. Or a bellyful of Spanish wine. Well, in an hour or two he would know. Whatever happened, he had a feeling that if he and Pasang were going to eventually leave with the goodwill and assistance of Sunita and her people—something they would need for the next stage of their mission—he was going to have to go along with whatever it was they wanted. And satisfactorily, for all concerned.

Wildman dried himself with the towel and then put on the clothing that the man had given him. It consisted of a pair of dark brown cotton trousers that he tucked into his Gokeys, a long-sleeved, green, cotton shirt with a thick peasant weave, and a dark blue silk scarf that he tied around his neck. There were no socks and so he took his old stockings, washed them in the stream, rung them out and slipped them on. They would dry inside his boots and it would not be the first time that he had dried a pair of socks by wearing them inside his Gokeys.

He gathered up his dirty clothing, walked back to the little tent, dropped the clothing outside the tent and went in. Inside there was a single native bed with a thin blanket on it. He laid down on it, fully clothed, stretched out, put his hands behind his head and within half a minute was asleep. His sleep was deep and restful. But he opened an eye instantly at the sound of a soft footfall and, without moving, watched a man enter his tent and stand by the door. "It is time to come, *sahib*. The Rani is ready for you now."

He swung his legs off the bed, stood up and followed the man out of the tent. Outside Pasang was waiting for him, also dressed in a clean set of clothes but wearing his own red cloth sash with the *kukri* stuck in it. Together they followed their guide down to the centre of the encampment.

<<>>

In the middle of the encampment was a circular clearing, about fifty feet in diameter. Its floor was of hard, beaten dirt. About a hundred men and a scattering of women were grouped around the clearing. On one side of it, and close to the edge, a small campfire was burning. By its light and with the assistance of a gibbous moon that was laboriously climbing out of the hills to the east, Wildman saw Sunita. She was seated in a wicker peacock chair and the firelight glowed on a voluminous gold sari, one end of which covered her raven hair. The remainder of it covered all of her body with the exception of her midriff, which was bare.

As Wildman and Pasang approached the circle of standing men and women, all conversation died and there was a silence. Sunita waved her hand and, as she did so, a man placed another chair beside her. Wildman started to walk towards it but Sunita raised her hand. She spoke in English, which Wildman guessed none of her people understood. "After the ceremony, Wildman. After my people here see what they have gathered to see. Then, in their eyes, you will be entitled to sit beside me."

She clapped her hands and two men appeared at the side of the clearing carrying a large basket. The crowd parted to let them through and they walked carefully to the centre of the clearing and slowly, almost reverently, put the basket down. The murmuring of the crowd, which had grown again after Wildman and Pasang had arrived, again ceased and if on their arrival it had been quiet, now the silence was absolute. Some of the men, Wildman noticed, seemed to edge back a little after the basket had been placed in the centre of the clearing.

Now all eyes turned towards Sunita, who reached behind her and drew out a long, thin, bamboo pole. She stood, walked out past the little campfire, leaned far forward and with a quick movement of the pole flipped the lid off the basket.

For a second or two nothing happened. Then slowly, accompanied by a deep and powerful hissing, the head of a King Cobra rose out of the basket.

Wildman heard Pasang drawing in his breath. "The *nag* saap, *sahib*. The King Cobra. Very dangerous!"

Wildman felt his throat go dry. He swallowed and hoped that no one would notice it before he replied to Pasang, "You don't have to tell me old chap. The bloody Hamadryad, the biggest and deadliest of them all."

To himself he said, oh shit. A bloody King cobra. I might have known it. So that's it folks. That's Little Shiva.

"Wildman?" Sunita's voice was sharp and clear.

"Yes, Rani Sunita?"

"Wildman, this is Little Shiva. And if you look over your shoulder you will see that the moon is rising. Little Shiva, my friend, is waiting to be kissed."

Wildman's attention was totally occupied with the huge snake in front him. But there registered on his mind, in spite of his preoccupation, a note of sadness in Sunita's voice. Something that reached out to him touched him, as though in regretful anticipation of what was happening. Then Pasang's voice cut in, low and urgent. "*Sahib*, don't do it. It is very big. One bite *sahib*, even if it has already eaten today. One bite...*Sahib*, we could run, if you wish..."

Wildman, half hypnotised by the sight of the huge snake, did not reply. After rising from the basket it had flared its hood and commenced a sustained and powerful hissing. Its attention was attracted by the little campfire and it had turned in that direction immediately it rose from the basket. But Wildman had a horrible feeling that it was also aware of his presence and was just waiting for him to move before turning and launching its deadly attack. His voice, when he answered Pasang, sounded hollow and distant. It was as though he was speaking to himself.

"Run, Pasang? I can't. I've never run from anything in my life. It's something I just can't do, if only because I know that if I run now then I will run the next time, and the time after, and the time after that...until there is no place left to run to."

A faint breath of air seemed to touch the back of his neck. Perhaps it was the hairs back there beginning to stiffen as his shoulder muscles tightened. Whatever it was, he suddenly snapped out of his reverie. He glanced quickly at Pasang, smiled a grim, hard smile and with a wave of his fingers said, "A quick kiss, Pasang, that's all they want. Nothing to it. And think, Pasang. Look around you at these simple people. At the presence of their women here. Probably children too, back in the tents. Do they look like people who would keep a fanged snake with its sacs full of poison in their camp? I don't think so. My bet is that it is defanged and about as harmful as a grass snake. A quick kiss? A piece of cake. Just wait and see."

Saying this he smiled again and stepped forward and walked to within four feet of huge serpent.

<<>>

At his approach, the cobra slowly turned its head in his direction. Its hissing increased in volume, the huge hood flared out another quarter of an inch on either side and its body rose further out of the basket. In the basket itself, another six feet of the creature—two thirds of its total length—

twisted and turned as it groped against the wickerwork sides for a better grip.

Wildman halted when he was still a good four feet away from the snake and slowly, very slowly, lowered himself to his knees. He stayed in this position, on his knees, for a full minute and then, with a slow, shuffling movement, began to inch his way towards the basket and its grim contents. As he came closer he leaned back and when his supplicant-like shuffle came to an end, though his knees were within twelve inches of the basket, his upper body, bent backwards, was still a little more than three feet from the snake.

The watchers around the clearing stood like statues of stone. Not a whisper was heard, not a finger moved. Sunita, her body arched in her chair, her fingers biting into its arms, watched Wildman, a look that was half dread, half sorrow, etched on her beautiful face. Wildman, glancing quickly up before he closed with the snake, saw the look and it registered in his mind. Sorrow? That he was going to die? Or dread, that he would fail her and destroy the legend of courage that they were all waiting to see demonstrated? Realising that whatever she was thinking was not going to affect the outcome of his situation, he quickly put his wandering thoughts aside, to concentrate on what he was going to do next.

Now, moving his arms back and locking his hands behind his back, and keeping his knees and legs quite still, he slowly began to straighten up. When his body was fully vertical, he did not stop but continued its forward movement, very slowly, downwards, in the direction of the snake.

The cobra had aligned its hooded head with Wildman's face. Its hissing continued, unbroken, and Wildman, every nerve tense, every muscle of his body under control, listened to the powerful hissing and could not but wonder how it did it without seeming to draw breath.

The snake now looked at Wildman with cold, passionless eyes. Its head was absolutely still. Wildman moved his face closer. Six inches. Closer. Four inches. Closer, until his lips were within three inches of the deadly serpent. Two inches. One inch. Then, his eyes locked on the cold, black pupils of the Hamadryad, and holding his breath, he moved his face forward the last inch and gently, ever so gently, kissed the cold, cruel lips of Little Shiva.

The instant his lips touched those of the snake, the hissing stopped. Wildman slowly and carefully drew his head back, straightened his body, stood up and walked towards Sunita.

A man screamed. “Shiva knows. Shiva knows,” and instantly there was a wild uproar of shouting, hand clapping and stamping of feet.

<<>>

Wildman stood in front of Sunita and looked at her. Her mouth was slightly open and the look on her face was one of drained relief. Pasang joined him and whispered, “Well done *sahib*. First class. People all very happy now. Now we have much help getting on up the road to Nepal.”

Wildman turned towards Pasang and smiled. “No problem, Pasang. I told you. Defanged. Obviously. No doubt about it. They would never keep it here otherwise. Not with all these people in the camp. Women and children too.”

Pasang shook his head and smiled and the crowd roared its approval. As it did so a big black rat, hunting for food on the outskirts of the clearing, and panicked by the sudden shouting, ran between the feet of the onlookers and into the clearing. It moved with speed as it passed the cobra’s basket. The great snake was still in its erect position and it had not moved since Wildman had touched its cold mouth with his lips. Now it moved and it did so in a blur of speed. One second the big rodent was racing past the snake. The next it had been struck, bitten and bowled over. It immediately scurried to its feet and started to continue its run across the clearing. It made about another three feet, slowed, fell, got up, fell again and then lay on the ground thrashing. Its feet lashed backwards and forward for about another five seconds. Then it stiffened, stretched out and died.

Pasang looked at the rat and then turned slowly to Wildman. “Defanged, *sahib*, did you say?”

Wildman shrugged with a exaggerated nonchalance, smiled a sad smile at Pasang and said, “Ah well, old man, we all make mistakes, you know.”

Now Sunita beckoned for Wildman and Pasang to come and sit with her. Wildman took the chair on her right and Pasang was given one on her left. The King Cobra had picked up the rat and sunk back into its basket. Now this was lidded and taken away.

Fuel was added to the campfire and soon a roaring blaze lit the clearing. The men settled down by the edge of the clearing, squatting and talking, while the women left to prepare the food for the feast. Sunita clapped her hands and watched with a smile as two women approached bearing trays and glasses. On one of them was a bottle of dark, almost black, Kukri Rum from Nepal. Pasang’s delight was obvious as it was presented to him. On the other, a tall bottle of Glenlivet, and as the man bearing it stopped in front of Wildman, Sunita leaned over and whispered, “You see, I told you that I knew more about you than you realised.”

Wildman, accepting the tray with a gracious nod, mused to himself, she could be right. Personally, he thought, I could have done with a snort or two before going down on that dammed cobra. Pouring himself a generous measure from the bottle, he added a little water from a jug and then raised his glass to Sunita and Pasang.

From the gloom beyond the campfire, dimly lit by the yellow moon, women now appeared, bearing metal trays of food. There were great heaps of rice, yellow with saffron. Chunks of pork, wild boar from the surrounding jungles, roasted to a crisp. Wild jungle fowl stuffed with succulent raisons and spices. And a dozen kinds of curried vegetables.

They feasted. The moon strengthened as it rose above them. Then it peaked and slowly began to slide down the night sky. About a dozen men, Sunita’s chiefs, joined Sunita and her guests for the food. But they took no part in the conversation and it was obvious that this was expected of them by Sunita, for she spoke only in English and Nepali to Wildman and Pasang, thus excluding them.

After a while the talk turned to Vask and Wildman noticed the chiefs leaning forward expectantly. Then, and only then, did Sunita switch to Urdu and include them in the talks. They nodded their pleasure at this and listened carefully when Sunita talked of Vask. “An evil man,” she said. “And now, with what you have done, a vicious enemy to have. He has returned to his house, I am told, and he is there now, planning his next step. Whatever it is, you may be sure that he will now act with the added impetus of revenge. When you leave here you are going to have to be very careful, Wildman. And you too, Pasang. You see, although those around us here do not know why Vask captured you and took you to his house, I know. I know what it is he wants and how determined he is to get it. He knows now of your brotherly relationship with Pasang and he will use that to full advantage. You can be sure that if he gets you into his clutches again, it will be Pasang who will suffer first. Then, when he has what he wants from you, you will be next. Next time there will be no escape. Yes, for the remainder of your journey to the north, you are going to have to take great care.”

The subject of Vask dealt with, Sunita switched back into English. When she did so the men around her rose, bowed, thanked her for the feast and left. As soon as they had gone Sunita picked up a glass and held it out to Wildman.

"I do not drink in front of my people, as you have noticed. But now I will join you, if only to toast your future and the safety of the remainder of your journey. To you both, then. To your courage. And to your success."

She raised the glass and drank, and after a while she allowed Wildman to pour her a second measure. Then Pasang stood up and bowed and said that he would turn in for the night. Wildman waved him good night and the little Sherpa stepped out of the firelight and disappeared.

The moon eased slowly down towards the dark blue line of the western horizon. The campfire burned low and soon the camp was silent. Wildman, the cotton shirt his only garment, felt the cold seeping into his back. But a fire burned inside him, a fire stoked by the golden alchemist that was the Glenlivet, that and the scent and sound of the beautiful woman who was his companion. A fire that moved from his solar plexus down through the muscles of his stomach and into his groin. He looked at the woman. Since they had met he had not touched her, nor she him. And the time had come, he felt, to make a move to rectify this. He leaned towards her and took her hand in his. She let him have it and turned to look at him.

"Sunita, the hour is late. The moon is dying and soon the night will be dark. There is a question on my mind, one to which only you will have the answer."

"Yes, Wildman?

"The question of what you said when I first arrived. About the two Wildmans that puzzled you. The Wildman of courage and the other one. About your need to know about both?

"Yes?"

"Well then, one I have given you, to the best of my ability and as your people demanded it. What was the other?

For an answer the woman suddenly rose and, keeping his hand in a firm grasp, led him across the clearing, away from the fire, through the silent encampment, to her tent.

<<>>

The crowing of a Grey Jungle Fowl awoke Wildman in the dark, just before the dawn. He opened one eye and looked at the woman sleeping beside him. Her raven black hair flowed across the satin sheets that covered the huge bed, and on her face was a look of innocent pleasure, the look of a sleeping child that has just enjoyed a beautiful dream. And Wildman smiled, knowing the source of that pleasure.

Their lovemaking had been prolonged and to the point of exhaustion. Entering the tent, Sunita had closed the canvas door and then led Wildman into a second canvas walled room, behind the first. The second room was her bedroom almost all of which was occupied by a huge bed. It was covered with gold-coloured, satin sheets, which, like the bed itself, were at one time the property of some fat moneylender who had crossed the bandit queen. The room was lit by half a dozen tall red candles standing in brass containers.

For Sunita there had been no preliminaries. She had kicked off her sandals, thrown off her gold sari, flung herself down on the satin sheets and held out her arms to him. It took Wildman about ten seconds to get his clothes off and while he did so she watched him with impatient eyes. Then he stepped quickly to the bed and without waiting for an invitation lowered himself down on top of her. He felt the power in her sinewy legs, closing around him, telling him that she was ready. He was ready too, hard and straight, and as he entered her she moaned and drove her fingers deep into the muscles of his back, locking his body to hers, pulling him in.

Their first orgasm came quickly and when Wildman's back arched in the frenzy of his physical release, she screamed and sank her teeth into his ear lobe. His body throbbing in ecstasy, he did not feel the pain. But he did feel her magnificent breasts pulsing against his chest, as her orgasm coincided with his. And when her body arched against him in a powerful spasm, her twisting, thrashing strength told him that he was matched with what for him was a rare thing, a woman whose passion equalled his own and whose physical strength was not far behind his.

Half in play then, and to see what she was capable of, he pinned her wrists to the bed in a vice-like grip and put all his weight on top of them. He saw a startled look flash across her face and at the same time her body began to arch upwards in an effort to throw him off. Slowly, and with a strength that Wildman would never have believed possible in a woman, she raised her body upwards, forcing both his hands, with all of his weight on them, off the golden sheets beneath them. When her arms were more than a foot from the surface of the bed, she suddenly looked at his face, saw the smile there and, relaxing, let him fall on top of her. As he did so she reached up and pulled his face down on to hers and drove her tongue deep into his mouth. The power of her body had already aroused him again and now the long, seeking tongue transformed his arousal into a series of deep, driving thrusts. She cried out with pleasure and continued to do so until a final thrust left her wide-eyed and gasping underneath him, her hands beating like fluttering birds on the satin sheets, her head lashing from side to side in a veritable torrent of passion.

They lay together after that for what might have been an hour. Then, half drugged with pleasure, half asleep, half awake, Wildman felt her lift herself up and climb over his body and position herself between his legs. For a few seconds nothing happened. Then, softly, as delicately as the wings of a butterfly touching his skin, he felt her hands touching the insides of his thighs. He felt the pleasure beginning to build as the sensation she created moved up into his groin. Her hands climbed and found his testicles and softly she began to massage each hard little sphere, one to each hand, squeezing, releasing, stroking, squeezing again. Suddenly he was erect and as quickly as his organ came to the vertical she leaned down and drew it into her mouth, deep, far back, so that its head was tightly cushioned by the soft membranes of her throat. Then, slowly, she began to massage it with the muscles of her oesophagus, sending a fire of delight racing through his body.

Wildman groaned and lay back. His hands gripped the sheets and waves of pleasure surged through him. Then Sunita quickened her movements and as she did he felt himself beginning to build towards another orgasm. Just as he was close, so close that, he knew from experience, there was no turning back, she stopped, withdrew her mouth and reaching between his legs seized both of his testicles in a firm grip. She drew them both outwards and downwards and held them there, keeping a firm pull on them with her slim, strong hands. Instantly his onrushing orgasm subsided and came to a halt. Astonished, he raised his head and looked down at her. Her oval face glowed in the candlelight and she smiled back at him from the end of the bed. For another ten seconds she retained her firm grip on him, never slackening the steady downward pull. Then suddenly she released him, bent over and took him again in her mouth.

Wildman gasped with pleasure. There had been many women in his life, much passion, much pleasure. But never, ever, anything like this. To be brought to this incredible peak of delight and to be held in balance there like this for agonising seconds was rapture beyond measure. Then, when it was certain that this was the final summit, beyond which lay nothing but passionless snows, to be shown that there was another summit and to be allowed to start for it with the same desire, ah, that was ecstasy.

Three times she allowed him to ascend to his Everest of delight and three times she used her deft and clever hands to draw him back from the summit. The fourth time she led him once again to his peak and then, with exquisite timing, withdrew her luscious mouth, threw himself down beside him, dragged him on top of her and with quick eager fingers thrust his throbbing member deep inside her. This time, when he exploded into her body, she was silent, and when, after a long series of spurting, throbbing ejaculations he withdrew and looked down at her, she lay still, her eyes closed, slowly sinking into sleep.

Just before dawn she awoke and demanded him again. She climbed on top of him and with supple movements of her nimble, knowing fingers quickly had him aroused and inside her. Sensing that he was sexually exhausted from the night before, she worked him gently, sitting on top of him, thrusting her buttocks up and down and letting him lie supine beneath her. Only when she felt his orgasm building did she move. She fell on him, seized him in her slim muscular arms, rolled with him until he was on top of her and then, wrapping her legs around him, lay back and allowed him to penetrate to the full depth of his manhood. She gasped when he came inside her and her gasping quickly grew into a series of long, sobbing moans as his orgasm died and she felt him collapse. Moans that seemed to carry a note of despair as they filtered through the thin canvas walls of the tent and out into the primeval jungle, out to where the gods of the forest gathered them up and wove them into the delicate fabric of the dawn wind that rose at their bidding to herald the arrival of another day and the end of her night of passion.

The jungle cock crowed again and its call was answered by a challenge from another, closer at hand. Wildman, naked, walked to the canvas door of the bedroom, opened it, passed through the main room, opened the second door and looked out. A grey mist hung across the encampment and the air was damp and cold. Dawn was breaking and an eerie band of light streaked the eastern sky. It would be another two hours before the sun was up. The little trees that stood between the tents shed the night dew in a steady series of drips and the canvas of Sunita's big tent sagged under the weight of their accumulated droppings. The sickly fog limited visibility to less that fifty feet and the two men who came pounding out of it were within thirty feet of him when Wildman first saw them.

<<>>

He tensed in the doorway and watched. Then he recognised one of them from the campfire feast of the night before—one of Sunita's chiefs. The two men came up at a fast run. Just in front of the tent they cut to the right and made their way around to the back. At once Wildman heard them calling to Sunita in low and urgent voices and as they did so other figures appeared, hurrying towards the tent out of the mist.

Wildman walked quickly back into Sunita's bedroom. She was sitting up in bed wrapping a light woollen robe around her body, her head cocked to one side and all of her attention directed towards the urgent voices outside the tent. Wildman listened.

"Coming from the west, Rani. Thirty, maybe forty men. Half of them Vask's people and the remainder policemen in uniform. They crossed the Lalit River twenty minutes ago."

For a moment Sunita sat still and looked at Wildman. Without saying anything, he could see the turmoil of her mind. Vask's thugs were on the way accompanied by local policemen. Had word leaked that Wildman was in her camp? Or had the cunning Vask simply guessed where his escaped prisoners might be? One of Sunita's patrols had spotted the group not long after they had entered the hills and thus a surprise attack had been averted. But that there would be an attack, she had no doubt. And its object would be to capture Wildman and Pasang. Which meant that they must leave immediately. Which in turn meant that she must say goodbye to Wildman.

For a brief moment she looked at him, lovingly. Then she rose quickly, walked to him and with her hands tenderly cupped under the source of her night of pleasure, kissed him long and hard on the mouth. "You heard my men. You must go. Quickly."

She turned and, facing towards the wall of the tent, issued a stream of orders. Among them, as he struggled into his clothes, Wildman heard her calling for a guide to take him and Pasang across the hills.

Now the sounds of pounding feet surrounded the tent. Men shouted and Wildman heard the rattle of rifle bolts and the clink of bandoleers. Sunita seized him by the hand and pulled him to the door. She looked up at him for a last time and spoke. "I wanted to have more time with you. If nothing else to help you make preparations for your journey north. But now there is no time. There is going to be a fight. Vask is on the way and he has bribed local policemen, probably from Nagpur, to come with him. The old man who brought you will guide you out of here. I do not need him just now. He will lead you. North and west. Where the forest ends, he will leave you. About fifteen miles from here. From the forest edge it will be about ten miles to Nagpur. Open country all the way. Due west. All right? Stay out of the villages. Keep in the open. Vask has people everywhere. When you get to the first roads try and get on a truck. Do not use a local bus. And when you get to Nagpur stay away from the big tourist hotel and spend the night down in the bazaar. There are many small hotels, some of them quite old. When you have a room send Pasang out. Tell him to go to the Nagpur City Garage directly in front of the railway station. The owner's name is Golwar. He is a friend of mine. Tell Pasang to give him this."

She thrust a small black stone into Wildman's hand. "When Pasang gives him this he will know from whom it came. You will need another car. A Jeep or a small truck. It will be the only way to go on to the north. Vask will have men watching the trains and the bus stations. Golwar will find a vehicle for you. Now, do you have enough money?"

Wildman's hand touched his money belt. "Yes. Enough. If your friend can handle American dollars?"

"He can. Now go. And if Golwar can get a vehicle for you tonight, then use it tonight. Leave the minute you get it. Make your own decision about which route you take. But do not stay in Nagpur. Nagpur is, and well you know it, Vask's hometown. For him, or rather for his money, there are eyes everywhere, watching, waiting to run to the master with babbling tongues and outstretched palms. Kiss me now, my beautiful tiger, my unbelievable lover, my gorgeous demon of the night. Kiss me once and kiss me hard. For we shall not meet again."

Wildman seized her in his arms and drove his mouth down, hard, on to hers. Again and for the last time he felt the steel of her body as she pushed it against his and drove her fingers into his back. Then she suddenly pulled away and pushed him through the doorway without a word. The tent flaps swung together and he was outside, where Pasang was waiting, and with him the little old man who had brought them to the encampment. Without a word their guide turned and set off down the valley at a fast pace. When he was about a hundred yards from Sunita's tent, Wildman turned and looked back once. Sunita was standing in the doorway, watching him go, her face framed in the great black mass of her hair. Then suddenly she was surrounded by her chiefs, eager for conference and for orders for the fight. She turned and passed into the tent and they thronged behind her. He did not see her again.

BOOK SEVEN

NAGPUR

Once again their guide ran like a deer for the first mile. Then he slowed the pace, stopping to listen every five minutes. The route he chose was north and west, away from the encampment and whatever trouble was going to take place there. They had gone about two miles when they heard the first gunfire from behind them. At once their guide again quickened the pace and for the next half-hour they kept up a steady, jogging run. Then the sounds behind them faded and once again they resumed an easier pace.

Because of frequent stops to listen for pursuers, it took them almost seven hours to reach the edge of the forested hills east of Nagpur. There, wishing them good luck for the remainder of their journey, the old man left them.

After he was gone they rested for a while, and, from a concealed position at the edge of the forest, scanned the country ahead that they would have to cross. It was open country, with rice fields. Men were visible, working the crops. Women walked the separator ridges between the fields with brass pots on their heads and children herded buffalo in areas where the crops had been cut. Waiting until a minimum number of people were visible, they made a slow and careful exit from the forest, and once out set a course due west for the city. In order to attract as little attention as possible they moved slowly, zigzagging between the many villages that dotted the flat country. The sun was setting when they reached the first road east of the city. There was a grove of small trees close to the road and they waited in these until a bus, four rickshaws and a dozen buffalo carts passed. Then a truck appeared and they ran out and Pasang flagged it down by standing on the side of the road and holding up a bundle of rupee notes. They declined a ride in the front where they would be expected to chat with the driver, climbed into the back and with the shades of night fast closing across the flat plains, rode into the city of Nagpur.

They stayed in the truck until it was deep into the heart of the city. It had still not reached its destination when a stoplight allowed them to slip off the back and, in the murk of the ill-lit city streets, merge with the teeming people who thronged them.

Nagpur. Population two million, give or take a couple of hundred thousand or so either way. Narrow streets, teeming bazaars thronging with people, dilapidated tenement buildings bursting with human life, dirt, disease, squalor and hundreds of wandering, seemingly ownerless cows, buffaloes, goats, pigs, horses. And pariah dogs by the thousand, many of them rabies carriers. And noise.

Noise. Some years ago India discovered the transistorised, power-operated, loudspeaker. Within months, or perhaps it was weeks, every shopkeeper seemed to think that he had to have one, both inside, to keep his customers happy, and outside, to musically blast the marvellous values of his wares into the street. Soon, every truck driver had one in the cab of his truck. Public buses followed suit and they, in turn, were followed by rickshaws and trishaws and vans and even private cars. The noise this created, added to the normal noise level of the street, was, is, to the western ear, unbelievable. Every time he entered an Indian city Wildman wondered how on earth the people who lived there could stand it.

Immediately after leaving the truck Wildman decided that instead of trying to find a place to stay, they would go straight to Sunita's contact, Golwar and ask him about the possibility of buying some wheels. If he was unable to come up with something that night, they would try and persuade him to put them up for the night. Somewhere, quiet, discreet. This seemed a better plan than booking into a hotel. For no matter how they tried, they would not be able to disguise themselves as anything other than what they were, a big white *feringhee* and a Nepali hillman. And Indian hotels throughout the subcontinent were, as both he and Pasang knew, a hotbed of underworld spies and police informers.

With this in mind they made their way towards the railway station. Twice they had to ask the way. Wildman let Pasang do this while he hung back in the gloom. Then the railway station appeared ahead and within another few minutes they were standing in a darkened doorway close to the station and sizing up the activity at the brightly lit Nagpur City Garage on the other side of the street.

They waited until they were fairly certain that there was nothing more than normal activity around the garage. Then they crossed the street quickly, dodging the teeming rickshaws and wandering cattle, walked into the front

Sunita's men in conference in the forest, planning their defense, before the attack by Vask and his thugs.

Sunita's fighters roll a log to block a road, before the attack by Vask.

Sunita in later years. Professional portrait taken in a studio in Bombay.
Credit, Modi Photo Studios, Marine Drive, Bombay.

of the garage and then right through it to a door at the back marked **OFFICE.** Wildman opened the door quickly, waited for Pasang to slip inside and then closed it and put his back to it.

The office was small and most of it was taken up with a single table. On it, an antiquated black telephone fought for space with stacks of battered ledgers and tattered files. There was no window and the walls were covered with old calendars, pictures of modern automobiles torn out of American magazines and diagrams of gearboxes, radiators and steering assemblies. Behind the table, in a battered wicker chair, sat a small man with a thin, lined face, steel-rimmed spectacles and short, cropped greying hair. It was only after he had spoken that Wildman realised he was in his forties, and not in his sixties.

When they entered the office the man's head was down and he was concentrating on a line of figures in a small ledger in front of him. One hand held a ballpoint pen with which he was tapping the edge of the ledger. The other rested on top of his head where his fingers slowly scratched his cropped scalp. When the door opened he paid no attention. But when its closing was followed by silence and not the customary jabbering of one of the garage grease monkeys, he looked up slowly. When he did it seemed to take him a little time to comprehend what he was seeing. A white man, big and dangerous looking, with his back firmly against the door and a nasty looking Bhutia, or Tibetan, or some such wild caste, with the handle of a huge knife sticking out of the front of his cummerbund. His eyes widened, his mouth dropped open, and the ballpoint dropped from his fingers and whatever he tried to say came out only as a gasp.

Wildman stepped forward and put out his hand, palm upwards. "We are friends. And also friends of a friend of yours, who gave me this to give to you."

His eyes wide, the little man dragged his gaze down from Wildman's face to look at his hand. When he saw what was there he slowly relaxed, reached out, took the stone, rolled it between his fingers and then, nodding and smiling, his breath still coming in short gasps, said, "Any friend of the Rani is welcome here. Especially any friend who brings this."

He put the stone into his pocket and, reaching out a thin hand, shook hands first with Wildman and then with Pasang. Standing quickly he dragged his chair, the only one in the room, around to the front of the desk, motioning to Wildman to sit in it. Then he moved quickly to the door and locked it. This done he came back and stood in front of Wildman and, rubbing his worn hands together, said, "Please. I am your humble servant. Tell me what I can do for you."

<<>>

It was several hours later. Wildman's Rolex told him that it was after twelve. Omitting much detail, he had told the garage owner what it was they wanted and had stressed the urgency of their need. The man had listened carefully to what he said and then had nodded and, after a moment to think, had taken a small black book out of a drawer under the table. He opened it, looked carefully at a page containing half a dozen numbers and then began telephoning. He looked up at Wildman after dialling the first number.

"You must forgive me sir if I speak now in Urdu. You do not speak Urdu I am sure. I hope that you will understand my need to do this."

Wildman did not enlighten him to the fact that he spoke several Indian languages fluently, one of them being Urdu. Using his knowledge, he listened intently as the diminutive Golwar made calls and spoke to his contacts.

There were several long conversations. Wildman heard the word "friend" used many times by Golwar and at one point there was a prolonged argument over what must have been the price of a vehicle. Twice Golwar hung up and allowed others to call him back. Then, after the six or seventh call, he smiled and hung up and said, "I think that I may have something for you. A good Jeep. Not an Indian Jeep that will fall into pieces ten miles down the road. But an old Kaiser. Old, yes. But with a reconditioned engine and some good work done on the steering and brakes and other parts. And the price will not be too high, I have been promised. A favour. Beeziness in this country is all favours, you must understand, sir. A favour done for me is one that I will owe back in return. A favour done by me means something in return owing to me. Favours. Some call it a corrupt practice. But we for want of a better word call it favours."

The phone rang at that point and Golwar picked it up and listened carefully. He shook his head from side to side and said *achaa*, meaning yes, a couple of times. Then he told his caller that he would ring him back in two minutes. That if he did, the deal, whatever it was, was on. And if he did not then it was off.

"Yes sir. We have the Kaiser. My friends can get it here within two hours. There is the matter of tyres to be put on it. It will need new tires. The price they want is rupees fifty thousand. In cash."

One hour later a buzzer sounded in the office. Golwar rose quickly, unlocked the office door, walked through the garage to the main door and peered through a crack in the panelling into the street. What he saw obviously satisfied him. He slid the locks on the main door and two women entered carrying aluminium *pots* wrapped in cloth. He led them back to the office and, as they entered, introduced them to Wildman and Pasang as his wife and daughter.

Wildman looked at the older woman. She was even smaller than her husband. Her threadbare sari was of plain cotton and the cheap glass bangles that she wore on her wrists confirmed Wildman's feeling that as a small garage owner his 'Humble servant Golwar' made barely enough money to live on. The daughter was equally drably dressed and her thin face and bony arms seemed to cry out for nourishment. She was young, probably sixteen, but already she looked thirty. A quick, shy look she shot at Wildman stirred him and he resolved that if the vehicle that Golwar was getting for him was any good then he would certainly give the little man his fifty thousand and a generous bonus on top.

Golwar picked the ledgers and files up off the table and piled them on top of a metal cabinet in the corner. His wife unwrapped the pots and drew out metal plates, metal cups, spoons and forks. There was a pot of tea and a little sugar wrapped in newspaper. As soon as the food was spread on the table the women left the office and went out into the garage. Smiling at Wildman and Pasang and telling them to eat, Golwar followed them.

The food was good. Saffron rice laced with coconut shavings and raisons. Chunks of mutton heavily curried in a thick yellow sauce. Lentils cooked thick and condiments wrapped in little pieces of newspaper. There were two mangoes, two bananas and an apple. Wildman made a mental note of the food. It was expensive food, the meat itself a luxury for a family like Golwar's; they had gone out of their way to bring him more than they could afford.

They had almost finished and were washing down the last of the rice with the warm tea when the buzzer sounded in the office. Pasang, who had been eating in a squatting position on the floor, rose instantly to his feet, went to the office door and opened it a half inch. He peered through and watched while Golwar opened the big front doors of the garage. He saw a dark green Jeep being driven in and he watched while three men got out. When he was satisfied with their appearance he turned to Wildman and gave him a quick nod. "The man's friends. With the Jeep."

Wildman tossed down the last of the tea, wiped his mouth on his sleeve, stood up, went to the office door, opened it and stepped into the

Sunita's friend, Golwar, who negotiated the sale of the Jeep for Wildman: with his wife, in Nagpur. A poor man, he and his wife were richly rewarded by Wildman for their assistance to him.

dimly lit garage. He walked up to the vehicle that had just arrived, nodded at the three men who stood beside it and looked at it. It was a World War II Kaiser Jeep. Golwar joined him and said, "This is the vehicle, sir. Please look at it and decide if it is what you want."

Wildman spent half an hour going over the Jeep. He would have spent longer but there was not much point to it. Because firstly the Jeep was in quite good condition and secondly he felt that it was probably the best that he was going to get. Again, he was anxious to get out of the city as soon as possible and if he could conclude the deal satisfactorily he intended to leave without delay. The longer he spent in the city the tighter Vask's invisible net would draw.

The three men who came with the Jeep, for instance. They may have been associates of Golwar's. But what allegiance did they owe the Rani, if any? And once they got their money, what did they owe a passing *feringhee* and his man? Nothing. Which left them wide open, as far as Wildman was concerned, to Vask's enticing system of reward for information. No. The Jeep's condition seemed fair and the engine, when he ran it, sounded smooth. Take it, he thought. Take it and get the hell out of Nagpur as soon as possible and while the going is good. Now…

He waved to Golwar. "OK. I'll take it. Now who do I pay, you or them?

Golwar hesitated and looked nervous. "You must pay them, sir. I am not part of the arrangement. I have only fixed the price and I have done that in the best of my conscience because of my friendship with the Rani. They will accept payment directly from you, sir."

Wildman led the way into the office and Pasang handed him the money belt that he carried. Golwar hung back as the three men who had come with the Jeep gathered around the table. As they did Pasang quietly and unobtrusively moved behind the office table and stood with his back to the wall. Wildman noticed the movement and smiled to himself. Ever the watchful Pasang. Trusting nobody. He zipped open the money belt and counted out twenty-five, one hundred-dollar bills and put them on the table. There you are, gentlemen," he said, indicating the money. "And how much extra for the gasoline. And the cans?"

The men looked at one another. Wildman, without waiting for a reply, pulled another hundred-dollar bill and threw it on the table. "That cover it?"

They nodded and took up the money. They counted it twice, nodded again, and left the office together, mumbling. Wildman heard them passing through the garage and closing the big doors behind then. Then he nodded to Golwar and, keeping Pasang's money belt in his hand, led the way out of the office. As in Bombay, when he bought the Scout, there had been no talk of papers of any kind. Ah, Wildman thought. India.

He already had the Jeep keys and now he nodded to Golwar, swung into the seat of the Jeep, started the engine and waited until Pasang was in beside him. Then he waved his hand at Golwar, who ran to the double doors to open them. While Golwar was doing this Wildman, with some difficulty in the small space, turned the Jeep around to face the double doors. He kept one hand on the wheel and the other on the money belt in his lap. When the doors were open and Golwar was standing beside them, his wife and daughter hovering in the background, waiting for him to drive out, he waved at the little man. He waited until he was close and then quickly drew fifty hundred-dollar bills out and thrust the bundle of notes into the startled man's hands. Wildman's last view of Golwar was as he ran to his wife and daughter to show them the fortune the gods had brought them.

<<>>

Wildman glanced at his Rolex. It was fifteen minutes before four. Dawn in about forty-five minutes. They had raced through the cold, misty streets of the city, the tires of the Jeep whining on the wet, dew-soaked surface of the roads. There had been little traffic. A sign had said, VARANASI, 350 MILES and twenty minutes after leaving the Nagpur Central Garage they were on the narrow main highway and heading north for the great city on the Ganges.

<<>>

The Jeep ran well. Wildman guessed that it was twenty-five to thirty years old and that probably little other than the frame was original. It had recently been painted a dark green and the canvas that made the cab in which they sat was new. The dashboard contained only three instruments. A fuel gauge, a speedometer with a built-in mileage recorder and a temperature gauge. The fuel gauge showed that the tank was full. The speedometer needle, wavering a little, recorded their speed in miles per hour with a reasonable degree of accuracy. And the temperature needle seemed content, so far, to sit close to the C of its dial and well away from the H. The fuel tank filler cap was under the driver's seat; the seats themselves were covered with a pliable plastic and filled with what felt like packed straw. The canvas top had clear plastic on either side at the back and there was a rear window, also of clear plastic. The windshield had a single air-driven wiper on the driver's side and inside the cab, set above the dashboard, was a small rear-view mirror.

The front seat had a metal back and bolted on to this was a spare wheel. Like the other wheels, it also had a new tyre. The remainder of the space in the back was taken up with the ten, five-gallon fuel cans that had come with the Jeep. A quick check by Pasang soon after they started showed them to be full. The cans were painted bright red and it was with some misgiving that Wildman noticed that they were not metal, but plastic. The vehicle had no doors and at their travelling speed of fifty to fifty-five miles an hour, the cold morning air roared into the cab. It cut through the thin clothing Sunita had given him and chilled him to the bone.

He drove steadily for three hours and just after seven, with a weak sun stretching long, thin fingers of light across the flat, barren land, they pulled into a small, roadside truck drivers' restaurant. He parked the Jeep fifty feet away from the building, got out and looked around. There were two trucks parked off the road beside the restaurant and around them stood their drivers, chatting and sipping tea out of thick-walled glasses. Wildman nodded to Pasang. "Tea, Pasang and we'd better eat while we can. Go and see what they have in that lovely little place."

While Pasang was in the restaurant, Wildman took out one of the fuel cans and topped up the Jeep's tank. He also opened the hood and checked the oil and then, using a rag over the cap to protect his hand, carefully opened the radiator. All seemed to be in order and the engine was not overheating, the one thing that he had worried about in the newly reconditioned engine. Pasang appeared. "They have food *sahib*. Rice and lentils. And also some coffee."

The coffee turned out to be instant, which Wildman abhorred. But, any port in a storm, he thought, and drank three cups of it with the food. Pasang stayed with the tea. They ate on a small porch in the front of the restaurant, from where they could watch the Jeep. After eating, they paid for the food, added a small tip for the grimy-faced, six-year-old waiter, walked separately to the back of the building, used the restaurant urinal—the back wall of the building—and then returned to the Jeep, climbed in and left.

They drove all day, stopping only twice. Once on the outskirts of a town to buy four cotton blankets. The second time, outside an old British post office building, to take a brief rest. But they had hardly stopped when a surly, greasy-haired man came sidling out from behind the building, to sit with his back to them and watch them over his shoulder. Wildman did not like the look of him and with a quick nod to Pasang started the engine, and moved on.

Wildman pushed the Jeep hard, keeping its speed, when road conditions allowed it, up in the sixties. Soon after leaving the restaurant he had allowed Pasang to take over the rear-view mirror, twisting it to the right so that the Sherpa could watch the road behind through the clear plastic of the rear window. Traffic was normal. Many trucks, a few private cars and the usual stream of buffalo carts and rickshaws and cyclists and pedestrians. As the day grew it increased, and when it did their average speed dropped. By six, with the dying sun a violent orange sphere in the dust haze of the plains to their left, they had put a good two hundred plus miles of road behind them.

<<>>

Soon after dark they stopped at a small roadside restaurant and ate again. After eating they drove on for another twenty miles and, when the road was clear of traffic, and there were no headlights ahead or behind, turned quickly off the highway. Shifting into second and then down again into first, Wildman took the Jeep down three miles of rutted, dusty road until he came to a small, thick patch of scrub. Pasang jumped out to check for holes and stumps and then slowly, in first gear and four-wheel drive, with Pasang walking ahead in the light of the headlamps, Wildman forced the Jeep deep into the centre of the thicket. He immediately cut the lights and the engine and then walked back with Pasang to rebuild the brush crushed by their passage into the thicket and to conceal the Jeep.

When this was done they returned to the Jeep. Pasang, as usual, insisted that Wildman sleep in the vehicle and, taking his *kukri,* chopped out a small sleeping area in the bushes next to the vehicle. This done he walked back into the brush, urinated, came back, wrapped two of the thin blankets they had bought around him and sat down with his back against the front bumper of the Jeep. Wildman stretched out on the front seat, put the other two blankets over him and, with most of his legs dangling out over the side of the narrow, vehicle, prepared for an uncomfortable night. He wondered if Pasang would sleep, decided that he probably would not, and was still thinking about this when sleep overtook him.

BOOK EIGHT

GHOSE

Ghose knelt on the dirt floor of the cell, his hands covering his face as though to shut out the approaching horror. He had only one thought left now, one beseeching prayer to his gods that ran like a soundless scream through his mind...that whatever it was that Vask had in store for him, that it would be painless and quick.

When the cell door opened he remained kneeling, the palms of his hands tight-pressed over his eyes. He recognised the voice of Vask and he knew that the shuffling of other feet meant that he had brought some of his henchmen along, to hear him pronounce the death sentence.

The harsh, cutting voice jerked him upright. But he remained kneeling, hands covering his face.

"You have made too many mistakes, Ghose. The foolishness that sent me and my team to Bangkok, when we should have been in Bombay. The brainlessness that let the American and his caste-less one get away. And now the destruction of a prize buffalo herd, something that is going to cost me much money. One mistake we may allow. Perhaps two. But three? Never. There is no place for fools among my people. So die. Die the death of a fool and a muddler and let your death be an example to others, so they may learn from it."

He tightened his hands across his face and waited for the silk kerchief. He would hear it, he knew. The quick hiss as the coin-weighted rumal snaked around his neck. Then the knee between his shoulders and the grunt of the executioner as he leaned back and, cross-handed, exerted the pressure that would quickly cut off air, blood, and life. Then silence. He would not try to fight it. There was no point. Vask's executioners were quick and strong and for Ghose to try and resist would be like pitting a pariah dog against a tiger. Thus, he would drop his arms down when he heard the hiss and allow the silk to close quickly on his carotid arteries.

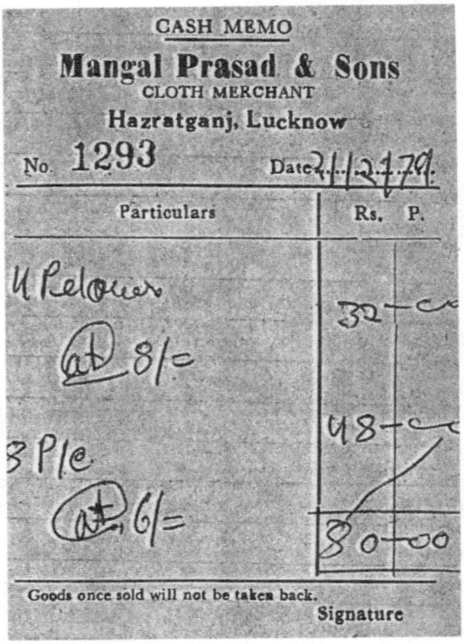

CASH MEMO
Mangal Prasad & Sons
CLOTH MERCHANT
Hazratganj, Lucknow

No. 1293 Date 21/12/79.

Particulars	Rs.	P.
4 Pelomer @ 8/=	32	—
3 P/c @ 6/=	48	—
	80	00

Goods once sold will not be taken back.
Signature

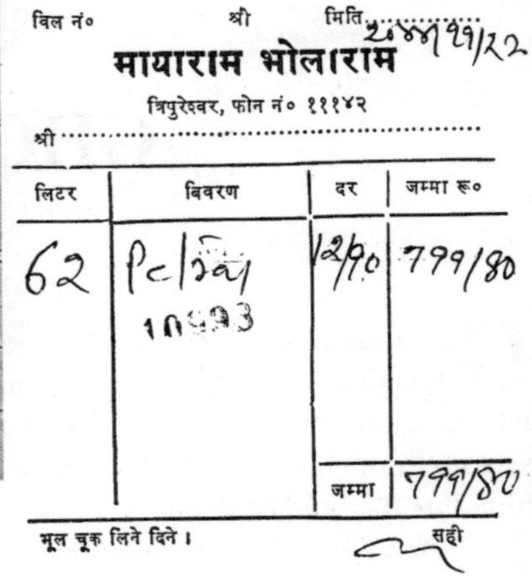

बिल नं० श्री मिति 2036/11/22
मायाराम भोलाराम
त्रिपुरेश्वर, फोन नं० ११९४२
श्री ....

लिटर	बिवरण	दर	जम्मा रू०
62	Petrol 10993	12/90	799/80
		जम्मा	799/80

भूल चूक लिने दिने। सही

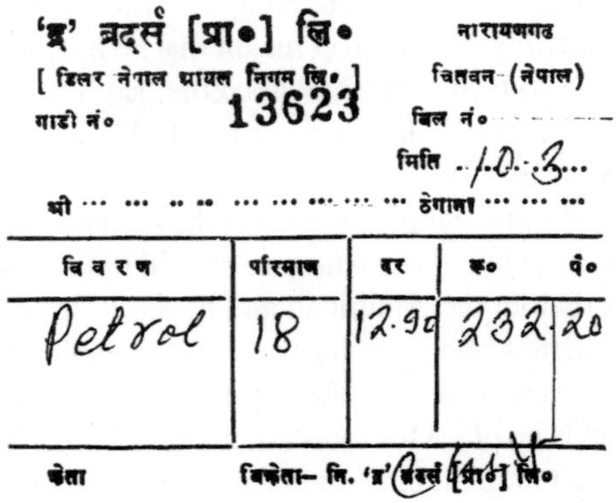

'ब्र' ब्रदर्स [प्रा०] लि० नारायणगढ
[डिलर नेपाल आयल निगम लि०] चितवन (नेपाल)
गाडी नं० **13623** बिल नं० ....
मिति 10.3...
श्री .... ठेगाना ....

बिवरण	परिमाण	दर	रू०	पं०
Petrol	18	12.90	232	20

क्रेता बिक्रेता– लि. 'ब्र' ब्रदर्स [प्रा०] लि०

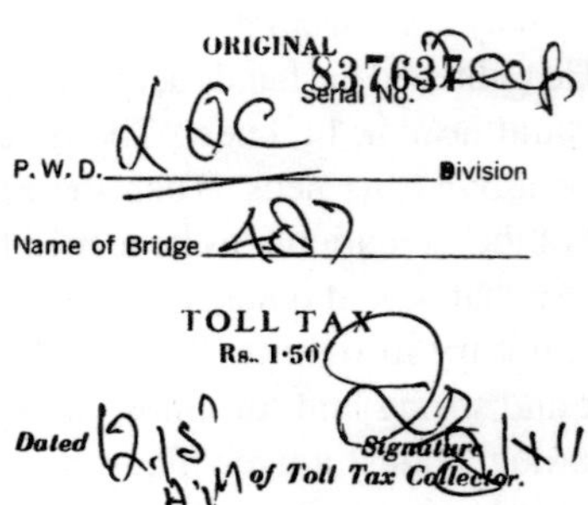

ORIGINAL
83763 Serial No.
P.W.D. LOC Division
Name of Bridge 487
TOLL TAX
Rs. 1·50
Dated 2.1.80 Signature of Toll Tax Collector.

Gasoline and road toll tax bills collected by Wildman during his race across India. Photo credit, author's private collection.

With blood flow to the brain cut off, he would be unconscious in five or six seconds, after which he would know nothing.

He waited. He heard the cell door slam shut and for a few seconds there was silence. Now, the rumal. But nothing happened. He heard a sound and waited. But the sound he heard was not the swish of the deadly silk, but something else. Something that turned his bowels to jelly and burst his bladder and sent the stinking urine gushing between his legs into the dirt. The sound was that of the shuffling, dragging tread of the black-faced monster that was Vask's brother. Ghose opened his mouth to scream and as he did so, Little Gunga opened the cell door, entered and began to whine.

<<>>

The giant played with Ghose for a long time. The man's screams definitely seemed to excite him. The dull cracking sounds that his bones made, as they snapped, one by one, had the huge, grotesque head nodding with pleasure and the whining rising to a pitch that penetrated the walls of the cell and sent a shudder through those who heard it. But at last, when the screams came to an end, and the thing that had been his latest toy was nothing more than a sodden, red, rag doll, Little Gunga lost interest in it and stumbled, head nodding, the whining slowly diminishing, back to his own cell.

<<>>

Vask sat at the head of the table in the front room of his house. It was one hour before dawn and the fifteen men who stood around him were silent with exhaustion and fear. Fear generated by what had happened to Ghose, something that could, at the drop of a pin, happen to any one of them and exhaustion from being now more than thirty hours without sleep.

When Vask came back from the temple and found that Wildman and Pasang had escaped, he had exploded into a veritable paroxysm of rage. Ghose, the senior man at the house while he was gone, was at once held responsible. Vask, looking ahead, had already marked Ghose as one of the people to be eliminated when he got the Eye. The man was clever and he knew too much. Again, Vask knew that if he thought he could get away with it, Ghose would undoubtedly double-cross him in a minute. Here was an excuse, an opportunity, not just to get rid of the man, but also to justify his disposal in the eyes of the gangs. Not that Vask had to justify anything he did. But of late the *rumal* had been swinging with a savagery that had had the men muttering. In Vask's mentality, loyalty and obedience were things that money bought. But at the same time he was clever enough to know that there was a limit to what his money could buy. Ghose therefore would be used as an example of what could happen to anyone who failed him, anyone. He was flung into a cell and the gang chiefs were made to listen to Vask pronouncing his sentence and, Vask hoped, mentally acknowledging it as justified. And then Little Gunga was unleashed on him. What was left of him when the giant was finished with him was to be flung into the street for the vultures to eat. And that was that.

Ghose disposed of Vask sat down to study a map of the area. He knew that once Wildman and Pasang got into the deep forest, they would be almost impossible to find. But he also knew that the jungles east of his own holdings belonged under the rule of the Rani Sunita and he guessed that her men might well pick up the fugitives and take them to her encampment. At once he ordered an attack on the encampment. His men rounded up twenty local policemen who were in Vask's pay and quickly put together a force of forty in all. Late on the night of the escape they set off into the eastern jungles for Sunita's camp. Vask had thought of going with them. But he knew that Sunita's scouts, ever watchful, would spot the attackers long before they reached the encampment. If Wildman and Pasang were there they would be spirited out of a jungle backdoor. This would mean a pursuit and to plan this and stay on top of the situation, whatever happened, Vask needed to stay at the centre of command. As well as which, a coward at heart, he had no desire to face Sunita's jungle fighters, even though he was fairly sure that forty men, twenty of them armed policemen, the other twenty his best men, should certainly be able to overwhelm her camp.

So he stayed behind with the remainder of his gang, underlings, drivers and messengers, the runts of the pack, while his principal men, assisting an "Official" police drive against the notorious bandits of the hills, cut through the forests for the attack on Sunita's camp.

<<>>

The battle, when it came, was a rout. Within minutes of Wildman's departure, Sunita, dressed in khaki trousers and an old army jacket and armed with a US Army 30.30 carbine, was racing through the jungle at the head of forty-five of her best men. The Lalit River, they had said. She knew the area well and she knew that just east of the Lalit and in a direct line to her

The death of Ghose. After Little Gunga had finished "playing" with him, his body was flung into the street and left there.

Later, Ghose's body was picked up by street cleaners and thrown into a nearby paddy field, where vultures and pariah dogs soon disposed of it.

camp was a long deep ravine, an obvious route for an attacking force. The ravine was deep, its sides covered with thick brush, its bed filled with huge boulders that could easily hide half a hundred men. She had her fighters in position on both sides of the ravine, at its head, when the first of Vask's men entered it from the west. Her orders were simple. Wait until the whole party was in the ravine and then open fire. She would fire the first shot. Any man who fired before her would answer dearly for his impetuosity.

When the firing started and the advancing thugs and their police escorts realised that they had been ambushed, there was immediate panic. Those behind immediately doubled their pace and ran forward in the hope of finding cover. Those in the centre of the ravine turned and bolted back. A few dropped to the ground and tried to find targets to return the fire. But all that they could see were grey boulders and brown brush, out of which the bullets whined and ricocheted and cut them down. Within fifteen minutes there was nothing more for Sunita's men to fire at.

Sunita rose and put her hand above her head and the firing stopped. The she climbed out of the ravine, up on to its high bank, and gave precise orders. She wanted one and only one prisoner. She stayed up on the ridge and listened to her men dispatching the remnants of Vask's thugs and their uniformed escorts. Single shots. Killing shots. No quarter.

Soon, four of her men came up the hill with a single prisoner. He was a tall, thin policeman in a tattered uniform. They led him to her and he stood with his knees shaking in front of her, certain that he was about to be executed. She looked at him with contempt, spat on the ground and looked away. The man was unharmed and when the attack began he had dropped his weapon and thrown himself on the ground. They had found him cowering under a bush while they counted the dead. One of theirs. Thirty-nine of the enemy.

Sunita looked at him. "You will go back to your master. You will tell him that we were happy to be able to entertain the swineherds that he sent to try and fight us. Tell him to send more, any time. My men enjoy the exercise and the contributions of weapons that he makes to us are gratefully accepted."

She turned quickly and spoke to one of her men. He smiled and pulled a pair of police handcuffs from his pocket. Grabbing the captive by the hair he forced him down and quickly locked one ring of the handcuffs tightly to his right wrist and the other around his left ankle. Then he turned and kicked the man in the rear, seeding him stumbling and rolling down the side of the ravine, to the laughter of Sunita's men.

Sunita did not join in the laughter. The handcuffs had been put on the man for a purpose. She wanted Vask to know what had happened to his raiding party. But she did not want him to know until she was sure that Wildman and Pasang were out of the forest and at least into the city of Nagpur. Hobbled as he was, the man would not be able to get back to Vask's house until late that night. By which time, she hoped, Wildman and Pasang, with little Golwar's help, should be on their way north.

<< >>

Now, while Wildman and Pasang were making their way towards Nagpur, Vask sat at the table in the front room of his house in a black rage. His men, in terror of him when he was like this, stayed out of his way unless he summoned them. When he called them in to ask if there was any news from the raiding party, or of the escapees, knowing that they would rush to him with news if there was any, but needing to have someone just to vent his rage on, they stood in front of him with legs trembling and mouths that were dry with fear.

Vask stayed at the table, waiting, seething, late into the night. At midnight they brought him food. But he snarled and smashed the tray out of their hands and on to the floor. The tray bearers fled. And he was still sitting there, brooding, one massive fist slowly pounding the table in front of him when a man was seen, coming up the hill from the direction of the forest. Vask jumped up and rushed out, and he was standing with his huge frame filling the doorway of the house when the wretched, handcuffed policeman staggered up and collapsed in front of him. Vask leaped forward and grabbed the man by the front of his shirt and pulled him up and hissed in his face.

"Well, fool, what have you to say? Where are the others? Where are my chiefs?"

The man could barely speak. "Gone, Raja. All dead. All finished by the Rani. A huge army, Raja. Five hundred men. We had no chance. I myself fought like a tiger, Raja, but was wounded..."

Vask's lips curled around his teeth as he heard the news. His raiding party wiped out. His chiefs slaughtered. His best men gone. And one miserable cur left to bring him the news, one snivelling pariah who had allowed himself to be captured and made a fool of by Vask's archenemy.

Now Vask's fury mounted to a crescendo. He hurled the man away from him, reached in his pocket, whipped out a weighted silk handkerchief and grabbed the wretch by the shoulder. He swung his arm back and the silk flashed. But at that moment the telephone rang.

Sunita's men building a pit trap to protect their jungle camp.

Vask dropped the cowering wretch in front of him and ran back into the house. He hurled himself into a wire chair at the head of the table, grabbed the antiquated phone off its cradle and put it to his ear.

"Raja *sahib*?" came a wheedling voice, speaking in whispered tones. "Raja *sahib*. Two men. One a big American. The other maybe from Tibet. They took a Jeep from the Nagpur Central Garage. Not more than one hour back. They drove north. The Varanasi road."

Vask listened carefully. "You have done well. Now listen. What number is on the Jeep?"

"Here it is, Raja, I have written it down. DLI 509."

"And the colour of the Jeep?"

"A dark green, Raja. With a cloth top."

"Good. You have done well. You will be rewarded."

"Oh thank you, Raja, I knew that I could..."

But Vask had slammed the phone down and was shouting for men and drivers. "The Jeeps. Bring the Jeeps around to the front of the house. Quick, you fools. Every man, everyone. Here. Now. We leave at once."

Vask turned and raced down a central corridor. Taking a key from his pocket he opened a thick wooden door leading into one of the side rooms. He emerged within minutes carrying an ugly-looking Kalashnikov automatic rifle and a leather pouch of ammunition.

<<>>

Three Jeeps roared around to the front of the house. Vask ran out of the front door. Still lying on the ground where he had thrown him was the handcuffed policeman. Vask's immediate reaction was to kick him out of the way. But when he looked up he saw that the total number of the men gathered around the Jeeps was only eight and it was suddenly brought home to him that this was all he was now left with, after the destruction of his raiding party by the Rani. Eight men, three of them drivers. Nine if he included the handcuffed policeman. He hesitated for a moment and then he barked an order. Two of the men ran off in the direction of the back of the house to reappear within a few minutes, dragging, one to each arm, the ponderous bulk of Little Gunga. Vask looked at his brother and shouted, "Get in the Jeep. The third one. There. In the back. Quick. In the Jeep and you shall have toys to play with. And we'll get you something to drink also. Quick. Get in."

As Gunga climbed slowly into the Jeep he shouted another order and two of the men picked up the handcuffed policeman and threw him unceremoniously into the back of the second Jeep. Vask climbed into the front of the third Jeep with his brother and then barked a single order at the driver. "North. Varanasi."

BOOK NINE

THE CLUTTERBUCK HOTEL

Long before dawn had yellowed the eastern sky, Wildman and Pasang were on the road. Wildman, a blanket wrapped around his shoulders against the early morning chill, drove fast. By nine they had another hundred miles under the wheels and were within fifty miles of the metropolis of Benares, renamed, after the partition of India, for reasons locked deep in the inscrutable minds of the Hindu priests who ruled it, as Varanasi.

It was when he saw a sign, **VARANASI 25 MILES**, that Wildman realised that the time had come to make a decision about Lord Carew's granddaughter. It was a decision that he was finding difficulty in making, as a result of which he had been putting it off for days.

On the one hand there was the promise he had made to the old man, that he would meet the young woman and after meeting her give consideration to taking her along with he and Pasang to Nepal. He had given his word to the old man in that promise and any deviation from that was out of the question. On the other hand, since he had talked with Lord Carew, a totally different set of circumstances had arisen and his mission now had about it an aspect that was far, far different from when he started out. That aspect, as well as the thing that had set the new chain of circumstances in motion, was the arrival of Vask on the scene.

What had started as an exciting and unusually challenging mission, now had about it an atmosphere that was entirely different, an atmosphere of deadly danger and a brooding aura of death. Not the kind of thing in which to involve a young woman, even if she was a so-called blithe spirit. Or was it free spirit? No. Not at all the kind of thing for some faint-of-heart and tender creature from the cushioned comforts of some Nob Hill, upper echelon home in Sydney, Australia. Some waffling blonde whose

Map showing the location of Vask's house. (Ringed.) And, immediately south of it, marked with dotted line, Sunita's bandit territory.

idea of adventure was a race downtown in Daddy's Rolls Royce followed by a four-hour stint in an Elizabeth Arden beauty salon. Some snotty, fickle-brained, chattering ex-débutante who would in the first place not believe him if he tried to tell her about Vask and company, and in the second place probably accuse him of inventing them as an excuse to get out of taking her along.

No. He didn't like doing it, but he was going to have to break his word to the old man. Well, he could explain later. In any case—and the thought eased his conscience a bit—he and Pasang were now way behind schedule and it was very unlikely that the sweet young thing was still waiting for them in Varanasi. That's if she had been able to find Varanasi. Which was doubtful. Wildman had a quick flash of her ensconced in the Imperial Suite at the Varanasi Sheraton surrounded by her luggage and her make-up, tapping her fingers on the cocktail table and glaring at the telephone while she waited for the adventurer man, whatever his name was, to call. So that she could cut loose from the Imperial Suite—it was so boring, she had been there three interminable days already—and tag along with him and tootle up the jolly old road to jolly old Nepal. Women. Wildman sighed and made his decision and as they closed down the last twenty miles into Varanasi, fighting the traffic pouring out of the huge city, he told Pasang what he had decided to do and why. The little Sherpa listened carefully and then nodded and made his comment and closed the subject.

"Good decision, *sahib*. Best thing not to take *memsahib*. Much too dangerous now with the Vask man looking for us. Better we go alone."

Wildman turned to look at Pasang speaking and as he did, a bright red, Indian-made Ambassador sedan came straight at them out of the dust and drove them right off the road. There is a distinct disadvantage, Wildman thought, to driving a left-hand drive vehicle on roads where the driving is—supposedly—on the left. It particularly emphasises itself when one has to pass something like a large truck going in the same direction. Normal passing is of course to the right of the vehicle in front. But to be able to see the road ahead and make sure that it is clear, the passing vehicle, with its driver sitting on the left, has to swing far out to the right for a clear view ahead. The only alternative is to keep tucked in tight to the left and endeavour to see the road ahead by looking up the left side of the vehicle in front.

They had been behind a huge Mercedes diesel for ten minutes and its driver was making no attempt to allow them passing space. The hard surface was narrow, one lane, and the verges on both sides of it were rutted and broken, with rocks and roots that effectively prevented the passage of a passing vehicle. Dust boiled over the Jeep and Wildman's eyes smarted and watered with the effort of trying to see the road. A dozen times he had swung far out to the right, sounding the Jeep's rather puny horn and flashing his lights in an effort to get the truck to move over. The truck driver paid no attention and the verge continued rough and impassable. Suddenly, returning from a swing to the right, Wildman noticed that the grass verge on the left had opened up. It was narrow and only just wide enough for the Jeep. But unlike the right side, which ran rutted and broken, its surface was smooth and clear of brush and rocks. Moreover it appeared to continue like this for a hundred yards.

The road ahead was clear except for one small, red approaching car and this would pass the truck on its left, so there was nothing to impede the passage of the Jeep if Wildman made a run for it up the left hand grass verge. He decided to take a chance, dropped the Jeep into second gear and floored the throttle. The vehicle leapt forward and they began to pass the truck. Wildman had almost cleared the truck and only needed another few yards and another few seconds before swinging back on to the road again. But at the last moment, the driver of the approaching red car, seeing that the truck driver had no intention of giving up his position in the centre of the road, and seeing that the left side of the road was deeply rutted, swung hard right and came straight at the Jeep down the wrong side.

Wildman cursed. The bloody Indian highway chicken game. Shit, he thought. If I was been driving something a little bit bigger and a little bit heavier I'd have taken you on, you witless idiot. But he was not. He was in a very light vehicle and, something of which he was very aware, he was also carrying almost thirty-five gallons of fuel in the back, something that made the little Jeep, in the case of an accident, a veritable bomb. The klaxon of the truck blasted through the dust and there were wild shouts from its cab. Behind the cracked windshield of the red car, Wildman had a quick glimpse of its driver, mouth open, shouting, and behind him a dozen wildly grinning faces. Then he swung the Jeep off the verge, hard to the left, giving way to the red car. It flashed by with inches to spare.

Directly in front a huge tree loomed, massive, with a gnarled grey trunk. Wildman swung even further left. The Jeep lurched wildly, its left wheels, front and rear, left the ground and then they were dropping down, down into a four-foot deep ditch at the edge of a rice field. If the bottom of the ditch had been smooth, they might have survived the fall without injury to the Jeep. But it had a scattering of large rocks in it. When the Jeep landed in it, with a thunderous crash, an extra large boulder took the vehicle amidships and Wildman and Pasang heard a loud metallic clang as the full force of the fall drove the boulder hard against the drive shaft.

When the dust had settled, Wildman reached slowly down and turned off the ignition. He sat for a moment, his body taught as a steel spring, his hands like steel vices on the steering wheel while he fought to contain his anger. Then he relaxed, turned to Pasang, smiled a rueful smile and said, "OK, old man, let's get out and have a look at the damage."

Twenty minutes later they were back on the road and driving slowly towards Varanasi. Speed, fifteen miles an hour. The Jeep shuddered violently. Every nut and bolt in the frame rattled. The canvas top lashed from side to side and the plastic fuel containers danced a staccato two-step on the floor of the rear compartment. With Pasang heaving and shoving and with the engine screaming in four-wheel drive, they had managed to get the vehicle off the boulder on which it had landed, out of the ditch and back up on to the road. But a quick glance underneath revealed the damage. The drive shaft had been bent like a bow from the tremendous blow of the fall on to the boulder. The universal joints at either end of the shaft had held and there appeared to be no damage to the oil seals, either at the front, where the shaft connected with the transmission case, or at the back, where it transferred its torque into the rear differential. But at anything more than fifteen miles an hour the bent shaft lashed violently against its bearings, both in the transmission case and the rear differential, and Wildman knew that it was only a matter of time before it snapped. If this happened they would be stranded. As it was they could still drive and so, vibrating like a wooden-wheeled soapbox being dragged across a sheet of corrugated iron, they limped into Varanasi.

Three hours after the accident they were deep in the heart of the teeming city on the Ganges, quietly lodged in an old, small, once beautiful, one-time British hotel, in the heart of the city. A hotel where no tourist in his right mind would ever even visit, let alone book lodgings. A hotel that Wildman had used before, and that he chose now for the sake of anonymity. A place that had a quiet compound where they could work on the Jeep without attracting too much attention. A hotel where, Wildman hoped, Vask and his thugs would never think of looking for them. And he had little doubt that Vask would be looking for them and that now, spurred by revenge for what Pasang had done to him, he would be furiously expanding his search.

Trying to think as Vask might, Wildman surmised that as soon as he found out that he and Pasang had left Sunita's camp, as no doubt he would, he would start his new search by sending word out by phone for watches to be set up at railways stations and bus depots. He would follow this up through the truck depots with information to be passed to all truck drivers on the highways north of Nagpur, to watch out for two strangers, one a foreigner, one a Nepali hillman. Through the truck driver highway grapevine, word would go to roadside cafes, shops, and fuel stations. From there the lure of Vask's reward system would spread it even further, to the big hotels in the cities and from them, through the hotel telephone operators, to the smaller hotels and boarding houses. Vask's contacts with the police would be used to their full extent and, within twenty-four hours, the evil spider that was Vask would have an ever-spreading web laid far across the highways and towns and cities of the north, all the way to the borders of Nepal.

But the Clutterbuck Hotel, set at the far end of a sleazy, cobble-stoned alley off a mean back street stinking with the refuse of the vegetable market? No one would think of looking for them there. Not even the cunning Vask.

And hardly, thought Wildman, breathing a sigh of relief, a high-minded, clean thinking, uppah class, nose-in-the-air, and society lady from the posher parts of down under. No. Wildman imagined that any inquiries that the old man's blithe spirit—or was it free spirit, dammit? —might make would extend themselves about as far as the nearest other tourist hotel from the one where she was languishing. And that would be the extent of them. Wildman smiled to himself, as a picture flashed into his mind of Lord Carew's little princess trying to make her way down the foul alley that led to the Clutterbuck Hotel, her Balanciaga, crocodile-skin handbag clutched in her delicate fingers, a lace-trimmed, white linen hat perched on her head—broad-brimmed, of course, against the pitiless glare of the noonday sun—her pink Shantung silk dress with cute little bows front and back, her high-heeled Dior shoes...up to her ankles in buffalo shit, fruit peelings, human faeces, dead rodents and pools of urine. His quick flash did not include the look on her face. But he had no trouble imagining its horror as the dear young thing sank to her kneecaps in the green, glutinous ooze of the fetid, flyblown alleyway.

<<>>

The Jeep wobbled its way down the filthy alleyway, its tires ploughing through the stinking quagmire of discarded vegetables, cow dung and human waste. At the end of the alleyway was the entrance to the hotel compound, a shattered hole in a high, tottering brick wall that at one time had completely encircled what must have been the trim, flower-filled compound of the old hotel. From leaning stone pillars set in the wall, the rusting remains of a huge, ornate iron gate sagged on its hinges. They drove through, bumping over broken brick and the cracked pavement of a leaf-strewn driveway, and pulled up under the portico of the hotel. There were half a dozen steps leading up to the front door of the hotel. Like the gates, the big wooden door sagged on its hinges, and Wildman noticed that from its ancient and rusting lock dangled a thick chain and a huge padlock. Above the doorway hung a rusting metal sign that said **THE CLUTTERBUCK HOTEL**. Wildman smiled when he read, underneath the sign, half-eroded with the rust of the years, ***RESERVATIONS ONLY***.

Pasang stayed with the Jeep while Wildman went in to see about a room. Wildman walked up the steps, passed through the front door and found himself in a small foyer. Directly in front of him, where a marble-topped reception desk might once have stood, was a large, crudely built table with rusting legs and a metal top. Behind the table was wooden board with three-inch nails sticking out of it, on which hung a dozen keys. At the table itself was a single chair and in it a large, fat, round-faced clerk in a black jacket, a grey-white shirt with a greasy black tie, blue-and-white check pyjama trousers and black rubber sandals on bare feet.

As Wildman approached, the man looked up with complete disinterest and said, "Yes. What you want?"

Wildman smiled what he secretly called his anti-apathy smile and said, "Any chance of a room?"

The clerk yawned, made a pretence of looking at a paper in front of him and said, "How many peoples?"

Wildman kept his smile broad. "One, as a matter of fact."

"How many days staying?"

"Oh, let's say, three or four."

"Five rupees day. No food. Four days twenty rupees advance also rupees five deposit against dirty room cleaning refundable on departure."

Wildman fished in the pocket of his shirt and pulled out the equivalent of two dollars and put it on the desk. The clerk reached out with his right hand, opened a drawer in the table with his left and swept the money in. With the same movement he turned around and pulled a key off the board behind him and threw it on the table. "Room five you want food best food Kashmiri Food House down thee street good food owned by my cousin door closed midnight open seven bathroom toilet upstairs right."

Wildman smiled to himself. There had been no request to register. The Indian government had a strict ruling about registration in hotels. All guests had to register, especially foreign visitors. But registration meant that the guest's stay in the hotel was recorded, not just for the government, but also for the hotel owners. With no registration there would be no record of his stay for the owners of the hotel, which meant that the clerk would be able to pocket the money.

Wildman picked up the key and walked back outside. Pasang was standing, leaning on the front of the Jeep, watching the gate, looking at the gaping holes in the old brick compound wall, relaxed but alert.

"OK, Pasang. We have a room. Now here's what we'll do. I'll take the Jeep around to the back of the hotel here and stay with it. And you? Well, you know what we need. A mechanic, tools and a machine shop or garage where they can straighten the dammed shaft. You know how to go about finding what we need, so I'll leave it to you. And it goes without saying, offer enough money to get things moving and get someone here as soon as possible. But at the same time not so much that it will attract any attention."

Wildman pulled a bundle of rupee bills out of his shirt pocket and gave them to Pasang and with a quick, "Very good *sahib*," the little Sherpa was off.

As soon as he was gone, Wildman got in the Jeep and drove it carefully around to the back of the hotel. There the old brick wall, slowly disintegrating in the grip of massive roots systems from the trees that grew along it, formed a small alcove that partially concealed the Jeep. He backed in, cut the engine, cursed and settled down to wait. Cursed because he knew from experience what it was going to be like to try and get a job they needed done quickly and efficiently. 'Quickly' was a word that left India with the British, he decided and 'efficiency' was a word that had never existed in the subcontinent. He looked at his Rolex, cursed again, curled his long frame across the front seat of the Jeep, stretched out and, with one eye open, allowed himself to doze. The flies buzzed, muffled sounds came from the inside of the old hotel building, and someone threw a bucket of water out of one of the windows. Crows cawed listlessly from an old, dusty, dried-up tree in the corner of the compound. The winter sun, shedding its thin light over the back of the dead but unburied hotel, slowly and silently eased itself down behind old brick wall, as it had done for just over a hundred years. Wildman might have smelled the food before he saw Pasang. He was not sure. But when Pasang placed metal containers of hot food on the front of the Jeep and said, "Some food, *sahib*," he suddenly realised how hungry he was. He also realised that it was dark and that Pasang was alone.

"Pasang. What's happening?"

If Pasang's English had been equal to it, he would have said something along the lines of, 'the usual bloody nonsense. Bloody shifty bastards want ten times the usual amount because it is after hours. It is after hours because they spent an hour arguing about the work, thus making it after hours when we got around to talking about costs. Then the usual bloody demands. Money down in advance and extra money because it's after hours and extra money because it is dark and more because it is away from their garage and more because it is a long way to come. At least four hundred bloody yards. Then as soon as they get the advance they find that they have several priorities. A. They have to go and eat. B. They have to go home and tell their wives that they are going to be working late. C. They have to have a rest after eating. D. They need more money to buy tools because they do not have any.'

But the Sherpa, his command of English limited, simply said, "Lazy buggers, *sahib*. Coming soon. Meantime *sahib*, you should eat. Food is here."

He unwrapped several metal bowls of food. Inevitably, it was boiled rice, curried vegetables and lentils. There was one tin plate and a spoon. Pasang spread the dishes out on the Jeep and Wildman, his stomach groaning with hunger, ate it standing up.

"You have eaten, Pasang?"

"Yes, *sahib*, when the mechanics went to eat I went with them. Otherwise they take many hours. So instead of standing watching them eat, to save time, I also eat. Thus I have eaten, *sahib*. I thank you."

The compound was quiet now, the only sounds, those that filtered in from the surrounding streets, the subdued murmur of people talking, the cries of children and the rasping noise of transistor radios playing Indian music. The sounds, coming in over the old broken brick wall, were curiously muted.

Pasang heard the men first. His head jerked up and he slipped away from the Jeep and stood against the wall. Wildman was just finishing his food, and he looked up to see two mechanics, distinctive in their greasy, oil-stained trousers and tattered shirts, approaching with a metal box of tools. One of them waved a hand when he saw Pasang and said, "Agia. We are here."

They dumped the toolbox on the ground beside the Jeep and one of them immediately crawled under the vehicle. As soon as he was under it he realised that he needed some light to see and he shouted something to his companion. The second man opened the toolbox, produced a small stump of a candle, closed the toolbox and then stood looking at the piece of candle in his hand. He looked at Wildman and then at Pasang and said, in Urdu, "Matches? Yes?"

Pasang produced a box of matches from his pocket and gave them to the man. The man took the box carefully, opened it, took out a match, struck the match away from himself against the side of the box and when it spluttered into life, lit the candle. He handed the matchbox back to Pasang and then bent down and passed the lighted candle to the man under the Jeep. Wildman groaned inwardly. There was a fuel tank under there with probably ten gallons of gasoline in it, and just above it in the vehicle another twenty or so gallons. Christ. What a way to work. But…this was India and this was the way it was done.

"S*ahib*?"

It was Pasang. "*Sahib*, I can watch the work here. Why not go and get some rest in the hotel. No need for you to stay here. I think everything OK. I think we safe now for a while."

Pasang meant safe from Vask and company, and Wildman was of the opinion that he was right. Vask was out there somewhere and no doubt desperately trying to get on their trail. But they had made fast progress since leaving the Nagpur area, getting the Jeep and racing up the road to Varanasi. Thank Christ they had not bent that bloody shaft a hundred miles back.

"OK Pasang, I'll leave you for a while. But I'll be in the hotel if you need me. Just give me a shout, OK?"

"Very good, *sahib*. Will do."

Wildman walked around to the front of the hotel, mounted the steps and started to walk through the foyer towards the staircase to the second floor. The foyer was empty, the clerk gone for the night. He was just about to mount the stairs when he saw a light shining through the glass panel of a small door off to the left. He looked and saw, dimly etched on the glass of the door in faded but beautiful Gothic script, the word **BAR**. A bar? In a place like this? No. Not much chance. He was about to dismiss the possibility and go on up the stairs to his room when he thought, what the hell, I'll have a quick look; nothing ventured, nothing gained. He stepped to the door, opened it and peered in…at something that was like a scene from Kipling's India.

<<>>

The room was small. But the ceiling was high, and suspended from it were two enormous pieces of carpet. Running down from them were string pulleys, attached to hooks in the wall just above little wooden stools. The carpets were old-fashioned *punkah*s, ceiling fans, and the pulleys were for the purpose of pulling them back and forth to create downward drafts of air. The stools were where the *punkah wallahs*, the men who operated the ancient fans, used to sit. On the left was the bar itself. It consisted of a huge back mirror, beautifully inlaid with floral etching, with glass shelves running across it for its full length. On either side were solid mahogany pillars as thick as an elephant's leg, standing floor to ceiling.

The bar itself was set on set on a solid mahogany base. A brass rail, thick enough to support the weight of an elephant, ran around the base of its dark wooden front, and the bar itself was topped with brown and white marble, a single piece, end to end, four inches thick. On either side of the bar, each set on oval-shaped oak plaques, were the musty and decaying heads of two tigers, and in front of it were half a dozen, old-fashioned, brass-legged, leather-covered bar stools. And behind the bar, his face shining in the light of two tall thin candles was a very large, very fat barman, a south Indian by the look of him. Very black, very white-toothed, smiling a white-toothed smile and vigorously polishing a glass as he nodded towards Wildman and said, "And good evening to you, sir. Please. Please come in and sit down."

Wildman, in a daze, walked up to the bar and sat on the leather stool as the barman gave the glass a last polish, placed it carefully with three others on the glass shelf behind him, turned to Wildman and said, "Yes sir, and what will you have?"

Wildman smiled, shook his head in disbelief, smiled again and said, "I don't believe it."

He waved his hand around, at the bar, the shining glass mirrored wall, the tiger's heads. "I still don't believe it. But OK, what have you got?"

The barman placed his hands on the cold marble in front of him and with a visibly cynical curl to his mouth said, "I don't blame you, sir, for not believing it. Not the kind of thing you would expect to find in the old Clutterbuck, eh? Well, it's a long story and maybe we'll get around to it later. In the meantime let me enthrall you, sir, with a recital of the marvellous and wonderful drinks that we have to offer a travelling gentleman like yourself in these marvellous and wonderful post Raj days.

"Firstly, sir, we have gin. It is made here in Varanasi. A pariah dog would not drink it, and if it did, it would be dead in five minutes. We have rum, made in Doolalli, down near Bombay. Guaranteed five years old and, I would guess, probably four days old and at the most five. In other words the time it takes to ship it up here from Doolalli. We have vodka, made in Madras. Quite colourless, not a bad bouquet and guaranteed to lay flat on the floor in ten seconds the biggest, meanest Russian this side of Kabul, Afghanistan, if you know what I mean.

"We have beer. It is made with glycerine, which is probably cancer causing, but which is supposed to preserve it. But as well as tasting of this preservative, as we have no refrigeration, it is hot. Hot beer. You like hot beer sir? Of course not. Then we have whiskey. Scotch whiskey. Indian scotch. Made in Calcutta. I use it myself, sir, all the time. My hobby is old furniture restoration and I use it to strip paint from old tables and chairs. Need I say more?

"God!"

"You have called on God, sir. And God will come to your aid. No. I am not a religious man. But God told me to look out of the window here at the back when you drove in today. I saw you out there when you arrived and I closed the bar here and I went home and picked up something which, like a ship at sea, you might say, has been seeking an appropriate port for a long time. A long, long time. It is a bottle of real scotch, sir. The name I am not sure of because it is so old, maybe twenty years or more, that time and the mice have eaten off the label. Now, sir..."

"Did you say, a bottle of scotch?"

"Yes sir. As I was saying, the…"

"Young man."

"Sir?"

"Will you do me an enormous favour?"

"Yes sir, of course, sir?"

"Shut up and produce. The scotch. The without label whatever it is that you brought from your home, the ship at sea looking for any port in a storm, etc, etc."

The barman leaned down and groped under the counter in front of him. Then he stood up holding an oblong object, wrapped in tattered newspaper. He carefully unwrapped it and placed it on the bar in front of him. Wildman took it in his hands. The bottle was dark green and the label, as he had been warned, was almost gone. But a little remained and Wildman, holding it up to the light, felt his mouth go dry when he saw, in faded black lettering against a gold background, the word **GLENLIVET.**

The barman leaned forward and started to say something. But Wildman quickly raised a hand and stopped him. "A glass, young man, a glass, and by all that's holy, if this bottle contains what I think it contains, you, young man, have made yourself a month's wages this very night."

The barman took a glass from behind him, wiped it carefully with a white napkin and put it on the counter in front of Wildman. Wildman took the bottle in his left hand, twisted out the cork, which had a tinfoil covering, poured a half inch of a golden liquid that came sparkling out of the bottle, sniffed it and then sipped. He sipped it again and then lowered the glass a couple of inches from his lips looked straight at the fat barman and smiled.

"By God, I never would have believed it. But I'll tell you one thing. Your bottle sans label has found itself a home port and you have a found yourself a harbourmaster who will not argue its price and, as you are the first civilised chap that I have met in the last week, I insist that you join me in a drink."

The barman smiled and said, "In that case, sir," and reaching under the counter pulled out a large bottle of Canadian-made Captain Morgan black rum. He poured himself a generous shot, touched glasses with Wildman and threw the shot straight down his throat.

When the barman, after a couple of hefty belts, told Wildman that he seldom drank, simply because he could not afford it, Wildman made it clear that the bottle of Captain Morgan was his, price regardless. At that the barman promptly started doubling his drinks. And while he drank he told Wildman about the bar, how his father, an ex-army man, had been the Clutterbuck bartender for twenty years. How, when his father died, he had managed to buy the concession from the hotel owners and why he had stayed on.

And customers? He had certain arrangements with the two big tourist hotels in Varanasi. Private arrangements for two of the bartenders there to steer the odd group of tourists down to the old Clutterbuck. Private because the hotels in question would not be happy about losing their own bar business. No, the old bar did not make much money. But he had his own army pension—twenty-five years, in at fifteen and out at forty—and that kept him going. Enough to live on, if not quite enough to drink on. And the old bar? Well there was something about it that touched him, something deep inside, he said, something calling out to be preserved. Something from the old days. The good old days of the Raj, when there was justice in the land of the *sahib* and when people knew what was what. And so he kept the old place going. Five nights a week. And occasionally, if he was lucky, he got a client generous enough to share a drink or two with him.

"Like your good self, sir. So, down the hatch sir. Or, as Humberry Bogart used to say, drink it again Sam."

They talked into the small hours. The barman, delighted to have some company, did most of the talking, and Wildman let him enjoy himself.

They drank, drink for drink, until slowly, with a happy drunken smile creasing his face into a mass of wrinkles and with the Captain Morgan nothing more than a wetness in the bottom of the bottle, the bartender slid slowly down behind the counter and collapsed in a heap on the wooden planks. Wildman leaned over and looked at him. He was smiling and clutching the empty bottle of Captain Morgan to his chest. After a few minutes he started to snore with a noise that vibrated the marble top of the bar and rattled the glasses on the shelves above.

Wildman began to chuckle when the snoring started. As it increased to full volume, he began to laugh. It was the loudest snore he had ever heard, and somehow or other it was also the funniest. His laughter mingled with the snores and he threw his head back and let himself go. He was leaning back on the leather-topped stool, hands dangling at his side, his head thrown back and his laughter pealing off the walls when a tall, fair-haired, beautifully tanned young woman thrust open the door behind him, walked in, walked up to him, folded her arms and stood silently staring at him.

Cover of wine list for the Clutterbuck.

CHAMPAGNE

		Quarts	Pints
19	MOET & CHANDON, DRY IMPERIAL, 1919	$5.50	$2.75
18	HEIDSIECK, MONOPOLE RED TOP ..	5.00	2.50
18	POMMERY & GRENO, EXTRA SEC. ..	5.00	2.50
18	MUMM'S, EXTRA DRY	5.00	2.50
18	CHARLES HEIDSIECK, EX. QUALITY 1920	5.00	2.50
18	LOUIS ROEDERER, EX. DRY	5.00	

CLARET

24	CHATEAU PALMER	2.00	1.00
39	CHATEAU ROMEFORT		1.00
25	ST. ESTEPHE	1.80	.90
25	MEDOC	1.80	.90
25	ST. JULIEN	1.80	
25	MARGAUX	1.80	.90
27	HAUT SAUTERNE	2.50	1.25
28	GRAVES	2.00	1.00
29	BARSAC	1.80	.90
29	PORPHYRY SAUTERNE	1.80	.90

BURGUNDY

21	RED CAP, SPARKLING	3.50	1.75
22	CHAMBERTIN	2.50	1.25
23	BEAUNE	2.00	1.00
23	POMMARD	2.00	1.00
23	CHABLIS	2.00	1.00

HOCK

			Quarts
63	HOCKHEIM NEUBERG ..	Deinhard & Co.	2.00
52	SPARKLING HOCK ..	Deinhard & Co.	2.25

MOSELLE

73	BERNCASTELER EST. WINE	Deinhard & Co.	2.00
94	SPARKLING MOSELLE ..	Deinhard & Co.	2.25

CHAMPAGNE
CLARET
BURGUNDY
HOCK
MOSELLE
SHERRY
PORT
VERMOUTH
LIQUEUR BRANDY
LIQUEURS
WHISKY
GIN
RUM
BRANDY
SAKE
ALE, STOUT
LAGER
MIXED DRINKS
MINERAL WATERS
MEDICINAL WATERS
CIGARS
CIGARETTES

Part of the incredibly comprehensive (one time) wine list of the Clutterbuck.

Cover of dinner menu from the old Clutterbuck Hotel.

HORS D'ŒUVRES

Olympia Oyster Cocktail — Iced Casaba Melon
Royan a la Bordelaise — Royan a la Vatel — Bismark Herring
Smoked Kippered Herring — Smoked Bloater — Black Alaska Cod
Sweet Mixed Pickles — Pickled Walnuts — Dill Pickles
Sardines in Mustard — Sardines in Tomato — Sardines in Oil
Table Celery — Ripe Olives — Green Olives

SOUP

Cream of Tomato, Cabrillon — Consomme, Trevise
Cold Essence of Tomato

FISH

Broiled Fresh Mackerel, Sardelles Butter
Tranche of Columbia Salmon, Sauce Bearnaise, Sliced Cucumber

ENTREES

Roast Prime Ribs of Beef au Jus, Kidney Pudding, Broiled Tomato
Filet Mignon, Pera Palast Hotel
Boiled Fresh Ox Tongue, Sauce Piquant, Rissoto
Tenderloin of Pork, Cauliflower Pre-vert, Anna Potatoes
Cold: Filet of Beef, Mexican Style

Hawaiian Dishes

Special Malolo Poi Cocktail — Kamana Pakaai, Poi, Roast Sweet Potatoes

POULTRY

Fried Chicken a la Maryland
Roast Long Island Duckling, Sauce Rouennaise, Orange Salad

FROM THE GRILL (10 Minutes)

Pork Chops, Naturel — Veal Steak, Major domo

VEGETABLES

Cauliflower, Cream Sauce — Stewed Corn, Mexican — Fried Egg Plant
Baked Italian Squash, au Jus — New Wax Beans — Boiled Rice
Potatoes: Boiled — Baked — Mashed — Anna

SALADS

Heart of Lettuce, Kirghis Dressing — Cucumber Salad

"A BIT OF SWEET MAKES THE MEAL COMPLETE"

Peach Pie — Neapolitan Ice Cream
Cabinet Pudding, Fruit Sauce — Plain or Fruit Jello
Assorted Cakes — Petits-fours
Cheese: Gorgonzola — Philadelphia Cream — Roquefort — Brie
Liederkrantz — Edam — Imported and Domestic Swiss
Neufchatel — Oregon Cream — Camembert
Coffee — Tea
Fresh Fruit
Salted Almonds — Assorted Nuts — After Dinner Mints

DEMI TASSE SERVED IN THE LOUNGE AND SMOKING ROOM

The sumptuous dinner menu, the Clutterbuck.

BOOK TEN

GAEL

She was tall and slender almost to the point of being thin. Her hair was blonde. Not light or dark blonde, but that lovely in-between colour that so few women have naturally, and that hair stylists call honey blonde. She wore it combed back from her forehead and parted in the centre so that it fell evenly on either side of her face. She had a warm, generous mouth which, when parted, showed even white teeth. Her nose was slightly large for the face in which it was set, but it was very straight. Long ago she had learned to hold her head high and show it off, and its fine line helped to set the character of the face itself. But it was the eyes that took and held Wildman's immediate attention. They were very large and seemed to glow with a passionate joy of life. In the flickering light of the bar candles, Wildman could not make out their colour. Later he discovered that they were dark green, flecked with gold. They were the kind of eyes that few women have, the kind that, cleverly used, can captivate a man. They were the kind of eyes that a man might see, briefly, in passing and afterwards remember nothing of their owner, not the colour of her hair, not the clothes she was wearing, not how tall she was. Nothing. Nada. Just the eyes.

The woman had a light, belted, corduroy jacket slung across her shoulders. She wore a khaki shirt, its sleeves rolled to reveal slim brown arms ending in small but capable-looking hands. Around her neck was a dark green silk scarf. There was no jewellery. A pair of light brown corduroy trousers were belted at her waist with a narrow leather belt, and their lower ends were tucked into dark brown, knee-high leather boots. The upper half of the boots glowed with the sheen of well cared for, high quality leather. The lower half were encrusted with the slime and filth of the alley and from them, faintly, the sickly smell of buffalo dung wafted up to Wildman's nostrils.

Slowly and sadly sinking into ruin, the old Clutterbuck Hotel in Varanasi, where Wildman and Pasang spent a memorable night on their way north.

Wildman was trying to control his laughter and was having great difficulty. The fact that he was half drunk did not help. But the problem was that he could not decide which was funnier. The way the fat bartender slid like a dying whale over the edge of the bar and down to the floor. Or the rolling waves of thunder that emanated from his prostrate figure. But then the problem was suddenly thrust out of his mind by something else…the sudden, sobering realisation of the identity of the person standing in front of him, staring at him. Oh God. Oh no. It can't be. Oh yes. It has to be. A young white woman in a place like the Clutterbuck in the middle of the night? Christ, it couldn't be anyone else. Well, let's find out. Let's see if she speaks the Queen's English. He swung around towards her on the bar stool, gave her what he imagined was his most devastating smile, held up the bottle of Glenlivet and said, "Well, hi there. And what about a little drinkypoo?"

The young woman, arms still folded, remained standing exactly where she was and her gaze on Wildman did not waver. Wildman, his devastating smile slowly beginning to freeze at the corners, raised his eyebrows a fraction, shook his head from side to side and said, "No drinkypoo then?"

Afterwards, Wildman realised that he had made a very bad start with the young woman. He should have looked more carefully at her face before he spoke. The lighting in the bar was poor, of course. But perhaps if he had looked closer he would have seen that the look there was far from friendly. Her mouth was set in a thin, tight line, her chin was thrust out and her eyes blazed with anger. Then she spoke.

"You bastard. You rotten bastard. I knew it. I knew it all along. I knew exactly what you were going to be like the minute my grandfather told me about you. A professional adventurer, yes? A professional crook is more like it."

"Now look here, young lady, firstly I'll have you know...."

"No. You look here. You listen to me, do you hear me? Shut up and listen."

She unfolded her arms and placed her hands on her hips and leaned forward.

"I waited for you at the Taj Hotel for three days. You didn't show up. I've been waiting for you at the Varanasi Sheraton for three days. Again you do not show up. Nor, obviously, do you have any intention of showing up. You've taken my grandfather's money, you've been pussyfooting across India and this," with a wave of her hand at the ancient bar and its surroundings, "is how you are spending your time. And my grandfather's money."

"My dear young lady, the fact is…"

Ignoring his attempt to explain, she continued. "Right, I'll tell you what the score is. At six-tomorrow morning you are going to be outside this hotel, packed and ready to go. I am going with you. I am going to see that my grandfather's wishes are carried out, and, matey, that he gets what he paid you for. If you are not ready tomorrow morning at exactly six, regardless of what excuse you try to trump up, by six thirty I'll have the police here and I'll file charges of grand theft against you. I'll have you held until my lawyers fly in and then I'll see you thrown into an Indian jail for the rest of your miserable life. Have you got that? Six. Or else."

She whirled around and, before Wildman could say a word, was out of the bar and gone. He watched her as she went through the door and then turned back to the bar. So that was the old man's granddaughter. Well, he had to grant her one thing, that she had to have something going for her, by gad, to have been able to find him down at the jolly old Clutterbuck. Well then. Have to talk to her about that later. Very much later. So she thinks that she is going to the climb on the jolly old bandwagon and drive up the jolly old road to Nepal with me, does she? At jolly old six o'clock in the morning? Ho ho ho. Six o'clock my foot. Have to be up a lot earlier than that to catch Wildman's bandwagon. Yes sir. Five o'clock or maybe even four. Six o'clock? Ha! By six he and Pasang would be fifty miles up the road and she could stand on her hands and scream her bloody little head off and a lot of good it would do her.

As for reporting him to him to the police and charging him with grand theft? In India? Well, that was the funniest thing he had heard of in years. Funnier even then the mighty snores thundering up from behind the bar. Wildman began to chuckle again. Grand theft? The police would be delighted. Of course, madam. Immediately. At once. We are more than thee happy to assist thee you. They would soak her for all the cash she had—to assist in thee investigation, madam, to pay thee contacts and that sort of thing, isn't it madam—conduct an "immediate investigation" that would go on for days and then, in the mysterious way that can only be managed in the mysterious East, mysteriously disappear. Oh yes indeed. Grand theft. Now that was really funny.

Wildman suddenly began to feel tired. It had been a long day and perhaps a little sleep might be in order. He was thinking about this when he felt a little draft of air pass over the back of his neck. He whirled around. The bar door was open and Pasang was standing just inside it, barely seen in the dim light of the bar's dying candles.

" Pasang, everything OK?"

The road to the Clutterbuck Hotel, the refuse strewn and filthy lane down which Gael struggled at night, knee deep in mud, to find Wildman.

"Yes *sahib*. Everything OK. About another two hours to finish job. Maybe three. Maybe good thing to get some sleep, *sahib*. Start early in morning?"

"Pasang, that is a good suggestion. And you? What about you?"

"I will stay up and watch those two out there and when they have finished I will pay them and get rid of them and sleep in the Jeep. No problem *sahib*."

"All right then, Pasang. Here's what we'll do. We'll get an early start. I'll come down and wake you at four and we'll head straight out. We'll get something to eat up the road. Good thing to get out of the city while the traffic is light. OK?"

"Very good *sahib*. I will also get more gasoline tonight, if you wish. I have enough money."

"Good thing, Pasang. Then we'll have no delay in the morning."

"Very good *sahib*. Goodnight then. Until the morning."

Like a shadow—God that man could move quietly—Pasang was gone. Wildman picked up the bottle of Glenlivet and looked at it. Three-quarters empty. Ah well. A better way of looking at it was one quarter full. He stood up with the bottle in his hand and was just about to leave the bar when a particularly loud snore reminded him that he had a small favour to bestow on his drinking companion of the evening. He opened his money belt, pulled out five one-hundred-dollar bills, folded them, and, going back behind the bar, leaned over the sleeping figure and stuffed the little wad into the front of his shirt.

Then he left the bar, climbed the stairs to room number 5, unlocked the door and entered the room. Locking the door behind him, he felt his way in the dark to the room's single large window, unlatched it and opened a pair of heavy wooden shutters to allow in some air and a little light. He then went to the wooden-framed rope bed the room provided, picked it up and jammed it tight against the door. The he lay down on it, fully clothed, pulled the single thin cotton blanket with which the bed was adorned over himself, stretched and, having set his in-built alarm to wake him up at precisely five minutes to four, eased himself into sleep with two last thoughts. One, that he hoped that the little rope mattress bed did not have bed bugs. And two, that anger did marvellous things to a woman's eyes. Especially when they were very beautiful eyes in the first place.

Just before he closed his eyes he noticed the moon. The foul air of the city, mostly smoke from the hundreds of body-burning *ghat*s along the river, yellowed its light and weakened it. But it was still strong enough to band the dusty floor of the old, high ceiling room with the parallel shadows of the thick iron bars set in the window frame.

At three minutes to four Wildman opened one eye and looked up at the ceiling. He opened the other and remained perfectly motionless until he had registered everything around him. The sounds. The light. The smells. It was a habit that a dangerous life had taught him. Sleep soundlessly and without moving. Wake without moving. Wait, look, smell, listen. And then move. Satisfied with what he saw and heard—the distant crowing of cocks, a faraway blare from a loudspeaker somewhere down in the city, the twittering of a few early rising birds from the compound outside—he swung his body off the bed, stood up and stretched.

The air was cold and he shivered. The thin blanket had not kept him warm and he swung his arms around a few times to get his circulation going. Then he picked up the blanket from where it had fallen on the floor, laid it on the bed, pushed the bed away from the door and unlocked it. Putting his head out carefully, he looked up and down the darkened corridor that led to other rooms, turned, had a last look around to make sure he had left nothing, stepped quietly into the corridor, closed and locked the door and made his way downstairs to the lobby.

The old hotel was cold and dark and the ancient wooden stairs creaked and groaned under his feet. In the lobby, all was silent. He leaned over the table that served for a reception desk, hung the key on the nail marked 5, turned and crossed the lobby to the front door and put his hand against its heavy wooden panels and pushed. Nothing happened. He pushed again and as he did so something large and metallic rattled down in the region of the door's handles. He bent over and peered down in the dim light of the lobby. Ringed through the solid brass handles of the door, locking them together and making the door impossible to open, was a huge brass padlock.

Wildman swore and turned towards the reception table. He walked up to it and looked at the wooden panel behind it. There was one key, the key to room number 5 that he had just hung there. He turned and looked at the door again and, walking over, felt it with his hands. It was old, cracked and warped. Its paint hung in curling flakes, and all around the frame there was a gap almost big enough to get one's fingers through. But in spite of its age and general decrepitude, the door, built in better days, built to be the front door of a proud old British hotel, was as solid as if it had been made of steel.

Wildman stood looking at the door and wondering where the hell he would find the day clerk who had signed him in. Signed him in? Well, let him in, when he arrived. The bugger probably slept miles away in the bloody city. And then, thinking of him, the man's words came back to him and he ran them through his mind the robot-like way the clerk had recited them. 'Five rupees day no food four days twenty rupees advance also five rupees cleaning room deposit refundable good food my cousin Kashmiri Eating House door closed midnight open seven.'

That was it, dammit. Door closed midnight, open seven. Not the bloody eating house door. The bloody hotel door. And then Wildman remembered how once before when he had run into the quaint Indian custom of locking hotel doors at night. A hotel up in Halduwani, in northern Utter Pradesh, years ago, after a neat little border crossing that he had made with a wealthy client who had an allergy to immigration officials. He and the man had tried to leave the hotel at two in the morning to catch a train south and had run into the same problem; locked doors. The reason behind the practice was simple. It was to prevent Indian hotel guests—the kind who used small, cheap hotels—from leaving with the furniture. Steel-barred windows on the guest rooms were also part of it.

<<>>

Damn. Wildman swore again. He remembered that last time and how he had spent two hours trying to get out and in the end had given up and had had to wait until broad daylight and the arrival of the hotel staff.

And the Clutterbuck? His mind had a quick flash of the window of his room and the massive bars that enclosed it. Damn, again. But there had to be a way out, somewhere, somehow. A window left unbarred, a kitchen door, something. If there was, then he had to find it. Even if it took an hour. He glanced quickly at his watch and as he did so he remembered the words of the fiery-eyed young woman in the bar and her threat. Six o'clock or else. Or else? The police, she had said. Better get moving. He had little fear of the police under normal circumstances. They were easy to deal with if one knew the ropes, which meant, simply, bundles of large-denomination rupee bills changing hands, quickly, with no questions asked. . But if the young woman was serious about her threat and if she was allowed to carry it out?

Wildman could handle the police and he could also handle, or later make up for, a brief delay. But how far out did Vask's tentacles reach, where the Varanasi police were concerned? If a report were to be made by her and if the police decided to act on it—and with foreigners involved they certainly would, because foreigners meant money, big money in bribes—Wildman suspected that in a police investigative team might well be one that was on Vask's payroll, or at least know of him and his rewards system. Even if no one in an investigative group was connected with Vask, or knew of him and his system, the word of an investigation involving foreigners would quickly go out. Vask would pick it up just as quickly and that would put him on their trail again. No. Whatever happened he had to get out of the hotel, fast, and get going up the road before, among other things, that fiery-eyed female with her holier-than-thou need to protect her old grandfather got back to the dear old Clutterbuck.

Wildman bounded up the stairs to the second floor and the corridor that led to room, number 5. The corridor had ten doors set in it, all similar to the door to his bedroom and all, presumably, leading to other bedrooms. He started at the first, number 1, and tried the handle. A gentle push and the door swung inward. The room was empty, derelict. Cobwebs laced the window frame between broken wooden shutters and a rat scurried through the dust. But the window nevertheless was firmly barred, like the window of his own room. He tried the next room, number 2. The same. Room 3, locked. He put his shoulder against the door and pushed. He felt the lock going and pushed harder. Something splintered and he lunged forward. A storage room. Thick dust, old chairs, tables with broken legs, broken kitchenware, lumber. And another barred window. He left and tried the next room. number 4. Locked. He put his shoulder against the door and pushed. The door was firm. Something propped against it? He put his ear to the door and listened. Soft breathing. Someone sleeping with the bed set hard against the door. A guest. A knowing guest who, like himself, did not trust old hotel room locks. He put his eye to the keyhole and peered through. Dimly against the dawn light he saw the room's window, heavily barred, as he had expected.

The dawn light! Darn. He looked at his watch. Fifteen minutes before five. Had he really spent forty-five minutes searching for a way out? Damn. He turned and ran lightly to the end of the corridor. There was another floor. He dashed up another flight of stairs. Ten more rooms. Some locked. Some open. Two with men sleeping in them, furniture jammed against the doors.

He ran downstairs through the reception area and into what at one time must have been the kitchens. Rusting iron-cooking ranges, brass taps green with age and disuse, old marble basins streaked with grime. Dust, debris, a smell of decay and two big wooden back doors leading into a yard, both solidly barricaded with heavy wooden planks secured by thick nails driven deep into the frameworks. Wildman cursed and ran back into the lobby. The barman. Dammit, why did he not think of him earlier?

He ran to the bar, opened the door and dashed in. But the big man was gone and all that there was to mark his passing—or his presence of the night before—was a dead soldier, the Captain Morgan rum bottle, forlorn on the floor behind the bar.

Pasang! He would be outside, waiting for him. Dammit, he had to attract him in some way. Maybe Pasang could find a crowbar or something and get to work on that front door. Or use his kukri on one of the panels and cut the lock out.

He ran back into the kitchen and began a steady pounding on the planks that sealed one of the kitchen doors. Stopping, he listened and then started again. His Rolex caught his eyes as he pounded on the old but solid wood. Damn. Another thirty minutes gone. Five fifteen.

He stopped and listened again. Silence. Dammit Pasang, where are you. You know that you were supposed to meet me at four. But no. That's not quite true, Wildman, old chap. You were supposed to meet him at four, not the other way around. And Pasang, being the reliable man that he is, is now waiting for you to appear in the back compound where the Jeep is and is not going to leave the Jeep—especially as it is getting lighter by the minute—until you appear. Christ!

Wildman turned and ran back up the stairs to his room. He lunged against the door. Locked, dammit. He ran back down, grabbed the key off the number 5 nail and ran back up the stairs again. A quick twist in the lock, the door slammed back and he was in the room, now bright with daylight. He ran to the window and looked out and down. Patches of half dead grass gleamed wet from the night's dew and the few skeletal trees dripped disconsolately. He jammed his face against the bars in an effort to see downwards and back towards the rear of the hotel, where the Jeep was. But the jutting edge of the rear wall cut off his view. He looked at his watch again and, wrenching himself away from the window, turned and raced for the door and half way through it, one foot in the corridor and one foot still in the bedroom, he collided head on with Pasang.

"Pasang!"

"Good morning, *sahib*."

The little Sherpa stood looking up at him, a half expectant smile on his hard, flat-cheeked face that said good morning indeed, *sahib*, and why at almost six o'clock are we still running around the hotel when we are supposed to be out of here at four?"

"Pasang, how did you get in?"

"I, *sahib*?"

"Yes. Into the hotel?"

"Ah. Up your pipe, *sahib*."

"I beg your pardon, Pasang?"

"Sorry *sahib*. Poor English. I mean, I meant, up thee pipe."

"The pipe? For God's sake, Pasang…"

"The drain pipe, *sahib*. To the roof. Across the roof and in through the what do you call it, sky lift, sky..."

"A skylight?"

"Yes *sahib*, the skylight."

"Then for God's sake let's get out of here the same way. And pronto, right now, if you know what I mean. Another ten minutes and that damned..."

"Damned what, *sahib*?"

"I mean that damned, er, traffic, will, er, be building up. Let's go, let's go. Now!"

Pasang turned and ran down the corridor. From its end he took the second flight of stairs to the third floor. From there he raced down the third floor corridor and where it came to an end stopped and pointed upwards.

"There, *sahib*. Way out. After you, *sahib*."

Wildman looked up. In the ceiling of the corridor was a small trapdoor. He did not hesitate. He leaped upwards, grabbed the edge of the opening and pulled himself up and through. In a second Pasang had joined him and together they made their way through a dark and gloomy attic to a skylight set in a sloping wall. Newly smashed glass indicated that Pasang had used his *kukri* to break and lever it off its hinges. Wildman eased himself through, ran to the edge of the flat roof and looked over it. There was a single iron drainpipe, leading downwards. It looked firm. He swung himself over, grabbed the pipe and, with his elbows thrust against the wall and his feet spread wide for balance, lowered himself to the ground. Pasang, catlike, landed with a thump beside him and together they raced around a corner to where the Jeep was parked. Parked and waiting, its rear piled high with luggage that included eight large, red velvet suitcases, assorted boxes and bags and a large, monogrammed, red leather makeup case. In its front, firmly ensconced and calmly polishing her nails, sat Lord Carew's honey-haired granddaughter.

<<>>

She gave Wildman the briefest of glances, was about to say something and then saw Pasang. Instantly her face broke into a dazzling smile, she swung two long and shapely legs out of the vehicle and, standing up, took both of his hands in hers and said, "Pasang. How nice to see you after all this time. And how are you?"

If Pasang was surprised at finding the woman there, he did not show it. Instead he raised his hands, bowed, touched both of his hands to his forehead and murmured, "Oh, greetings, *memsahib*. How happy I am to see you. How wonderful to find you here and for you to find us. Now you will travel with us, yes?"

For an answer the young woman swung herself back into the front of the Jeep and gave Wildman a cold, imperious look.

"Of course, Pasang," she said, and promptly turned her attention back to her nails.

<<>>

It was three hours later and they were sixty miles up the road from Varanasi. Wildman, angry at the young woman and the way she had judged him, angry at himself, angry at the world in general, drove like a man possessed. He completely ignored his female companion and spoke only once, to Pasang, to tell him to keep an eye on the rear-view mirror. For her part she stared straight ahead and, if his high speed driving made her nervous, she did not show it. Just after nine he pulled in at a small wayside teahouse. He cut the engine, got out, said, "Tea," to Pasang and, completely ignoring the young woman, walked into the teahouse and left her sitting in the Jeep. But if he thought to leave her tealess in the Jeep, he had reckoned without Pasang and the little Sherpa's good manners. Plus the fact that there was already—probably due to visits by the young woman to Lord Carew's estate while Pasang worked there—an established relationship between he and the young woman. Pasang scrambled over the driver's seat of the Jeep, got out and turning, bowed courteously.

"Would you like some tea, *memsahib*? I can bring you some if you wish? Or you can come with me into the teahouse?"

"Why, thank you, Pasang. I think I'll come with you."

Pasang led the way into the teahouse and seated her next to Wildman. He quietly ordered tea for her and then went back to the Jeep.

Wildman sat and tried not to look at the young woman. When a grinning urchin had brought the tea and they had both thanked him, simultaneously, he sensed the situation as being rather ridiculous to the point where someone was going to have to break the ice, if only as a prelude to his telling her about Vask. He had to do that soon, so that he could clarify the situation he was in, and its dangers, and persuade her to leave. He turned to her and spoke. "OK, we'd better talk. Right?"

Her answer was to tip her head back almost imperceptibly and look him directly in the face. Now, in the daylight, he saw the real colour of her eyes; a deep green, almost the emerald green of the Eye itself, but flecked with gold. She raised one perfect eyebrow approximately a tenth of an inch and, her gaze level and unflinching, waited for him to speak. When she said nothing he said, "So, no talkee?"

After he'd said it he thought, damn, that's too much like the 'no drinkypoo' of the night before. He immediately switched to another tack.

"OK. There are certain things that you have to know. Alright?"

The level, unflinching remained directed at him and Wildman thought to himself, there was ice behind those eyes.

"OK. I'll start at the beginning and I'll try and make it as brief as possible."

He looked around carefully to make sure that no one was within earshot and then leaned forward and whispered, "The mission is to get the Eye, your grandfather's emerald, back to the temple of the Yellow God in Nepal. Right? You know about this, yes. Your grandfather told you about it?"

She must have looked at him for half a minute before she replied. But when she did the reply was in the form of a question and the tone of her voice was such that any hope that Wildman had of coming to an understanding with her immediately flew out the window.

"Yes?"

Gritting his teeth in the face of what was close to a deliberate snub, Wildman forced himself to continue. He told her about Vask. He told her what kind of a person the man was, the organization that he controlled and the lengths to which he was prepared to go to try and get the Eye. He watched her as he spoke and slowly, as his story unfolded and as he saw the look of incredulity on her face, one that slowly turned to scorn, his heart began sink. When he had finished she sat silently. Her 'yes', when he had started, was it. That was all he got. One word. Yes. And now, nothing. But her face told him the rest. It wore a look of total disbelief. Worse, her look and the way she tipped her head sideways conveyed to him something that looked almost like maternal pity. So that when he came to the point where he was going to tell her about their capture, and Pasang's torture, and their escape, and Little Gunga, he thought, damn, forget about it, so far the whole story has gone down like a lead balloon.

"You don't believe a bloody word of it, do you?"

For an answer she stood up, took three one rupee bills from a pocket in her khaki shirt, laid them on the table, walked back to the Jeep, got in and silently resumed her seat in the front. Wildman, angry before but now fuming with frustration waved Pasang into the Jeep and then climbed in himself. He glanced at his Rolex—the time was nine-thirty—fired the engine, rammed the gear lever to first, floored the throttle and roared out on to the highway.

<<>>

Back in the city of Varanasi the door of a sleazy tenement building opened and a man emerged. He blinked in the morning, sun, scratched his head, and scratched his crotch. Then, before going to work at the miserable Clutterbuck, where he was employed as receptionist, chief clerk, accountant, morning door opener and evening locker-upper, headed for his favourite teashop, the Kashmiri Eating House. Being owned by his cousin, he could get a cup of tea there at a cut-price rate. He might even have a small cake with his tea this morning, he thought, and spend a little of yesterday's windfall. Stupid foreigners. They never asked. Just dug in their pockets and paid. Five rupees a day. Instead of three, the regular rate. Well, he'd wait and see if the hotel owners came around while the American was still there. If they did he would have to tell them that he forget to register the American and hand over the difference between four days at three rupees a day and four days at the five that he had collected. If they did not, he had made a windfall. Yes, a small cake this morning with the tea would be very nice. Maybe even two cups of tea. And what would be even nicer would be when he told his smart cousin with his big restaurant and his fancy waiters how he had put one over on a stupid *feringhee* and made himself a very nice little profit. Oh yes, he would enjoy seeing his cousin's face when he told him that.

<<>>

Ten minutes later he entered the restaurant and sat down. A waiter hovered as with a wave of his hand he ordered tea with milk and sugar, and a large raisin cake. The waiter sped away and gave the order to the cook and the restaurant owner, seeing who it was who had made the order and sensing something unusual in it—tea *and* a cake this morning—sauntered slowly over to the table and, with a knowing smile, sat down.

The little clerk enjoyed his moment. He sipped his tea and slowly, so that he would not finish it too soon, munched on the cake. As he did so he watched his cousin's face and inwardly, maliciously, smiled at the man's visibly impatient curiosity. When there was nothing but crumbs left on his plate he felt that he might be overdoing it if he waited any longer. So, leaning forward, a look of gloating satisfaction on his pallid face, he told his cousin all about his cleverness and how he had put one over on, not just an ordinary hotel guest, but an American hotel guest, one with a Jeep and a Nepalese manservant.

As he happily related his little tale of success, his cousin, never one to ignore a story that involved money, listed intently. Then slowly the cousin's his face lost colour. The fat clerk, repeating the story of his incredible business acumen a second time was so enjoying himself that he noticed nothing until his table companion suddenly leapt to his feet and thrusting his face within an inch of his glared at him and hissed, "You imbecile. You idiot. You turd-eating fool," and with a shout to his head waiter to watch the cash drawer, ran out of the restaurant, down the street and around the corner to a tailor's shop. A tailor who was a cousin. A cousin with a phone.

<<>>

Vask's convoy had made its second stop for fuel when the news reached him. It had been relayed three times and the last caller had spread it by phone to five roadside fuel stations, three sub-police stations and the managers of two roadside bus stations. In one of the fuel stations the manager was just putting the phone down when, to his delight, Vask's three Jeeps drove in and the Raja himself got out and walked into his office.

When the excited fuel station manager babbled his information at him Vask remained outwardly calm. But inside he seethed with renewed intent. The Clutterbuck Hotel in Varanasi? He had never heard of it. But that did not matter. What mattered now was that they were out of Varanasi and somewhere north of it and on the road to the Nepal border. The question was, which road?

He walked back to his Jeep and pulled a map out of the glove compartment. Taking it back to the fuel station office, he spread it on the manager's table and began to study it. The direct route to Nepal out of Varanasi was not north, but northeast. Northeast up the main highway via the cities of Chausa, Dumroan and Arrah. Then across the Gagra river at Bankipore, north to Muzaffarpur and then north again through Kantai, Kesaryia, Motihari and Segauli, to the border town of Raxaul.

Raxaul lay on the Indo-Nepal border, and if Wildman managed to get across the border before Vask could cut him off, that would compound the problem of stopping him. True, he could pursue him across the border. But the other side was the Kingdom of Nepal and, while he did have some contacts there on whom he could depend, his main network pretty much phased itself out at the international line. North of the border it still operated, but not as well as in India. Once across the international line the net thinned, and Vask knew that if Wildman got across the border and he, Vask, was forced to pursue him into Nepal, then Wildman's chances of getting away would be greatly enhanced. No. He had to be stopped before he got to the border and the way to do this was to find out which route he was taking to Nepal—the direct route, or another one—keep after him, catch up with him and then deal with him.

Vask delved in the front of his shirt and pulled out a large, flat folder. From it he extracted a handful of rupee bills and, counting them, laid them on the table. The fuel station manager, licking his lips, looked at the money, two thousand rupees, for him a fortune. With a heavy look, Vask told the manager that one thousand was his reward for passing on the information and the other thousand was for phone calls. He was to start at once and call every gasoline station north and northeast of Varanasi. He was to direct all return calls to a central number in Varanasi. Vask wrote down the number. There would be another thousand rupees for him if his work produced results, in other words if one of the gasoline stations that he alerted reported back positive information on the movements of the American and his servant.

Vask left the gasoline station, got in his Jeep, waved to his other vehicles to follow him and continued up the road towards Varanasi. Inwardly his anger seethed. But it was tempered now to some extent. His network was working. Money talked and, as long as there was greed and avarice in the land, it would produce results. And greed was eternal. Yes, mister Wildman, he said to himself. I am on your trail. I am catching up. This time there will be no mistakes. This time we will not let that little monkey you call a friend even get near me. Little brother Gunga will deal with him very quickly. No. Slowly would be much better. And if my guess is right and you really do care for that brown-faced nothing, then I'll soon have to you talking. Talking? By the gods I'll have you eating out of my hand by the time Gunga is finished with him. And the Eye will be mine and with it all that I have worked so hard for, all that I truly deserve, after so many years of waiting. Yes, I'm after you mister wild person, or whatever your name is. Let's see if one *feringhee* and one stupid Nepali nothing can outrun the network of the Raja Vask!

BOOK ELEVEN

HIDE AND SEEK

Her hair was beginning to mat with the thick brown dust that poured into the Jeep every time they were forced off the road by a truck, or by a car playing chicken, or by a line of wandering rickshaws, or a herd of buffalo, or bullocks, or cows. Or a group of people walking down the centre of the road going to market. Or stray dogs. Or goats. Or pigs. Or supine bodies lying in the centre of the highway. People asleep? Unconscious? Dead? Who knew? Wildman wondered, who cared?

The tan was gone, layered with a patina of Indian dirt and the freshly laundered and carefully pressed clothes of the morning were wrinkled and dirty and, in places where no lady should show it, sweat-stained. And she was hungry. Goddamit, she was hungry. It was now three in the afternoon. Too early to get anything to eat at the hotel, she had had one cup of tea since the night before and her stomach was beginning to groan. And the moron who was driving showed absolutely no inclination to stop. Goddamit, he would probably keep on until midnight unless someone did something or said something. But she was not going to. No siree. That was just what the big galah was waiting for. 'Excuse me, but do you think we could stop for some food,' was obviously just what he was waiting to hear. He would give her a pitiful, condescending look, raise his eyes to heaven, mutter something about women and then just keep driving. No. She would not give him that satisfaction. Not if she were to die of starvation between here and Nepal. Bloody macho twit and his ridiculous story. And this was the man her grandfather had picked to carry the Eye, that priceless jewel and all that it meant to the old man, to Nepal? Stone the bloody crows. What a choice. But then, the old man was getting on in years and, much as she loved him, she had to admit the possibility of a little senility creeping in. God, if only she had been there. Yes indeed, matey. She would quickly have seen through his caper, exposed his con game and put the cops on to him. Bet that would have made him run for cover. And what had the old man told her he was willing to pay him for the mission? Tie me kangaroo down...a bloody fortune!

Well, she would do what she could. The old man had been good to her. She owed him a lot. As well as which she was very fond of him. She would do what she could; do her damnedest in fact, to see that the Eye got to the temple. She would watch mister macho man, see where he kept the jewel, take it while he slept—maybe with Pasang's help—and then split, up and away, rent another Jeep, or get on a train or a plane or something and get up to Kathmandu on her own. Maybe with Pasang. But...something was beginning to puzzle her. She had known the little Sherpa for more than fifteen years, ever since he became a permanent member of the establishment of Himalaya House. The old man really trusted him and she had always looked forward to seeing him when she visited. Indeed, having him there helped to brighten the brooding atmosphere created by the creepy Ghose.

And now there was something very odd going on. She had watched him when he was with Wildman, when they were together, driving, talking, working, and filling the Jeep with gasoline. And the little man seemed to like the damned crook. Like him? He even seemed to have an unusual respect for him! And she knew that in spite of his lack of education and his status as a servant in the house of her grandfather and his peasant background, that Pasang was above all things a first class judge of character. Odd. Very odd indeed. In the meantime, with her stomach crying out for food, she wondered if there was some way that she could indicate to Pasang, without Wildman's noticing it, that she was bloody hungry and that unless she got something to eat soon she was probably going to faint.

They stopped at last at a combined gasoline station and roadside-eating house. The place was crowded with parked trucks, truck drivers eating and drinking tea and locals hurrying back and forth. Because of the crowd they were not able to park the Jeep close to the restaurant and so Pasang elected to stay with it while they ate. Wildman promised to send him some food from the restaurant and, leaving the Jeep and followed by Gael, led the way into the interior of the flyblown eating house and sat down at a small metal table covered with a greasy, black plastic sheet. He had not waited for her nor asked her to join him and she was fuming as she lowered herself on to a wooden bench opposite him and waited for a waiter to appear. Wildman saw this and thought to himself, maybe if I goad her, make her even madder than she obviously is—if that is possible—she will start thinking about throwing in the towel and heading back to down under. He decided to try it and leaning forward, picked up a small piece of paper, half a page torn out of a child's copybook, from the table in front of him. He frowned, raised his eyebrows and pretended to read.

"My goodness, guess what they have on the menu today. Just look at this. For an aperitif, Canadian smoked salmon with Russian black bread. For the entrée, beef Wellington, swimming in a rich brown gravy and straight from the expert hands of the master chef in the kitchen. New potatoes from the auld sod—they must mean Ireland, where my ancestors come from—garnished with mint sauce and set in little beds of green peas. Wow! And for desert, my goodness, I never would have believed it in a place like this...bomb Alaska with a meringue topping. Now that's yummy. Oh, and look here, look at what's to drink...ice cold, imported Fosters lager, straight from Sydney in the land of the wombat and the wallaby Now, if that doesn't warm your happy little down under heart, what would?"

She sat and scowled at him and it took a tremendous effort of will power for her to hold back what she wanted to say to him. She was tired, she was dirty, she was bloody hungry and the bastard knew it and was using it to goad her. To what end? Oh, that was obvious. 'Dear Mr. Wildman, I really think that I have had enough and, if it's OK with you, I'll just drop off at the next bus stop and head home with my tail between my legs.' Oh yes indeed. That's exactly what you want, isn't it. Well, not on your bloody life Mr. Crookman. I'll stay with you if I have to go without a bath and a decent meal for a week. I'll..."

"Not interested in the beef welliwoo? Don't drink beer? Not even Fosters loverly ice-cold lager? Nope? Then what about some nice rice and curried vegetables, eh?"

She might have gone for him just then and she started to look around for something large and heavy to throw at him, or hit him with. But at that moment a waiter appeared, all of six years of age, and, reaching up, started sliding plates of hot rice and curried vegetables and metal spoons on to the plastic covering. Wildman leaned over to him and, in perfect Urdu, told him to take another meal out to the man by the Jeep, the hillman with the big knife stuck in his belt with which, if the meal were not of ample proportions, and well cooked, he would lop off the waiter's head. The urchin grinned a half-frightened grin and sped away to get Pasang's meal.

Wildman watched Gael eat. She wolfed the food down like a starving Bulgarian and it was gone and she was finished long before him. She used the metal spoon the child waiter had given her to eat and when the food was gone used it again to scrape the metal plate clean. Quite an appetite for a frail young thing, Wildman said to himself. He wondered if she had other appetites. But then he caught the steely glint in her eyes, the touch of ice and decided, probably not. Well, maybe for someone else. But not for him. Not by a long chalk.

She waited until he was finished and, when he stood up, followed him out of the eating-house. Pasang was standing by the Jeep and something about his attitude made Wildman quicken his pace. When he reached the vehicle Wildman bent over the front tyre and from there, pretending to see something, whispered to Pasang to join him. Pasang knelt down beside him and peered intently at the tyre. "Something wrong, *sahib*. Two men in the gasoline station over there. Inside. See, through the window. They have been watching the Jeep since soon after we arrived. Not working. Waiting, I think, for something."

Wildman pretended to look at the front of the tyre, running his hand over its surface and so bringing his head around to the front of the vehicle. Across the road was the gasoline station yard and office. There were two pumps, one for gasoline and one for diesel, and behind them a small cement building with an office fronted by a large glass window. Through the window Wildman saw two men sitting at a table. They were not working, just sitting there, looking across the road towards the restaurant. He decided to test their reaction. He stood up and raising his head looked directly across the road at the gasoline station office. Immediately both men bent over and looked intently down at papers on the table in front of them.

Moving casually, pretending not to hurry, Wildman motioned Pasang to get into the Jeep and turned to look for Gael. She was gone. He swore.

"Pasang, where did the *memsahib* go, dammit?"

"Behind restaurant, *sahib*, to peepee."

Bloody woman. Come on, hurry up. He waited another three minutes and when there was no sign of her told Pasang to stay with the Jeep and went to look for her. He met her coming out from behind the eating-house, walking slowly, trying to run a comb through her matted hair.

Wildman turned and walked quickly back towards the Jeep. She followed him slowly, irritatingly slowly and when she got to the Jeep he was already in and had the engine started. "Goddamit, come on. Hurry. Don't you understand the word hurry?"

She climbed in the Jeep and turned on him in a temper. "As a matter of fact, yes, I do understand the word hurry. I know for instance that if one hurries it does not take seven days to get from Bombay to Varanasi. I also know…"

But Wildman was paying not the slightest attention to her. Swinging the Jeep out onto the road he was watching the two men in the station

Heavily overloaded trucks on the Indian highways, and the consequences of this illegal practice. These were some of the hazards Wildman faced in his race for the Nepal border.

office out of the corner of his eye. They waited until he was up on to the hardtop and pulling away. Then one of them reached for a phone on the table in front of him.

"I also know, sir, that when one makes an agreement..."

"Shut up. Do you hear me?"

Her eyes blazed and her lips drew back over her teeth.

"What did you say to me? Did I hear you say...."

"That's right. I said shut up. And I meant it. Pasang?"

"Yes *sahib*?"

"Get back and clean that rear window. If you can't clean it cut a hole in it. Then sit where you can watch the road behind. Don't take your eyes off it. Any sign of anything unusual tell me immediately. Even if you are not sure what it is. Watch out for Jeeps. Vask had Jeeps, didn't he?"

"Yes *sahib*. Grey ones. At the house where they took us."

"Good, Pasang. Then that is what we will be watching for. The minute you see anything like a grey Jeep you tell me, OK?"

"Very good *sahib*. Will do."

Wildman heard Pasang scrambling over the suitcases in the back, heard him scuffling at the rear window. Then he heard the swish as the *kukri* came out of its scabbard, followed by a rasping sound as Pasang cut a view hole in the plastic of the rear window, one that would give him the visibility that he needed.

In the front, Gael groaned to herself. God almighty. Here we go again. Cops and bloody robbers. And grown men playing at it. Who was Wildman trying to fool? Did he really think that she was actually going to fall for this bloody nonsense? Next thing she knew he'd be putting on a cowboy hat and leaning over and telling her in a Gary Cooper drawl that they were going to have to be careful they were not headed off at the pass, if y'all know what I mean, little missy. Jesus Christ. She ground her teeth in frustration. And in perplexity at Pasang. Wildman and his games she could understand. But the straight and serious and totally honest Pasang? What the hell was going on here?

Her frustration increased when, another twenty miles down the road, just after roaring through a town named Causa, Wildman swung the Jeep hard to the left, drove off the main road and raced off at high speed down a gravel-surfaced secondary road that went, as far as she could see, due west. But Nepal was north! Not west. She saw a sign that said Buxar and another that said Ahmadabad and then the thick brown dust pouring into the Jeep made her eyes water so badly that she saw little else. Later she remembered a river—a branch of the Ganges?—a town that might have been Ghazipur and then a series of small villages through which the Jeep roared at high speed over roads that were worse than anything she ever imagined. By evening they were still, as far as she could make out, heading west. Maybe a bit north. But definitely not due north. And the roads if anything got worse. As the sun began to redden the horizon to the west, Wildman allowed the speed of the Jeep to drop a little and when it was almost dark he leaned back and told Pasang to relax.

<<>>

Apart from his goading game with the menu back at the eating-house, and telling her to shut up when they got back in the Jeep, he had not spoken a word to her all day. If he had she would not have answered him. Her body ached. It felt as though it was bruised all over. She was filthy, caked in thick brown dust; her face was streaked with rivulets of brown mud where her sweat had plastered it on to her skin. It was hours since she had eaten and she was hungry again. She was also very tired, very angry and she wished the hell she knew where they were going and why. But she'd be damned if she was going to ask anyone. Well, maybe she would ask Pasang, if she could get him alone later.

They were off the beaten track. The roads that they drove on were little more than cart tracks. Some stretches were gravelled. But most were of hard, baked dirt from which the dust swirled upwards in thick, choking clouds. There were no eating-houses on these back roads, no human habitation other than tiny villages set far back in the fields.

Wildman kept driving until long after dark. He seemed to know where he was going. But he remained silent and if he did feel that he owed his lady passenger an explanation of what he was doing, he was not about to allow this to persuade him to speak to her. He knew that she did not believe his story of Vask and his thugs and that, as far as he was concerned, was that. If she was not going to believe him, then what was the point of telling her anything more, or of trying to convince her of the reality of the situation.

Suddenly, without warning, the road came to an end. It ran straight down a steep, sandy bank and into the waters of a broad, deep-looking river. Wildman slowed, turned off into a little grove of trees on the edge of the riverbank, stopped the Jeep and cut the engine. He looked at Gael abruptly, said, "We'll stay here tonight," got out and walked back towards where the road entered the river. He walked down the bank to the water's edge and looked upstream. About fifty yards away was a big, wooden ferryboat, big enough to carry a Jeep. It was moored to a tree by three thick, coconut-fibre ropes. There was no sign of life anywhere near, no boatmen. But Wildman did not expect any. River ferryboats in Indian seldom operate after dark. With sunset the ferrymen went home to their villages. They would be there in the morning, some time after dawn. Until then, they would sleep. And food? Well, they would just have to do without it tonight. Unless his hoity-toity passenger had something to eat in one of her five hundred bloody suitcases. And was willing to share it. Which was doubtful.

<<>>

He walked back to the Jeep. Pasang was standing talking to Gael. They both turned to him as he approached. "Don't happen to have any food in one of those splendid suitcases of yours, I suppose?"

"Of course I don't. Why?

"Why? Because if you did that's what we might have for dinner. As you don't, it's no din-dins tonight, my lovely. No food. Got it?"

He walked back to the Jeep, reached inside, pulled out the blankets that Pasang had rolled and packed behind the front seat, opened the roll and gave two to Pasang. Then he climbed into the Jeep, laid down across the two front seats, pulled the other two blankets over himself and stretched out. He saw her looking at him and in the dark he was not sure but he thought her mouth was open. He spoke to her without looking at her. "Well, you're going to sleep aren't you? Then kip down. On the ground somewhere. Anywhere. You've got a blanket or something to put over you, haven't you? We know you have no food. But surely you thought of bringing a blanket with you? Yes? Gets cold out here at night, you know."

With this sally, he leaned back, put his head down on the hard plastic cover of the front seat, pulled the two blankets up over his body and composed himself for sleep. Within three minutes he was far away, dreaming, against his will, and somewhat to his irritation, of a huge steaming platter of beef Wellington, new Irish potatoes and a tall, beaded, tankard of ice-cold, foaming, frothy, Fosters lager.

<<>>

Wildman slept well through the first part of the night. After midnight a pair of nightjars began to hunt around the Jeep, and the steady clicking of their beaks as they caught the insects that were their food interposed itself on his dreams and he dozed rather than slept. Just before dawn, a group of jackals burst into territorial calling on the far bank of the river, a chorus of yipping and wailing and barking that within minutes was picked up by another group, half a mile away. Wildman listened to the calls being passed down across the flat countryside and as they died away he saw, looking through the open doorway of the Jeep, the sky beginning to lighten in the east. At the same time he felt the Jeep shake, ever so slightly.

He was instantly alert, fully awake. Keeping his eyes half closed, he remained perfectly still and waited to see what had touched the Jeep and made it move. There it was again, a faint juddering, almost a trembling. It was not accompanied by any sound and he was about to attribute it to some passing animal, a jackal sniffing around for food, or a porcupine, when he heard a distinct groan.

He sat up slowly and, levering his body forward, craned his head and neck over the side of the vehicle and looked down. In the grey dawn light he saw the shape of a body, curled up against the front wheel of the Jeep, its head buried in its arms, legs drawn up to its chest. He looked closer. It was Gael.

She lay hunched against the front wheel. She was dressed in the filthy clothes in which she had travelled from Varanasi, and nothing else. No blanket. No sleeping bag. Her clothes, from what he could see in the dawn light, were thoroughly soaked by the night dew and she was shivering violently. The bodily vibrations caused by her shivering, conducted to the vehicle through the wheel against which she was resting, were what he had felt. He sat up and looked at her. Damn silly woman. Now she'd probably get pneumonia and have to be carted off to a hospital. Bloody females. Didn't they have any sense at all? No sleeping bag and no blankets? Not even a sweater? Come to think of it, he hadn't noticed her opening up the back of the Jeep and getting into her suitcases there. Dammit, he would have given her a blanket if she had asked him.

He sat up, swung his legs out of the Jeep, folded his blankets together and spread them over the shivering form, carefully tucking in the ends under her feet and back. Straightening, he looked around. Where was Pasang? He should be sleeping somewhere close to the Jeep. He moved slowly to the front of the vehicle and peered around it. No Pasang. He looked down the other side. The little man was not to be seen.

The light was strengthening and, as it grew, Wildman noticed how flat the country was. A thin mist, generated by the cool night air condensing over the surface of the warmer ground, reduced visibility; as he left the campsite to walk over to the edge of the river, to relieve himself, he could see probably three-quarters of a mile. Pasang, squatting fifteen feet up in the fork of a thorn tree, could see further.

"Good morning *sahib*."

The sound was a whispered hiss. Wildman jerked his head up and his eyes met those of the Sherpa. As they did Pasang whipped off the two blankets in which he had wrapped himself, tossed them to the ground and with quick, catlike movements came ten feet down the tree and dropped the remaining five to the ground.

"Pasang. Were you up there all night? Did you get any sleep?"

"Flat country *sahib*. Good visibility from a little bit up, a little bit, what you say, eela, ela…"

"Elevation?"

"Yes *sahib*, elevation. Some moonlight last night too. I was able to see more than half a mile at times. I hope that you slept well, *sahib*?"

"Pasang, Pasang."

Wildman reached out and put a hand on the Sherpa's shoulder. "You just don't believe in taking any chances do you? I bet you didn't sleep all night."

"Not good to take chances now, *sahib*. Indeed, we must be very careful. We have made a very bad enemy. It is my fault, for what I did to him and because of this I feel very responsible for you. And now for the missy *baba* also."

"I agree with you Pasang. But I want you to know that I do not think you are to blame for what happened. It could just as easily have happened with me, or with someone else."

"Nevertheless, *sahib*, I feel I am responsible. And he is after us now. Not just for what he wants from you, but also because of what we did to him. That is to say, what I did to him. He has a, what do you call it, a net, a web, like a spider, which he spreads ahead of him as he moves. And no matter what we do, or how fast we travel, or which road we take, the net is there, all around us, on either side, behind us and ahead of us. We have to eat, yes? And we have to get gasoline as we travel. That is where the net, the web, will touch us. That is where it will begin to close, to send information back to Vask. As soon as he gets that information he will act, like a spider, hurrying down the lines of the web to the centre, where he will hope to find us.

"May I say, *sahib*, that you are doing a very wise thing in taking the back roads and leaving the highways. May I also say that I hope that you will continue to do this, cutting east or west, or even south, as you see proper. By doing that we will make a twisted knot of the information that will be going back to Vask. He will act on it, *sahib* that is for sure. And he will keep following. By the zigging and zagging, if that is good English, we will not stop him, *sahib*. But we will slow him down and, if the gods smile on us, then we may reach the Nepal border ahead of him. He will follow us across the border, no doubt. But we will have many advantages once we get into my country, many good things working for us. Good things that will get us to the temple of the Yellow God before him, to complete our mission. But for now, *sahib*, and until we reach the border, we must be very careful. Especially, *sahib*, now that we have the *missy baba* with us.

<<>>

When Wildman and Pasang got back to the Jeep, they found Gael standing beside it, combing her hair. She had her large, red makeup case open on the hood of the Jeep and a mirror propped against it. She smiled at Pasang. "Good morning, Pasang. I hope that you slept well. But you are naughty. You should not have given me your blankets. I was quite all right without them."

Wildman she ignored completely and, as he walked past her, he groaned inwardly and said to himself, "Here we go. Another bloody day of it."

Wildman waited until the young woman was finished on the hood of the Jeep—goddamit, better not aggravate her while she is trying to pretty herself up—and then, when she had closed her make-up case and taken it around to the back of the vehicle, opened the hood to have a look at the engine. He checked the engine oil, the battery acid level and the radiator water. Running his eye over the engine, he used his fingers to tighten the engine leads where they attached to the plugs and them tamped them down in their sockets on the distributor head. He pulled on the fan belt to make sure it was tight and then opened the distributor and checked to make sure that it was clean. Satisfied, he closed the hood and turned his attention to the tires. He was still inspecting them when two men appeared, walking up the riverbank. Approaching, they raised their hands to their foreheads and gave him a greeting. They were the ferrymen from the river crossing and they told him that their crew was pulling the big ferryboat into place and that as soon as he was ready to cross, they would take him. The fee would be five rupees.

Five minutes later, Wildman carefully eased the Jeep down the bank and up two thick planks and on to the flat deck of the ferryboat. Once abroad he cut the engine, put the vehicle in first gear and pulled the handbrake. Pasang walked aboard the ferry with Gael, the men cast off and the ferry was rapidly poled across the turgid stream. On the other side the loading procedure was simply reversed. The bank was a little steeper on this side and so Wildman put the Jeep in four-wheel drive. The vehicle, its tires spinning briefly, quickly made the climb. Pasang jumped in, Gael climbed in the front and Wildman paid the ferrymen and gave them an extra two rupees as a tip. Then they were off.

<<>>

They drove all day across the monotonous flat country of U.P. as it was called. Uttar Pradesh, the Northern Province, at one time the Kingdom of Oud and the bailiwick of the powerful Maharaja of Oud, until he ran into a little trouble with the British for soaking a couple of his dancing girls, who displeased him, in gasoline and putting a match to them. As punishment, the British simply annexed his kingdom and added it to their vast Indian empire.

Endless paddy fields of rice, interspersed with squares of dark green sugarcane, rolled away to the horizon on either side. One of the most heavily populated areas of India, the villages averaged a quarter of a mile apart and from dawn to dusk the Jeep and its occupants were never out of the sight of people. Traffic was heavy, even on the back roads that Wildman was following as he continued north and west. But it was cart and pedestrian traffic for the most part and there were few trucks and buses.

They drove until sunset, stopping only once for a quick meal of soggy rice and even soggier vegetables, washed down with lukewarm tea. But no one complained about the food. They were glad to get it and once again, to Wildman's amusement, Gael ate like a starving Bulgar. As the sun was setting they merged with a main road, followed it for a mile and then crossed a bridge and entered the city of Faizabad.

A dark red sun etched the skyline of the city as they drove into it across a deep, wide river, the mighty Gagra, which has its sources high in the Himalaya of Nepal. Wildman felt an old thrill at the sight of the ancient domes of the old Moghul palaces and tombs, black against the setting sun. Then they were in the city and all his attention was taken up with finding a way through the teeming, narrow streets, trying to get through it and out the other side as quickly as possible. It took him a full hour. Then the houses and factories and tenements and city traffic began to thin and they were north of the city and into the country again. They made one more stop, to fill up with gasoline. Wildman filled the Jeep's tank and topped up all of the cans. He noticed the gasoline station manager's curiosity as he and Pasang opened up the back of the Jeep and, to get at the plastic fuel cans, unloaded their passenger's custom-made red leather suitcases, all eight of them, from the vehicle.

Pasang carefully screwed down all of the caps on the fuel cans and then helped Wildman pack then into the back of the Jeep. He and Wildman loaded the eight suitcases in on top and then Wildman went to pay the gasoline station manager. When he did, Pasang whispered to Gael that he had something to do and that she should not leave the Jeep until either he or Wildman got back. Then he disappeared quickly around the back of the station office.

He was just getting back into the Jeep when Wildman returned and they drove off into the gathering dusk without a word. But Wildman was a little curious. There had been one or two men hanging around the gasoline station and this was the first time that he had ever seen Pasang leave the Jeep when there were people around. He glanced in the mirror a couple of times to see if Pasang wanted to talk to him, and offer some sort of explanation. But all that he could see of the little Sherpa was the back of his head as he sat facing backwards, his eyes glued to the small square hole he had cut in the plastic rear window of the Jeep. It was not until four hours later, close to eleven, when he pulled off the road into a mango grove, to camp for the night, that his curiosity was satisfied.

"Stop here for the night, *sahib*?"

"Yes, Pasang. Get some sleep. Get an early start again and with a bit of luck we might make the Nepal border by tomorrow evening."

"Very good, *sahib*. All clear behind. Maybe because," he hesitated and smiled, "Maybe because I help to delay them a little also."

"Delay them? What do you mean, Pasang?"

"That last gasoline station. There was a telephone in it. On the table. While you were paying for the gasoline, I went around the back of the building and climbed up and cut the wire."

<<>>

She lay on the ground with two of the thin, half cotton, half fibre blankets wrapped around her. She had taken a silk dress out of one of the suitcases and rolled it up and made it into a pillow. She chose a place under the front of the Jeep where, she found, there was just enough room to lie down as long as one did not raise one's head more than a couple of inches.

If one did, the bottom of the radiator was liable to smack one right in the centre of the forehead. Just as the tow rod, or was it tie rod, was equally ready and willing to reward a careless movement by knocking out ones front teeth. But the overhang of the vehicle would do one thing; it would keep the dew off her.

She had accepted the blankets from Pasang. Not from Wildman. She knew very well that one of the blankets was Pasang's and the other Wildman's. But she pretended not to.

She and Wildman had not spoken all day. When he approached her soon after they had made camp and asked her if she would like to sleep in the front of the Jeep, she had actually been startled at having him speak to her. But she recovered quickly and, with a cool no thank you, told him she was perfectly comfortable on the ground outside. She waited until he had climbed into the Jeep and settled his long frame across the front seat and wrapped himself in the single blanket, before crawling under the front of the vehicle and wrapping her own around her. As she did so, a shadow crossed the front of the Jeep. It was Pasang. "All right *memsahib*?"

"Yes, Pasang. Thank you. Thank you and good night."

"Good night *memsahib*. Until the morning, then."

<<>>

She lay on the ground and looked up at the underside of the Jeep. The night was clear and the bottom of the radiator and the line of the front bumper formed a clear-cut rectangle that slowly, as her eyes adjusted themselves to the light, filled with stars. For a while there was no sound. Then, as the little creatures of the grass and the brush recovered from the impact of their arrival, and returned to their nocturnal activities, a number of small sounds began to register themselves on her hearing. From an old stump nearby came a steady gnawing as a wood beetle carved himself a new home. Nearer at hand a tiny lizard gently rustled the leaves as he stalked the insects that were his prey. A continuous sharp snapping sound puzzled her, until she saw a shadow flash across the night sky, and realised that it was a night bird of some kind, catching moths. An occasional metallic click puzzled her even more, until she identified it as the metal of the engine above her, contracting as it cooled.

From above, faint but audible, came the sound of Wildman's steady breathing. Bloody man. What the hell was he up to? What the hell was going on anyway? She had had no time to get Pasang alone all day. She had hoped to do so when they made camp for the night. But again there

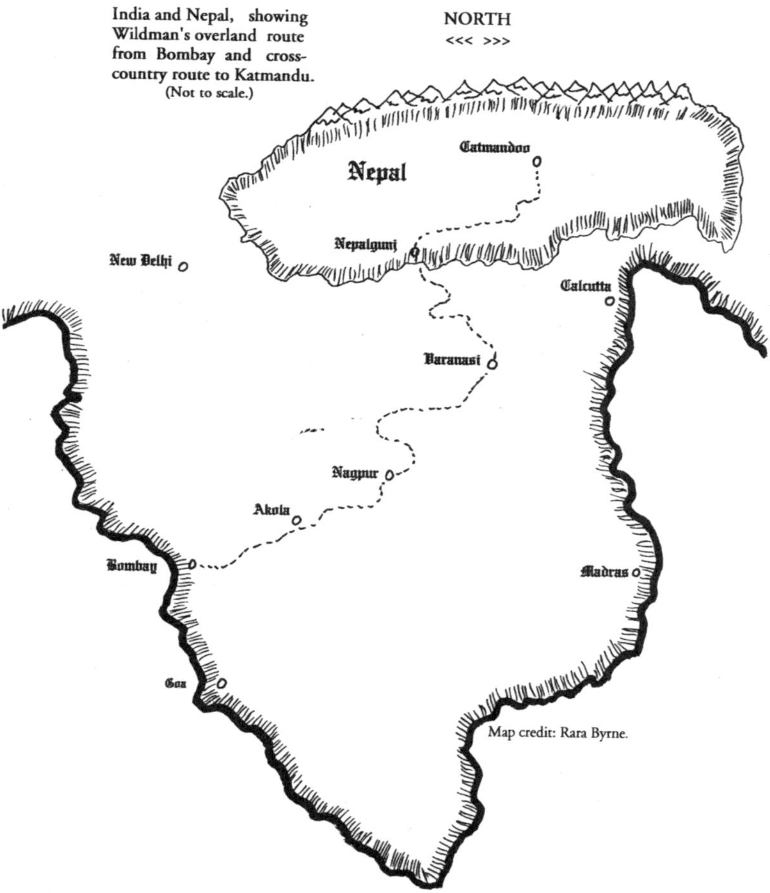

Map showing Wildman's route across India and into Nepal.

had been no opportunity. Dear God, it had been like an army drill. Drive off the road, stop the engine, here are your blankets, forget about dinner, goodnight, don't bother to salute. And they seemed to be heading further and further west. And what *was* all this bloody nonsense about thugs and bandits? And why was Pasang playing the game with this bloody con man who had probably taken her poor grandfather for thousands of dollars. The good Pasang, whom she had known since she was a little girl and whom she trusted absolutely?

She was tired. She had never, ever, felt so filthy in all her life. Her hair was a matted mess. Her skin itched. She had not had a wash in three days. Or was it four? Her nails were broken and clogged with black dirt. She had had no time to change and in any case had nothing to change into. Oh yes, the khaki outfit had been a great idea when she bought it in Bombay. But why the hell didn't she buy two sets? Shit and damnation. And shit again. And she was hungry. God, she was hungry. That filthy food they ate was the pits. And there was always so little of it. One plate and then it was up, up and away chaps, let's go, let's go, the enemy is closing in. God, what she would not give for a hot bath. And that lovely, lovely suite back at the Varanasi Sheraton. And that endless hot water. And that lovely room service. And…

Her mind wandered. 'Thank you, I'm feeling just a little peckish this morning. That's right, my good man, peckish. So I'll have four eggs instead of two. Scrambled. On toast. And lots of extra toast. Not too dark, that's it. And two pots of coffee and cream and make it the nice thick cream you gave me yesterday morning. Oh, and while you're at it, throw in about half a dozen, I mean a dozen, of those beautiful, scrumptious, mouth-watering, melting-on-the-tongue croissants, the ones that you make down there in the kitchens, fresh every morning. What was that? Right now? No. Just give me ten minutes. I'm going to have a jolly good soak in the old tub, first. Wait. Make that twenty. You see, I've just spent three days being pounded to jelly in the front of a mechanical monster called a Jeep, racing over the world's worst roads in a solid cloud of throat-choking, lung-filling Indian dust in the company of a total madman who is also a con man and a crook. I. Oh God, oh God, what she would not give for a cup of hot coffee and one old, stale croissant.

And Pasang. Was he part of the deal? Was he in on it for a cut of some kind with Wildman? Had Wildman seduced him with an offer so enormous that the straight little Sherpa had been swayed had faltered and then bent? 'Here you are Pasang, your once-in-a-lifetime chance. Enough money to retire, go home, buy up the whole goddamn village. How about it, buddy boy?' No! Not Pasang. No! No! No! She clenched her fists and felt her cracked and filthy nails biting into the palms of her hands. But then? What if it was all true? What if there was a bunch of thugs after them? What if Wildman's story, that he started to tell her and that she rudely interrupted, was true? Dammit, she should have let him tell it all and at least pretend to take it in. Then she could have...but what if it was true? A leaf creaked as a lizard pounced on a fat beetle and she felt her body jerk.

If it was true, then this would explain everything that had happened to now. All the artful dodging. Pasang sitting like a statue peering through that damn hole in the rear window of the Jeep. All the precautions every time they stopped. And Pasang, dammit, was he really telling the truth tonight? Did he really shinny up that roof and cut that man's telephone line? But Pasang would not do a thing like that unless there was a very good reason. Unless....

She felt a little bead of sweat running down the side of her neck. If, just if, mind you, Wildman's game was on the level, then everything that he was doing must be on the level. Every hour of fast, cool, and, she had to admit, expert driving. Every carefully considered decision about what routes to take, and what not to take. The whole master plan of heading away from the main roads in an effort to shake off the baddies. Baddies? But if they were what all of Wildman's and Pasang's actions suggested, then they were a lot more then just plain baddies. They were...thugs? No, they couldn't be. The thugs were eradicated by the British, seventy-five, a hundred years ago. Every student of Indian history knew that. Then what were they? And who were they that would make a tough character—oh yes, she had to admit that he was tough—like Wildman literally run for his life? And Pasang? Pasang was not a man to run.

Pasang...She remembered an incident in a village, years before, up near her grandfather's place in Scotland, when a hulking two-hundred-pound farmer's boy had staggered out of a tavern and grabbed her by the arm. How he had laughed when Pasang stepped up in front of him and told him to let her go. Laughed and looked down a height of well over six feet at the diminutive Sherpa, whose whole body suddenly exploded into a hundred and twenty pounds of concentrated energy, all of directed into a single, snapping blow to the man's solar plexus. A blow so fast that afterwards she could not remember actually seeing it. The man suddenly stopped laughing. He started to go down like a falling chimney stack when Pasang, almost apologetically, leaped forward and took the man's head and eased it gently to the ground. Pasang run? No. Not unless...not unless...And the shadows of the tales of the thugs of old and their vile

The Scout being ferried across one of the many rivers that Wildman had to cross to reach the Nepal border. In the background a new bridge is being built; in the foreground, abandoned ferry boats of a bygone age.

deeds crept across her as she drifted into sleep. And her dreams were not pleasant ones.

<<>>

Wildman had an established pattern of sleep to which his mind and body adhered with disciplined regularity. When he lay down, he went to sleep almost immediately and regardless of the time, he always slept soundly for three to four hours. He did not dream during this time and normal sounds would not awaken him. Then, after this brief period of sleep, he would awaken, fully alert and refreshed. He would stretch, make himself comfortable and then go to sleep again for the remainder of the night. But during this second period, his sleep was entirely different. It was a very light sleep, more like dozing, and the smallest sound would awaken him instantly. The crackle of a dry leaf. The faint, very faint swishing sound the grass made when an animal passed through it. The distant alarm call of a bird, or a deer. A sudden switch in a pattern, as when the cicadas, droning endlessly through the nocturnal hours, suddenly sensed rain, or the approach of wind, and changed the tempo of their sounds.

Now, on this third night out, some time after midnight, his mind and body moved into their second phase of sleep. He dozed, drifting in and out of light dreams, part of his mind looking inwards at the dream sequences, part of it alerted to look outwards, to watch and listen for the slightest indication of any change in the normal pattern of night sounds, something that would trigger him into immediate and full awakeness.

A jackal pack had been calling back and forth for some time. Their calls had been challenged by a hyena and when its cackling laughter cut across the flat rice fields, the jackals were momentarily silenced. When the hyena's calls died away, they started up again, and now their calling had continued for more than an hour. Obviously, somewhere out there in the corner of one of the fields was the carcass of a dead animal and what Wildman was hearing, or rather having imprinted on his subconscious mind, was a dispute about ownership. When a fox joined in with a series of long, high-pitched screams that cut the air like a knife, these too just registered as part of the pattern. But when, a short time later, the jackals in full chorus suddenly stopped, abruptly, leaving an eerie silence in the dark night, he was instantly awake, uneasy, listening, both eyes wide open. When their calling did not start up again, he pushed the blanket down off his body and sat up in the Jeep, every nerve tense, every sense straining to penetrate the grey mist that had crept across the sodden landscape.

A steady cascade of drips fell from a small tree on to the canvas hood of the Jeep above him. A frog croaked in the grass about twenty feet away. An owl hooted gently. But from out across the flats, out where the jackals and the fox had been calling, there was only silence. A damp, cold silence, smothered by the mist. A silence that was ominous.

<<>>

"*Sahib*, something wrong. Somebody coming, I think."

It was Pasang, looming out of the fog. Wildman did not hesitate. To encounter the enemy in daylight was one thing. To have them suddenly come charging out of the darkness of the night and be on them before they could take some kind of defensive action, would be bad. Very bad. He leaped out of the Jeep, leaned down, grabbed Gael by the shoulder, and shook her violently until she was fully awake. Whispering at her to get up quickly and get in the Jeep, he pulled her upright and pushed her in. He saw Pasang scrambling into the back, fumbled the keys out of his pocket, got them in the ignition, fired the engine—it faltered, died and then started—and rammed the gear lever down. With the headlights on low beam he powered the Jeep out of the campsite through the trees that enclosed it, dodging the bigger ones and smashing down the smaller ones. Then, the tyres spitting gravel, he accelerated down the road until the speedometer needle touched sixty…all within three minutes of hearing the song of the jackals interrupted.

He drove as fast as the road allowed, his only fear being that they would be delayed by a river ferry crossing, or a broken bridge that might require a slow detour through a muddy ditch, or stream. Pasang huddled in the back; his eyes glued to the hole in the rear-view window, silent, his body tense.

Gael, one of the blankets they had given her wrapped around her, the other lost in the wild scramble to get in the Jeep, braced her body with her feet hard against the sloping flooring that was the engine bulkhead. One hand clutched the body cowling of the open doorway the other gripped one of the metal bars of the framework of the front seat. Her mind was numb, confused by the impact of the rude awakening, and she was frustrated and angry at once again being a part of something she did not understand. The cold damp wind screamed in the open doorway of the Jeep, the engine roared and here they were again, racing like escapees from a lunatic asylum down a godforsaken road in the back of beyond in the middle of the night. Being pursued by something that was either an evil nightmare from the darkest side of eighteenth century India, or a crazy figment of the imagination of the Jeep driver. When, hours later, on a highway that seemed to be taking them north again, Wildman suddenly turned off the road and, in a cloud of dust boiling brown in the first sunlight of the day, pulled up outside a small tea shop, leaned across and spoke to her, she found herself bewildered to the point of being tongue-tied.

"Pasang, stay with the Jeep, OK? Keep an eye out down the road. Gael, stay in the Jeep, OK? I'm going to get some tea and something to eat. Whatever they have. I'll bring it back to the Jeep here and we'll eat it here. Don't get out, OK? If you need a pee, hold it until we get a little further up the road."

Wildman had parked the Jeep close to the road. Pasang stayed in the back watching through the rear-view window hole. Gael, numb, her body aching with the ride and shivering with the cold of the bleak November morning, a damp cold that the sun had not yet succeeded in dissipating, did as Wildman said and stayed where she was. She would like to have said something to him. She would like to have been able to say, 'up yours buddy,' and jumped out of the Jeep and gone behind the teahouse for the pee that she so badly needed. But her mind, like her body, was exhausted. By the lack of food, the cold, the discomfort and a night of nightmarish dreams in which she had run across endless paddy fields, her feet sinking deep into the thick brown mud, pursued by black-robed, silent figures. Figures that ran without effort and without sound and carried brightly coloured, weighted silk handkerchiefs in their hands; swinging them, reaching out for her, reaching for her throat, until in the end she had found herself in a dark alley the floor of which was deep in slime and filth. In the alley she staggered through the quagmire, sinking to her knees. The thugs closed in. She screamed. At the end of the alley was a gateway and behind it, the old Clutterbuck Hotel. In the gateway, silhouetted against the ghastly yellow light of the street lamps, stood the tall figure of Wildman. She screamed again and reached out her hands to him for help. He looked at her, a sneer on his face that said, quite frankly my dear, I don't give a damn, and then, ignoring her, turned and walked away.

She blinked the sleep from her eyes, ran a grimy hand across her dirt-streaked forehead and looked up to see Wildman leaning over her with a tall glass of hot, milky tea and a handful of dried salt crackers. He handed another glass to Pasang and returned to the teashop to get his own. When he came back he got into the Jeep beside her and sat, silently sipping his hot tea and chewing on the dry, stale crackers.

"I'm sorry. This is all that they have to eat. They can make food for us, they say. But it will take half an hour and we can't wait that long. We have to get on."

She sipped the hot tea and used it to soak pieces of the dried crackers. By doing this, she was just able to swallow them. The tea was hot, though, thank heavens, and sweet. Wildman must have made them put ten teaspoons of sugar in it. She avoided sugar normally. But what did normally mean out here? What was normal about all this? What was reality? What...

I'm sorry, he had said. She had not heard him use that word before. Probably had to cough it all the way up from the bottom of his stomach. I'm sorry? It indicated...what did it indicate? Feeling? Yes. Feeling. Feeling for someone other than himself...Well, she had seen some concern for Pasang, come to think of it. For her? Nothing. To a degree of male chauvinism that she would hardly have thought possible. But now...I'm sorry. She slurped down the last of her tea and turned her head to look at him. He caught the movement in the corner of his eye and for a moment continued to look straight ahead, down the road. Then he turned to look at her, slowing taking in what he saw.

She was a mess. She had tied her hair back with a little piece of string. Honey blonde, was it, when they had started out? Honey mud would be more like it now. And not too much honey either in what looked like a bunch of rats' tails hanging down her back. Her right cheek had a large purple bruise, where something had hit her. Probably forgot she was sleeping under the car and shot up when she heard that hyena and banged herself on the tie rod. Her eyes, well, they were still gorgeous, even if the redness of the whites detracted somewhat from their pristine beauty. Under them were dark, lilac patches that showed her exhaustion.

Her lips were dry and cracked and the corners of her mouth were lined with little streaks of dried mud, where the moisture had collected and watered the dust. The rest of her? Well, the rest hardly warranted description. Her clothes looked as though they had been washed in a muddy roadside ditch and then dragged through the dirt for ten miles behind the Jeep; her boots were caked with mud, the leather dry and cracked. Her hands, curled around the tea glass as she tried to draw a little warmth from it, were grimy, the fingers tipped with blackened nails. She had been shivering so violently with the cold when he brought the tea that she had spilled some of it down her front between the folds of the blanket, and crumbs from the broken crackers had stuck to her wet shirt.

'Bloody woman,' he wanted to say. 'I told you that I didn't want you along. I told you what it would be like.' But then, he hadn't, had he? Well, that was not his fault. The only two times he had tried to speak to her, when they first met in the Clutterbuck bar, and again the following morning—when he should have picked her up and thrown her bodily out of the Jeep—she had turned up her snooty little nose at him and told him to go take a flying jump. More or less. Bloody woman. The only thing going for her was that she had not complained yet. And considering what she had been through so far, and what she was going through now and, God knows, what might yet lie ahead, this was, well, no great thing, but, well, something to her credit.

He looked at her. 'Go on, burst into tears and tell me you want to run home to mummy and daddy. Go on. I won't hold it against you. Pasang and I will drive you to the nearest railway station and put you on a nice little train and get you a nice, first class ticket and you'll be back in the Varanasi Sheraton before you can say billabong'. But she hadn't complained, had she? Come on, Wildman, admit it, you bloody stubborn man. A first for you, you'll have to admit, with the women you've had out on some of your wonderful little trips. Up in the snow and down among the crocodiles and deep in the jungles of wherever. Oh yes, you put them through it all right. And they stubbed their little toes and barked their tender shins and they got their little migraines and their backaches and their gippy tummies and they sank to the ground and howled for their mummies and their daddies. And this one? Well, she would crack, just like all the others. Hadn't done so yet? So what. It was just a matter of time. Still, it would be nice to get her somewhere where she could have a bath and decent meal and some clean clothes. Sort of deserved it, not having screamed for mummy so far. A little different from the others in that respect. Maybe, just maybe, in another time and place, maybe…

But no. He closed his mind to that possibility. In the meantime, lack of complaints notwithstanding, considering the background that her clothing and manners and poise and, yes, her eight red velvet suitcases suggested, she probably did deserve a little consideration. Just a little, mind you. No need to overdo it. And wrenching the words up from the lower pit of the lower end of his stomach, he had said, 'I'm sorry, this is all they have to eat.'

They looked at each other now and, if Wildman was successful in erasing all feeling from his face and eyes, anything that might be construed as emotion, or, God forbid, sympathy, she was even more successful. And between them their pride was a ten-foot thick wall of solid ice and in the end it was Pasang who provided the opening that put the first crack in it.

"Would you like some more tea, *memsahib*? I can bring some?"

"Oh, thank you, Pasang, but I...."

Wildman leaned across. "Have another cup. It'll warm you up. Yes, Pasang, quick as you can."

He jumped out to allow the Sherpa to get over the front seat and out of the Jeep. Pasang was back in a couple of minutes with another glass of the hot milky tea, and when he handed it to Gael, she thanked him. But when she did so, she looked both at him and at Wildman. And the little crack in the ice suddenly widened.

<<>>

"Look, I think you should know something about what is happening."

They were on the road again but had stopped in a clump of trees for a snake check. Snake check. A safari term. Known in other parts of the world as a pit stop, or peepee stop or, for those who preferred to give it a more genteel name, an imperative call of nature. They had drunk their tea without another word. A small boy had come to the Jeep for the glasses. Wildman had given him a coin and then they had left and were on their way again. The teashop was a mile behind and the place Wildman had chosen to stop, on a straight stretch of the road, gave them a clear view up and down it in either direction for more than a half a mile. When Gael returned to the Jeep he let her get in and then spoke. "I think you should know more, because I have the feeling now that you are, shall we say, more open to, er, more willing to lend some credibility to accept, er, what I told you about...."

He searched for words. Dammit, he wished she would not look at him like that. Those bloody eyes. He found his mind wandering, picturing her as he first saw, back at the Clutterbuck.

"You mean the man Vask and what you told me," she smiled, if bleakly. "Or tried to tell me? About his being after us?"

"Yes. Look, it's real. I mean it bloody well is. So far, what have you seen that might in some way support what I told you? Nothing. Absolutely nothing. We race through the night. We peer around corners. We leap up in the dawn and go tearing off across the country. We are two, three hundred miles off the direct route to Nepal. Pasang sleeps in a tree with one hand on his knife and sneaks around the back of fuel stations and cuts people's telephone wires. We eat and sleep with one eye on the road in front and one behind, and we jump a foot in the air every time we hear an odd sound. OK then, believe me when I say that I don't blame you for what you must be thinking. That you are dealing with a complete madman who has somehow or other seduced, Pasang, your old family retainer, into joining him in some kind of mad road spree half across India. But believe me also, please, when I try to tell you that what we are dealing with is very real. Incredible? Yes. But real, truly. And because I want you to believe this and particularly because I want you to be assured that Pasang has not been subverted in any way ¯ dammit you know he could not be—I want you to ask Pasang how he got that hole in his cheek while I, if you will excuse me for a couple of minutes, will go and indulge in a brief but necessary requirement of nature. OK?"

He was gone before she could reply. As he disappeared behind a convenient tree, she turned to look at Pasang, crouched in the back of the Jeep, sitting sideways to her, his head moving from side to side as he watched the road ahead and behind. He had been listening to Wildman and had heard what he had said to Gael, and now when she turned to look at him, he took it as his cue to speak.

"Yes, *memsahib*. It is true, what he says. Every word of it. Why we took so long to come up to Varanasi. That we did try to find you in Bombay. And we did try, in fact we waited for you I think more than half an hour and then had to go. We parked at the gardens and..."

"The gardens, did you say, Pasang? What gardens? The Taj has no gardens? But never mind, go on."

"Yes, *memsahib*. And when you were not there the *sahib* sent a telegram to your grandfather to arrange another meeting in Varanasi. And then we were delayed on the road."

"What happened on the road, Pasang?"

"The man Vask. The one that the *sahib* told you about? He managed to put some sugar in the tank of the car that we got in Bombay. When we broke down, they were waiting for us. They had guns. They took us to the man's house, near Nagpur. We managed to escape and get away and get into Nagpur itself and get this Jeep there. Then we came on up to Varanasi."

"And the man, Vask, is he really a thug and does he really have a gang working with him?"

"Yes, *memsahib*. A real thug. And a gang. A big gang. He has much money and so he has many people working for him. He has many, what do you say, contacts, many arms and legs, like a spider. With the police, with people working on trucks, with the bus services, with the gasoline stations. This is why the *sahib* is running like he is. This is why we have left the main roads and come this way to get into Nepal. The man, Vask, is not after us, *memsahib*. He is after the stone, the Eye. And he will do anything to get it. Anything. And this means great danger now, to you, and to the *sahib*. Yes, *memsahib*, what Mr. Wildman has told you is all the truth."

Pasang, his honest face turned towards Gael, his steady gaze holding hers, unconsciously allowed his hand to brush his cheek. Thinking of Vask and what had happened brought back a flash of mental pain.

"And your cheek, Pasang? Did Vask do that to you?"

"Yes, *memsahib*. He did."

<<>>

Wildman reappeared, jumped in the Jeep, got a quick, nodded OK from Pasang to say the coast was clear, fired the engine and they were off. He looked at Gael once and the look he got in return, half scared, her teeth biting her lower lip, her eyes wide, showed him that the talk with Pasang had done the trick. Above the roar of the engine he turned his head sideways and, keeping his eyes on the road said, "We'll talk some more later. OK? After we get through Baraich, the next big city. We're going to have to make one more stop to fill up before the border. There may be no gasoline available in Nepal. There are few if any gas stations on the main east-west highway, the highway to Kathmandu, which is where we are heading. So we'll have to carry all we can."

She nodded to show that she understood.

"As to how we stand now, I mean, in regard to the enemy, we don't know what it was that was moving out there in the mist this morning, when we took off the way we did, like jackrabbits. But something was. Or somebody. Pasang sensed it, as I did. That's why we dragged you out of bed so rudely. My feeling is that Vask may have tabs on us and know where we are. It's the damned fuel stations that are our weak area. Vask's listening posts, as it were. Our problem is that we have no way of avoiding them. Which means," he said, as he swung to avoid a bus coming straight at them on the narrow lane, "that now it's a race for the Nepal border. They will probably try to follow us across it. But once in Nepal, as you will see, we will have all sorts of advantages over them. Their spy network comes to an end at the border. No gas station network, among other things. And few if any people willing to work for them. So we've got to make it to the border before them."

The Jeep hit three potholes in a row and bounced into the air. A string of buffalo carts appeared and Wildman slowed. Instead of sounding the born and waiting for their sleepy drivers to laboriously move them off the road, he drove off the hardtop and roared through the dirt of the verge, sending a huge plume of choking dust out behind the Jeep and, until they regained the road again, filling it with a stifling cloud.

"OK. Have you got the picture?"

She shouted back at him. "Yes."

And that was all that he needed. He gave her a quick smile and she half turned her head and gave him one in return. An equally quick one. But nevertheless, a smile. And between them the last of the ice suddenly melted and was washed out of the open doors of the speeding vehicle, to be whipped away in the wind of their passage.

<<>>

The countryside grew lush. Northern U.P. The northern part of the Northern Province. Tiny villages lay buried in banana and mango groves. The rice fields were a rich green with the coming harvest, and tall stands of sugar cane waved in the wind. The trees that bordered the road were huge, with spreading branches from which long, twisted roots dropped to the ground, turning the road in places into long, shaded tunnels. The winter sun shone brightly in the dark blue sky and far to the north a line of white cloud rimmed the horizon.

A scattering of tea houses and shops marked the outskirts of the city of Baraich and within minutes they were in the city, winding their way through streets that teemed with thousands of people, with cows and carts and rickshaws and cyclists and dogs and children. There were few if any road signs. But since they had regained the road, north of Gonda, Wildman was back on familiar turf and he took the Jeep through the narrow, winding streets without having to ask anyone for directions.

Again he chose a fuel station out on the edge of the northern side of the city, and after they had stopped, Gael realised why he did this, rather than stopping at the first one they came to in the city itself. A fuel station on the north side of the city meant the beginning of the highway north again, the comparatively clear road that would allow them a quick getaway if danger threatened. They had just driven through the city itself and she had seen what it was like and realised how impossible it would be, in a getaway, to move at any speed in the incredibly crowded streets.

At the fuel station, without being told to do so, she stayed in the Jeep and watched Wildman work. He had an alertness about him that made her think of a wild animal, a big cat. He moved quickly for a big man, with a fluid grace that indicated perfect physical fitness.

From Wildman her eyes moved across to Pasang. He slid out of the Jeep the moment it stopped and had taken up a position about twenty feet away, from where he could see the vehicle, the men working on it, and the area behind it. She watched his eyes flicker from time to time towards the station office and the three men who occupied it. One sat at a table and the other two sat on gasoline drums stacked on the floor. Typically, both the men sitting on the gasoline drums were smoking, and she marvelled at the mentality that would allow a man to smoke while sitting on a forty-gallon drum of gasoline. She could smell the cigarette smoke from where she sat in the Jeep, the pungent odour of the little brown *bidis* that Indians smoked by the million. But suddenly the smell was different, and she was mentally trying to analyse why, when she noticed a little Punjabi restaurant tucked behind the back wall of the fuel station. The smell was of cooking food. She did not know what kind of food. Probably the inevitable curried vegetables and rice. But oh God, it smelled good to her.

<<>>

Her thoughts were interrupted by Pasang scrambling over the front seat and into the back of the Jeep; the vehicle lurched as Wildman followed him, dropping his one hundred and ninety pounds of muscle and sinew behind the steering wheel. Then the engine was roaring and gears were snapping and engaging and the seat was pushing her hard in the back as the vehicle accelerated out of the station parking area and back on to the highway. She glanced quickly at Wildman and saw his face, serious, intent, his attention to the road total, his body behind the wheel relaxed and yet at the same time like a coiled spring. And she knew that he had seen her looking at him in his peripheral vision when he leaned towards her and, still keeping his eyes on the road said, with a quick smile, "Yes, I smelled it too."

<<>>

Wildman, his attention totally focused on keeping the racing Jeep in the centre of the road as it dodged between carts and wandering pedestrians and stray dogs, found his eyes drawn to the thick line of white cloud that edged the horizon to the north. He blinked his eyes a couple of times to clear them of the dust that caked his eyelashes and looked again. Gael noticed the movement and wondered if he had seen something ahead that she had missed. Then, when he leaned back and shouted to Pasang, "Nepal,

Pasang. The mountains," she knew what it was he had seen and what she suddenly found her own eyes drawn to.

The towering mass of what looked like cumulus, that soared to the heavens, far to the north of them, was not cloud, but mountains, and what she was looking at were the snow-capped peaks of great mountains that rose to the roof of the world. The Himalaya of Nepal...She leaned towards Wildman and pointed and shouted above the roar of the wind and the engine. "How far?"

Wildman replied. "The mountains? About a hundred miles. The border? About another thirty."

They slowed to pass through a small town. The sign said Nanpara. There was one long street lined with shops, teahouses and tin-roofed shacks. Wildman did not stop. A string of wandering buffalo carts, a thousand milling people, a dead cow in the middle of the road, a line of buses loading and unloading people, a single fuel station with rusting pumps, a sign that said **NO GASOLINE** and then they were clear of the town. Wildman's heart lifted as he saw a signpost that said **NEPALGUNJ ROAD, 30 MLS**, the name of the town that straddled the Indo-Nepal border and marked the end of the Indian highway. His heart lifted, his eyes lifted again to the great mountains and he felt a surge of elation that as quickly turned into something else, something almost fearful, as Pasang's quick, excited voice shouted from behind him.

"*Sahib*! Jeeps. Coming behind. Coming fast. Two. No. Three. Grey Jeeps, *sahib*."

Wildman did not hesitate. He rammed the throttle flat to the floor, hunched himself over the steering wheel and, as the vehicle leapt forward, gave his complete attention to what he knew was going to be a race for life, a race the outcome of which would only be one of two things. Escape, and the sanctuary of Nepal. Or capture, torture and death.

<<>>

The engine of the Jeep screamed as they hurtled up the road. Another sign said **NEPALGUNJ. 20 MLS**. Wildman drove like a madman, giving way only to objects that were larger than the jeep. With everything else it was look out, I'm coming through, get out of the way, or else. A wandering crowd of men, women and children occupied the centre of the road. Wildman drove straight at them. Screaming with terror they leapt for their lives. One man was not quick enough and Gael felt his body slam against the side of the car and had a quick peripheral vision of him as he somersaulted into the verge. A bus came at them, head on. But you did not challenge something as big as a bus. Wildman whipped the Jeep off the road, down into the verge and back up again in a boiling cloud of dust.

Close behind the bus, too close for Wildman to see it in time, another vehicle suddenly appeared. It was a motor-powered rickshaw, built to hold five people plus the driver, but with the usual fourteen or fifteen people in it, crammed in with the driver, jammed in the back and hanging on outside. There was little that he could do in the split second between when he saw the thing and when he knew he was going to hit it. He had a brief flash of terror-stricken faces and, just before he slammed into it, he saw its occupants exploding in all directions as they leapt for their lives with wild screams. The Jeep hit the contraption head on, with most of the impact being taken on its front bumper and radiator. The rickshaw disintegrated. Bits and pieces of it flew in all directions and one wheel curved high in the air and then landed in front of them and rolled down the road ahead of them until they caught up with it and crunched it under their tyres. The Jeep staggered under the impact of the collision, lurched sideways, hesitated, straightened and then roared on.

"*Sahib*, they are catching up."

Another signpost flashed past. **NEPALGUNJ. 15 MLS**. The road cleared briefly and Wildman gave the Jeep everything it had. The needle climbed to sixty, to sixty-five and then steadied at just under seventy. It would not go any faster. But seventy was good if only the road would stay clear. But almost immediately a truck appeared ahead, and he was forced to drop his speed, lurch off the road, roar down the verge, let the truck roar past and then accelerate back on to the road again.

They covered another five miles. Another sign flashed past them, **NEPAL BORDER, 10 MLS** and Wildman struggles to maintain his speed. But according to Pasang's terse commentary from the rear, the pursuing Jeeps seemed to have closed up a little and Wildman, pushing his vehicle to its absolute limit, suddenly knew why. It was the weight they were carrying. The extra fuel and eight bloody suitcases. He had lifted the cases in and out of the Jeep several times to get at the gasoline cans and he knew how heavy they were. What the hell did she have in them? He glanced in his rear-view mirror. But it had a thick layer of dust on it and in any case Pasang's hunched-over figure obscured the view to the rear.

"Pasang!"

"Yes *sahib*, I think getting closer."

He saw Gael twisting in her seat, her eyes wide and for a second he hesitated. Then he shouted back at the crouching Sherpa. "Pasang. The suitcases. Throw them out. Quick. If you can't get the back open cut it open. Fast now."

He felt Pasang move above the swaying of the Jeep and then heard a ripping sound as his *kukri* sliced through the canvas that enclosed the rear of the Jeep. Another ripping cut and then the back canvas was gone. As it did, Wildman reached up and gave his rear view mirror a quick wipe with his hand. After that, for the next three minutes, which is all that it took for Pasang to heave the eight huge suitcases out of the Jeep, he saw a sight that were it not for the gravity of the situation would have had him in fits of laughter.

The suitcases had been beautifully made. High quality leather laid over thin wire frames and then covered with hand-stitched red velvet. Custom jobs, every one, made with care and without any concern for cost. But not made to withstand the impact of a hard road hitting them at sixty miles an hour, bouncing them, spinning them in the air and then hitting them again.

As each suitcase hit the road it burst on impact. Or it bounced, spun through the air and then burst on the second impact. The first suitcase must have been one that contained mainly lingerie and when it burst there was an explosion of silk, mostly white, as bras, panties, short slips, dress slips, pantyhose, stockings and sundries sailed into the air. The second might have been nightdresses. They leapt from their confinement like escaping birds and, in a glorious cascade of colour, pinks and blues and the palest rose and red and black and green and lavender, went sailing into the air. Some floated back to the road. Some seemed to prefer the roadside trees, settling quickly to decorate their branches in long colourful drapes. A third, or perhaps it might have been a fourth, must have been designed for shoes only. It had been built with neat little wooden compartments inside, each one just large enough to contain one pair of shoes, twenty-five compartments to the case. Alas the little handmade plywood boxes were no match for the force with which the road punched them. For a brief while, twenty-five pairs of shoes leaped and danced in the air as though trying to keep up with the Jeep. Then they were gone.

The rest of the cases quickly followed, and Wildman saw books, notebooks, writing paper, what looked like a portable typewriter, pens, pencils, staplers, erasers and typewriter ribbons fill the air. He heard Pasang grunt as a particularly heavy one went out and hit the road with a heavy metallic crash. He saw black objects spinning in the air and recognised them as cameras, lenses and light meters. Yellow among the black were dozens of boxes of film and flying with them went half a hundred packets

The view of the Himalaya that Wildman and Gael and Pasang saw as they approached the Nepal border. In the foreground is the edge of the Terai forest into which, after surviving the fiery explosion on the bridge, they ran for their lives.

An Indian jackal. In the night it was the presence and calling of a pack of these clever canines that alerted Wildman and Pasang to the approach of Vask's gang.

of lens cleaning tissue, a dozen bottles of lens-cleaning fluid and two silver tripods. There was one case left, a smaller one. Pasang had seen Gael getting toiletries out of it a couple of times and guessed it might be special. He shouted at Gael. "*Memsahib*, the *lal jolla.* The small red case. Yes or no?"

Wildman saw Gael turn, caught the agonised expression on her face and then heard her shout. "Yes, out with it."

Pasang heaved the smaller case out the back and, as it burst, Wildman heard a great crash of breaking glass as bottles of hand lotion and facial lotion, toilet water, eau de cologne, mascara, eye shadow and nail varnish shattered on the road. Fifty shining brass lipstick tubes flashed briefly in the air and then disappeared in a foaming cloud of shampoo, hair conditioner and liquid soap.

The bursting spray caught Wildman's eye and for a tenth of a second he flicked his eyes up to the rear view mirror and down again. When he did he saw something that sent a shiver down his back…a grey Jeep bearing down on him, coming fast and no more than a hundred feet behind him. He saw white-shirted forms crouched behind its windshield and what looked like rifle barrels sticking out the front, poked through an opening under the windshield, flat to the hood of the vehicle and pointing in his direction.

<<>>

Wildman looked back in desperation at the Jeep behind him. It seemed to be closer. He could see the rifles clearly now. They could start to shoot at any moment. And then he had an idea.

"Pasang."

"Yes, *sahib*."

Pasang rolled forward in a half crouch and looked at Wildman sideways. "Pasang. The gasoline cans. I'm going to slow a little. Let them get closer and as soon as I give the word chuck 'em out. One by one. OK?"

"Right, *sahib*."

Wildman eased his foot on the throttle and Gael swivelled around to look back. "I'm going to hit them with some gasoline. Keep your head down, OK?"

He watched the mirror and prayed that the goons with the guns would follow the instructions that he felt sure Vask would have given them, which was not to shoot. Above everything else, Vask would want him alive. A dead Wildman meant a dead end to Vask's search for the stone, if Wildman

Main street of Arrah, north India, near the Nepal border, typical of the cluttered and crowded city streets through which Wildman had to force his way.

Pasang (center) watches very carefully as a petrol station attendant fuels Wildman's International Scout.

did not have it on him. For Wildman it was a hunch, nothing more. But he felt it was a good one, because there were four or five men in the Jeep behind and he had seen two rifles sticking out and they could have got in twenty or thirty shots by now if they had wanted to do so. He also had a feeling that Vask might know about his cargo of gasoline. Fifty gallons of it in ten and five gallon cans with more in the tank. Enough to blow them sky-high with a single stray bullet through one of the cans. He slowed. The lead Jeep came closer and suddenly, when it was no more than a hundred feet behind—no shots, he was right in his hunch—Wildman shouted to Pasang. "NOW. HIT THEM WITH IT!"

Pasang already had both hands on one of the cans of gasoline. He picked it up and hurled it out of the back of the Jeep. The can sailed through the air, bounced and rolled, and the Jeep behind them seemed to swallow it as it rode over it. Wildman heard a dull, heavy thump and looking back saw a rolling ball of flame and black smoke silhouette the vehicle. He saw a second Jeep, behind the first, skidding wildly off the road to avoid the flames, and then his attention was back to driving. When he looked again, the lead Jeep was back in place. Far down the road he saw the second Jeep roaring along the verge and then corkscrewing back on to the road. The third Jeep—he saw it only briefly, it was another hundred yards back—had slowed to allow the second Jeep to stay in its position.

"Pasang. Give them another. This time throw it up in the air and try and make it break on the road."

The nearest Jeep, its engine screaming, again began to close the gap. Pasang waited until it was seventy-five feet away and then, half standing in the back of the pitching, rolling vehicle, used both hands to throw the second gasoline can out of the back and up into the air. The method worked. The can rose some ten or twelve feet in the air, curled down, hit the road, burst and exploded. Again there was a flash and the dull thump of the gasoline igniting. But the driver of the lead Jeep was ready this time, and instead of going straight through the black smoke and flame that rose from the road, he roared off on to the dusty verge, bypassed the fire and quickly regained the road again. When he did this, his Jeep briefly created a boiling plume of thick brown dust and the sight of it gave Wildman an idea.

Shouting to Pasang to keep throwing the cans out, he wrenched his vehicle off the road and into the thick brown dust of the verge. Indian dust! How many times had it slowed him down when he could see nothing in its dense, billowing clouds. If he stayed in the verge he would create a dust cloud that not only would slow Vask's goons but might also keep them from closing on him.

<<>>

Wildman's vehicle lurched and pounded through rocks and debris and the six-inch deep dust of the verge. There was an orange flash as another can of gasoline exploded on the road behind them. In the semi-darkness of the huge brown dust plume that trailed them, it was muted and Wildman realised that his game plan with the dust seemed to be working. So he kept the Jeep off the highway and on the dusty verge. He was roaring down it in the pounding, leaping vehicle, fighting the rocks and broken branches and deep holes, when suddenly the long tunnel of trees that they had been in for miles, opened up and came to an end. Ahead of them was a wide, deep river and beyond it a small town with what looked like factory sheds in the foreground. Squinting with the dust in his eyes, Wildman saw a bridge and, leading down to it, a narrow, single lane ramp.

The bridge was made of metal and, like the ramp that led to it, designed for single lane traffic. It had a deck of thick wooden planks laid edge to edge, all the way across.

Wildman did not know the name of the river that the bridge spanned. But he did know that it was deep. He had stopped here once on a blazing hot day in May, and swum in it and now, at the latter end of the monsoon, it flowed deep and brown.

From the wooden deck of the bridge, to the surface of the water, was about twenty-five feet, and the bridge itself was built as a single span, supported on concrete slabs at either end.

On both approaches to the bridge, at each end, the road ran straight. Then, just before entering the ramp, it curved sharply. Trees had been allowed to grow at each end of the structure, obscuring it from the view of approaching vehicles until they were actually on the ramps. This was particularly evident at the north end, where a thicket of thorn interlaced with vines blocked any immediate view of the ramp.

A hundred feet from the bridge, at the south end, the verge that had flanked the road for so many miles and that had allowed Wildman to use its dust to slow his pursuers, suddenly came to an end. Here the ramp to the bridge began. It was a short, fifty-foot causeway with steep, forty-five degree angle dirt banks on either side. As soon as he saw it, Wildman whipped the Jeep up out of the verge, swerved on to the ramp and started

Vask's men work to repair one of his Jeeps on the road.

Villagers pulling one of Vask's Jeeps out of a mud hole.

to race down it for the bridge. As he did so, the thick brown tail of dust that had been following the Jeep was abruptly cut off and the road behind was suddenly clear again. He was half way down the ramp when he saw the first Jeep emerge from the last of the dust plume and roar down the slope after him.

He looked ahead. The bridge was clear. A family of people stood at the near end. They had been about to cross, but hearing the roar of the approaching vehicles, had decided not to take a chance with them on the long, narrow structure. Wildman saw them, saw them hesitate, registered the decision they had made and floored the throttle. The Jeep roared through the little grove of trees standing at the near end of the bridge. It bounced on the wooden rim, where the ramp to the bridge began, squared itself for the run across the bridge and then, with the wooden decking rattling wildly under its wheels, began to race across. As it did so, Wildman's mind registered two things. The first was the thumping crash as Vask's lead Jeep, right behind them, hit the end of the bridge and came thundering down after them. The second was a much heavier thump one that shook the bridge from end to end, as a much larger vehicle came thundering out of the blind corner at the other end. Wildman saw glaring headlights as a huge vehicle, its klaxon horn blasting its right of way, came straight at them, at high speed, across the one lane structure.

The approaching truck was a gasoline tanker. It had a large, yellow radiator fronted with a thick steel bumper from which hung a dozen heavy steel chains. The cab was made of wood, the standard box-shaped affair common to all Indian trucks; it was gaily coloured and from its upper edge hung a thick fringe of glittering tinsel. Inside the cab, the walls were decorated with dozens of brightly coloured Indian calendars, ribbons, bells, plastic dolls, a large plastic image of a deity and a dozen bottles of Ganges holy water hanging on strings. Bolted to the back wall of the cab was a large transistor radio with four huge loudspeakers.

The enormous yellow tank that comprised the body of the truck began immediately behind the cab. It too was painted bright yellow. On either side, and at the back, in bright red letters, it carried the legend: **INDIAN OIL. FLAMMABLE**. The capacity of the truck was six thousand gallons and it was full. The cubic capacity of the tank was calculated in the old British way, a carryover from the days of the Raj. The gallons were therefore Imperial gallons, with a weight of ten pounds per gallon. The weight of the truck itself, engine, cab and chassis, was a mere ten thousand pounds. But with its fuel load, the gross weight of the whole unit was seventy thousand pounds, or thirty-five tons. This is what made the bridge shudder when, at speed, it came thundering down the ramp and on to its plank decking. This is what Wildman felt as he started his run across the narrow, one lane structure.

<<>>

There was no time to stop. And there was no way of avoiding what, if he continued, would obviously be nothing less than a head-on collision. And so Wildman acted as he had trained himself to act, for many years, with quick, cool thinking supported by near instantaneous reflexes.

Gael froze when she saw the approaching truck. For a moment she thought there must be a way past it. The she realised that there was none, that the bride was a single lane structure and that unless Wildman stopped and backed up, fast, they were heading for disaster. Then, just as quickly, she realised that they were going much to fast to stop and she was half turning towards Wildman to see what he was going to do when his hand suddenly lashed out, giving her a stinging, backhanded blow on her left upper arm. The blow, painful and totally unexpected, rocked her sideways. But the pain and the impact on her arm instantaneously transmitted itself to her brain so that when Wildman shouted at her, "JUMP! OUT! QUICKLY! JUMP FOR YOUR LIFE!" her body was already tensed and poised to act.

<<>>

If Gael hesitated it was for no more than half a second. Then she grabbed the door framework with her right hand, the corner of the windshield's metal frame with her left, levered herself up and flung herself through the doorway, over the edge of the bridge and into space.

Then it was Wildman's turn. If he had had the time, and the inclination, something quite far from his mind at this moment, he could have consulted his worthy Rolex and seen that from when he left the road, and started his run across the bridge, that what he had was in effect a ten second countdown.

Thundering down the bridge ramp and crashing onto the wooden bed of the bridge took two seconds. Then, with eight seconds to go, he had shouted at Gael, backhanding her on the arm. One second after that, at seven seconds, he had her through the door and clear of the Jeep and falling to the river below. At six, having shouted a similar command to Pasang, he felt rather than saw the agile Sherpa grab the metal framework that formed the back of the Jeep cab, swing himself out and leap for his life. At five, he took his foot off the brake, where it had been literally grinding the pedal into the floor, pulled himself up in the seat, swung his long legs through the opening, got one foot on the bottom of the metal door frame for leverage and, with the imaginary clock calling four, jack-knifed himself through the doorway and out into space. At three, he hit the water, sank, and thanked his gods that the river, which would have a muddy bottom, was deep. At two seconds, after a fifty-foot fall that thrust him almost ten feet down, his head broke the surface. At one, his vehicle, still travelling at something in excess of forty miles an hour, hit the fast moving truck head-on with a combined velocity of close to eighty miles per hour.

<<>>

Wildman's Jeep travelled another hundred feet after he and his companions bailed out, and before it hit the tanker. It might have swerved on the deck planking of the bridge, once steering control had been relinquished. But it did not, for the heavy wooden pedestrian railings, made of old railway ties laid one on top of the other, stabilized its direction…straight at the oncoming tanker. So that when it hit the tanker truck, it did so head-on.

It was, at first, the enormous weight of the tanker that took control of the physical forces created by the collision. It shuddered under the blow. But with its immense weight and momentum, it lost only a little of its forward speed. However, the effect of the collision on the Jeep was quite the opposite. Its whole front end crumpled and in a shattering of glass, the windshield blew out. Its engine was driven back into the cab. The chassis buckled and lost its gravitational grip on the bridge and rose upwards. The twisted frame leapt into the air and then, travelling backwards at the same speed as the tanker, did a back somersault that for an instant had it upside down in the air, directly in front of the tanker.

It was in this position when the first of Vask's Jeeps, its engine screaming, arrived on the scene. With its braking tyres tearing long, sharp splinters out of the bridge planking in trails of the black smoke of burning rubber, it roared underneath the airborne vehicle and slammed into the front of the tanker. As it did so, the airborne Jeep came down on top of it, enveloping it in a crumpled mass of twisted debris, boiling hot radiator water, battery acid, torn canvas and raw gasoline from its shattered fuel tank.

<<>>

The impact of Vask's Jeep, coming immediately after the collision with Wildman's vehicle, slowed the tanker a little more. But it did not stop it as, with a terrible grinding and snapping of twisting and breaking metal, it continued its forward movement. The tanker's engine was ripped off its mounts by the impact and its engine casing was fractured. When the casing cracked, the racing pistons did the rest, tearing it to pieces, instantly. When the combined mass of Vask's Jeep, with Wildman's vehicle on top of it, ploughed into it, the whole mass of the huge engine block was driven back out of its original mounting and through the bulkhead behind, right into the cab. Doing this, it took all of the lower part of the cab with it, including the steering wheel and its power steering mechanism, the gear box, all of the dashboard and, in a deadly spray of glass particles, the one inch thick, non-safety glass of the tanker's windshield.

<<>>

There were twelve men packed into the cab of the truck. It had been designed to seat four only and so they sat on each other's laps, on the floor, or up on the back of the seat, a scrambled eggs mass of arms and legs and sweating bodies. The group included the driver, a mechanic and a cleaner. The driver normally drove with both hands on the steering wheel, one foot on the throttle and one foot on the brake pedal. He steered the truck and applied the brake when he thought it necessary; this was all his elevated position, as a professional driver required him to do. The mechanic sat beside him with one foot on the clutch and one hand on the gear lever. It was the mechanic's job to work the gears and the clutch. The cleaner, as was usual a boy of ten, did the rest, his job being to keep water in the radiator, diesel in the tank and oil in the engine, plus an occasional wipe to keep the windshield clean.

The other nine people in the truck cab were passengers. Oil company regulations specified no passengers. But regulations were a word that faded half a mile after the truck left the company yards and the nine men additional men in the cab were paying passengers, being picked up and dropped off at various destinations for fees which went to enrich the driver's pocket.

Apart from superficial injuries, all of the men in the tanker cab survived the first impact, that of Wildman's Jeep. The shock of the jolt hurled them all forward against the dashboard and only the driver, his hands braced against the wheel, was able to hold himself back. There were broken kneecaps and smashed noses, accompanied by wild cries of pain and surprise.

But the double impact of the second Jeep, carrying Wildman's Jeep on top of it, wrote a different story and it did so in words of deadly intent. It picked up the whole mass of the huge diesel engine, all eight hundred pounds of it, wit its trailing wires and broken pipe and jagged metal and drove it straight back into the huddled mass of bodies in the cab. From there it went on, right through the back wall of the cab to where it lodged, wrapped in bloody gore, against the thick metal plating of the huge tank behind the cab. The men in the cab did not even have time to scream. But even if they did, and even if for a second or two they might have managed to survive the smashing blow that took them all into eternity, it would not have made much difference. Because now, to add to the massive collision that had set the shattered tanker up like a punch drunk boxer for the knockout, came the third Jeep, second in line in Vask's convoy, to deliver the killing blow.

<<>>

It was the sharp curve and the trees at the south end of the bridge that hid what was happening on the bridge from the second of Vask's Jeeps, and its driver. His eyes were on the road ahead, rather than the Jeep in front of him and his whole attention was occupied in getting his lurching machine through the curve at the entrance to the ramp, and then on to it. He slowed a bit, coming down the slope, but as soon as he got his vehicle on to the ramp, and aligned for the bridge, he accelerated and he was actually increasing speed as he came out on to the bridge itself. After that, what happened was all too quick for any timely reaction from the limited ability of his reflexes.

He did manage to get his foot off the throttle. And he did manage to get it on to the brake pedal. But his mind was still telling his foot muscles to start depressing the pedal when he, and his vehicle, and all inside of it, including one unfortunate man crouched in the back with his right hand still handcuffed to his left ankle, were engulfed in the mass of the tanker and the metal carnage that enveloped it.

The third collision stopped the tanker. Vask's second Jeep, travelling at over forty miles an hour when it hit, disintegrated to become part of the wreckage that had wrapped itself around the front of the huge vehicle like a mass of crumpled tinfoil. The men in it, like the others in the Jeep in front of them, all died instantly. But again it would not have made much difference if any of them had survived the triple blows of the collision. Because the third Jeep, at the split second of impact with the mass of wreckage, touched metal to metal and produced the spark that ignited the gasoline-soaked wreckage of the whole.

<<>>

There is a common conception, among people who have had no experience with its dangerous potential, that gasoline burns when ignited. It does not, and its liquid, exclusive of its vapour, can actually extinguish a naked flame. It is the vapour, its gasses, which are flammable. Again, the vapour does not actually ignite when brought into contact with a heat source; it explodes. And its lethal power is amply illustrated by the physics involved, which tell us that the vapour produced by one gallon of gasoline has the explosive potential of ten sticks of dynamite.

When the gasoline-soaked mass of the wreckage wrapped around the front of the now motionless tanker ignited, it did so instantly. A roaring, orange ball of flame exploded outwards and then mushroomed up into the clear winter sky accompanied by a billowing cloud of oily black smoke. The explosion itself lasted a mere one second and then the flames settled down to burn, at a fierce two thousand degrees, the cab of the truck and its occupants, the mass of the wreckage of the three Jeeps, and the bodies inside them. Following the vapour trail like a hound of death, the fire reached far back into the wreckage and as its heat touched the wet gasoline with which it was soaked, this speeded its evaporation, creating more vapour on which it fed hungrily. It melted aluminium casings and spars, brass and copper piping. It instantly dissolved bakelite and plastic and battery casings and the lead inside them. It consumed wood, rubber, human flesh and clothing, without distinction.

When all of the liquid wetness of the burst tanks of the three Jeeps had evaporated, burned off by the fierce heat, the flames started to die down. But if they did, they died, as does the applause that greets the arrival of champions to the ring. The real applause, the thunderous ovation, was being held back, nurtured and fortified in anticipation of the main event, an event for which an invisible audience now watched and waited.

Poised in tiered rows of seats, breathing hard, bodies tense, they had watched the drama on the bridge rapidly develop, from onrushing vehicles, to shattering collisions, to a roaring fire. But now, as the fire died, so did their interest in it. Now their eyes, bright, greedy, glittering with the need for violent entertainment, were on the big, yellow metal container at the back of the tanker, with its six thousand imperial gallons of gasoline. And their attention was totally directed towards what was going to happen when the dying but searching flames of the initial fire pushed inquisitive fingers through the minute but slowly widening cracks in the super hot, rapidly heat-fatiguing metal of the huge yellow tank. And reached inside.

<<>>

The third Jeep of the convoy, the one carrying Vask and his monolithic brother, Little Gunga, was just entering the long ramp down to the bridge when the wreckage of the collision caught fire. Vask's vehicle was coming fast. But its driver, Metha, had seen the black smoke of the fire, its underside tinted red by the gasoline flames, before he left the road and was able to stop his vehicle, just in time, before it got on to the bridge. However, panicking, he hit the brakes too hard, putting the Jeep into a long, screaming slide that carried it out to the steep edge of the ramp where, with half of its body hanging over the edge, it came to a halt. It hung for a moment, two fast spinning wheels off the ground and then it slowly slid down the forty-five degree angle bank of the ramp to the dirt verge below it. There, in a movement that was almost in slow motion, it slowly toppled over on its side.

With shouts of anger, Vask and his men scrambled out of the overturned vehicle. With a smashing backhand blow, Vask knocked aside one man who tried to get out before him.

Little Gunga, jammed in the back of the Jeep, panicked. He had not liked the ride. He had not been given the toys he had been promised and he had had no liquor for two days. He did not wait for space to be made by the other men so that he could get out through one of the openings of the vehicle. He simply levered himself upwards and, using his huge, bullet-shaped head, spilt the canvas of the Jeep's roof. He then stood there, enveloped in canvas from the waist down, gibbering, the huge head nodding up and down, the purple-lipped mouth slobbering mucus, a thin whining voicing his displeasure.

With the Kalashnikov in his hands Vask clambered up the ramp and ran down to the edge of the bridge. There he stopped. A solid wall of flame made an impassable barrier in front of him and there was no way

Smoke from the burning tanker on the bridge.
In the background is the town that
Wildman glimpsed briefly before he and
Gael and Pasang dived into the river.

Credit, Uttar Pradesh State Police, Motor Vehicles & Highway Division.

The bridge where the multiple crash took place.
Photo Credit: Uttar Pradesh State Police, Records Section, Lucknow, UP.

Remains of the tanker which burned in the crash,
killing all who were on board.

around it. Metha and the others, followed by Gunga, quickly joined him. They stood in a tight group and faced the roaring flames, as though by watching them they could make them diminish. A light wind blew some of the ash laden, oily black smoke towards them and as it enveloped them they staggered back, choking, eyes watering.

Vask moved quickly to the edge of the ramp and looked down at the river. Had Wildman escaped? Waving at the others and Gunga to follow him, he ran off the bridge and down to the waters edge. Where was Wildman and his accursed Nepali? Killed in the wreckage? Up there in the flames? In which case his chances of getting the Eye were gone, now and forever.

Vask cursed and wiped his eyes with the sleeve of his filthy shirt. As he did, he saw something that sent his rage soaring. The far bank of the river was edged with flat rice fields. They were green with the coming harvest and they stretched away for more than half of a mile to a dark, thick wall of forest, where they came to an end. Within two hundred feet of the forest, running like the wind, were three figures. Above Vask's head the black smoke billowed out of the burning wreckage and Vask suddenly realised that it was the smoke blowing in his face, while he was on the bridge that had prevented him from seeing the three running figures. Had he seen them then…He fingered the Kalashnikov and cursed. But there was still a chance that he could stop them. They were a good thousand feet away and within seconds they would be into the woods and out of sight. But with a little elevation, he might be able to hit them. One or two bursts of the Kalashnikov, sprayed into the ground ahead of them, might well stop them.

He turned and ran back up to the ramp. When he got to the top, ignoring the smoke coming off the burning wreckage, he slipped the safety catch off his weapon, raised it to his shoulder and, setting the front sight just above and in front of the three running figures, brought the back sight quickly into line. He was just about to squeeze the trigger when something on the bridge caught his eye. Something that sent a shiver of instant fear racing through his whole body. It was the red sign on the yellow side of the tanker. **INDIAN OIL. FLAMMABLE.**

The smoke from the burning wreckage billowed, closed on the sign, opened again. But Vask was not looking at it. Cursing in panic, he was running for his life, away from the bridge and, typically, he was doing it without warning his men, all of whom were grouped around Gunga, down at the water's edge.

The men below him saw Vask raise his gun and take aim. They too had seen the running figures and now their attention was divided between

Vask, about to shoot, and the fast disappearing figures in the distance. When Vask suddenly lowered his weapon, to turn and run, they were confused. But not for long. Within seconds they were running with him. But in their case it was not the sign on the side of the tanker that sent them racing after their master. It was the heat and flame of a gigantic fireball, roaring up from the exploding tanker, that sent them fleeing in panic, running for their lives, scrambling, falling, shouting in fear and alarm. Oddly, the only one who did anything sensible about the threat of the flame was Gunga, who, left alone, and feeling the heat beginning to envelope him, turned and threw himself into the river.

<<>>

When the tanker blew, the explosion was accompanied by a tremendous roaring whoosh as it compressed the air around it in the initial expansion of the blast. A second roar followed, when the air rushed back into the vacuum caused by the imploding ball of flame, rushed back to feed the fire of the burning vapour as the gasoline from the ruptured six-thousand-gallon tank poured down across the bridge. In seconds the whole structure was wrapped in fiery orange flames that enveloped its entire length and seeped through its wooden planks to fall to the surface of the river, there to splutter and hiss in multicoloured pools that the gentle current slowly carried downstream.

BOOK TWELVE

KATHMANDU

Wildman, Gael and Pasang were almost at the edge of the forest when the tanker exploded. They broke their stride, stopped and looked back. They saw the huge orange fireball roar into the sky and the mushrooming cloud of black smoke that followed it. As they watched, the fire raced down the bridge in either direction and, within seconds, the whole structure was wrapped in scarlet flames.

It was Pasang, with his sharp hillman's vision, who saw Vask as the man ran up the bridge ramp and turned towards them and raised the Kalashnikov. His quick look also took in the men with Vask and the huge shape of Gunga. Then, his voice urgent, he was telling Wildman and Gael to run for the trees and get under cover.

Without hesitation they turned and with seconds were at the thick outer wall of the forest and bursting through it to take advantage of its welcoming cover. Once inside it they did not stop, because although the forest offered them concealment, it also shut off any view of possible pursuers, something that was of immediate concern.

Wildman doubted that Vask himself would try and follow him on foot. The man was big and muscular. But he was also very heavy and, if he came after them, it was unlikely that he would be able to exceed the pace they intended setting, and catch up with them. Gunga they did not worry about. A menace at close quarters, it was doubtful that he was able to move any faster than the slow shuffling walk they had witnessed back at Vask's house. But Vask might just order a few of his men to go after them, and the way to circumvent the possibility of their catching up was to go fast, and keep going.

And so they ran, leaping over clumps of fern and small bushes, seeing deer and small animals darting ahead of them in the dappled light that penetrated the canopy of trees above them. The only rests they took were short panting ones, doubled over, to catch their breaths. Then it was on again, through small clearings, across shallow streams, their beds carrying the last of the monsoon water, bypassing stands of thick, nearly impenetrable elephant grass and thorn breaks, on and on again until suddenly the ground began to rise, almost imperceptibly. When this happened Wildman knew that they were leaving the Terai and entering the Bhabar, the terrain that marks the end of the great plain of the Indian subcontinent and that is itself eventually terminated by the escarpments, the great rock walls behind which lie the foothills of the Himalaya.

<<>>

"I think we'll sleep well tonight."

Wildman was standing by the edge of a small stream. Gael was sitting on the bank, her feet in the ice-cold water. She had washed her hair and her face and then tied her hair back with a small strip of cloth torn from the tail of her shirt. Pasang was off on his own. He had said something about food and had melted into the jungle and disappeared. Wildman had taken off his shirt, washed it in the stream, rung it out and put it on again. In the cool air of the darkening evening it felt good on his skin.

They were exhausted. They had run, and walked, and trotted, stumbling, tripping and falling, for eight miles. Pasang had set the pace and Wildman, with an occasional mental check on their direction, had allowed him to lead. When the sun sank down into the trees to their left and long dark shadows began to band the floor of the jungle, he decided to call a halt. They had come to a small clearing, the floor of which was covered with thick green grass and a scattering of leaves. A little stream ran down one side and here he told them they would camp for the night.

Immediately on arrival, and telling Gael not to wander far from the clearing, he and Pasang had gathered wood for a fire. When they had enough stacked by the stream, and with night settling fast in the dark halls of the trees, Wildman had washed and Pasang had gone off to find something to eat.

The jungle was quiet. Off in the trees to their left a peacock wailed, and once Wildman heard the piping alarm whistle of spotted deer. But there were few other sounds apart from the gurgling of the little stream.

The light had completely gone when Pasang materialised out of the gloom. He whistled softly before he appeared, so as not to alarm them, and Wildman returned his whistle. He was carrying all that he had been able to find in what little light there was left. He had six small, green, wild bananas and a couple of handfuls of dried figs. They shared them carefully between them and this was their dinner. After they had eaten, they lay down on the grass beside the stream and stretched out to sleep. It was agreed that they would light a fire later, probably close to midnight, when the cold damp air would seep down into the trees and the temperature would drop. Until then they would do without it.

They were confident that no one would be able to track them from where they had entered the forest after leaving the river. Confident that for this one night at least, and until Vask found a way to get across the river and make his next move, they were safe. But in the cool damp air of the winter night of the Terai jungles, smoke from a campfire does not rise. It hangs above the fire until a little wind picks it up and starts to move it along. When this happens it will travel a considerable distance, low to the ground, before it dissipates. Anyone with a little knowledge of jungle lore can backtrack it to its source. Thus they would hold off lighting the fire until they needed it, later in the night, when the temperature dropped and the lowland dew began to soak the forest. In this way they would avoid showing a light in the early part of the night when there might still be a villager travelling on a jungle trail and also avoid sending out a long grey finger that could point the way to their camp.

Late in the night Gael was awakened by a pattering sound on the grass around her. She guessed the time to be about midnight. Rain, she thought, feeling small droplets of water falling from the tree canopy above them and touching her face. She sat up and stared into the blackness and as she did so a dark figure moved a few feet away. A voice spoke. "It is I, *memsahib*. I am lighting the fire. Getting cold now. The dew is coming in."

She should have known. It does not rain in the Terai in November. The pattering was drips from the dew, gathering on the high canopy above them and then spilling off it to fall to the ground. She heard a scraping noise and, as she watched, saw a tiny series of sparks close to Pasang's chest. For a moment she did not know what he was doing and then she realised that he was making fire with flint and moss, striking the back of the blade of his *kukri* downwards against the flint and flashing the sparks into the dried moss. As she watched she saw a tiny glow and heard Pasang hissing. He was holding the moss close to his lips, almost inside his mouth, and blowing on it very gently. The glow grew into a little flame and, when it did, the Sherpa quickly crouched down and touched it to a little bundle of dried grass. There was a crackling sound, the smell of burning grass and, within seconds, a small glowing fire. As the flames leapt up, she realised that she was cold. She got up and moved to the fire and, as she did so, Wildman joined her. Pasang added sticks to the flames and the three of them huddled around it. A little later, when it had warmed them, they alternated between lying down and sitting up, close to the fire, to try and keep warm. An hour before the dawn the temperature dropped down into the forties, the coldest part of the night. In the open country through which they had come, it would be even colder, down in the thirties and dropping down close to the freezing level just before dawn. But the forest, where the temperature was always more even—cooler during the day and warmer at night—gave them an extra ten degrees of warmth and made their night in it more tolerable.

<<>>

Gael was dozing in front of the fire, just before dawn, when the air suddenly vibrated with a deep, powerful, drawn-out rumble. She awoke instantly and sat bolt upright. Wildman was awake, sitting hunched looking into the fire and Pasang was sitting opposite him, a handful of small sticks in front of him as he tended the flames. She looked quickly at both of them. They had not looked up. She was about to ask if either of them had heard the noise when it came again. The sound had great power and seemed to roll away down through the halls of the jungle for miles. Wildman turned to her and said, briefly, "Tiger. A big male I would guess. Calling for a mate. This is the mating season for tiger up here. November. With a bit of luck you might see him as he passes."

Pasang nodded his agreement, and he and Wildman turned their attention back to the fire. Gael looked at them and from their appearance of total calm in the face of the tremendous waves of sound coming through the jungle, learned her first lesson in the lore of the big cats. It was obvious, from the attitude of her companions—one of them born here, the other with years of experience in these jungles—that essentially, left alone, they posed little danger.

She relaxed and sat back and listened to the sounds. Now that she knew there was no danger, the calls seemed to lose their menace. Indeed, there seemed to be something ineffably lonely about them, especially as they died away into the distance. She heard them for the last time as the first streaks of daylight began to grey the trees, and her reverie was interrupted when Wildman stood up and stretched.

"Well, time to roll up the tents and get going. How about a quick breakfast first? Bacon and eggs and some jolly British muffins and a nice big pot of hot coffee. How do you like your eggs done, Gael?"

She felt a surge of annoyance as his glibness. She was bloody hungry again—God, when were they going to get a decent meal—and she thought that this was stretching her sense of humour a little too far. But she suppressed her anger, tossed her head back, flashed him a quick smile and said, "Oh, I'd love to, but I couldn't. That southern fried chicken in the spicy sauce and the herbal mashed potatoes that we had for dinner was bad enough. But it was the strawberries and ice cream afterwards that did for me. Not to mention the coffee and cognac."

She watched his face as she spoke and then fired another little sharp pointed arrow at him. "Mind you, I could, possibly, if I was pressed, look at one small mug of coffee with a little honey and a healthy dash of Glenlivet in it."

His mouth opened and he began to say something. Then he grinned ruefully, gave her a mental touché and turned to help Pasang kill and bury the fire under some kicked-up dirt. Minutes later they were making their way north again, through the sodden, dew-soaked jungle, the sun grumbling under the eastern horizon and the five-thousand-foot escarpments, that marked the edge of the foothills, looming ahead.

<<>>

They walked for ten hours, stopping only to drink water from jungle streams and to rest for brief, five-minute periods. Longer breaks than this, Wildman would not allow. He carefully watched Gael's progress, measuring her strength and energy levels and, as the lack of food made them ebb through the day, tried to gauge their pace accordingly. Which is to say that he pushed it to the limit. But he felt that he had to, because his plan was to get as far as possible from the border as quickly as possible, and there were two reasons for this.

The first concerned being seen by villagers. At one time, years before, the jungles had stretched in an unbroken belt right across the south of Nepal, right up to the edge of the escarpments. But over the years the population of the Terai had been swelled by migrations of people from the hills, driven down by the loss of their land to erosion. As a result, large areas of jungle had been cut down to allow for cultivation, creating treeless clearings sometimes a mile square. These contained new villages and rice fields and during daylight hours, there were always people working in them. Crossing this open country meant being seen, and being seen would lay a grapevine trail that Vask might just be able to follow, once he was across the river and into Nepal.

Wildman's second reason for moving fast was to get to a highway as soon as possible, one that would provide them with transportation to Kathmandu. The temple of the Yellow God lay north of Kathmandu and Wildman's route to the temple therefore lay through the capital city. But Vask knew where the temple was and Wildman guessed that if he did not try to follow them through the forest, he would head for Kathmandu, knowing that to get to the temple Wildman would have to pass through there.

Vask would probably first look for them on the highway—there was only one in southern Nepal, a single road that ran all the way across the country from east to west—and failing contact with them there, he would try to get ahead of them in the city. There, using a surveillance web, he would try and ambush them when they arrived. Speed was therefore what counted now, because whatever Vask did would take time, especially the organising and setting up of a watch in the city, a place where, being out of his own territory, he had few contacts.

This was something they could take advantage of, and this was the reason for the gruelling pace that Wildman set for himself and Pasang and Gael. If they could reach the highway before Vask got his insidious report and reward system in operation, and if they could keep going, fast, all the way to Kathmandu, then they stood a good chance of getting there safely, of thwarting the thug leader's plans and staying out of the reach of his long and deadly tentacles.

<<>>

By four o'clock Wildman estimated that they had covered something close to twenty miles. A shouted question by Pasang to a villager in a rice field had elicited the information that the highway was a mile ahead, and when Wildman heard this, he put up his hand and waved Gael and Pasang to a halt. Now they were resting in a small bamboo thicket at the edge of the forest. Pasang squatted on the ground, facing back the direction they had come. Wildman stood with his back to a tree, bent over, breathing slowly but heavily and looking down at Gael. She had lain down on the ground the instant he called the halt, put her head on her arm and fallen asleep within seconds. He wanted to talk to her, to try and explain the importance of the brutal pace. He wanted to tell her of his contacts in Kathmandu, one of whom, a close friend, was the influential manager of one of the big hotels, something very advantageous to their plans. Of how, once they got there, the odds of Vask being able to find them and harm them were greatly lessened. Of how…

But to talk to her would mean waking her up and, looking at her, he changed his mind. Her face was drawn and the shadows under her eyes were deep and dark. She looked close to exhaustion, and Wildman knew that now she was drawing on her last reserves of strength and that these in turn were fast running out. She had held the brutal pace all day and, apart from brief conversations when they halted to rest and drink, had remained silent. If her leg muscles were groaning with pain, if her back felt as though it had been broken, if her whole body screamed for rest and for sleep and if her stomach seemed to have dried up into a small hard knot, she kept it all to herself, without a word of complaint. Wildman looked down at her, at the delicate eyelashes covering her closed eyes, at the slim brown arms tucked under her head. He thought to himself that, at another time and place, someone who could take this kind of punishment—lack of food, lack of sleep and the grinding pace—and not even issue one word of complaint, might well be worth knowing better. In fact...But at that moment Pasang stood up and looked at him meaningfully. And so he reluctantly woke her and, pushing her gently ahead of him, made for the highway.

<<>>

They emerged from a small stand of trees. A little dust hung in the air and suddenly the highway was right in front of them. Ahead of them was a twenty-foot embankment on which grew small clumps of brush. They scrambled up, almost to the top and then, concealing themselves in one of the little clumps, had Pasang go out and sit on the edge of the highway and wait for the first truck. It was not long in coming, and the sight of what looked like a Nepali man standing on the side of the road holding up a big bundle of hundred rupee bills, quickly brought it to a halt. Five minutes later the three of them were stretched out on top of a huge pile of rice sacks in the back of the truck. They were exhausted, coughing in the swirling dust sucked in by the open back but grimly content in the knowledge that, with the pace they had set in the forest, and the speed with which they had been able to commandeer a truck, they were almost certainly ahead of Vask. They realised, of course, that as soon as he discovered this, or even speculated it, Vask would head for Kathmandu and try to find them there. But the fact that they were now very probably ahead of him, with the principal danger—of being captured and taken back across the border into India to face torture and death—now behind them was what mattered.

The truck stopped three times for fuel and food for the driver and his half dozen companions. Once in a city named Butwal. Once in another city called Narayanghat, where a road to the north left the east west highway and headed up into the hills. And once in some nameless place where the driver had a sweetheart for whom he had brought a packet of candy from a shop in Butwal. Each time the truck stopped, Wildman and Pasang were on their feet, instantly, alert, watching, listening, ready at the slightest sign of danger to wake Gael and leap straight out of the open back of the vehicle and run for their lives. But the long journey, taking them far into the night, passed without incident. Through the hours of darkness Gael never moved, and as the night grew older and the air, roaring in through the slatted sides of the truck, dampened and chilled, Wildman covered her with extra rice sacks and kept watch on her.

Seventeen hours later, in the bright sunlight of a new day, in swirling clouds of dust and to the roar of trucks, buses, private cars and the voices of hundreds of people, the truck pulled up on the edge of Kathmandu's Ring Road, a highway that encircled the whole of the teeming city. They came to a stop. The driver and his men scrambled out, grinning, and Wildman paid what he had agreed to give them. Pasang woke Gael and, lifting her bodily, handed her down from the truck to Wildman. Laying her gently on the ground at the edge of the road, Wildman turned to Pasang to tell him to start looking for a taxi. But the little Sherpa already had one rolling towards them. They lifted Gael carefully into the back and then Pasang looked questioningly at Wildman.

"To the house, *sahib*?"

"No, Pasang. To a hotel, the Shangri La, in Lazimpat, where my contact is. We'll go to the house later."

Forty-five minutes later they were standing at the reception desk of the Shangri La, a beautifully built, rose brick building in the northern part of the city, with a cobble stone courtyard, manicured flowerbeds, staff in well-tailored uniforms, security guards and a fierce-looking stone lion guarding the front gate. Propping the somnambulant Gael between himself and Pasang, one of her arms over each of their shoulders, Wildman asked for the manager, Mr. Utpal Sengupta to whom, Wildman said, he had an introduction. For a moment or two the desk clerk, his face registering disdain, made it obvious that he believed that the three filthy, smelling, dust-covered creatures in their tattered and stained clothing, standing in front of him, were obviously candidates for one of the five-rupees-a-day hippie joints in the teeming heart of the old city. But Wildman's being able to name the hotel manager made the difference and, reluctantly, but with a nod to one of the hotel security guards to keep an eye on the wild-looking trio, he picked up the phone and called the manager. There was a pause.

"Wildman, sir, from London. But I think maybe there's some mistake, sir. The gentleman..."

But at the other end of the line the manager had dropped the phone. They heard a door slam. Heard a shout. And the next thing they saw was a young, beautifully dressed, smiling young man racing out of a side door, taking one look at Wildman and rushing up to him with open arms. Wildman grinned and grabbed his friend in a bear hug. Pasang smiled and nodded. Gael passed out, cold, on the floor of the foyer.

<<>>

Talking about it all later, what Gael remembered best about the manager of the hotel were his eyes and how they twinkled with mischief to dominate a warm and humorous face. She guessed that he might have been about thirty. He was always, while they were with him in Kathmandu, impeccably dressed, super efficient, fast talking, fast moving, the soul of honour when it came to maintaining a confidence and a bottomless pit of information on what was happening in Kathmandu. A man of many contacts and tremendous energy, he proved to be exactly what they needed to get whatever they wanted while they were in the city. This included private, very private, accommodation while they were there-no names, no registration-and no record of their stay after they left. A vehicle, which they could use to get up into the mountains, to the temple of the Eye. And, immediately, clothing and toiletries for both of them.

Now, in the hotel's comfortable foyer, Sengupta bowed to Gael, shook hands with Pasang and gave Wildman a bear hug that spoke of former friendship. Whatever he thought, he asked no questions. He simply clapped his hands, room keys appeared as if by magic and ten minutes after they had met him, Gael and Wildman were soaking in hot water in huge tubs, Gael with a glass of ice cold white wine in her hand and Wildman with a healthy looking double *peg* of scotch balanced between his knees as he attempted to scrub ten days of dirt off his body.

Pasang left to go to a small hotel called The Snug, owned by a friend of his, deep in the heart of the ancient city. He promised to check back early next morning. Wildman and Gael were given rooms, adjoining rooms Sengupta pointed out, with a twinkle in his eye, and snacks and drinks were sent up in minutes. A bottle of '67 Saint Emilion Bordeaux for Gael.

And a tall, familiar green bottle of Glenlivet for Wildman, at the sight of which Wildman decided that as a hotel the Shangri La had all the makings of a very civilised watering hole.

<<>>

While they soaked in their tubs, Sengupta rushed back in his car to his house in the suburbs and, with the help of his attractive French wife, put together some sets of clothing for them. He was back in the hotel in thirty minutes.

After his bath Wildman showered in cold water and then used the room telephone to call for dinner. A scarlet-uniformed dinner waiter quickly appeared, flourishing a menu containing a veritable forest of print. After Wildman had made his choice and asked that it be served in his room, he called Gael to ask if she would like a menu and if she would like to join him. Her reply made Wildman chuckle.

"My dear sir. Would I like a menu! And what do you think I have been looking at for the last five minutes? Of course I'll join you. But have you ever, ever, seen such a positively scrumptious looking menu in your entire life!"

Sengupta had sent up the clothes that he and his wife had managed to put together for them. There was a dark blue silk dress for Gael, with a pale blue sash and evening shoes that fitted reasonably well. There was also a pair of light corduroy trousers, a long-sleeved, cotton shirt, a woollen sweater and a pair of canvas sided hiking boots. And there were two complete sets of underwear, French, silk, and very sensuous. But then, Gael remembered being told, Sengupta's lovely wife, whose name was Caroline, was French.

For Wildman there was a dark green cotton shirt with a Paisley scarf, a razor, two pairs of socks and a pair of dark tan, ripcord-cotton trousers accompanied by a rather venerable-looking Harris Tweed jacket. From the large size of the trousers and the jacket, he could see that they did not belong to their bright-eyed host but had been borrowed. He still had his Gokeys, of course, and after some mysterious person, unseen, had slipped into his room while he was wallowing in the tub and taken them away and cleaned and oiled them, they looked as good as new.

Gael brought her wine with her from her room and offered to share it with Wildman. But he told her that he preferred to stay with his Glenlivet for the moment. What he did not tell her was that he had a small task to perform later that night, one for which he would need a clear head and all of his wits. She guessed that he might be up to something when, dinner over, he made signs that indicated it had been a long day for him and that, pleasant though her company was, he had other things on his mind. She left him and when he walked with her to the door of her room, she turned and looked at him with a new softness in her gaze and said, "Be careful, whatever it is you are up to."

He told her that he would. He also told her to lock her door carefully and not to open it to anyone without prior telephone contact and identification. Then he said goodnight.

<<>>

Two miles away, far down among the maze of streets of the one thousand year old city, Vask stood in the doorway of the top floor room of an old, cut-price hotel called The Panorama and listened to what a young Nepali boy, a hotel employee, had to tell him. An Indian with whom he had made contact, a man who owned an auto parts shop, had called the downstairs reception desk, the boy said, to say that he would coming to the hotel later that night. Vask asked what time the man had said he would come. The boy did not know. Vask grunted and gave him two rupees and the boy grinned and scampered off down the ten flights of uneven stairs and back to his job at the front desk. Vask closed the door and walked back into the room. His contacts in the city were starting to get back to him.

<<>>

Vask had lost no time getting to Kathmandu. For a few minutes, back at the bridge, clear of the fire and with his men around him, he had considered going after Wildman. But he knew that the man and his companions would run like the wind and he doubted that he and his men could catch them. In any case, that was not his way. His way, always, was to look for and find the easier approach. Strategy was what counted in a game of hide and seek, which is what this was now. Follow your quarry for as long as you could, yes. But as soon as you lost him, abandon the chase, bypass the point where you last saw him and then try to get ahead of him and ambush him.

Now where would Wildman go, once he got into the forest? Obviously he would have a plan. He was smart, Vask had to give him that. But what would that plan be? Stay in the forest and hide? No. The jungle grapevine was as strong as the grapevine of the open plains of Vask's

Utpal Sengupta, manager of the Shangri La Hotel and Wildman's friend, with the Maharani of Rumblebellipur, in the beautiful formal gardens of the Shangri La. Photo Credit: NASA High Orbiting Satellite # PB-RM-207.

country. Within a few days, a week at the most, word would seep down through the villages of a strange white man and his woman, with a mountain man, staying in a village, hiding, waiting for something, sleeping and eating in a village hut, never coming out. And Wildman was smart enough to realise that. No. Wildman would move on and he would move fast. He would...yes, that was it. He would want to move fast and for that he would need transportation. And where to find transportation? The nearest highway, of course.

And unlike India, with its myriad road system dating back to British times, Nepal had only one highway in the south, something they called the east west highway. It ran through the Terai, just north of the border, all the way across the country. The solution then? Simple, get up to the highway and block it. Set up a road trap and wait for him to come along. He'd be on a bus or a truck. Get up there with his men and just stop the buses and trucks as they came through and search them. He'd soon find the American and his girl friend and...Ah yes, the girl friend. And what would their relationship be now, Wildman and the woman, and could it be used to advantage, once he found them? Very possibly. Unlike his people, Westerners fell apart when someone did something nasty to one of their women.

He would take them all back down to Nagpur, trussed up in the back of the Jeep like chickens for the market and as soon as he got them there, simple, just bring out Gunga, point him to the woman and ask Wildman for the stone. Maybe he'd let Gunga play with the little hillman first and let Wildman and the woman see what his little brother could do. Arm breaking seemed to be what Gunga enjoyed the most. But Vask had also seen him pull a man's arm right out of its socket and then tear it off his body. Oh yes, mister wild man would not like that at all. Probably send his little whore into hysterics. He could just hear her screaming. 'For god's sake, give him what he wants. Give it to him. Look what he is doing. And he's told you I'm next.' And so you will be, my little dancing girl.

Come to think of it, if he could get the American to hand over the stone on the basis of what Gunga would do to his little hillman friend, then maybe he could keep the woman around for a while. He had never had a white woman. He had heard that they were good in bed. That once a man got on top of them and got their legs apart, they automatically surrendered. Yes, that might be interesting. She might be very satisfying for a while. He had had only one glimpse of her, running across the fields. But she was fair-haired, and that was nice. Not like his Indian whores. All black-haired. Head, underarms, belly and crotch. All the same. Always. And what colour would her hair be, down there in her little holy of holies?

The Shangri La hotel in Kathmandu...First in Kathmandu for ambience, graciousness, service and style.

Kathmandu, city of temples, gods and goddesses.

Gold, like her head? And she had long legs, he had seen that. Long white legs that could wrap around a man's waist. Yes. And after he got tired or her? Well, Gunga would love to have her. He'd tell Gunga he had a special treat for him. Gunga of course had never had a woman of any kind and had never known sex. It would be very amusing to show him how to do it for the first time. Even more so with a white woman. Maybe he could have a party for his man and get them all to watch. Now that would certainly elevate his status in Nagpur. Oh yes indeed. But now…back to the Nepalese highway and the problem of catching them on it?

In actual fact, he realized, there were two problems. One was that this was not India and, come to think of it, he was not even sure that a Nepali bus or truck would stop for a flag-down in the night. Two, searching vehicles might also pose problems. He had heard that Nepalis were inclined to fight, unlike the meek and mild village Indians he was used to. Maybe the highway was not such a good idea. And again, if the American succeeded in getting to the highway before him and then got ahead of him, he'd find himself wasting his time on it, like flogging a dead horse. No, a better idea would be to bypass them now and get ahead of them. This of course would not be an effective strategy if he did not know their goal. But he did. The temple of the Eye lay due north of Kathmandu and to get to it, Wildman would have to pass through the city. Being westerners—oh yes, he knew their habits—they would obviously stop in the city to eat and to rest, at least for a night or two.

That was it. He'd bypass them and get ahead of them. There were a lot of Indians in Kathmandu these days, and he should have no trouble in making some contacts. Buying some contacts, that is. Should not be difficult. With his countrymen there was little loyalty to anyone. Outside of immediate family that is. Money was all that mattered, money that talked with a loud voice. But, oh Kali, the money he was spending on this accursed American! Rupees by the thousand and thousand. But then, all things considered, it was worth it. A ten million dollar reward was certainly worth it. A ten million dollar reward was worth anything. Thinking of which, and still standing in the stinking smoke of the burning vehicles, he shouted to his men and Gunga to start getting the Jeep back up on the road. This was quickly accomplished, with Gunga holding one end of the Jeep up off the ground and the remainder pushing and pulling from behind.

An hour later Vask was heading east, driving fast on the back roads that run along the Indo-Nepal order, heading for Raxaul and the Tribuvan Rajpath, the big highway that runs north from the Indian border, straight up to Kathmandu. Twenty-three hours later, Vask's Jeep turned into a narrow street in the Kichipokri district in the heart of the city of Kathmandu. It stopped at a sign that said **THE PANORAMA HOTEL**. Leaving Gunga in the Jeep, Vask went in and slammed a fistful of Indian one-hundred-rupee bills on the counter and demanded a room. Twenty minutes later, with Gunga quietly hustled in through a back door he was sitting in the hotel's top storey room, talking rapidly into an old black telephone.

The room was large, with big glass windows that overlooked the roofs of the surrounding houses and provided a distant view of the mountains. It had two beds and a number of chairs and settees. Gunga, nursing a bottle of rum in his hands and whining softly, sat on one of the settees, its short, wooden legs groaning in protest at his immense weight. Vask's two men, the last of his guards, sat on the chairs, watchful and nervous. Metha, the last of Vask's drivers, remained in the street, sitting in the Jeep to guard it against theft, his long cloth turban wound around his face and head against the cold.

<<>>

On arrival in Kathmandu, Vask had immediately set to work to find contacts. A few quick inquiries informed him that there were a number of Indians, some from the Nagpur area, living in the city. Several of them were in the motor vehicle parts business in the Kalimati district. He had immediately gone to see them and had selected two of them to work for him.

The contract he offered them was a simple one. It was money for information. However, his new contacts being Indians, and just as devious as he was, there was no agreement on the amount of money he would have to pay for the information he needed. Indeed, as Vask was about to find out, his new business associates immediately agreed among themselves to soak him for every penny they could get. Back in Nagpur, where Vask had great power, they might have been a bit more careful. But up here in Nepal they were not so vulnerable to the man and his vengeful tactics, and they intended to take full advantage of this.

The first task they were given was a simple one. Go to the temple of the little Yellow God and find out if the long-missing Eye had been returned. If it had, then whatever plans Vask made now would probably have to be directed towards the temple itself. Wildman, he felt sure, having delivered the Eye, would grab his money and disappear on the first plane out to Bangkok or Singapore. Or wherever. Of course, if the Eye

The Hotel Snug in the Bhimsenthan district of Kathmandu, where Pasang stayed when he and Wildman were in the city.

had not been returned, then he must keep after Wildman, find him, get the Eye from him and then dispose of him. In the meantime the most important thing was to find out if the Eye was back.

Vask's new associates told him that this would be a very difficult job. That it would involve travel, bribes, danger, etc., etc. In return, but without promising anything, Vask mumbled that if they got him the information he needed, they would be well paid. Anything reasonable. Of course what Vask thought was reasonable and what they thought would be fair coverage for 'thee much work and thee great dangers involved, oh great Raja,' were two different things.

<<>>

Vask's new contacts did not go to the temple of the Eye itself. They did not have to. They knew that if the eyeless image at the temple were to have its stone restored, the word would quickly spread among nearby villages. There would be rejoicing, pilgrimages to the temple, festivities. So they just drove up the road from Kathmandu a few miles and visited a couple of villages near the temple. The villagers told them that they had heard nothing about the long-missing Eye being returned; this was the information that they brought back to Vask.

Their total output in time and money, to get the information Vask wanted, was ten gallons of gasoline and six hours driving, three to the villages near the temple and three back again. Add to this another hour or so of waiting, while a couple of Nepali boys they had taken with them made inquiries in the villages. And that was it. But what they told Vask was an altogether different story.

"Much difficulty, oh great Raja. Many problems. Nepali peoples very nasty in thee villages. Not willing to talk to thee strangers. Therefore much money having to be paid. Altogether putting out ten thousand rupees, which we did so knowing that thee great Raja from Nagpur would be most willing to reimburse us, thank you, please, isn't it."

Vask, smiling his gratitude on the outside, but seething in anger behind the mask, paid them ten thousand rupees from his dwindling supply of cash. He had to. Because now that he knew that Wildman still had the stone, he needed these contacts—shit-eating spawn of monkeys is what he inwardly called them—to find Wildman in the city. And so he gave them their next task.

Without telling them why he wanted to know where Wildman was, or what he wanted from him, he described the big man to them. He added the possibility of a girl accompanying him, and a Nepali man, a Sherpa, and told them that if they could find the trio, in the teeming city, they would be richly rewarded.

Now the little Panorama desk clerk had told him that the Indians had called to say they had new information for him and were coming to see him again. With more very expensive information, no doubt, he thought. But if it was information about the accursed trio who had caused him so much trouble and expense to now, then it would be worth it, whatever the price.

<<>>

He looked at his watch. Ten o'clock. The Indians should be here soon. In the meantime he would eat. He told the guards to go down and buy food and bring it up to him. Then they were to leave and let him eat his dinner in private. When he had eaten, they could both go and eat somewhere. Then they were to come back up to his room.

He looked at Gunga sprawled on the sagging couch. The giant's eyes were half-closed as he slumped on the settee in a drunken stupor. Vask spat on the floor in disgust. There were the only two ways he could control his huge brother; locked up or dead drunk. Those, or a woman, or a man, to play with. His toys. He would talk with the Indians when they came and see if it might be possible to get a woman for Gunga. Not a man. He would kill the man and, in this accursed foreign city, that might mean trouble. Trouble out of which his currency might not be able to buy him.

A woman would be better. Gunga pawed them and then, not knowing what they were for, masturbated two or three times and then lost interest in them. Vask's only problem with a woman for Gunga was that he had to stand by while the giant played with her, ready to restrain him if he got carried away. If he did not do this, then he might well finish up with a dead whore on his hands. Easy enough to deal with, back in Nagpur, where another whore was just another dead body to throw in the river. But up here? And the accursed whores. They always took one look at Little Gunga and demanded ten or more times the going rate.

Yes. His brother was a problem. It might be time to start thinking of disposing of him. Certainly after he had the Eye, he would have no further use for him. He laughed at the thought of Gunga living with him in a foreign country. They'd lock him up on sight in the nearest violent mental institution and throw away the key. And then no doubt bill Vask for his keep. No. The time was coming to get rid of Gunga. But for now he'd better

The old Panorama Hotel in the Kichipokri district of Kathmandu.

keep him. In a fight Gunga stood alone and, as a menace, something with which to threaten his men and keep them under control, he was more than useful.

And who knows what the next few days might bring. Vask licked his lips as he thought about the possibilities; after he had the Eye nothing would give him greater pleasure than to set Gunga on the American and the Nepali and watch what he would do to them. He looked at his watch again. Ten past ten. He hoped the Indians would not be late, so that if the information they brought required action of some kind, he could get to it that night.

<<>>

Not long after night fell, Wildman walked out into the garden of the Shangri La Hotel. It was quite beautiful, with manicured lawns and profuse masses of flowers set in small, brick-walled beds. The high wall that enclosed it was decorated with terracotta figures of elephants and fronted with dozens of small flowering trees. In one place an explosion of mountain bamboo sent long, leafy stems reaching to the sky and in another, colourful Tibetan prayer flags on tall yellow, poles moved gently in a soft breeze. The entire garden itself was illuminated with soft, concealed lighting and the scent of the flowers that hung in the air was sensual and sweet.

He walked slowly, observing the layout of the trees and the shadows they cast against the wall. On his second circuit he walked a little closer to the thick clump of mountain bamboo and suddenly, with a quick, short run he was up and over the ten foot wall.

Dropping down from its outer side, he found himself in a small, dark back street, fronted by two-storey brick houses. There were no people about and there was no traffic. He walked quickly down the street, turned into another and, coming to the end of this, found himself on a main thoroughfare with traffic moving. He stopped a taxi and told the driver to take him to the Kathmandu zoo. He was told in reply that the zoo was closed at that time. He repeated his order, received a crazy foreigner shake of the head in reply, and was driven down into the heart of the city, through it, over a bridge across a river and then on for two more miles. The taxi stopped in front of the zoo gates. The driver indicated the closed gates and shrugged and waited. Wildman paid him the meter rate and added a tip.

The driver waited. Wildman told him that he could leave; he did not want the man to see where he was going. But the driver, hopeful of a return fare to the city when the *feringhee* found the zoo closed, waited. Wildman looked at him and smiled and asked him where he could get cigarettes. The driver told him, three blocks down and to the left. Wildman smiled again and gave the man a handful of rupee bills and told him to go and get him some cigarettes and bring them back. The driver shrugged—crazy foreigners, imagine sending a taxi for cigarettes—grunted and drove off with a crash of gears to get the cigarettes. When he returned his passenger had vanished. He looked at his watch and decided that he would give him ten minutes. The time was ten thirty. If he was not back by ten forty he would leave without him. And, quite rightfully he thought, pocket the cigarettes and the change. Crazy foreigners.

<<>>

The Indians arrived at the Panorama Hotel at eleven o'clock. They had a piece of information for which, they felt, the high Raja from India would be willing to pay a great deal of money. Though they had picked it up in the course of routine inquiries in the city, they did not tell Vask this. For Vask their story would be about long hard days of dedicated effort, bribes paid, money put out for men and taxis and gasoline, 'all very costly, oh great Raja, isn't it.' However, this time, in truth, they had applied a little more effort.

They had started by asking themselves where visiting foreigners would stay in a city like Kathmandu. The answer, of course, was the tourist hotels. The problem was that there were many tourists hotels now in Kathmandu, probably a hundred in all, and it would take days to go round all of them, one by one, asking for a single foreigner called Wildman. Again, being Indians, they might not get the co-operation that was needed in an inquiry like this, at a Nepalese hotel. Again, it was highly possible that the foreigner in question might not register under his own name, but under an assumed name. He might even not register at all. But they thought it worth a try and they started with big two hotels that had Indian barmen working in them, the Malla and the Annapurna.

At the Malla they picked up a little driblet of information from a pot-bellied Bengali bartender with greasy black hair that pushed their thinking off in another direction. If the man in question was a foreigner who visited Kathmandu from time to time, he said, and was therefore not your average tourist, he might keep a house in the city somewhere. That was interesting and maybe worth following up on. But at the Annapurna, from a weasel-faced, little Madrassi with a nervous tick in his eye and a tiny, pointed head that contained a veritable mine of information about what

Back door of the Panorama Hotel in Kathmandu through which, in the night, Vask smuggled his monstrous brother, Little Gunga, into the hotel. Photo credit, Kathmandu Metropolitan Police.

went on in the city, they did better. He told them that he knew of two *feringhees* who had houses in the city and who answered to the description they gave him. Big men, coming and going quite a lot, semi-permanent residents of the country. One had a house in a district called Nag Pokri, meaning the lake of the snake. The other had a place in Jawalakhel, up beside the zoo.

They drove quietly to Nag Pokri, found the house in question and on the pretence of needing directions to another area, managed to get in to the back area where the kitchen was, and talk to the servants. The house owner, they were told, was an American. A big man, a permanent resident. His name was Armington and he was the director of a trekking company. At first they were suspicious about what they were told. But then, from the way the man's servants talked about him, freely and without restraint, it was obvious to the Indians that they had not been cautioned about giving information to strangers, as would be the case with Wildman's servants, if he had any. So it was quickly apparent to them that Armington was not their man.

Leaving Nag Pokri, they drove to the Jawalakhel district. Arriving there they turned left at the zoo, drove three hundred feet down a dark street and then turned right into a narrow lane enclosed by six-foot high, brick walls. And at a little house, an old gatehouse to one of the ancient palaces, a small two-storied building with the name ***JULIA COTTAGE*** on the door on a brass plate, they got a reception that was entirely different from the one they had received at the Armington house.

A concrete wall prevented their getting around to the back, where they hoped to find a kitchen and talkative servants and so, taking a chance, but with their excuse ready—a box labelled **KATHMANDU AUTO PARTS**—they knocked on the front door. It was immediately opened by a fierce little Sherpa with narrow, suspicious, black eyes set in a tight, grim face. They saw a Sherpa woman hovering behind him.

"What you want?" he barked at them, the instant he saw them.

In reply one of them stepped forward. "We are from the Kathmandu Auto Parts shop. We came to tell Mr. Wildman *sahib* we have the parts for his car that were ordered from India. Please we would like to talk to Mr. Wildman."

The little man glared at them and at the same time looked quickly up and down the street. "Parts? What parts? Mr. Wildman does not have a car here now. In any case he is not here."

With that he slammed the door in their faces. But they smiled grimly at each other as they turned away, for the little man, fierce and uncooperative though he had been, had given them the information they needed.

Wildman relaxing at the Shangri La Hotel after the mission was completed.
Photo credit, South China Morning Post, Hong Kong.

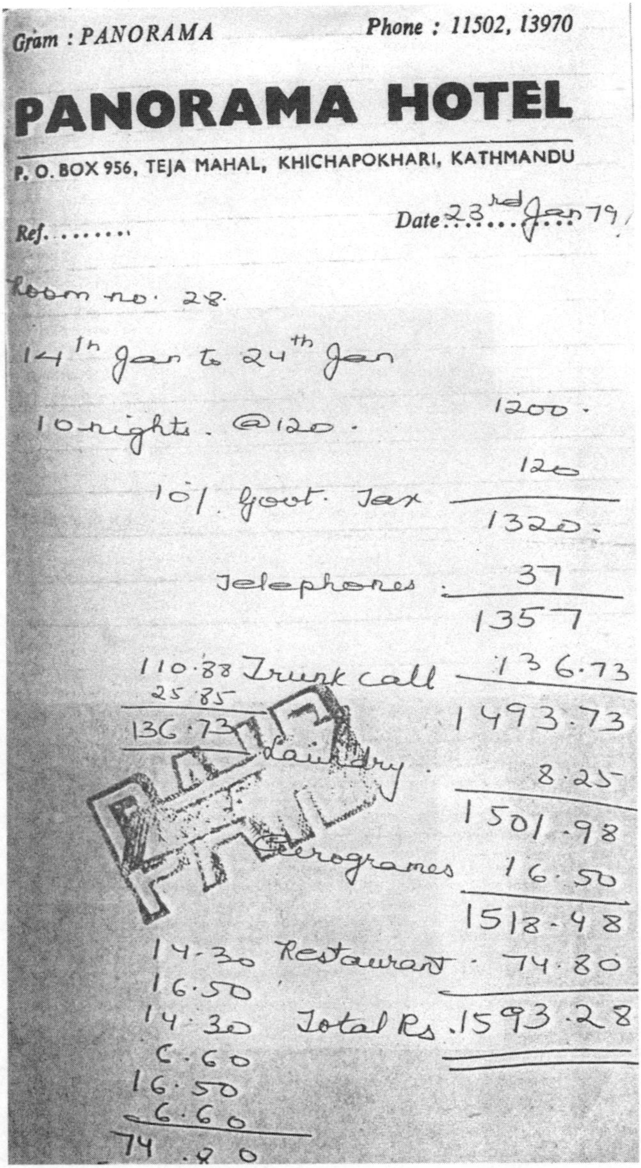

Gram : PANORAMA Phone : 11502, 13970

PANORAMA HOTEL

P. O. BOX 956, TEJA MAHAL, KHICHAPOKHARI, KATHMANDU

Ref. .... Date: 23rd Jan 79

Room no. 28.

14th Jan to 24th Jan

10 nights. @120.	1200.
10% Govt. Tax	120
	1320.
Telephones :	37
	1357
110.88 Trunk call	136.73
25.85	
136.73	1493.73
Laundry.	8.25
	1501.98
Aerogrames	16.50
	1518.48
14.30 Restaurant.	74.80
16.50	
14.30 Total Rs.	1593.28
6.60	
16.50	
6.60	
74.80	

PAID

A bill for Vask and his men at the Panorama Hotel,
where they stayed when in Kathmandu.
Photo credit, Kathmandu Metropolitan Police, Criminal files.

Forty-five minutes later they were climbing the stairs to Vask's room at the Panorama, rehearsing, for the third time, the story that they would tell the Raja. Oh great Raja. 'Ees very valuable information. Thee great find indeed. But the people who help us, they demand much money. Very greedy peoples, oh Raja.' And this time, in case the Raja might be a bit slow getting his hand into his pocket, they had agreed that their game plan was going to be, money first and information afterwards. They got to the top of the tenth flight of stairs, looked at each other, nodded in agreement and knocked on the door of Vask's room. The time was ten past eleven.

<<>>

Wildman spent thirty minutes watching his house in Jawalakhel from the concealment of the lane's high brick wall, before sliding over it, running quickly down the lane, bounding up the six steps to the front door and knocking gently. He heard a faint movement inside when he knocked and then silence. He knocked again, a little louder, at the same time keeping a watchful eye on the lane behind him and the street from which it came and on which some traffic moved. Then he heard the latches on the door being opened, he saw the handle move and with a jerk the door swung inward and he found himself looking into the scowling face of his housekeeper from whose right hand dangled a long-bladed *kukri*. They eyed each other for probably three seconds. And then the little man jerked his head back in surprise, opened his mouth and said, "Oh *sahib*, it is you. Oh *sahib*, I am so sorry. I thought it was those Indian thieves coming back for more questions. Oh come in, *sahib*. Come in. Come in."

Saying which he stepped back quickly, allowed Wildman to enter, and then shut and bolted the door behind him.

<<>>

Wildman sat in the kitchen of his house, with his housekeeper and his wife. In front of him was a big mug of instant coffee. Locks had been checked on the front and back doors and the single window of the little kitchen was closed and tightly curtained. Wildman's housekeeper was a tough little Sherpa named Tashi Kirong.. He was fifty years of age, stood five foot two in his socks and was a loyal, hard-working little man from Kirong, in Tibet. He had one wife, one small daughter, was the guardian of Julia Cottage, Wildman's Kathmandu house, and had been in Wildman's employ for twenty years.

Gael at the Shangri La Hotel after the mission.
Photo credit Life Magazine, New York, USA.

He told Wildman about the visit of the two Indians. Wildman listened carefully, his mind rapidly turning over contingency plans as he guessed that the two Indians were very possibly associated with Vask. When Tashi had finished, he told the little Sherpa that he was back in Nepal for a while, but that just now he would not be staying at the house. His visit now, tonight, was going to be very brief and after this he would probably be away for about a week. Then he would be back and when he did, he would probably stay at the cottage for a while. Until then Tashi was to tell no one that he had been at the house, was to keep the house locked and to admit no visitors with the exception of uniformed Nepalese police.

"Police, *sahib*?"

"Yes, Tashi. We have a problem, you see. Simply put, it's like this. Some very bad men want to see me. I do not want to see them. When they do not find me here at the cottage, they may get angry and they might try to hurt you. And so I am going to arrange for some police to come down and move in here with you for a few days. Let them in. Let them use the extra bedroom and give them whatever they want to eat. Try and make sure that at least two of them are in the house at all times. And keep your daughter in for the time being and at least until I get back. No school, no visits outside. The situation is a dangerous one. But after I get back it will be resolved, I promise you. Until then you must follow these orders. Yes?"

"Yes. Of course *sahib*. Everything you say."

Tashi nodded and his wife also bowed her head in agreement.

"And where is your little girl now? Sleeping?"

"Oh yes, *sahib*. Sleeping. But dreaming about the nice present you sent to her, still in its box, which she absolutely refuses to open until you come. It was with the things that you so kindly sent us from England."

"You mean she has not opened it yet?"

"No *sahib*. But that is all right. When you get back we can…"

"Listen, Tashi. Would you mind very much waking her up now? We'll open the parcel and I'll give her the present personally. Otherwise she will have to wait another week. Would you mind?"

The little Sherpa hesitated and then replied, "Not at all, *sahib*," and his wife hurried away to get the little girl out of bed.

While she did, Tashi stood up and opened one of the kitchen cupboards and took out a big white cardboard box with **HARRODS, KNIGHTSBRIDGE, LONDON,** emblazoned on the cover. With a smile he handed it to Wildman, who quickly opened the box. Inside was the big doll in the green dress that he had bought for Tashi's daughter in Harrods. He took it out and as he did, he heard the sounds of Tashi's wife returning.

Quickly he picked up his coffee mug off the table and handing it to Tashi, said, “Tashi, can you top that up with a bit of hot water please?”

The Sherpa took the mug and turned to the stove. As he did Wildman quickly spread the doll’s legs, and forced a finger through the narrow slit that he had cut there in the toilet at Harrods, three weeks previously. He got a finger around the thongs of the small leather bag that he had put in there, pulled it out and, as Tashi’s wife appeared in the doorway of the room, dropped it into his pocket. Then he stood up and gave the doll to a sleepy-eyed and delighted little Sherpa girl. Fifteen minutes later he was in a taxi and heading for the city’s police headquarters at Tangal, a mile south of the Shangri La Hotel. The time was fifteen minutes before twelve.

<<>>

The old man who guarded the front door of the Panorama was annoyed at having to open it, to let people out of the hotel at such a late hour. Especially the Indian from the top floor, who never tipped. The one with the huge, weird friend and the two grim-faced goons who walked behind him all the time, like guards. If he had not paid in advance, he would certainly not open the door for him. But the man and so he reluctantly let them out. The four men left the hotel, walked down the street to the parked Jeep, banged on the door to wake up Metha—sleeping inside with the doors locked—had him open the doors, climbed in and set out for Jawalakhel.

Vask was angry. The two Indians had demanded fifty thousand rupees for the information they had for him and after two hours of cat and mouse arguing he had had to give it to them. What persuaded him, what made him give in, in the end, was the value of the information. It was exactly what he needed, the one piece that might, if properly used, clinch the whole matter for him and bring it to a successful conclusion. Unfortunately for him, his informants guessed this and so played it for every penny it was worth. In the end, with ill-concealed rage, Vask had paid them fifty thousand rupees and in return they had given him the address of Wildman’s house in Jawalakhel. At the same time, smiling inwardly and exchanging quick, furtive glances with each other, they had held back another little piece of information, something, which they felt might well add a very healthy bonus to what the rich Raja from India had already paid them.

<<>>

That afternoon, one of the Vask’s informers or, as they liked to think of themselves, his business associates, had been approached by a sixteen

The Jawalakhel district in Kathmandu, where Wildman had his house, Julia Cottage.

year old cousin, looking for a job. He was promptly given one, on a commission basis, which meant that he got paid if he produced. He was supplied with a blanket to keep him warm, a packet of Yak cigarettes to keep him quiet, and a hundred rupees to be used only in an emergency and, if not used, to be returned. The job he was given was to go to Jawalakhel and watch a house there. Wildman's house.

His instructions were simple. He was to watch the house and if he saw a tall, foreign-looking man leaving it, he was to follow him, find out where he went and then get back to his new employers as fast as possible with the information. He was dropped off by taxi in the Jawalakhel area and he quickly found a small garden down the street from Julia Cottage, with a low brick wall behind which he could hide. Settling himself in, he wrapped himself in the blanket against the night cold, opened up his packet of Yak coffin nails and commenced his watch.

He was lucky. He had been in position only a couple of hours when Wildman—a tall foreign-looking gentleman—arrived and he saw him go inside. Following his instructions, as he thought best, he did not leave at once to inform the others of what he had seen. He waited, as he had been told to, for the man to leave. When the man did, he followed him. He saw him flag down a taxi and get into it and for a moment he panicked. The man might get away. But he was he was lucky, there was another one following, a small, blue, late-night taxi, cruising forlornly for a fare. He flagged it down, jumped in and told the driver to follow the *feringhee's* cab, still in sight.

Wildman's cab headed north, back across the river, through the heart of the city, past the royal palace and then east to the city's central police station, where it stopped. When he saw Wildman get out and go inside, he told his taxi driver to wait, hoping that the hundred rupees he had been given for emergencies would be enough for the added fare.

After twenty minutes the big *feringhee* came back out of the police station, accompanied by two policemen. He saw them salute the big man and watched him get back into his cab, telling his own driver to follow as Wildman's taxi sped away from the station, west, and then north, up through the Lazimpat district to a big foreign looking hotel, with a fierce looking lion statue outside and tough looking security men hanging about.

When he saw the big man pay off his taxi and go into the hotel, he told his own driver to park in the street, well away from the hotel entrance and its watchful guards.

He waited for an hour and when the man did not come out, guessing that he might be staying here, he went racing back to his masters with his information. As his taxi rattled down through the dark and silent streets of Lazimpat and back into the heart of the city, the clock in the university tower struck the hour of two.

<<>>

At he police station, Wildman had met with a Chief Inspector and had made specific arrangements. Everything was understood. A four-man guard would be placed on his house. At once. A Jeep had been sent for and the guard would leave for Jawalakhel within twenty minutes. A junior inspector would accompany the men and see them to the house, and into it, and would then come back and report. The guard would stay there until Wildman's return from a short trip, probably a week. The duty of the guard would be to protect the house and its contents and the family who lived in it as housekeepers, a Mr. Tashi Kirong, and his wife and their little daughter. And the inspector was repeating himself when he said again that Mr. Wildman's most generous contribution to the Policeman's Benevolent Fund was totally unnecessary but nevertheless thankfully received. Considering the hard times everyone was going through.

<<>>

Vask's driver, Metha, had to stop four times to inquire the way to the house in Jawalakhel. Part of his problem was the lateness of the hour and the lack of people moving about. The night was cold. A grey mist hung in the dark and gloomy streets and the whole city seemed to have gone to bed. The few fuel stations they saw were shut tight and the hundreds of shops and restaurants that lined the narrow streets were barred and bolted as though in the face of an impending riot. It was some time after twelve-thirty when, driving slowly, so as to attract as little attention as possible, Vask's Jeep turned into the little lane just beyond the zoo and started down it towards Julia Cottage.

They had gone no more than thirty yards in the direction of the house when Vask saw a police Jeep parked outside it, with a uniformed driver guarding it. Two uniformed constables were standing on the steps of the house, waiting while an inspector talked to a tiny little man dressed like a Sherpa. Quietly, to the sounds of Vask's cursing, Metha stopped the Jeep and backed it out of the lane. Once out of the lane he looked to Vask for instructions. Vask thought quickly. Then he dropped off one of the guards, told him to walk around and try to keep an eye on the house and see what the police were doing there. He told him that he would come back in an hour and pick him up at the gates of the zoo.

When the guard got out, Vask ordered Metha to leave the area at once and drive around the streets, anywhere, but slowly, so as not to attract attention, and to keep driving until he gave him further orders.

<<>>

When Wildman re-entered the Shangri La, the night receptionist greeted him with a smile and handed him an envelope. "Good morning sir. Your room key, sir? Of course. And here is a message for you. From our manager."

Wildman thanked him and opened the envelope as he walked up the stairs to his room. Inside the envelope was a Jeep ignition key and a note from Sengupta. The note read: *I have a Jeep for you. It is parked in the back courtyard. There will be a driver if you want one. If not, take it yourself. It is filled with gasoline and is in good condition. Take care and come have dinner with my wife and I when you get back.*

Wildman walked up the four flights of broad, heavily carpeted stairs to his room on the second floor. At Gael's door he stopped and listened for a moment. There was no sound from within. He opened his door and went in and closed it behind him, locking it carefully. In his absence the room had been tidied up, the bed drawn down and the lights switched off. Leaving the lights off, he went to the window and drew back the heavy drapes and looked out. His room overlooked the forecourt of the hotel, beyond which he could see the street.

A few cars were parked in the forecourt, and the big, dark grey flagstones of its surface, damp with the night dew, gleamed wetly in the subdued light coming from the street. Down at the main gate below him, three uniformed security men huddled over a brazier filled with burning charcoal. The high wall of the courtyard blocked much of his view of the street. However, the open front gate allowed a view of the roadway, on the far side of which, just visible, was the front end of a small blue taxi. He watched it for a while from the darkness of his window. It was very late for a taxi and he wondered why a taxi driver would be sitting out there in the street at this hour. There were no tourists moving at this time of night, no sign of life at all, apart from the security men. Well, perhaps the man was waiting to catch an eager beaver early morning foreigner. One of those gushing little old ladies with their cameras and their straw hats and their tourist guide brochures and their eager questions and their fat little pocketbooks filled with one dollar bills and their total ignorance of how a Kathmandu taxi meter worked.

He stripped off and put his clothes on the floor beside the bed. He took the little leather bag from of the inside pocket of his jacket and slid it under the pillow. About an hour later, sleeping lightly, he heard the sound of a car engine starting up. He jumped out of bed quickly and moved to the window and was just in time to see the little blue taxi driving off. He looked at his Rolex. The time was three a.m.

<<>>

The Indians at the auto parts shop were excited with what their sixteen-year-old cousin had to tell them. He told them what he had found out, and how he had followed a big foreign-looking man from the house in Jawalakhel to a police station and then to a hotel called the Shangri La, in the Lazimpat district. The bit about the police station worried them. What was the American doing there? Had he been alerting the police to the doings of the weird Raja at the Panorama Hotel? Might they be involved? The thought worried them and they hesitated about going out again. But greed, plus the thought of the Raja's money, soon got the better of them and after a quick conversation they went downstairs, got in their Jeep, backed it out of the rusting tin shed next to their shop, where they kept it, and drove to the Panorama…

Leaving their young cousin outside with the Jeep, they then tried to get into the hotel. It took a while and it was only after a long argument, plus an exchange of ten rupees, that the old man, who guarded the hotel's front door, agreed to allow one of them to come in and go up to the room on the top floor, where the Raja from India was staying. The man he allowed in went racing up the stairs to the top floor and banged on the door of Vask's room. There was no reply. He banged again on the door, several times, to no avail. It was only after he came downstairs again that the doorman remembered to tell them that the Raja had gone out some time before. When would he be back? The old man, closing and locking the door in their faces, had no idea.

The two Indians returned to the street and stood by their Jeep for a while. They thought of waiting for the Raja to return. They also thought of driving out to the Jawalakhel district, to the foreigner's house, to see if Vask was there. But then they remembered the story their young cousin had told them of the big foreigner and of how, before going to the hotel in Lazimpat, he had visited a police station. It made them realise that they really did not know exactly what the Raja from Nagpur was up to. Better to stay away from the foreigner's house just now, especially if the police were involved in some way. Better to restrict themselves to providing the Raja with information and getting whatever they could for it. As much as they could, and preferably behind the closed doors of the Panorama Hotel, and not in the street.

And anyway, it was cold now. A nasty, damp cold. The kind that seeped into the bones of an Indian lowlander. They got in their Jeep and drove back to the parts shop, put the Jeep away in the tin shed, told the cousin to sleep under the shop counter, climbed up to their living quarters above the shop and went to bed. The stupid Raja could wait. The new information that they had for him would be just as valuable in the morning.

<<>>

Vask returned to Jawalakhel just before three thirty. He saw his man standing at the gates of the zoo from some distance away and, without stopping, had the man scramble into the Jeep on the run. While they drove up the road past the zoo, and towards the city, the man told him what he had seen. The police Jeep had driven away some time after Vask had left. But four policemen, who had come in it, went into the house with blankets and bedrolls. The house door had closed behind them and they had not come out again. It was the opinion of the guard that the policemen had moved into the house on some kind of semi permanent basis. The bedrolls and the blankets supported this.

Vask listened to what the man had to say and then snarled at his driver and told him to drive to the auto parts shop, over in the Kalimati district. Maybe his informers knew something that he did not. He looked at his watch. It was fifteen minutes before four. They would not like being wakened at this hour. The hell with them. He had paid them enough to wake them at any hour.

Arriving at the shop Vask got out of the Jeep and went up and banged his fist on the steel shutters that closed off its front. As he did so, he stepped back and looked up at the small windows of the living area above. That was where the owners lived, he knew, and that was where they would be sleeping. Nothing happened in response to his knocking and so he tried again, pounding the heavy shutters with his big fist and making them rattle loudly. A voice from above an adjacent shop attracted his attention. He stepped back from the shutters and looked up. A man's head had appeared through a small window. A voice said, in Hindustani, "You are making a lot of noise. What do you want?"

Vask told him, whereupon the man replied, "There is no one there. They are out somewhere. Now go away and let peaceful people sleep. Or I will call the police."

The man withdrew his head and closed his window and Vask was left in silence again. He got back in the Jeep and, with his rage seething, told Metha the driver to take him back to the Panorama.

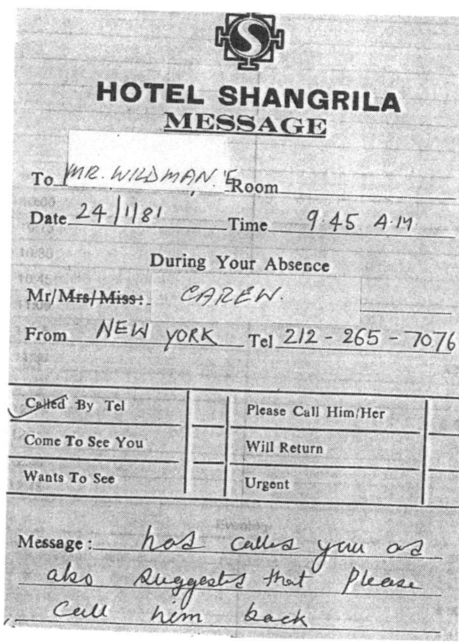

HOTEL SHANGRILA
MESSAGE

To MR. WILDMAN'S Room

Date 24/1/81 Time 9.45 A.M

During Your Absence

Mr/~~Mrs/Miss~~: CAREW.

From NEW YORK Tel 212 - 265 - 7076

Called By Tel	✓	Please Call Him/Her	
Come To See You		Will Return	
Wants To See		Urgent	

Message: has calls you as also suggests that please call him back

Shangri La Hotel telephone message for Wildman from Lord Carew or his estate executors in New York.

The driver turned the Jeep and drove off in the direction of the Panorama. The mist had thickened and the roadway surfaces glistened in the dim light of the street lamps. As they turned to enter the narrow street that led past the great pointing stone finger of Bhimsen's Tower, at the end of which stood the old Panorama, they passed the only other moving vehicle they had seen in the last hour. It was another Jeep with what looked like three men in it, driving off in the direction of Kalimati.

<<>>

Wildman's big, comfortable room at the Shangri La faced east and the first thin light of dawn, painting his windows in shades of pale, watercolour pink, awakened him just after five. He lay still for a few minutes, thinking. That taxi. It bothered him. What time was it when it left? Three? Four? Taxis do not cruise the streets of Kathmandu at that hour. Wildman had spent enough time in taxis in the city to know that. He used them a lot. They were cheap, they were fast and they were a lot more convenient than using one's own vehicle and fighting the parking space battle every day. Their only drawback was that after about ten o'clock at night their drivers simply packed up and went home.

He sat up in bed and looked out of the window. The faint light that crept through the spotless panes was growing, as the day dawned. Down in the city people would be starting to move around, shop shutters would be opening and men with huge basket loads of vegetables, fresh from the valley fields, would be converging on the market places. Dogs would be barking and thousand of pigeons and crows would be leaving their roosting places of the night and setting off on their daily search for food. Children would be grumbling at having to get up and women would be boiling water for tea and dressing, pulling on sandals and wrapping thin cotton blankets around their shoulders against the damp cold. Their husbands would be drinking hot tea and having a quick cigarette and listening to the chiming of the university tower clock telling them it was time to get ready to go to work.

Fully awake now and with his mind beginning to focus on the coming day, Wildman's thoughts turned to a consideration of the mind of the man Vask, the kind of person that he was, where he might be at this time and what he might be doing. Would he have guessed that Wildman would head for Kathmandu and had he followed him here? Was he in the city now? Somewhere deep down in the heart of the seething metropolis, in one of the hundreds of small hotels that had sprung up in the last few years to cater to the hordes of cheap travel tourists from all over the world? Like him, sitting up in bed, thinking, plotting, planning and in his case, quite possibly, with a huge, ghastly figure sleeping on the floor beside him, a giant creature that moaned and whined in its sleep?

If he was here, would he still be concentrating on ways and means of finding Wildman, and getting the Eye? Or would he now, having failed to stop him three times, and with the loss of most of his men at the hands of the bandit Rani and in the inferno on the bridge, as well as the huge amounts of money fruitlessly expended so far, be ready to concede defeat? Maybe.

But then Wildman's mind flashed back to what old Lord Carew had told him about Vask and when he added that to what he now knew about the man from personally encountering him, he quickly changed his mind about the chances of Vask throwing in the towel. For what came through to him, and what persuaded him was not so much the viciousness of the man, his total and complete lack of moral integrity, or the murderous ruthlessness with which he had people tortured and killed. No, it was something else, something that probably posed more of a threat to Wildman than any other part of the man's villainy.

It was his grim and deadly tenacity, spurred by his raging desire to obtain the Eye and, with it, all the rewards that it would bring. No, Vask was not a man to give up easily. Wildman, sitting up in his big, comfortable bed in his hotel room, listening to the cocks crowing and the dogs barking out in the fog-drenched streets and the pigeons cooing on his windowsill, suddenly felt an icy touch of impending danger. It was faint, intangible, brushing the subliminal reaches of his mind with its delicate fingers. But it was there and, sensing it, he immediately began to concentrate on it and then to nurture it. He forced it to move out of his subconscious mind and into the mainstream reaches of his brain and he kept enhancing it until his whole body tingled with it. Then suddenly he knew what it was. He had known it before.

Sixth sense was what some people called it. Wildman did not have a name for it and, if asked, would probably have said that it was simply a matter of putting together the salient points of a mental problem into a readable pattern, one that could be rationally viewed and interpreted. But he did have a name for the absolutely imperative follow-through necessary to what his subconscious mind had suddenly thrust into the forefront of his thoughts. Action. The kind of action that had whisked him safely out of several very nasty situations in his life. The kind that allowed him, he thought grimly, to stay in one piece until now. To stay alive. The kind that one took when one had a ten-million-dollar emerald tucked in a little leather bag under one's pillow in a hotel room in an exotic foreign city.

<<>>

He stayed quite still for another thirty seconds. Then he swung around and picked up the telephone and dialled room service and ordered breakfast for two, hot coffee, croissants, butter, marmalade, fruit, and honey for his coffee. When the order was taken, he pressed the receiver down for a second for a disconnect and then dialled Gael's room. He listened while the phone beside her bed trilled four times. When a sleepy voice said, "Yes?" he spoke quickly and sharply. "It's me. You-know-who. Get up. Get dressed and get over to my room as quickly as you can. A bite to eat and some coffee and we are leaving. See you in five minutes."

He dropped the phone back into its stand and smiled. If nothing else, the thought of food would get her up. He leaped up off the bed and strode quickly to the bathroom and showered. Hot, then cold. The cold water took him by surprise. He had forgotten how cold Kathmandu water could be. Mountain cold, straight out of the ten-thousand-foot hills that ringed the valley. He had towelled himself off and was dressing when he heard the phone ring again. "It's me. I'm up and I won't be long. But, mister slave driver, I'm having a shower first, OK?"

Wildman looked quickly at his Rolex. Five twenty. The light, easing through his window, was brightening and the sky out towards the edge of the valley was tinged with gold. He dressed and took the little leather bag from under his pillow. He tucked it carefully into his money belt and tied it around his waist and he was pulling on his Gokeys and buckling them up when there was a knock on the door. He unlocked it and opened it cautiously to a smiling room-service man in a scarlet, gold-braided uniform, balancing a tray loaded with food. There was a large silver coffeepot and two cups. Sugar in a silver bowl. Cream in a fat little jug. Fresh croissants, little brown muffins, butter, jam and marmalade surrounded by an army of shining knives, forks and spoons. Hanging on his arm the man had a basket of fruit that included a sliced pineapple, bananas, mangoes, apples, limes and a freshly cut papaya. Wildman stood aside and waved him in and, as he did so, Gael appeared with a cool, "Good morning, Captain Bligh, sir," and walked in after him...

Wildman nodded and smiled. "Hmm. Knew the food would do it," and they quickly sat down to eat. Now all they needed was Pasang and Wildman suddenly realised that he had not set a time for him to come this morning.

<<>>

In the cluttered apartment above the auto parts shop, Vask's informers awoke soon after dawn. They would have liked to sleep on a bit, after their late night excursion to Kichipokri. But the vast, swelling sound of the city, that began with the first paintbrush streaks of light on the eastern horizon and grew with amazing rapidity to a solid roar, effectively prevented any possibility of that.

They got up and draped thin wool blankets around themselves against the cold and shouted at the sixteen-year-old cousin, wrapped in his thin cotton blanket under the shop counter, to get up and make tea. Grumbling, half awake, the young man pulled a small kerosene stove out of a cupboard and pumped it up and lit it and put a kettle of water on it. When he served it a few minutes later and several cups of the hot liquid had gone down their gullets, thick with sugar and milk, they felt a little more capable of facing the new day. They dressed and went down and outside, to the back of the shop, where there was a small, brick-paved yard and a water tap. Here, on the bricks, they defecated and urinated and afterwards used the cold water tap to wash their hands.

As the light grew stronger, the first trucks began to roar through the Kalimati district and past the shop, heading for the edge of the valley and up and over its rim and down into the great basin of the Trisuli River, to take the roads west to Pokhara, in the mountains and south to Raxaul and the Indian border. Soon the sunlight began to creep across the valley, touching the golden spires of the temples and reddening the ten thousand tiled roofs of the ancient city, warming the faces of men and women working in the fields and turning the night dew on the road surfaces into dancing grey ghosts that rose up to be swallowed by the radiators of the trucks.

Time to move, the Indians thought. Time to visit the great Raja again and see what we can get out of him. And with this thought uppermost in their small minds, and shivering in the damp cold, they climbed again into their Jeep and backed it out of its tin shed and drove slowly towards the Panorama for another hopefully profitable meeting. The sixteen-year-old cousin was left to guard the premises; the minute they were out the door he fired up the kerosene stove to make more tea for himself.

They drove carefully in the thickening traffic, down to the end of the Kalimati road and then left and north towards the centre of the city. As they turned away from the Tundikhel, the big, open, grass-covered area that marked the centre of the city, to enter the maze of streets that was Kichipokri, the tower clock of the university tolled the hour of five.

<<>>

Wildman and Gael left the Shangri La through one of the rear staff doors. Sengupta had told them he would hold their bill until they got back and now, in the growing light of the newborn day, they were standing in one of the walled back yards of the hotel checking out the Jeep that he had provided for them. It was another World War II Kaiser vehicle, bright green, with a steel cab top. Fuel, oil, tyres, brakes; all were as they should be. It looked like a reasonable vehicle and, even though it was probably thirty years old, it was probably the best that Sengupta had been able to find in the city. Wildman fired the engine and sat and listened to it for a couple of minutes. It ran smoothly and he felt confidant that it would serve them well enough for their immediate plans.

He need not have worried about Pasang. The second they came out of the back door of the hotel he had materialised from the shadows of a storage shed. He greeted them with a smile and a brisk good morning as the three of them climbed into the Jeep. A security man opened the yard gate for them and they drove through and out into the street and then turned left, north, towards the city's Ring Road.

"To the temple, *sahib*?" said Pasang, from the back.

Wildman nodded and then they were off on what he hoped was the last leg of their journey. To the temple of the little yellow god. With the Eye.

Reaching the Ring Road they turned right and after a couple of miles turned left on to what was called the Bodhnath road, a road that ran past a giant *stupa* purported to contain, deep in its stony heart, a hair of Gautama Buddha. The Jeep engine ran smoothly despite its age. The sun promised a fine day. There was no sign of the enemy. And that they had been successful in making an early start was confirmed by Wildman's sturdy Rolex, which, scratched and scraped by river stones and jungle thorns and rocks and sand and hard usage, told him, battered but unbowed, that the time was fifteen minutes before six.

<<>>

Vask was horrified at what his Indian informers told him and at the price that they demanded for their information. "May the gods shit on you," he said to himself, looking into their lean and hungry faces. "So the *feringhee* has another accommodation? He is no longer at his home in Jawalakhel? He has gone somewhere else?"

They did not at first tell Vask that they had followed the man they thought was Wildman to a hotel. All they said was 'another accommodation.' They did not know how time was running out for Vask. But they sensed that if they told him that Wildman had gone to a hotel, even without telling him its name, and particularly because the hotel in question was one catering mainly to foreign tourists, he might well be able to track the big *feringhee* down without any further help from them. And if he did that, then, obviously, he would not feel that he had to pay them. So all that Vask got from them was 'another accommodation.'

They watched his face shade with rage to a tinge of light purple when they told him this. Seizing the advantage, and while he was still reeling from the news, they added, almost nonchalantly, as though it was not of any great importance, that they would need a further fifty thousand rupees to tell him the location of the 'accommodation' they were talking about.

But time was indeed running out for Vask. Thoroughly frustrated by his failure to find Wildman, he was now giving serious thought to what might be involved in breaking into the temple himself and, helped by Gunga and his two guards, forcing a way through its custodians, to take the Eye. He thought that he could do it. The Kalashnikov would speak on his behalf and it would speak with an authority that could not be denied. But then there would be the road back. Back to Kathmandu, through the city, and then south. The timing was the problem. Probably, from what the Indians had told him, it would take three hours to get back to Kathmandu from the temple on the hill. And then seven or eight hours south to the border. There would be pandemonium. A hue and cry. And the accursed country had telephones. And telephones reached out ahead of one and helped the police to build roadblocks and barriers. It would be a race against time. Against what the police could do. It would be a very risky race.

No. He would fall back on an attack on the temple if all else failed. The thing to do now, the obvious thing, would be to stop Wildman before he got to the temple and before he delivered the Eye. And the best plan would be to try and catch him on the way there because, it stood to reason, if he was heading for the temple, he would have the Eye on his person.

He looked again at the cold, jackal-like faces of his informers and then spoke. "All right then. I will pay you what you ask. But only yesterday I paid you a fortune for the address of a house where the *feringhee* was *not* to be found. If you do this again, and give me the name of another place where he is not to be found, then I shall come after you for a reckoning. And I know where you live and I know that you are bound by your livelihood to stay there. And that is where I will find you if you again give me useless information."

With his men watching and with Gunga slobbering and whining on the groaning hotel room couch, Vask reached into his shirt front and pulled out a cloth bag with the last of his money. When he had counted out fifty thousand rupees and put it on the table in front of him, there was very little left in the bag. Probably less than a thousand. Barely enough to buy gasoline to get back down to India. And he had no way of finding or raising more cash in this accursed foreign city.

The Indians rose together and grabbed the money and stuffed it into their pockets. “He is at a hotel in the Lazimpat district, north from here about two miles, called the Shangri La. He has an upstairs room on the second floor, at the front. He went in there this morning, very early, and we think that if you hurry you may find him sleeping there.”

<<>>

Vask had Metha drive him slowly past the high, red brick wall of the Shangri La Hotel. He shuddered at the sight of the huge stone lion, blue and orange and gold, with glaring eyes, mounted at the gate. The watchmen eyed his Jeep suspiciously as he approached, but lost interest when he continued past them. Vask told Metha to keep going until they were a hundred yards beyond the gate. Then he had the Jeep pulled in and ordered his two men to get out. They were given precise instructions. They were to feel their way around the gate watchmen and see what they could find out. If possible, they were to try and get into the hotel through the back, into the kitchen if possible, and question some of the staff there. A big American foreigner, an English or American woman staying with him. And a Sherpa servant.

They were to keep a careful eye out for the Sherpa. He might possibly be hanging out at the back of the hotel. He would probably not recognise them. But they should remember him from Nagpur. And they were to be careful. They were Indians. They would stand out as Indians among the Nepalis and the Sherpa was known to be dangerous.

Vask personally did not give a damn what happened to his two men. They were mere gun fodder to him, to be fed to whatever god chose to swallow them up in the needs of the chase. The only reason that he wanted them back was that if they did not return, he would be left without the information he needed. In addition, they were the last of his men. Losing them would leave him with his timid and near useless driver, Metha, and Gunga. And Gunga, he had to admit, had his limitations. So he told them to be careful, for what that was worth.

<<>>

The steel cab of Wildman’s Jeep had a glass window in the rear. The minute they left the Shangri La, Pasang, sitting in the back, turned wholly around in his seat and commenced giving his undivided attention to the road behind. Wildman, driving at a moderate speed, watched the road ahead and Gael, silent, alert, sat beside him, ready to do whatever he asked. Thirty minutes after leaving the hotel, they were out of the city and into the great patchwork quilt of the farmland of the valley, green and yellow with winter wheat and ripening mustard.

<<>>

Vask's guards did a lot better than he expected. They were back in twenty minutes and they had vital information. It was exactly what Vask wanted and the confidence with which they gave it to him supported its credibility. But at the same time it threw him into a panic and he felt himself break out in a sweat when its full meaning got through to him.

One of the watchmen at the front gate was a young man with junior security status. On being told that a Raja was looking for some friends of his, staying at the hotel, and after they had been described to him, he told Vask's men that he had just seen three people leave from the back of the hotel in a green Jeep. A big man, probably an American. A fair-haired young woman. And a Gurkha, or Sherpa, sitting in the back.

Vask did not hesitate. Ramming his men into what space the huge Gunga left in the back, he shouted at Metha to get going. The Jeep took off with tyres squealing and two hours later, after a wild drive that left two unlucky peasants maimed on the road and a rickshaw smashed to pieces, he found himself peering in wild excitement through the dusty windshield of the vehicle. He saw, far ahead of him, but travelling at what looked like a moderate pace, a bright green Jeep with a red Kathmandu number plate.

"We've got them," he shouted, slapping Metha on the shoulder and urging him to even wilder and more reckless speed. "We've got them. At last!"

Pasang, looking back through the Jeep's rear window, saw the long plume of grey dust far behind them. He watched it for about two minutes, noted the speed at which it was approaching and then, without turning around and without taking his eyes off it, said quickly to Wildman, "*Sahib*. They come."

BOOK THIRTEEN

THE TEMPLE OF THE YELLOW GOD

Wildman's reaction was instantaneous. He floored the throttle of the Jeep, settled down in his seat, told Gael to hang on and set his mind to drive what he knew would be a race for life. No gasoline cans to throw out this time. No luggage. Just the mountain road, about thirty miles to go and nothing but speed and hard driving to keep them ahead of what he knew was, without a shadow of a doubt, Vask and his men.

The mountain road might help. He had many years of driving experience on the hill roads of Nepal. From it, he knew that when speed was essential, the value of using the gears, changing down and accelerating into and through corners, for the added traction this provided, could not be underestimated. Likewise changing down in time for hills, and not waiting until the vehicle was actually on them. He knew that minimal braking on corners added a second or two here and there and that seconds, added up, eventually became minutes. And he knew that when the road ahead was clear, one could take hundreds of feet off the actual distance one had to travel by cutting across corners, swinging from one side to the other, as the road allowed. Did Vask's driver know this? Did he have mountain road driving experience? Wildman guessed, correctly as it turned out, that the man did not and as soon as he saw that he was holding the distance between them and the grey Jeep, for the sake of safety he eased his speed down a little.

<<>>

Soon after they spotted Wildman's Jeep, Vask reached down between the seats of his vehicle and pulled up the blanket and plastic sheeted bundle containing the Kalashnikov. He unwrapped it carefully and then stuffed the blanket and the plastic wrapping back down between the seats. Then he pulled out the bag containing the ammunition clips, took out a thirty-round clip, snapped it into the weapon and checked the safety catch. With the Kalashnikov resting comfortably across his lap, he leaned forward, eyes brimming with hate, to watch the green Jeep racing away up the mountain road ahead of him.

<<>>

Gael was the first to see the temple. On top of an enormous outcrop of rock, which rose from the hills like a giant, clenched fist, something gleamed. The reflection grew and flashed in the morning light, and slowly a cluster of towers and spires began to take shape. "There it is," she shouted to Wildman, over the roar of the Jeep's engine.

Wildman gave the edifice a quick glance and shouted back. "Yes. Couple of miles to go. Let's hope there is a road all the way there, so we don't have to get out and walk. Or more likely run."

The huge rock outcrop grew closer and, as it did, it seemed to tower over them. The whole of its front face was a sheer cliff, a thousand feet high, and it appeared to be almost vertical. At first there was no sign of a pathway up it and they were less than five hundred feet from it, before they saw the stone steps cut in its face. Then the Jeep was skidding to a stop in a boiling cloud of dust and they were scrambling out of it and running for the steps. Behind them the sound of Vask's Jeep grew louder. Then they were on the steps and racing up them, feet pounding on the hard rock, Wildman taking them two at a time, Gael close behind and Pasang, who had stepped back at the beginning with a murmured, "After you *sahib*, *memsahib*," bouncing up behind them like the human mountain goat that his name said he was.

<<>>

They were about one-third of the way up the cliff, a good three hundred feet, when they saw Vask's Jeep swing in below them and stop. They saw men piling out of the vehicle and running for the steps. All but one, who got out with the others but then stood beside the vehicle, looking up. Vask. Keeping up their pounding pace up the steps, climbing steadily, they glanced down and recognised him, now three hundred and fifty feet

The lion figure outside the Shangri La Hotel that frightened Vask and his men in the night.

A Varanasi rickshaw wallah who claimed to be Vask's brother. Although abandoned by Vask, and left destitute, fear of his brother's vengeance prevented him from giving the police information about his brother's criminal activities that would have been highly rewarded.
Photo Credit: Varanasi City Police. Anti Corruption Division.

The road north, through Kathmandu, to the temple of the Yellow God.

below them. Their quick glances also took in the giant Gunga, as the huge figure, arms waving, ran towards the base of the steps and then with surprising speed began to climb.

Suddenly the steps in front of them cut into a small tunnel, one of three in the face of the cliff and for a few moments, when they plunged into it, the men below were out of sight. The narrow tunnel was only fifteen feet long. But it was cool inside and Wildman instantly raised his hand to stop the others, for a quick rest. He knew the risk of stopping. But he also knew that if they did not keep up their speed, which they could not do without a rest, however brief, the men coming up behind them might catch up with them.

Wildman wondered, as they rested in the tunnel, why Vask had not joined the others in the chase. When he gave the signal to Pasang and Gael to go on, and they ran out of the tunnel and starting climbing again, he quickly found out.

Vask had stepped back from the Jeep and, watching him out of the corner of his eye, Wildman suddenly saw him raise something to his shoulder. As he did so, the air was split with the crackling roar of automatic fire, followed by the splintering whine of bullets ricocheting off the rock wall all around them. Wildman was quickest. "Down," he shouted and all three of them dropped to the steps and lay flat. In that position they were out of sight of Vask and the instant he lost sight of them he stopped firing. Wildman waited for a few seconds. "Now,"" he said and they rose to their feet and ran on up. The instant they did so the firing commenced again and twice Wildman felt rock splinters touch his clothing as the hot lead lashed into the rock around them.

Vask's aim with the Kalashnikov was good and he had a weapon that was perfectly suited to what he was trying to do. He had a good position where he was, fifty feet out from the base of the rock wall and the distance to his targets, no more than five hundred feet, was well within the range of his weapon. Yet Wildman noticed that instead of hitting close to them, the bullets were spraying across the face of the rock all around them and, each time Vask fired, they climbing up and away from them. When Vask fired again Wildman realised what was happening, what Vask was doing wrong, and why they were not suffering what should have been the deadly consequences of his shooting.

Vask was firing long bursts. Even as they looked down, they saw him rip a magazine off the automatic, throw it to the ground, and reach into the Jeep for another. But the Kalashnikov, an ominously accurate weapon when correctly used, was not designed for accurate aim with long bursts. What happened when more than half a dozen shots were fired in a single burst was that the barrel tended to climb up and away from its point of aim. A number of factors caused this and the main one was vibration from the recoil action of the bolt mechanism. No one had taught or told Vask about this, so that when he let go with a long burst, his rounds sprayed wildly across the rock face, with minimum concentration. Wildman hoped that he would continue firing like this because in addition to reducing the possibility of hitting them, he was probably also rapidly overheating the barrel of the Kalashnikov.

<<>>

They had dropped to the steps again and were hugging them as the rounds whined over their heads and screamed off the rock around them. Then, looking down, Wildman saw a movement below. It was the head of Gunga, no more than a couple of hundred feet behind them and suddenly, with a shiver, Wildman realised what Vask was trying to do. The man was clever, when it came to it; he was trying to pin them down and let Gunga catch up with them. Wildman looked again. Gunga was closer and now he could see two other men no more than a hundred feet behind him. The sun was hot and it had warmed the rock steps on which they were lying. But Wildman suddenly felt himself shiver at the thought of a face-to-face confrontation with Gunga on the narrow staircase. He had a horrible vision of bodies flying into space, picked up like dolls by those terrible hands and arms and flung into the void.

He made an immediate decision and, leaping up, shouted in a voice that brooked no argument. "Up! Run! No more stopping. RUN! RUN!"

Gael and Pasang did not hesitate. Better a chance with the Kalashnikov than a tussle with Little Gunga on the cliff face. Hearts pounding with the effort, breath coming in gasps, they raced on for the top and Vask, seeing them go, poured burst after burst at them from below.

There were two more short tunnels cut into the rock face and in these they had temporary shelter from the reaching fingers of the Kalashnikov. And when they came out of the last one, they were a good nine hundred feet above the ground, with Vask a diminutive figure, far below them. A hundred feet to go. They were almost there. Then Vask fired a last burst, they heard the chattering bark of the automatic and as the rounds came whining off the cliff around them, Wildman felt a stinging blow to his leg, felt the muscle collapse and fell with a bruising crash.

Pasang was at his side instantly and, together with Gael, seized him around the waist and dragged him back into the shelter of the tunnel. The firing below immediately ceased.

<<>>

Wildman lay on the rock floor of the tunnel, his breath coming in deep, hoarse surges, his eyes watering from the pain of the wound in his leg. He glanced down and saw the blood flowing. Gael took one look at the wound and with a coolness that Wildman, despite his condition, noted, took immediate charge.

"Pasang. I will look after him. I think you had better…"

But Pasang knew instinctively what he had to do and, without a word, ran back down to the entrance of the tunnel, whipped his *kukri* out of his belt and took up a position in its mouth. Gael saw the big knife flash from its sheath, knew that Pasang would do whatever he had to do—hopeless though it might be with the powerful Gunga—and turned her attention to Wildman.

Rolling up his blood-soaked trousers, she looked at the wound. The hole, she noted, was neat and clean. Probably a bullet rather than a splinter of rock. But it was bleeding profusely and the bleeding had to be stopped. Without hesitation she whipped off her shirt, ripped it down the back and then ripped it again into wide strips. Then she leaned over him, naked from the waist up, her firm, beautifully contoured breasts heavy with their fullness and shining with sweat in the bright morning sun.

She quickly bandaged the wound and, as she did, Wildman felt the pain ease and looked up at her face. Through the sting of the salty sweat in his eyes, he saw on it an expression of concern, of tenderness, that for a moment took his mind off their grim situation. Trying to smile against the pain from his leg he said, "So this is what I have to do to get you undressed?"

For an answer she reached out and gently touched his face. "Why don't we talk about that later? Right now the important thing is, can you walk?"

Grimacing with pain, Wildman lurched to his feet. Gael shouted to Pasang, who ran back to join them and then with her arm around Wildman's waist, the three of them staggered out of the tunnel and slowly, Wildman with streams of sweat pouring down his face, climbed the last few steps to the top of the cliff.

<<>>

The amphitheatre in front of the temple was extraordinary. It was oval in shape, with the high stonewall of the temple bordering one long side of the oval, and the cliff the other. Its surface was of rock, black, smooth, and perfectly flat. Wildman guessed that it must have been cut from the solid rock of the mountain itself. The surface may originally have been rough. But over the centuries, the bare feet of thousands of pilgrims had polished it to a glistening smoothness. On either side of it, to left and right, were jumbles of huge boulders. They were what had been removed from the hilltop when it was being levelled for the temple; they were piled in heaps on both sides of the oval.

Set in the face of the rock, their facades reflected in the glistening surface of the amphitheatre, were three massive doors. They were of gold, or a gold-plated metal of some kind, and were intricately embossed with figures of snakes, tigers, elephants and peacocks, all surrounding a seated image in the forehead of which was a single eye.

For a moment the doors held the attention of the panting trio as they came out into the amphitheatre. Looking at them, Gael felt like running towards them and shouting for entry. But then she remembered the legend, that only one of them allowed access to the temple, and that only for a chosen few. The other two held a deadly promise for the uninvited. A promise of death.

They heard a noise behind them. Men's voices. Quickly they looked back and down. A hundred feet below them, the huge, dome-shaped head of Gunga appeared and, close behind him, two men, followed by the driver, Metha.

Wildman leaned out and looked down, Gael supporting him with an arm around him. Three hundred feet below and behind the men, Vask, the Kalashnikov cradled in his arms, was also pounding up the steps. He would be at the top within two to three minutes. The men, with Gunga, would be up even quicker.

<<>>

Wildman looked across at the three huge doors reflecting their gold in the glass-like surface of the amphitheatre in front of them. They were a hundred feet away. A hundred feet that would take perhaps one minute to reach them. They could do it. But then what? Which door? He would have to sit down and go over the poem again, word by word. That would take time. And there was no time left. And to take a chance with one of the doors and get the wrong door? Well, he himself might take a chance. But if he was wrong, that would not be fair to Pasang and Gael. For who knows what lay behind the wrong doors. Caged tigers? A massive python? A couple of dozen Hamadryads, nine-footers, with their poison sacs loaded? Scorpions? Rabid bats? A black panther, trained to attack and kill? Men? Men armed with bows and poisoned arrows? Trip wires to guns set to blast into eternity anything or anyone attempting to enter? Whatever it might be, he was not going to take a chance with it. For himself, maybe. But not with Gael and Pasang. Slapping Pasang on the back to emphasize the urgency of the moment, he grabbed Gael by the arm and hissed. "Quick. Into the rocks."

They ran, stumbling, slipping, towards the piles of rocks to the right of the arena and they had dropped behind them, and were out of sight, just as the huge, imbecilic face of Gunga rose over the edge of the cliff. Crouched behind the boulders, heads down, they did not see him. But they heard his dreadful whining and with a shudder they pictured in their minds the wet, slobbering mouth, the beady black eyes seeking, searching, the ghastly head nodding up and down.

<<>>

Gunga halted at the edge of the amphitheatre. For a moment he seemed bewildered. The small black eyes set under the beetling brows darted back and forth. Then they were caught and held by the gleaming gold of the three huge doors, brilliant in the mountain light. He was still staring at them when Vask's men, with Metha close behind, scrambled up the last of the steps and joined him. He turned to look at them and then turned back towards the doors and pointed a thick forefinger at them. He whined and the huge head nodded up and down as much as to say, "There. They went in there."

The men stopped. Wildman and his companions were not in sight and they were not sure what to do. Metha looked back and spoke quickly to the others. "Wait. The Raja is coming. He will know what to do now."

They huddled together around Gunga and to an onlooker it was obvious, from the way that they kept close to him, that they were very nervous. Then Vask appeared, breathing hard, and joined them. Metha immediately pointed towards the doors and, presuming that Gunga had seen the trio go into one of them, told Vask this. Gunga, his mouth oozing spittle and his huge head nodding in seeming confirmation of what the driver was saying, continued to point towards the doors.

"But which door? Which door did they go in, you imbeciles?"

Vask held the Kalashnikov to his chest and snarled at them. They all looked at Gunga. Had Gunga seen which door? But Gunga, who had never learned to talk, and whose only sounds were his near incessant whine and the growls of pleasure that he made when he had a man or a woman to play with, could not tell them. All he could do was gesture and while in his childish mind the beautiful doors were something that he thought he should point out to the others, Vask presumed that he had seen Wildman and his companions go in one of them, and was trying to tell them this.

Vask looked quickly around the area. Then he raised the Kalashnikov, pulled off the banana clip magazine and checked to make sure that it had a full load of thirty rounds. Slapping it back into the weapon, he set the safety catch to FIRE and telling the others to follow him, walked slowly across the arena to the doors.

<<>>

Keeping the others close behind, he carefully examined each door. Bending down to peer intently at the scrollwork, he looked for a keyhole or a lock of some kind, checking the edges of the huge metal frames in which the doors were enclosed for a gap, a crack, anything that would indicate how they might be opened. When he had examined all three doors, he beckoned the men to join him and then took up a position in front of the middle door.

Transferring the Kalashnikov to his left hand, he dug into an inside pocket with his right and pulled out a sheet of paper. On it were written the verses that contained the riddle of the doors. Years before, back at Himalaya House, the cunning Ghose had found the verses in a drawer in Lord Carew's writing desk and had copied them and sent them to him. Now the time had come to look carefully at what was written, and find the answer to the riddle.

As he bent over to look at the verses, Metha, who could read English, joined him, leaning over his shoulder to look at the paper. Although normally Vask would have considered the action rude and insulting, now he said nothing. Metha was not very smart. But Vask had looked at the verses many times since Ghose had sent them to him and had never been able to make head nor tail of them. If Metha could find an answer to the questions they posed, that was all to the good. And so he said nothing and let the man read the verses, out loud, while the others stood and listened.

"Thee riddle of thee golden doors is what it says, oh Raja," said Metha, in a nervous, almost quavering voice.

"Yes, you idiot," Vask snarled at him. "I know that. Now read the rest, you fool."

"Yes Raja, yes. It says, Raja, forward stride, count not thee cost, he who hesitates is lost. For those who come to thee golden doors, thee question arises, which one is yours. And then it says, is it the left one, or middle or right and can entry be made by day and by night. But the left, it says, must be wrong if thee right is right, as in thee, er, opposing, thee, er, opposight, regardless of might.

"Well, you dolt. Read on. What are you waiting for? Read on and tell me what you see."

Metha continued and read the verses through to the end, stumbling over a few of the words but generally getting most of them right. Vask waited until the man had read the verses all the way through. Then he turned to look at him, to see if he had an answer to the riddle and, without saying anything, just stared questioningly at him. He knew how much now depended on correctly interpreting the verses. But at the same time, in spite of the urgency of the situation, he was not about to lower himself in the eyes of his men by asking a lowly driver for advice. Metha sensed this and quickly moved to speak. Stepping back to show respect, he pointed at the paper in Vask's hand and said, "Oh Raja, see what it says there. It says that left is wrong when right is right. That is the answer, oh Raja. The right door. Right is right. That's what it says in thee paper. There."

He pointed to the right hand door and continued. "It must be so because it clearly says that left is wrong, in thee writings. There. In thee second verse."

Vask thought for a moment. The man could be right. The verses clearly said something about left being wrong. That eliminated the left door. And the centre door was too obvious; a trap for anyone foolish enough to try and blunder through. It had to be the right one. That was it.

<<>>

When Vask and his thugs had moved away from the edge of the cliff and walked into the centre of the amphitheatre, to stand in front of the doors, Wildman and the others were able to see them through a gap between two of the boulders. Now they watched them standing there, with one of them reading from a piece of paper and Gael, with her mouth close to Wildman's ear, whispered a question. "The verses? The ones you told me about?"

Wildman whispered back. "Yes. I don't how Vask got them. If I had to guess, I would say that somehow or other Ghose got them to him. I would also guess that Vask is not going to have any more luck than I had, trying to interpret them. By the way, you know them don't you? I mean, you have them in your head, yes?"

"Yes. Why?"

"Well, I don't know what is going to happen here now, so what I suggest is that you start going over them in your mind to see if you can come up with any ideas about which door is the right one. The solution is there, I know it is, hidden in the riddle. Your grandfather would not have given the verses to me if they did not have the answer in them. Keep trying, OK? I'll do the same thing and, if we can work something out, and the opportunity arises, we might just be able to make a dash for it."

Gael nodded and sank down beside Wildman, the upper half of her body, naked now, gleaming honey gold in the mountain light. Pasang, flat on his stomach behind them, his *kukri* firm in his right hand, kept his eyes on Vask and Gunga. But he was very conscious of Gael in front of him, and of her nakedness, and with the inbred courtesy of his culture, resolved that as soon as they were able to move, she would have his shirt. It was not right that his *memsahib* should be without proper clothes, regardless of the circumstances.

<<>>

Vask decided that his driver might have found the answer. The right hand door. He also decided that the best person to send in first would be Gunga. There might be men behind the door, guarding it. If there were, Gunga would deal with them. If they had weapons and Gunga got hurt? Too bad. In any case his giant brother would probably effectively neutralize them before going down for the count. So Gunga it would be.

He turned to Gunga and spoke to him in a low voice, at the same time pointing towards the right hand door. Wildman, watching, saw the giant's head turn slowly around to look at the door. He hesitated and when he did, Vask placed a hand in the small of his back and, continuing to speak to him in a low voice, pushed him gently towards the door. Gael, seeing them move towards the great golden door, felt a shiver run down her spine as she imagined what would happen if they found the correct door and got into the temple. There would be a slaughter.

About five feet away from the door Gunga stopped. The huge head nodded up and down and faintly to the ears of the hidden watchers came the high-pitched whine. Vask again urged him forward. But the giant held back. Something was wrong. He did not know what it was, but something was not right. It was his brother who was telling him to go forward, his brother whom he trusted as he trusted no one else. His brother who housed him and fed him and gave him whiskey to drink and provided him with his little playthings, men and women, and who, of all people, would not expose him to anything bad. But something was not right. He sensed it in the dim recesses of his mind. And what he sensed was danger. He was not capable of analysing what he felt. But he knew it was there and he did not like what it was telling him.

Slowly, reluctantly, he began to move towards the door, Vask close behind him, his hand against the giant's back, his voice low and coaxing in the huge ear. The other men hung back. Vask, they could see, was not taking any chances; he was going to make his brother go in first. For their part they were of course relieved that Vask had not ordered them in first. Whatever danger lurked behind the golden door, Gunga, with his phenomenal strength, could probably deal with it. So let him go first. After he got in they would be glad to follow him. Behind Vask, that is, with his automatic weapon.

<<>>

Gunga was now at the door. His huge head nodding, he stopped and leaned forward to look at it. It was very big and he could see that it was made of some sort of metal. But there was no sign of a handle or a lock. So what did his brother want him to do? From behind him, growing impatient with the giant's slowness, Vask gave him a hard, jabbing push in the small of his back. Gunga jerked forward, putting out an arm to balance himself and in doing so, accidentally touched the surface of the door. When he did this it opened instantly, sliding smoothly, with only a faint hissing sound, into a deep recess in the side of its massive frame.

<<>>

With Vask close behind him, Gunga stood and looked into the opening revealed by the opened door. Inside, he saw a passageway of exactly the same dimensions as the door's frame. It led backwards, curved to the right and disappeared into darkness. Its floor, walls and ceiling seemed to be of the same, smooth, polished rock as the area where they stood. But because of the lack of light, he could not see more than ten feet into it.

Gunga peered into the darkness. He did not like it. Did not like what he sensed. There was something bad here. Something nasty. Vask stood a little behind him and, leaning to the right, peered around the giant's massive body into the passageway. Wildman and Gael, tense, silent, dividing their thoughts between the verses of the riddle and the actions of the men at the door, watched from the concealment of the rocks. Vask spoke again to Gunga, his hand on the giant's arm, urging him forward into the darkness of the passageway. As he did so he waved to the men behind him, ordering them to join him. Moving forward reluctantly, the men did so, to form a tight group immediately behind him.

<<>>

Gunga still hesitated. Vask, growing impatient, stepped back and, transferring the Kalashnikov to his left hand, placed his right hand on the giant's back and hissed urgent words into his ear. "The woman. The one you saw? The white woman. You shall have her. For you to play with for as long as you like. Just for you. After that, the man you saw. The big white man. And as much whiskey as you want both before and after. Now, do as I say. In. Inside. Now. You have to do this if you want your presents and your whiskey. Yes? Then in. Now."

For another few seconds the giant did not move. But then, with a firm hand from Vask urging him forward, he took one short step, then another, into the passageway. As his foot started to take the weight of his second step, it happened.

Their view blocked by the men crowding behind Gunga, Wildman and Gael could not see what took place. But Vask and his men saw it and with shouts of fear, falling over each in panic, they threw themselves backwards.

<<>>

His second stride had taken Gunga fully into the first few feet of the passageway and all of his enormous body was inside and perhaps six inches beyond the frame of the door when, with a deep hissing sound, the grim reaper laid his scythe across the giant's shoulders. He had no time to turn. No time to do anything. And death took him so fast that it is doubtful, as he died, if he even knew what had actually happened to him. The only thing that registered on his mind was a powerful hiss, something that to him might have sounded like a score of striking cobras but which an engineer might have interpreted as the sigh of powerful hydraulics. And that was all he knew.

The hissing sound was accompanied by the powerful stabbing movement of a score of steel-shafted spears that slid, with blinding speed, horizontally, out of the walls on either side of the passageway, to plunge their razor-sharp heads deep into his body. With the irresistible force of powerful machinery behind them, the shafts passed clean through the huge body, piercing the liver, the spleen, the stomach, the walls of the lungs and the heart in its chest cavity. They thrust in through one shoulder and out of the other and also through the huge neck, slashing into the carotid arteries on either side, slicing the trachea in two, cutting the jugular vein and brutally severing the spinal cord where it entered the cranial cavity.

Gunga's dying screams echoed across the rock arena. They ended in a deep, gurgling groan. Vask, horrified, not so much by what had happened to his brother as to what had nearly happened to him, watched with eyes wide with shock as the huge body stiffened in the steel embrace that help it upright, and then relaxed and sagged. As it did so the door, with a soft hissing sound, came sliding back out of its recess and with a faint but positive click, closed, effectively blocking any further view of the spitted and pinioned giant.

<<>>

Gael buried her face in her hands. The dying screams of the giant had unnerved her. Her view of Gunga as he entered the passageway had been partially blocked by the men behind him. But when Vask had leapt back, crashing into the men behind him and knocking all three of them to the ground, she had been able to see what had happened to him. Before the door closed she saw the huge, transfixed figure, the dark red patches growing on it like hideous crimson flowers as it jerked into immobility. Wildman, his own breath coming hard, inched towards her and put an arm around her shoulders. "You all right?"

She shuddered and whispered. "Yes, I think so. And what now?"

Wildman smiled grimly. "Now, I think, they'll try another door, Little Gunga's demise notwithstanding. Typical of Vask, though, wasn't it, to make his brother go first. Dammit, if it had been the other way around, with Vask in there, pinned to the walls, I think the others might have been demoralised enough to give it up."

He turned to Pasang, flat on the rock behind him. "Pasang."

"Yes, *sahib*?"

"Pasang, have you seen any sign of movement above the temple wall? Anybody up there?"

"No, *sahib*. And I have been watching carefully. Nothing. No sign."

"What about the wall, Pasang. Do you think that we could get up it?"

"We could try, *sahib*. But it is too high to bounce up. We would have to pile rocks. That would take time. We could not do that with Vask there. If I could get close enough to Vask and the others, I might be able to use my *kukri* on them. But Vask still has the automatic weapon and they are a hundred, maybe a hundred and twenty feet from here. A long run, *sahib*. But I will do it, if you say. We must do something, *sahib*. Soon."

"No, Pasang. It's too far. And I'm not going to lose you now. Not after all that we have been through. No. We will wait. Look, Vask has the paper out. He's reading the verses again. I think that he may be going to try another door. Let's wait a little longer and see what happens."

<<>>

Vask stood to the left of the door where Gunga had died, and once again read the verses. Behind him the men cowered together, and that they were fast approaching the end of their limited courage was obvious by their erratic movements. They were horrified at what had happened to Gunga; inwardly they envisioned the same thing happening to them. Metha kept very close to Vask's back, with a crouching posture that almost bent him double. The other two squatted on the ground, their backs tight to the wall behind them, darting fearful glances at Vask, at the top of the wall above them, and at the rocks around the arena. The movements of all three were quick and jerky, the movements of badly frightened men, men close to panic.

Vask put the sheet of paper with the verses back in his pocket and, stepping back a few paces from the wall, looked at the middle door. He looked away from it, to the left-hand door, and back again. Then he shook his head. To his cunning if not very intelligent way of thinking, the middle door was too obvious. It was too inviting. Too beckoning and, to his mind, one that only the unwary might use. The foolish. And he had not come this far by being foolish. Not by the gods.

As to the left hand door, the verses seemed to say that it was wrong. Clearly, in the second verse. Which meant, yes, wait a minute, but of course, that was it, that the writer of the verses was trying to draw attention *away* from it? Away from the real door, the one that gave entry to the temple.

That was the answer. Yes. He would try the left-hand door. Correction. His men would try the left-hand door. He would follow closely and safely behind them. Just as he did with Gunga, which clever thinking had saved his life. Which clever thinking would continue to keep him alive, even at the cost of the lives of the cretins who cowered around him now.

He turned and barked at the men, pointing at the left hand door.

"Get up. We are going to try another door. Get up and come with me. Stay close. We'll go in together. Up. *Jeldi.* Now!"

Raising the Kalashnikov to waist height, Vask waved to the men to follow him and walked towards the left hand door. The three men, slowly, reluctantly, hanging back to the limits of his order to stay close, moved after him.

Arriving at the door, Vask looked carefully at it from a distance of about three feet. It seemed to be exactly the same as the right-hand door. No keyhole, no handles, and no latches of any kind. The same embossed animals glistening in the sun, the same serene, one-eyed image, watching from the door's centre. He waited another few seconds and then reached out with the Kalashnikov and, using its muzzle, very gently tapped the centre of the door, just below the seated image. Within a split second of his tap, the door opened. There was a faint hiss, it slid sideways and, exactly like the other door, disappeared into a deep recess in the side of its frame.

Vask, wary, ready to leap backwards, crouched in front of the doorframe and looked in. Inside, behind the frame, it seemed to be identical to what he had seen when the right-hand door had opened. Another passageway cut into the rock, receding back into darkness. The available light showed that it was straight for about ten or twelve feet and then curved to the left.

Vask, careful to keep his body outside the massive metal frame of the doorway, leaned forward and peered in. He looked carefully at the sides of the passageway and the walls immediately inside the door. They were smooth and without holes or slits through which spears might flash out and stab. He looked at the floor. Solid rock, from what he could see. The ceiling, the same. Then he turned to Metha and the guards and stepping back and jerking his head towards the doorway, shouted at them. "Get in. Now. Did you hear me? Now. All of you. Inside. NOW!"

But the guards were very close to panic. Clear in their minds was the image of Gunga's bloody body, hanging suspended in the passageway behind the right-hand door. His terrifying screams as the spears took him still rang in their ears; with its sound, the last of their courage had dissipated. It was Metha, slowly beginning to edge backwards, who spoke.

"Oh Raja. No. 'Ees too dangerous. Very bad things happening here, Raja. Better we go home now and leave all this. Better..."

Vask took a step towards him, cursing him. "You yellow cur. You will do as I say. Now. You don't think that I am going to let a village dog like you interfere with my work. Now. Inside. NOW!"

But Metha, having to choose between the wrath of Vask and the terror that the gaping black hole of the doorway imposed on his mind, decided that Vask's anger was the lesser of the two evils and took another step backwards. As he did so, the other two men started to move with him, sidling slowly towards the edge of the cliff and the steps that would take them down to safety.

Vask swung around to face them and with his action, Metha's nerve snapped. He turned and with a scream of terror, ran for the cliff edge. The men hesitated, looking quickly from Vask to the fleeing man. As they did so Vask straightened up, spread his legs and raised the Kalashnikov to the waist firing position. The guards saw the movement and froze. But Metha had eyes for only one thing, the cliff edge and the steps beyond it as, mouth open and with his turban flying off his head in a wild tangle of cloth, he ran for his life.

Vask, a snarl of contempt on his face, held the Kalashnikov at his waist and waited until the man was six feet away from the edge of the cliff. Then he fired, a long, crackling burst that raked the mirror surface of the arena in front of him, raced out after the fleeing man in a dancing fury of splintering rock, caught up with him and then, like a giant hand, picked him up and flung him into space. Vask waited until the wretched driver's despairing scream had died out and then, spinning around, brought the Kalashnikov to bear on the other two panic-stricken men. He shouted at them. Two words. "INSIDE! NOW!"

<<>>

The men's eyes darted back and forth between the Kalashnikov and the dark mouth of the tunnel in front of them. They jumped visibly when Vask made a stabbing movement towards them with the automatic and then, shaking with fear, began to inch themselves towards what was to them the lesser of the two evils, the great golden frame of the left-hand door. Twice Vask reached out and jabbed them with the muzzle of the Kalashnikov. Then they were inside the frame and standing in the passageway and looking back at Vask for instructions. Their faces, a deathly grey under their dark colouring, oozed with the sweat of their terror as they peered fearfully into the darkness ahead of them.

Vask waited until they were well inside the doorframe before very carefully putting in one foot, and then another, and stepping in to join them. He looked past them into the passageway, the Kalashnikov ready for instant action, his finger curled on the trigger, his nerves as taut as stretched steel wires. Ahead of him the passage disappeared into darkness and after a few seconds, whispering, he ordered the men to go forward. When they hesitated he jabbed them again in their backs with the loaded and cocked automatic, making it clear that if either of them turned and tried to run, he fully intended to use it.

Slowly, inching their way with feet of lead, struggling to contain their terror, one foot sliding reluctantly ahead of the other, toes feeling the floor for anything other than its smooth rock surface, Vask's men, with their master ten feet behind them, moved down the passageway and into the darkness. The last that the hidden watchers saw of the three of them was the hulking figure of Vask, moving at a snail's pace behind his men. Then the darkness swallowed them and Wildman and Gael and Pasang could see nothing more.

<<>>

Gael began to raise herself upright. My god, she thought. They're in. They've made it. They…But Wildman's hand snapped out and took her by the shoulder, forcing her back down. "No. Not yet. Wait."

"But they're in. Nothing has happened. They've got into the temple. They'll…"

"No. Wait. They. chose the wrong door."

Wildman's voice was like ice and at the sound of it she sank back down, her eyes, wide in expectation, on his face.

"But how do you know? We haven't been able to crack the riddle. We…"

"Yes we have. I have. They've gone in the wrong door. I'm sure of it. And what is going to happen now is not going to be nice. In fact you might want to cover your eyes and…"

<<>>

The sound, when they first heard it, was like nothing they had ever heard before. Wildman's mind raced as he tried to analyse it and he felt Gael stiffen beside him as her hand reached out to grab his wrist. It began with a deep rumble, so deep it was almost a growl. It quickly grew in volume, filling the air around them. It seemed to be coming from the depths of the rock, under their feet. They thought they felt a faint tremor below them. Even as their minds registered this, the rumble deepened in tone and then, within the space of two or three seconds, transformed itself into something that for all the world was like the hissing roar of a huge, white-water rapid. Then the sound pinpointed itself; its epicentre was the dark hole of the passageway into which Vask and his thugs had just disappeared.

Wildman and Gael got to their feet, tense, barely able to breathe and slowly, *kukri* in hand, Pasang rose from behind to stand with them. The three of them stood, poised, staring at the dark hole of the open doorway, when suddenly a huge tongue of water, dark even against the dark of the passageway from which it emerged, came roaring out of it, a solid spout of liquid that completely filled its frame. From there, under what must have been tremendous pressure, it shot across the amphitheatre, a single, powerful jet of liquid. As it burst into the sunlight it lightened inside and as it did, they saw them, Vask and his men, arms and legs, a terror-stricken face, a mouth screaming a silent scream, seized, carried and hurled like rag dolls towards the precipice. So powerful was the force behind the great, tube-like funnel of liquid that it retained its shape all the way across the rock amphitheatre to the edge of the cliff and it was only at the cliff's very rim that it began to disintegrate and collapse. Locked in its cold heart, helpless, Vask and his men were still alive when it took them over the edge of the precipice.

As it plunged over the cliff, the solid liquid shape disintegrated and long before they were smashed to pulp on the rocks, far below, Vask and his thugs were falling through the air in a boiling and broken waterfall, able to see the sky above and the rocks below, tumbling helplessly, over and over, feeling the cold air of the mountains whipping at their clothing, biting at their skin. Then came the rocks, black teeth in a hungry mouth, reaching up for them in a silent snarl of death and oblivion.

<<>>

As quickly as it had erupted from the tunnel, the great jet of water was cut off and subsided. As it did so, the massive golden door slid out of its recess and closed with a soft hiss. Pasang jumped up and ran to the edge of the cliff and looked over. Gael rose shakily to her feet. Wildman rose with her and put his arms around her. "It's OK. It's all over. They've gone. Gone for good. We're safe now. We've nothing more to worry about."

She put her head on his chest. She was trembling violently. He tightened his arms around her naked upper body and looked towards Pasang. The Sherpa was standing at the edge of the cliff looking down.

Far below the great mass of water was still pouring over the ground and through the rocks, frothing and bubbling in thick brown rivulets where its tremendous force had torn up the dirt. His sharp eyes quickly picked up the sprawling figures of Vask and his guards and, a little to one side, the dead driver. Satisfied, he turned and walked rapidly back to join the others, taking off his shirt as he did so and holding it out for Wildman to give to Gael.

"All gone, *sahib*. All finished," he said, with a grim smile. Slipping his big knife into its sheath he added, "Now we go into the temple ourselves, yes?"

"Yes," said Wildman, gently releasing Gael, and stepping back. He took the shirt from Pasang, thanked him and gave it to Gael.

"Here, put this on," he said, struggling, in spite of the tenseness of the situation, to drag his eyes away from her voluptuous cleavage. "It's all over. We're at the end of our journey. Now let's have a crack at getting into the temple, shall we?"

Buttoning up Pasang's shirt, Gael darted a look across at the three doors. "Fine. But which door? The riddle is impossible. I've run it through my head a hundred times. I've...but wait a minute. You said something, didn't you? When Vask was going in? Now I remember. You said that you knew which door was the right door. No. Wait a minute. You didn't say that. You said...wrong door. That was it, wasn't it? Wrong door? So you knew it was the wrong door. But how did you know? Did my grandfather tell you? Did..."

"No. He did not," he said, watching the colour beginning to flow back into her cheeks and her confidence return. "I cracked the riddle. That's all. And I think that you could too, if you look at it very carefully. Not so much at the wording as to how the solution, its hidden meaning, is placed within the structure of the verses. Listen..."

"Forward stride, count not the cost.
He who hesitates is lost.
For those who come to the golden doors,
The question arises, which one is yours?"

"So far so good, yes?"

She frowned in reply. "Yes, although I don't see any pointers to a solution there?"

"OK. Then listen again. We'll skip verse two and go directly to three. OK? Ready?"

Herein lies a deadly riddle,
Is death awaiting in the middle?
Or are all three doors but a lethal warning,
From each of which there is no returning?

"So," he said, watching her intently, "have you noticed anything yet?"

"Well, it mentions the middle door. But only as a question. And a pretty nasty one at that."

"Alright. Then let me go on. But listen carefully."

A man of wisdom might quickly see,
That entry lies in number three,
But the doors their numbers do not say,
How then know the one safe way?

Wildman put a hand on her shoulder and looked into her face. "OK. So there is nothing in the first verse that tells you anything, one way or the other. Right? You can, if you like, look on it as simply an introduction to the riddle. Then comes the second verse. Same thing, introductory. But then the fourth…a man of wisdom will quickly see, that entry lies in number three. Got that? Number three. And therein lies the secret of the riddle. The answer to it. The…"

"Yes! Yes! I've got it. It's door number three. No. I mean it's verse number three! It's…"

"Yes. You've got it. It's verse number three. And…?"

"But of course. It's where it says that entry lies in number three. Not door number three, but verse number three. And the only door mentioned in that verse is the middle door."

"Yes. *The middle door*. Your see, you can disregard what the verse actually says about the middle door because what is said is not in the form of a statement, but as a question. Remember? Is death awaiting in the middle? And then…the answer lies in number three? Meaning it lies in verse number three, in which verse the only door mentioned is the middle door."

<<>>

They stood on the wet surface of the rock in front of the great golden door. The middle door. Pasang in the centre, Gael to his right, Wildman to his left. They looked at each other. Then Wildman nodded and Pasang slowly reached out and reverently touched the figure of the seated image in the middle of the door. For a split second nothing happened and then, with a faint hiss, the huge door slid smoothly sideways, into a recess in its frame, just as the left and right hand doors had done. But whereas the other doors had opened to dark passageways that held menace and death for the uninvited, the centre door opened to reveal a sight that was entirely different, one that made Gael gasp with surprise and delight.

Immediately inside the door was a spacious courtyard that stretched back for three hundred feet and standing silently in it, all looking towards them, were a hundred men dressed in the red robes and bright yellow hats of lamas of a sect of the Buddhist religion. They stood in serried ranks, forming a path that led back all the way across the concourse to a series of stone steps that climbed to a high rock platform. On the top of the platform was a wooden structure made of massive, beautifully carved beams, almost like a huge shallow box and in it, hands folded in its lap, legs crossed in front of it, sat the imperious figure of the Yellow God. The image had no eyes. But in the centre of its forehead was a single, round aperture, like an empty eye socket, from where, nearly a hundred years before, a young Englishman, mad with love for a beautiful young woman, had taken the Green Eye.

They stood and looked through the gold framework of the door into the courtyard. Suddenly, trumpets blared and the lamas, as if on signal, began to nod and smile and applaud and beckon them forward. They walked through the doorway and into the courtyard, the three of them, into the milling throng that immediately surrounded them. As they did so, the huge golden door slid silently shut behind them.

BOOK FOURTEEN

EPILOGUE

It was over. They had been fêted at the temple. Given rooms to rest. Food. Gifts from the young head lama of the temple. For Pasang, a sturdy Sherpa mountain pony with a richly ornamented saddle, and gold coins in a silken purse. For Gael, clothing in the form of Tibetan robes richly woven with brocade, blouses of the finest silk, felt boots embroidered with gold and silver thread. Wildman would accept nothing at first but in the end, as a souvenir more than anything else, he agreed to take a *thanka,* a hand-painted Tibetan scroll, very old, very beautiful.

The Eye had been returned and accepted by the lamas with due ceremony and appreciation. It was replaced in the forehead of the Yellow God; there to watch over all who had played a part in its return to its rightful owners.

They stayed for two nights at the temple. After the festivities of the first night, the young head lama and his temple custodians left them alone, to rest, talk and make their plans. Included among the rooms they were given was a small dining hall, deep in the main cluster of buildings and on the second night, after Gael and Wildman had dined there, Pasang knocked gently on the door and asked if he might join them. They welcomed him and Wildman bade him be seated at the dining table.

"Well, Pasang, we made it, eh?"

"Yes *sahib*, *memsahib*. We have done all we set out to do. And we have fulfilled our promises to the good Lord Carew."

"Oh, but Pasang," said Gael, "you have done more than that. Much more. If you had not been with us, Pasang..."

"Oh *memsahib*, what I did was nothing. In any case I now wish to speak, not of that, but of a more important thing. A special letter, which Lord Carew gave to me at Himalaya House just before we left. My instructions, from him, were to give it to you, *sahib*, after the mission was fully completed. And I think that means now, *sahib*, don't you think so?"

"Yes, Pasang. But I presume that you read the letter or memorised it. You don't have it on you, do you?"

"Oh yes, I do *sahib*, In fact..."

"But how could you? How could you have kept it all this time? Why, Vask had us stripped when he captured us, down at Nagpur. Clothes, shoes, money belts, everything. There was just nowhere left where you could have hidden anything?"

Pasang smiled and reached into the front of his waist sash. "No *sahib*. There was one place, one thing, he never searched and never thought of searching. Because I did not have it on me when they stripped me. You remember, *sahib*, how they took it from me on the road, when they captured us? Here *sahib*..."

With a practised movement he whipped his big Gurkha knife, in its sheath, out of his waist sash and laid it on the table. Smiling, he pulled out the knife itself and laid it carefully beside the sheath. Then he picked up the black, hand-sewn buffalo hide sheath and from the top of it pulled out a small pocketknife. Laying the sheath on its side, he carefully cut the stitching down its edge. When it was open almost all the way down, he dug his fingers in and pulled out two folded sheets of notepaper.

Wildman smiled. "So that's it. That's why you would never wash the sheath? And that's why you never put the knife back in it until you had cleaned it?"

"Yes *sahib*. I did not want to get the letter wet. Normally I would sheath the knife immediately after use and clean it and the sheath later. Anyway, *sahib*, here is the letter and I now follow my instructions by giving it to you."

Wildman took the pages from him, unfolded them, looked questioningly at Gael and said, "I'll read aloud, shall I? So that we can all share it? Then here goes..."

Dear Wildman, my dear granddaughter Gael, and my faithful servant Pasang...If all three of you are reading this letter, then this means that you are together, that you have been successful and that you have completed the mission with which you were charged. It also means that you have been able to defeat those who would have tried to stop you returning the Eye to the temple of the Yellow God. How you will have done this I do not know. But the fact that you are reading these notes means that you have done it, and that Vask and his men and his dreadful brother have failed in whatever attempts they will have made to take the Eye for themselves and, no doubt, to harm you in the process. I only hope that at the least you have been able to hand them over to the authorities for just punishment for their crimes. I hope also that you have been able to do this in Nepal, where Vask will not be able to use his money to buy himself out of the due application of justice.

As to Vask's people here in England, have no fears. I am only waiting until I hear from you as to the success of your mission to put into effect immediate arrests of Ghose's contacts in London—we have all their names now—and of course Ghose himself, who, as you may have suspected, has for years been biting the hand that has fed him here. Yes, I have known for a long time about Ghose and you may be interested, briefly, in hearing of how I first became suspicious of him, of how my suspicions were confirmed and of why, with this knowledge in hand, I kept him here.

As you know, Ghose was supposed to be the son of my old regimental batman. He was not, and I found out one day when he injured himself in the house here and had to spend a couple of days in hospital. I went to see him and found him sleeping with his feet sticking out from under the end of a hospital bed blanket. The feet were bare and carried no markings. And that was where my suspicions began. You see, in the old days, in India, native batmen were allowed to have their wives and children with them in barracks. There was a great deal of travel in the way the army moved around on the subcontinent. Over to Madras, across to Bombay, up to the frontier, the Khyber, etc. For native servants this meant a great deal of third-class train travelling, often under very crowded conditions. One of their natural fears, when travelling, was the danger of losing one of their children and so a custom developed of having the batman's service number tattooed on the sole of one foot of every child. We condoned the custom and in fact paid for it; there was even a little ceremony attached to it when a new child was born. And Ghose? No number. No tattoo. And as soon as I saw this I knew that he was not the son of my former batman, but an impostor. So I wrote some letters and set in motion an investigation to try and find out who he actually was and where he came from. It took almost a year, but the upshot of it was that I discovered that he was a protégé of Vask, who somehow or other had learned of my batman's dying wish and substituted one of his own people. What happened to the real boy? I do not know. My feeling is that he was probably murdered.

As to keeping Ghose on here after I discovered who he was, this required serious thought. He was Vask's man, planted in my house to be a direct contact with Vask and his thugs and obviously prepared to work with considerable dedication for his masters. But then I thought of the advantage that I had in my knowledge of who he was, and of the fact that he did not even suspect that I knew. I thought, why not keep him on here and use him, and this knowledge, to keep my own eye on Vask and his doings. So I did. I promoted him to butler and even gave him successive raises in salary and a small apartment of his own in the back of the house, with his own telephone. But I arranged to have all of his mail intercepted, incoming and outgoing and, naturally enough, I had a private detective agency tap his phone line for me and record all his messages, in and out. In this way I was able to stay one step ahead of the fellow, and of Vask, all these years. Ghose, unknowingly, supplied me with a great deal of information on the thug leader and his plans, as a result of which I was able to twice circumvent—without, I think, raising any suspicions of my private intelligence—the attempts on me at my home here. In fact I feel that the too clever Mr. Ghose is going to be very surprised when the cold hand of the law descends on his shoulder one of these days. Which it will do the instant I, or my lawyers here in the case of my absence, know of the success of your mission.

And my reference to the possibility of my absence? Alas, I am afraid that when you read this I shall almost certainly be gone. I am a very old man now and, even as I write this, I feel that my time is up. Have no fears for me. I have none for myself, having led a full and enjoyable life. Nevertheless, with the prospect of the last great adventure looming—which is, incidentally, how I view death—it is only circumspect that I make certain arrangements for those who have served me well across the years, those whom I hold dear.

Firstly, Pasang. Pasang, you have served me long and faithfully and I think that the best thing for you now is to go back to your own country and your own people. With this in mind I have set up for you a pension. It will be paid to you through the Central Bank of Nepal in Kathmandu and you can collect it on whatever schedule suits you, every month, or every six months. You can even arrange for it to be sent to you at your home in the mountains. Good-bye, Pasang. Go with God and may you enjoy a long and happy life."

Wildman stopped reading and turned to Pasang. "Did you understand all that, Pasang?"

"Yes *sahib*. I thank you. All understood. From the good Lord Carew. May God bless his soul."

"OK. The letter goes on…

The High Priest of the temple of the Yellow God, who befriended Wildman and Gael and Pasang and rewarded them for the return of the Eye, and for their courage and dedication.

Gael at the temple of the Yellow God in the beautiful Tibetan robes given to her by the High Priest of the temple.

The indomitable Pasang, Wildman's companion and protector through all of the hazards of the extraordinary mission. Photo credit, Wildman files.

Next, Gael. For you, dear Gael, if, as I believe, I will no longer be here when you return, I am leaving the bulk of my worldly possessions, including the manor here, Himalaya House, and its adjoining lands. You will find the legacy that will be deeded to your name ample for the costs of running this old place and, in addition, of sufficient proportions to provide for you on a most agreeable basis for the remainder of your life. God bless you, my child. Enjoy your life and may it be long.

As for you, Wildman, at the time I am writing this, a day or so before your departure, my only worry about you is that you may decide to go through India with the Eye, rather than through Thailand. I will not debate with you the differences or the degrees of danger involved, in the two routes. Whichever one you choose, I know it will be on the basis of a carefully considered decision. And I shall have confidence in you. In addition, though you may not suspect it, if you do choose the India route, may I say that that is just what I expect you to do, for a very private reason which, as this letter is addressed to all three of you, I shall leave to you to divulge to the others, if and when you choose.

Lastly, I conclude by saying that I surmise it is this same reason, your private one, that has prompted you to refuse any money for this mission? Very well then. I will respect your wish. But at the same time I am depositing the sum of five hundred thousand US dollars in your account at Grindlay's in St. James Square, in London. If you wish to accept it, as I feel you should, then please do so. If you do not, then you can leave it where it is, in which case it will revert to the bulk of my fortune.

Goodbye then, to all three of you. I leave you with the knowledge, on which you may care to reflect, that by doing what you have done you have made an old man very happy. You have also, by returning the Eye to its rightful owners, eased a troubled conscience of many, many years.

The letter was signed, simply: *M. Carew.*

<<>>

Gael was the first to speak. "What a wonderful old man he has been. So thoughtful, always, of others. Our only problem is not knowing if he is still alive, or if he is gone."

Wildman looked at her. "I hate to think it. But my feeling is that he is gone. Getting the Eye back here was very important to him. I think he knew that we could do that. At least, shall we say, he was confident that we could. And that we have been successful. In which case, with his life's last wish carried out, he may have found himself without any real desire to live on. And at that age one has to have something to live for, something compelling to hold on to."

Pasang nodded. "He is gone, *sahib*. I feel it. The good man has gone to his ancestors and to his God."

Gael, her eyes soft with tears, nodded. "I think you are right Pasang. But I also think that if he is gone then it is willingly and, as he said, with his conscience clear and at ease. And that is what is very important."

She turned to Wildman. "And I owe you an apology. You never told me that you had not asked for a fee for the work? And I accused you and indeed, even thought of you as having all sorts of mercenary ideas and intentions towards my dear grandfather. I'm so sorry. I do hope that you will accept my heartfelt apology?"

"There's no need to apologise," Wildman said. "Just as you do not have to apologise for not turning up at the Taj Mahal Hotel in Bombay when you were supposed to, which to some extent endangered us, because…"

"Not turning up at the Taj? But I did. At exactly nine in the morning. As arranged. Darn it, I waited an hour and then again next day and the day after, just in case there was a misunderstanding and I had the wrong date. I waited so long that in the end one of the hotel staff came out and gave me chair to sit on so I could sit and watch the ships coming in."

"Watch the ships coming in? But you can't see the ships from the front of the Taj? What are you talking about? The front of the hotel faces a closed street. It's…oh my god, now I know what happened."

Wildman began to laugh. "Forgive me, dear Gael. But you're not the first one to wait in vain for someone at front of the famous Taj. Its problem, you see, is that its front is its back. And via versa. Its front, with its formal gardens—which is where we waited for you—faces on to a little back street. And its back, where indeed you and probably many others have waited in vain over the years, faces the sea. The reason? It was designed by an English architect in London, who sent the plans out to the company that wanted to build the hotel. An Indian contractor won the bid to build the thing and started at once. By the time the architect came out, it was too late to reverse what he had done. Unbelievably, the contractor built it backwards!"

They laughed together. Then Wildman grew serious again. "But as to apologies, truly it is I who owe you one. A very big one, in fact. For endangering your life in India. By coming through India in the first place and not taking what was probably the safer and certainly the quicker route through Thailand. But as your grandfather says in his letter, there was a very private reason involved, one, which, at the time, seemed to me to justify what I was doing. Certainly it did before I met you and before I came to know you for the rather wonderful young woman you are. After I met you I thought differently, and realised that there was no justification for doing what I did, especially where it involved exposing you to the deadly hazards of Vask and his thugs. But by then we were half way here and, short of dumping you off along the way and hoping that they would ignore you to follow me—a risk I was not prepared to take—I had to keep you with me."

Gael had blinked back the tears in her eyes. Now she directed a steady gaze across the table at Wildman and gently placing one of her hands on top of his said, "And the reason? Is that the very private reason that my grandfather refers to in his letter?"

"Yes. It is. And now I think that you—and Pasang too—should know about it, know my reason for choosing an overland route through India. This was, simply, that I wanted to force a personal confrontation with Vask and, in the process, if the opportunity arose, kill him. I know it sounds brutal. But there is more to it than a simple desire for what I considered justifiable homicide, as I shall explain in a minute."

"In any case, in the course of my planning, I quickly came to the conclusion that the only thing that would give me any chance of getting to grips with the man would be to draw him out of his lair in central India and get him to a place where we might be, shall we say, be on more equal terms. In other words, Nepal. In his own territory I knew that I had little chance. He was too strong, too many people around him, too much power. So I chose a road route and...you know the rest. We made contact with him, stirred him up, provoked him, and then got him out of his lair to a place where, I am glad to say, instead of my having to kill him, he bought on his own destruction, as well as that of his men. And that is why I chose to come through India, right through the black heart of his territory, right into his clutches, as it were. And all the time he never suspected that this was my game plan. In fact I honestly believe he thought me a fool for choosing the route that I did."

"But what a risk you took. And the Eye? Supposing you had lost it?"

"The Eye? I never had it with me. I mailed it by registered mail to my Sherpa housekeeper in Kathmandu. That's where I went the night we spent in Kathmandu, while you were snoozing away in your room at the lovely Shangri La."

"You mean you actually mailed it? By mail? Something worth ten million dollars? By mail?"

"Yes. Because when you consider it, when you consider all that we went through, our capture by Vask, the race across India, the hide-and-seek we played with his thugs in Kathmandu, it was probably a lot safer than trying to carry it on me, right? As to registered mail, well, you know how that works? It's a sign and receipt system, and it was actually invented by British postal authorities in India, during the Raj. The way it works is that each man who handles the item in question, a letter, or a packet, has to sign for it and in turn has to get a signature from whosoever he passes it on to. A safe system. The Smithsonian used it not so long ago to send the Hope diamond, value, I believe, at a hundred million dollars, to an exhibit in San Francisco."

Gael, her green eyes wide with the wonder of what he had done, sighed her agreement. In the end, yes, it probably was the safest thing to have done. But one thing still bothered her and this was Wildman's desire to come to grips with Vask. She knew there had to be a strong reason. She had spent time enough with Wildman now to be able to read his character and to understand the nature of the man. And it was obvious that he was not a man given to unnecessary violence. Why then the urge to find Vask and destroy him? It bothered her. It was like a missing part in a jigsaw puzzle. Although she sensed it had something to do with what her grandfather was referring to in his letter, when he wrote 'a very private reason', one that Wildman might not want to talk about, she felt she had to know. And so she asked him, and it was with relief that she saw that he appeared to have no objection to her question. Indeed, his response was as though he had expected her to ask it in the first place.

"My real reason for wanting to get to Vask? It goes back a long way, I'm afraid. Back nearly eighty years, to the original Gael, the one after whom you are named. The colonel's daughter, that is, for whom Lord Carew, as a young man, took the Eye from the temple here. You know some of the story, yes? You will have been told why you were named as you were? But you don't know all of it and I'm sure you don't know where I fit into it."

"Where you fit into it? What do you mean?"

"OK. You remember the colonel's daughter and the whole story of the Eye and how your grandfather tried to give it to her and how she refused it and, later, refused him too? You know that a year after your grandfather left Kathmandu, she married another officer of one of the regiments there and subsequently had two children, a boy and a girl, Rupert and Rara?"

"Yes. My parents told me all about that, of course."

MINISTRY OF FOREIGN AFFAIRS

नं१।७-१२-३३८०(११) ।७२०२

KATHMANDU,
NEPAL.

मिति १६,मार्ग ०१५

स्लीक जोन्सन नामक निम्न लिखित जवानका एक दललाइ सुरक्षाको लागी देहायका वन्दक गोली साथमा लिइ पूर्वी नेपालको सोलो खम्बु क्षेत्र चोयाङ० म्यालो र थ्याङ० वोचे इलाकाहरूमा रही यो मंसीर २० गते देखि जेष्ट १६,२०१६ सम्मको लागि हिम मानव ।यती। को अनुसन्धान गर्न श्री ५ को सरकारबाट इजाजत प्रदान भएको छ । निजहरू जयनगर र विराटनगरको वाटो भै उपरोक्त स्थानहरूमा जाने भएका छन । यस अनुसन्धानको सिलसिलामा उक्त दलले कौनै कुराको मद्दत मागेमा आफ्नो खर्चबाट व्यहोर्नु पर्ने गरी मनासिव माफिकको जो चाहिने मर मद्दत दिन दिलाउन सम्बन्धित वडा हाकिम,गोस्वरा गौडा,चौकी तथा अफिसर मलादमीहरू संग अनुरोध गरिन्छ ।

✓ मिष्टर पिटर.सि.वायर्न
मिष्टर व्रायन वायर्न
मिष्टर कीर्क जोन्सन
श्री चक्रेटी ।भारतीय।

खर खजाना

१. १२ बोरको म्यान्चन २ नाले वन्दूक १ —— १०० टोटा
२. ३५५ बोरको म्यानलीकर राइफल १ —— ५० गोली
३. २२ बोरको वि.एस.ए.राइफल १ —— ५०० गोली

Foreign Ministry.

नजरमानसिं
नायव सचिव ।

Letter to Wildman from the government of Nepal congratulating him on the success of his mission and the return of the Eye to the temple of the Yellow God.

"And you know what happened to her and her husband in India, while they were on their way, overland, to Bombay? How the thugs waylaid them and murdered them? And how there were only two survivors, little Rupert, and Rara, who got away by running for their lives into the jungle and hiding there for days?"

"Yes. A dreadful thing. I know the story."

"Well, just as your dear grandfather did a fine tooth-comb on me before he considered me for the job of taking the Eye to Nepal, so I did an equally thorough job on Vask, on the history of his vile family and its criminal record going back a hundred years. And are you ready for what I found out? It was this…that Vask was a direct descendent of the man who strangled the colonel's daughter and her companions, the thug leader of the gang that committed the atrocity."

"My God. So that is why…No. Wait. You said something about you fitting into the thing, having a part in it? What did you mean when you said that?"

"When I said I fitted in? I'll tell you. The two survivors of the atrocity, Rupert and Rara, were eventually found and rescued by the British authorities and returned to England. Did anyone ever tell you their surnames, their last names?"

"No, no one ever mentioned their last names to me. No."

"I thought not. Otherwise you would have recognised mine as your grandfather did, in the course of his research. His letter's 'very private reason', which he left to me to explain and which is this. The British officer that the colonel's daughter married, in Kathmandu, after Lord Carew left there in despair, was a Brigadier Wildman. His children were Rupert and Rara Wildman. Yes. Wildman. My name. And when Rupert came of age, he eventually married. He and his wife had one child. Me. The colonel's daughter was my grandmother."

<<>>

They stand at the base of the cliff and the steps for a thousand feet above them are red and yellow with the bowing and waving lamas who have come to see them safely on their way. The ground around them is still scoured with the impact of the great fall of water from above. But the bodies of Vask and Gunga and their three companions have been taken away. Vask's Jeep is also gone and, somewhere in the hills, with the consent of the lamas of the temple, a Nepali family, possibly a family who had suffered from the depredations of the thugs in the past, is richer by one useful four-wheel-drive vehicle.

Wildman and Gael sit in the green Jeep that their host of the Shangri La, Utpal Sengupta, has loaned them. It is heavily spattered with mud from the pile of dirt hurled in the air around it by the falling water, but otherwise unharmed. The engine, after a bit of spluttering and gasping, has started and is now running smoothly.

Lord Carew in his latter years, loved and admired by all who knew him.

Pasang has mounted his pony. He made his decision the previous night, to go home to his village of Thami, high in the Himalaya, far to the east, and to settle down there. At least, he had said, smiling at Wildman, until the *sahib* needed him for another mission.

The smiling head lama of the temple has presented all three of them with white silk scarves, talismans for a safe journey home and there have been embraces and handshakes all around. Gael has had to force back a tear at Pasang's decision to leave, and even Wildman felt a pang when he realised that he might never see the little Sherpa again.

Then, with a shout of good luck and a wave, Pasang is gone. They see him twice more. Once on the curve of a ridge. Once on the top of a distant hill, when he stops to wave back. Then he rides on and the mountains swallow him.

Gael turns to look at Wildman. The two nights of rest have done wonders for her looks and her green eyes glow with health and vigour. The gorgeous Tibetan clothes she wears, a gift of the head lama, enhance her beauty. The full length, double-breasted coat of dark blue allows only the tips of her yak hide boots to show. A pale blue, silk blouse is pinned in the front with a gold pin and a scarf that matches it is knotted at her throat. Her hair is tied back in a thick, golden coil in the style of Tibetan women and she wears the clothes, as few westerners can, with style and grace. Wildman feels something tighten in his chest when she turns to look at him. The emerald eyes, the steadiness of the gaze, do something to him that no woman has ever done before. He is struggling to understand what it is and, secretly embarrassed at his failing to do so, tries to cover up his confusion with some light conversation.

"Well, now it's back to the jolly old Shangri La, I suppose. Hot showers and chicken in the basket and morning coffee and hot croissants and all that sort of thing. Maybe we'll also be able to get a couple of those adjoining rooms again, the ones that look out on the gardens."

Gael, sitting in the front of the Jeep, her body moving gently to the throbbing of the engine, turns to look at him. She lets her head sink down a little and then, to keep him in her gaze, raises her eyebrows, making her eyes appear even bigger than they are.

"Adjoining rooms, did you say? Separate rooms? I knew it! I knew there was something strange about you! And what is wrong with one of those big, beautiful suites that they have, the ones with the huge, soft, sumptuous, sensual, double beds? For both of us? Oh yes, there're big. The beds, I mean. I checked them out before we left the hotel, in case you don't know. Big enough for all sorts of nocturnal romps and high jinks, if

Wildman in the highlands of central Brazil,
cocaine country drug lord territory—January, 2003,
getting ready for another daredevil assignment.
Photo credit, Fifi La Griffe, Paris Match.

you know what I mean. Unless of course there really is something strange about you that you've been keeping a secret?"

For an answer Wildman reaches out and puts both of his long, muscular arms around her and pulls her to him and sets his mouth hard against hers. In an effort to show, in anticipation of things to come, that when it comes down to it, there is really nothing strange about him at all.

<<>>

A trailing finger of thick, brown dust points to the Jeep as it races towards Kathmandu. Far to the north a bronze-faced man on a pony pauses briefly on a high pass and looks back. He salutes once and then urges the pony on towards the great mountains. A mile to the east of the temple, in a dark ravine, the vultures snap and squabble over the remains of five men, one of them a giant in size. And from the temple itself, high on the great rock that rises out of the hills, its all-seeing eye burning with green fire in the morning sun, the Yellow God forever gazes down.

***** **THE END** *****

ACKNOWLEDGEMENTS.

I am indebted to a number of people for their gracious help to me in the writing of this little tale of daring do. I asked to be forgiven if, by chance-and of course not by choice-I have missed anyone.

Among those who have kindly contributed, in person as well as with time, advice and encouragement, are the delightful and perennially effervescent Sarah Fix, of Hood River, Oregon and her close friend, my companion of many a long and delightful sunlit day in the green mansions of the Terai of Nepal, my dear daughter, Rara (sometimes also known as Tara) Gael Byrne, of Parkdale, Oregon.

The sophisticated and inimitable international jet setter, Tom Dadras, of Brentwood, California, for, among other things, acting as Wildman's companion at a splendid lunch at the legendary East India Club, in London. (And for not drinking all the port!)

The gifted and accomplished artist, Stephen Lau, of Alhambra, California, for his positively superb work with the book's cover design, both its concept and its artwork.

Rick Austin, of NASA's Jet Propulsion Laboratories, Pasadena, California, for research and advice on the little known but highly volatile potential of everyday gasoline, and what can happen when this is misunderstood.

Kent Estep, of Marina Del Rey, California, stalwart jungle safari companion, for taking the helm of the author's fragile little boat and steering it to safety through the intimidating seas of the world of the computer.

Everest veteran, fearless adventurer and personal friend, attorney Wayne Annala, of Hood River, Oregon, for legal research in the crocodile infested swamps of the legalities of using real living people, rather than dead ones, in the tricky legal area of illustrated fiction.

John Beahler, MD, of Washington DC, for being a good campfire companion, even if he does have, as a fisherman, the longest arms I have ever seen.

Pasang Sherpa, of Kathmandu, Nepal, my old and courageous gun bearer of the hunting years, as the model for the indomitable Pasang of the book. And my one time *shikari* camp manager, Tashi Kirong, now passed away, as the model for Wildman's tough little housekeeper at his house, Julia Cottage, in Kathmandu.

Jeff Harvey, of Hood River, Oregon, designer of the cover of ***SHIKARI SAHIB*** (Pilgrims Publishing, 2003) for original TGE cover design contributions.

The brilliant and peerless Robert Rines, of Boston, Massachusetts for his trust in the young Wildman and for setting him off on the career that made him famous as an international courier.

Gael Moseley Cohen, of Byron Bay, New South Wales, Australia, without whom the book might not have had its glamorous and romantic Australian flavour, as well as not a little of its humour.

Bill and Beryl Green, of Touchen End, Berkshire, England, for admirable courage displayed in the face of the dangers threatened by the dreaded Vask and his thugs during their hazardous undercover research, under the guise of the Weens, in Varanasi, India. And their fine son Michael or, as he is known to the doormen of some of London's finer restaurants, Mikhail.

The beautiful, talented and ever charming Cathy Griffin-sometimes known to her friends as La Griff-of Brentwood, California, keeper of the compass that steers this writer on the literary straight and narrow, for concerned and endless encouragement for a war weary veteran of the battlefields of the publishing world.

Pilgrims Publishing editor-in-residence, Christopher N. Burchett, of Varanasi, India, for his patience with the author's vacillations and general literary incompetence, his assistance with the work and his sterling, book publishing directives.

And last but by no means least, Mr. Rama Tiwari, owner of Pilgrims Publishing-and also of two very attractive and well-worth-visiting bookshops in the Thamel and Phulchowk districts of Kathmandu, Nepal for his personal interest in the author's writings and for having the courage to take on an illustrated work of fiction, something very unique—perhaps precariously so—in the world of publishing.

Peter Byrne.
Los Angeles, California.
Kathmandu, Nepal.